Shojo Beat

La Corda d'Oro

Story & Art by Yuki Kure

Kahoko Hino
(General Education School, 2nd year)

The heroine. After participating in a school music competition with a magic violin, she discovers a love for music.

Len Tsukimori
(Music School, 2nd year)

A violin major and a cold perfectionist from a musical family of unquestionable talent.

Ryotaro Tsuchiura
(General Education School, 2nd year)

A soccer player and talented pianist who seems to be looking after Kahoko.

Keiichi Shimizu
(Music School, 1st year)

A cello major who walks to the beat of his own drum and is often lost in the world of music. He is also often asleep.

Kazuki Hihara
(Music School, 3rd year)

An energetic and friendly trumpet major and a fan of anything fun. He is in love with Kahoko.

Azuma Yunoki
(Music School, 3rd year)

A flute major from an ultra-traditional family who's very popular with the girls. Only Kahoko knows that he has a dark side!

Aoi Kaji
(General Education School, 2nd year)

A handsome, popular transfer student who doesn't try to hide his crush on Kahoko.

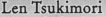

Story

Our story is set at Seisou Academy, which is split into the General Education School and the Music School. Kahoko, a Gen Ed student, encounters a music fairy named Lili who gives her a magic violin that anyone can play. Suddenly Kahoko finds herself in the school's music competition, with good-looking, quirky Music School students as her fellow contestants! At the end of the competition the violin loses its power and disappears, but Kahoko decides to continue studying music...

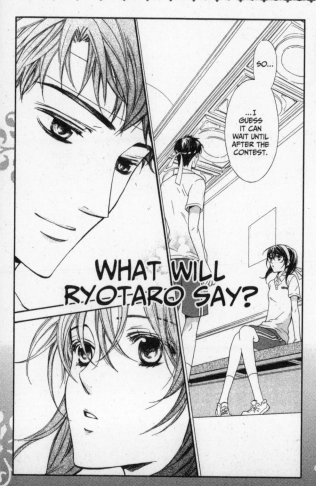

SO...
...I GUESS IT CAN WAIT UNTIL AFTER THE CONTEST.
WHAT WILL RYOTARO SAY?

Previously...

LEN'S FORMER TEACHER, MR. SAOTOME, AGREES TO TAKE KAHOKO ON AS HIS STUDENT IF SHE CAN PLACE IN THE BIG UPCOMING MUSIC COMPETITION. WHILE KAHOKO IS BUSY REHEARSING UNDER LEN'S GUIDANCE, RYOTARO TELLS HER THAT HE WANTS TO TALK. AND AT THE END OF THE ANNUAL SCHOOL FESTIVAL, AZUMA KISSES KAHOKO ON THE FOREHEAD!

The music fairly, Lili, who got Kahoko caught up in this affair. ↓

La Corda d'Oro

CONTENTS
Volume 15

ff

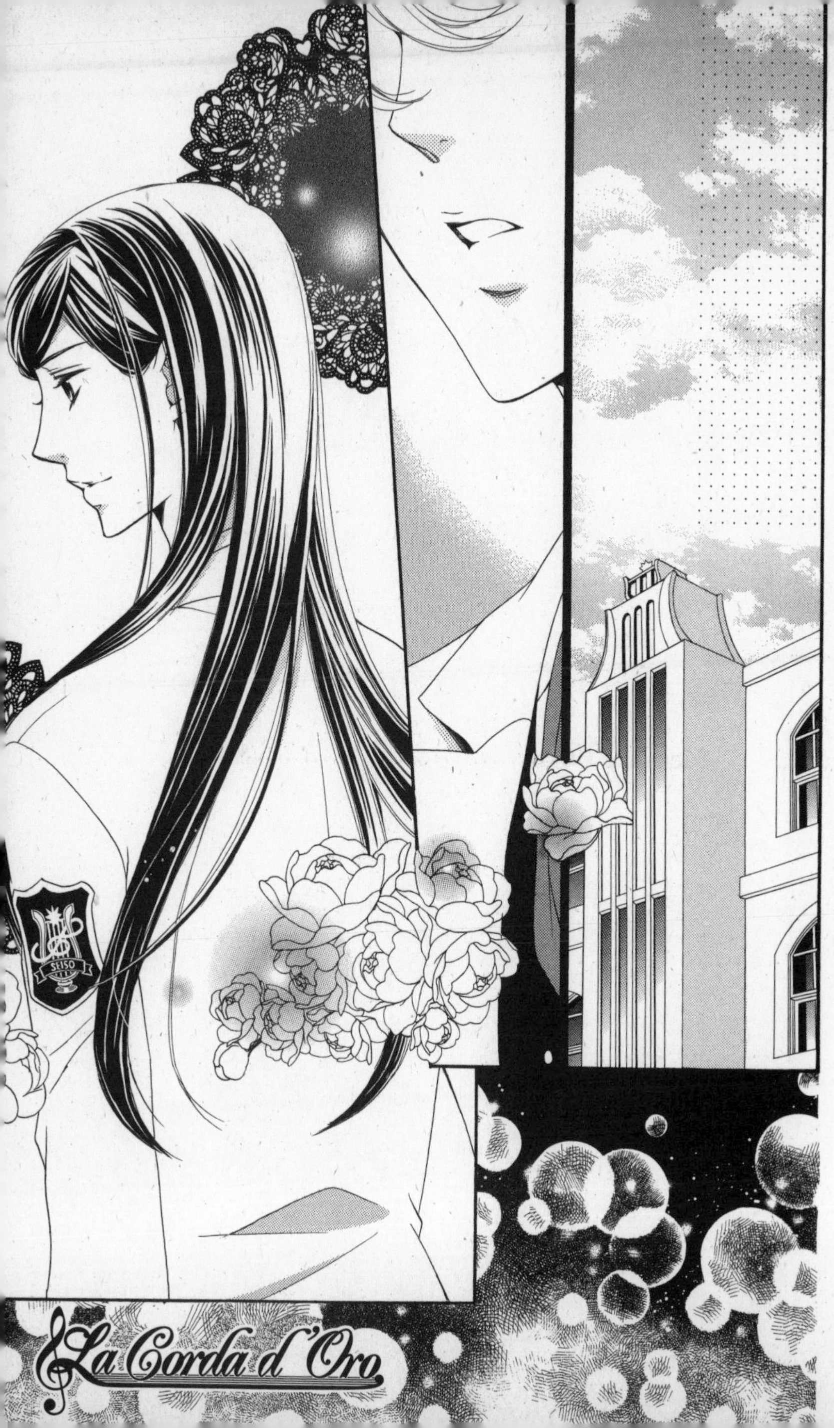
SEISO
La Corda d'Oro

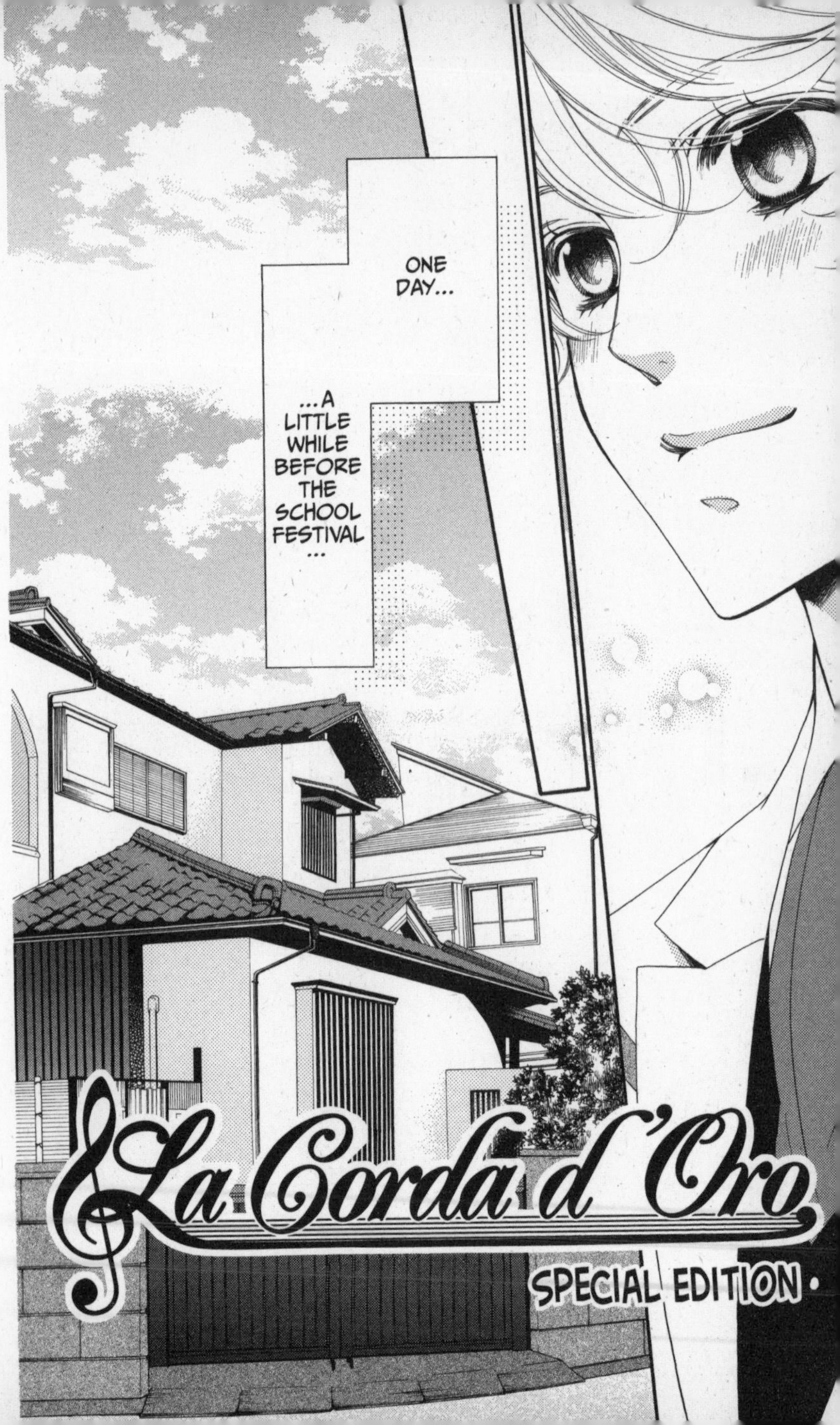
ONE DAY...
...A LITTLE WHILE BEFORE THE SCHOOL FESTIVAL...
La Corda d'Oro
SPECIAL EDITION

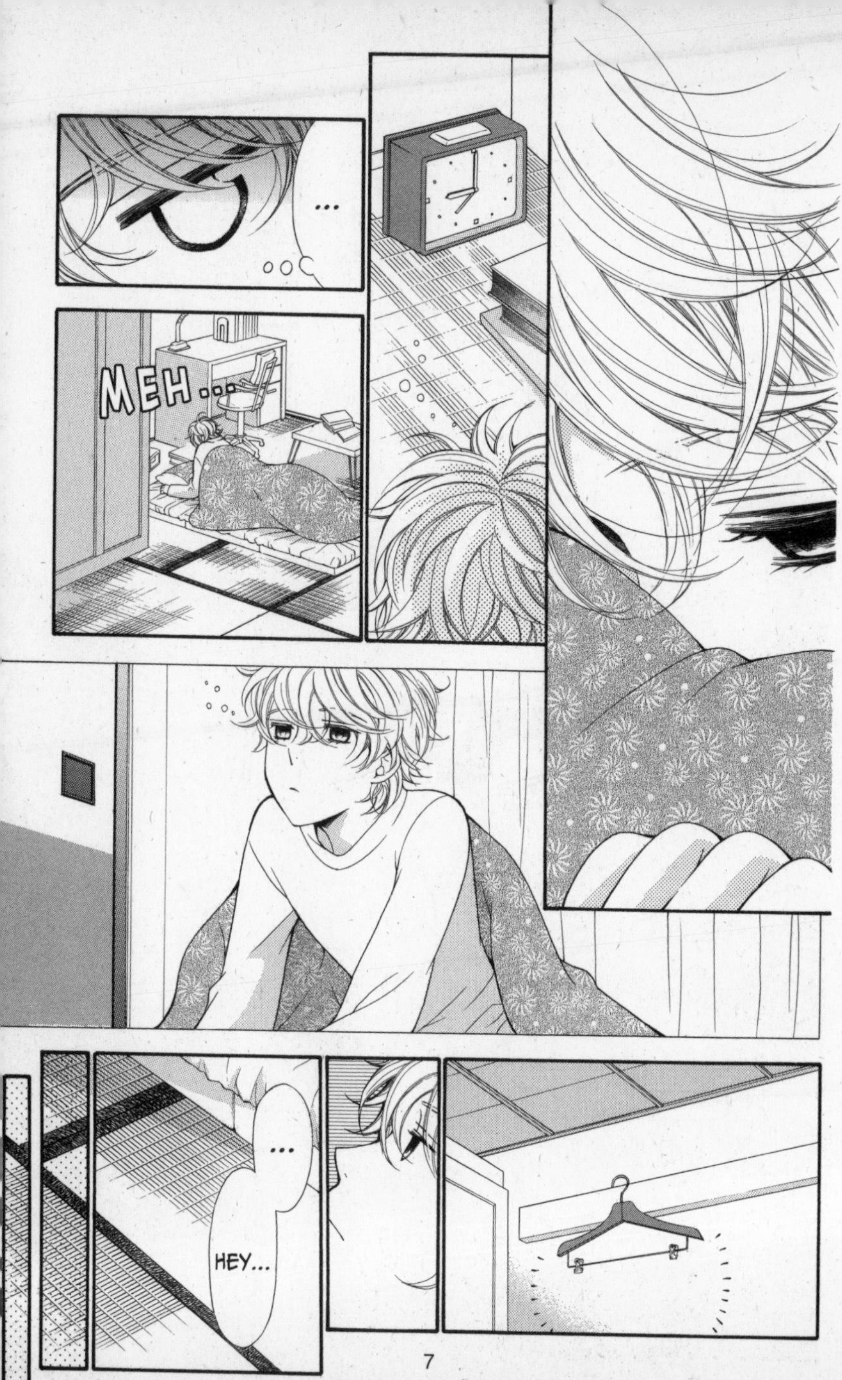
...
MEH...
...
HEY...

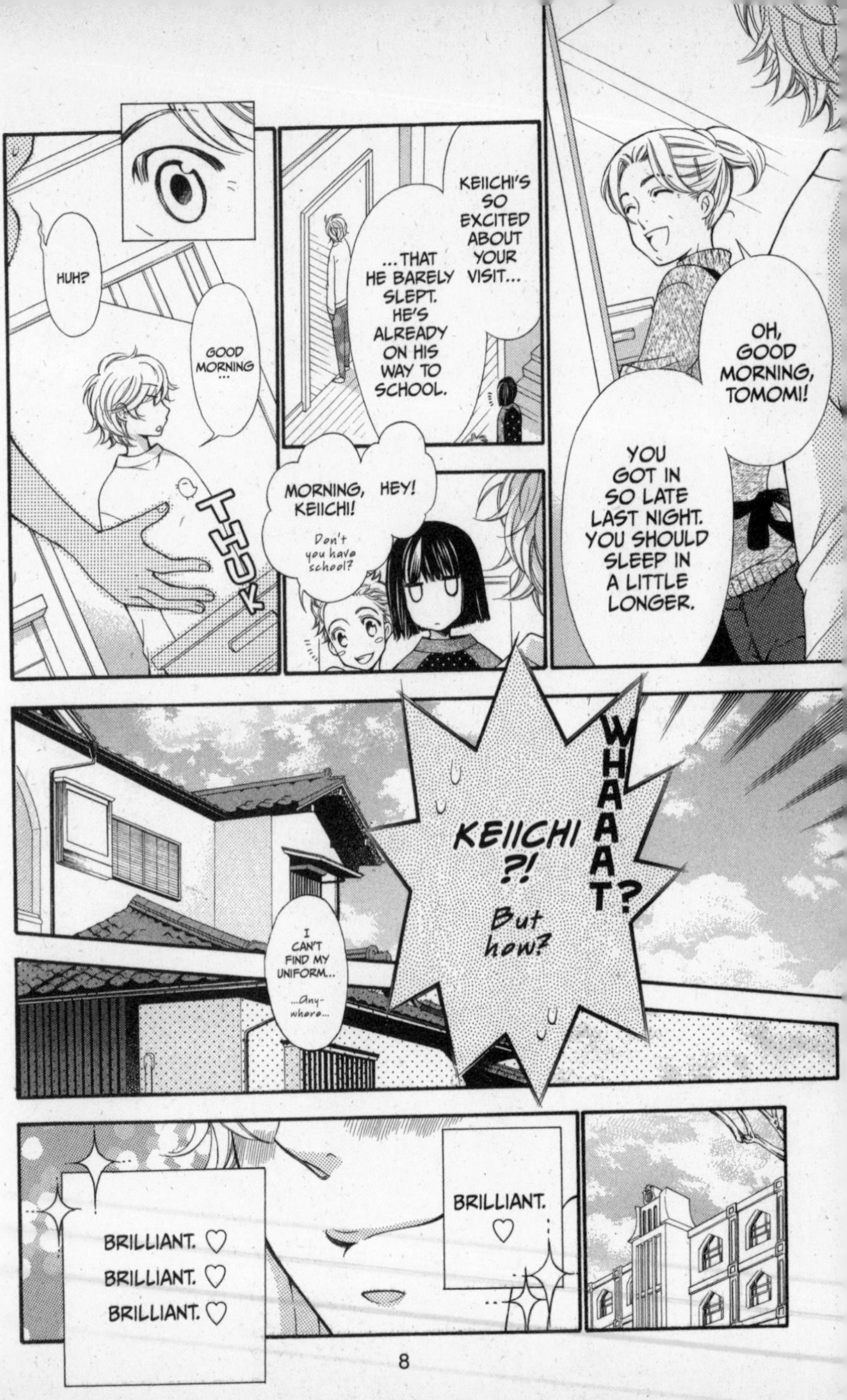
OH, GOOD MORNING, TOMOMI!
YOU GOT IN SO LATE LAST NIGHT. YOU SHOULD SLEEP IN A LITTLE LONGER.
KEIICHI'S SO EXCITED ABOUT YOUR VISIT...
...THAT HE BARELY SLEPT. HE'S ALREADY ON HIS WAY TO SCHOOL.
HEY!
MORNING, KEIICHI!
Don't you have school?
HUH?
GOOD MORNING...
THUK
WHAAAT?
KEIICHI?!
But how?
I CAN'T FIND MY UNIFORM...
...Anywhere...
BRILLIANT. ♡
BRILLIANT. ♡
BRILLIANT. ♡
BRILLIANT. ♡

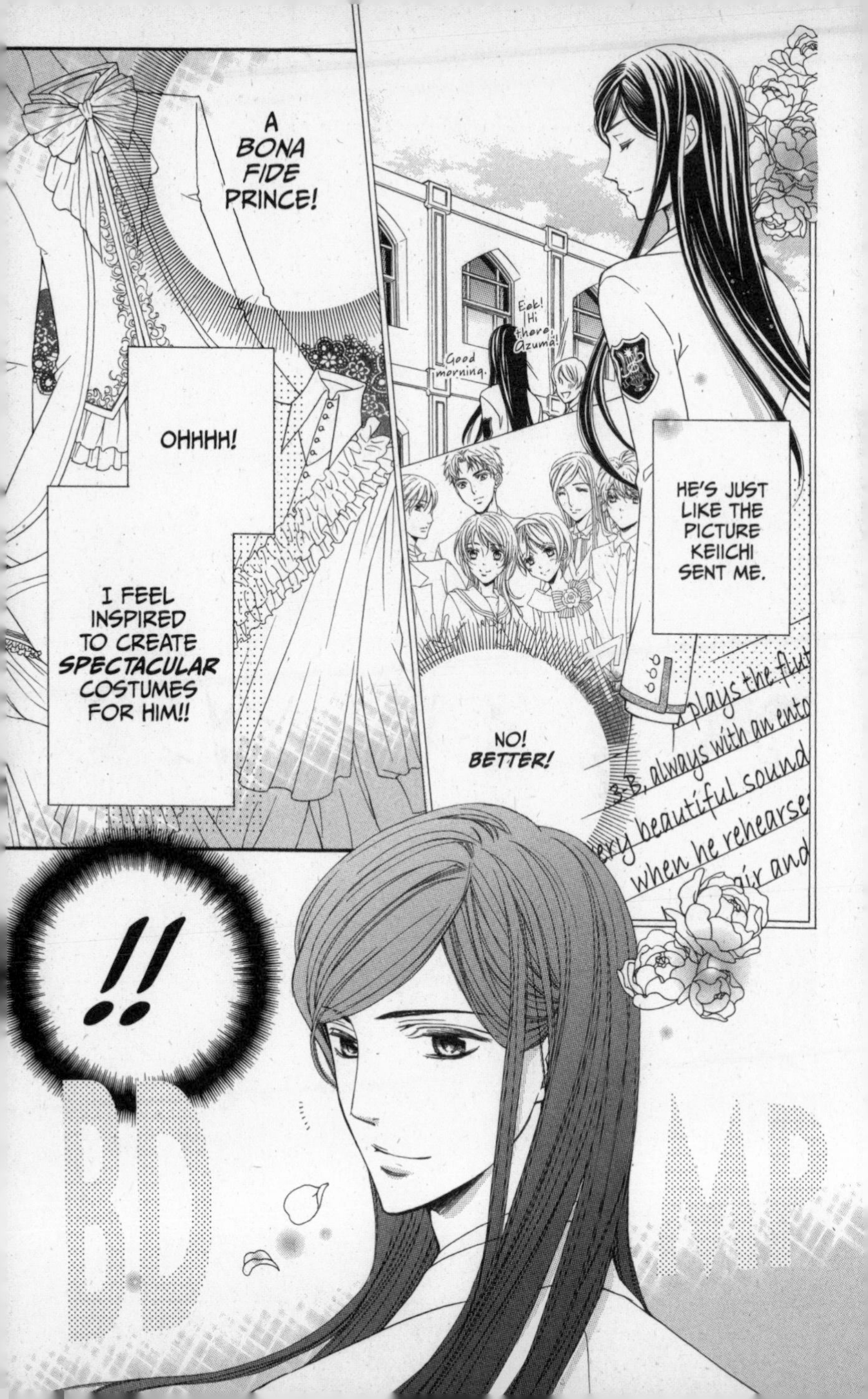
Eek! Hi there Azuma!
Good morning.
HE'S JUST LIKE THE PICTURE KEIICHI SENT ME.
plays the flut
3-B, always with an ento
very beautiful sound
when he rehearses
air and
NO! BETTER!
A BONA FIDE PRINCE!
OHHHH!
I FEEL INSPIRED TO CREATE SPECTACULAR COSTUMES FOR HIM!!
!!

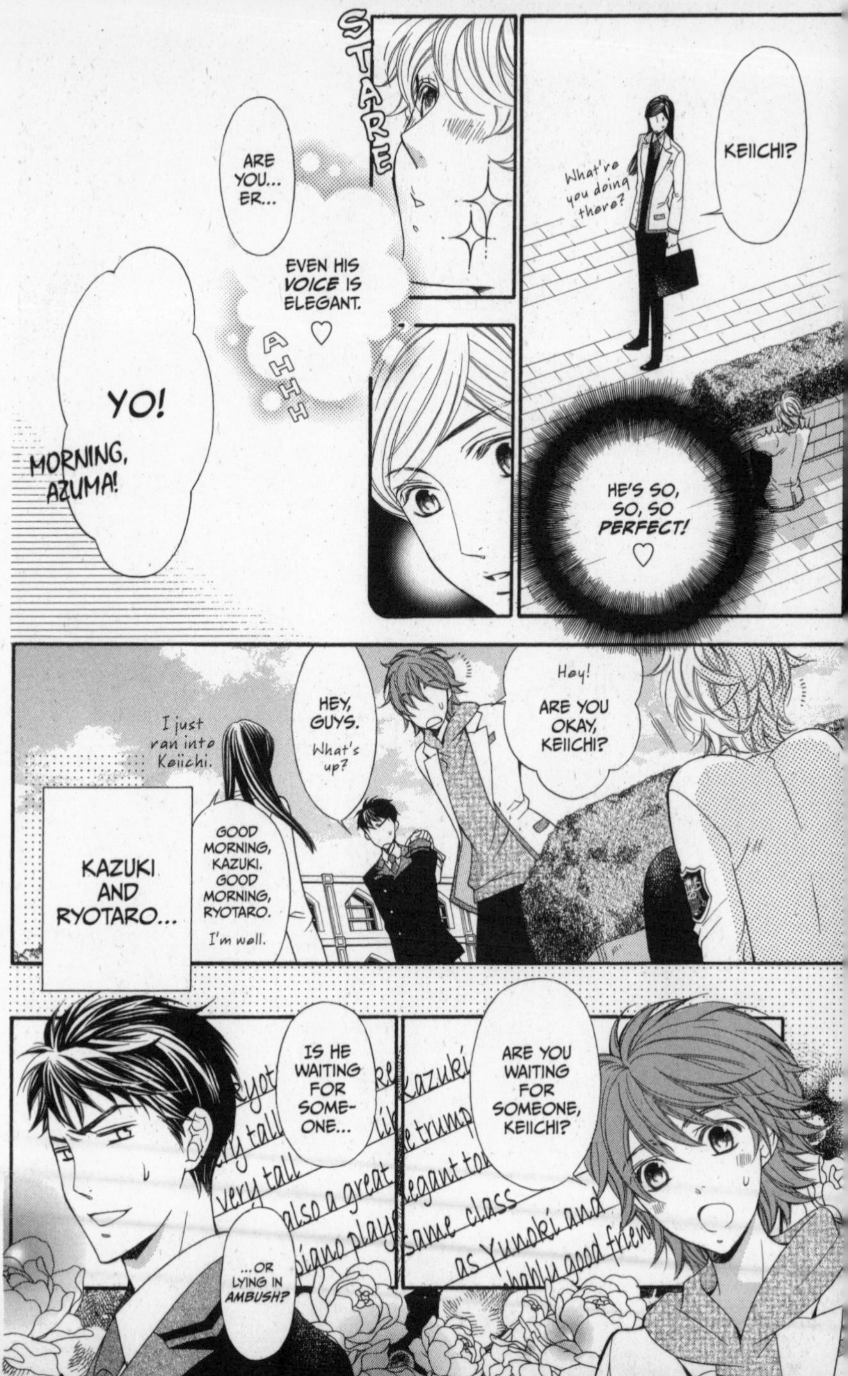
KEIICHI?
What're you doing there?
HE'S SO, SO, SO PERFECT! ♡
STARE
ARE YOU... ER...
EVEN HIS VOICE IS ELEGANT. ♡
AHHH
YO!
MORNING, AZUMA!
Hey!
ARE YOU OKAY, KEIICHI?
HEY, GUYS.
What's up?
I just ran into Keiichi.
GOOD MORNING, KAZUKI. GOOD MORNING, RYOTARO.
I'm well.
KAZUKI AND RYOTARO...
ARE YOU WAITING FOR SOMEONE, KEIICHI?
IS HE WAITING FOR SOME-ONE...
...OR LYING IN AMBUSH?

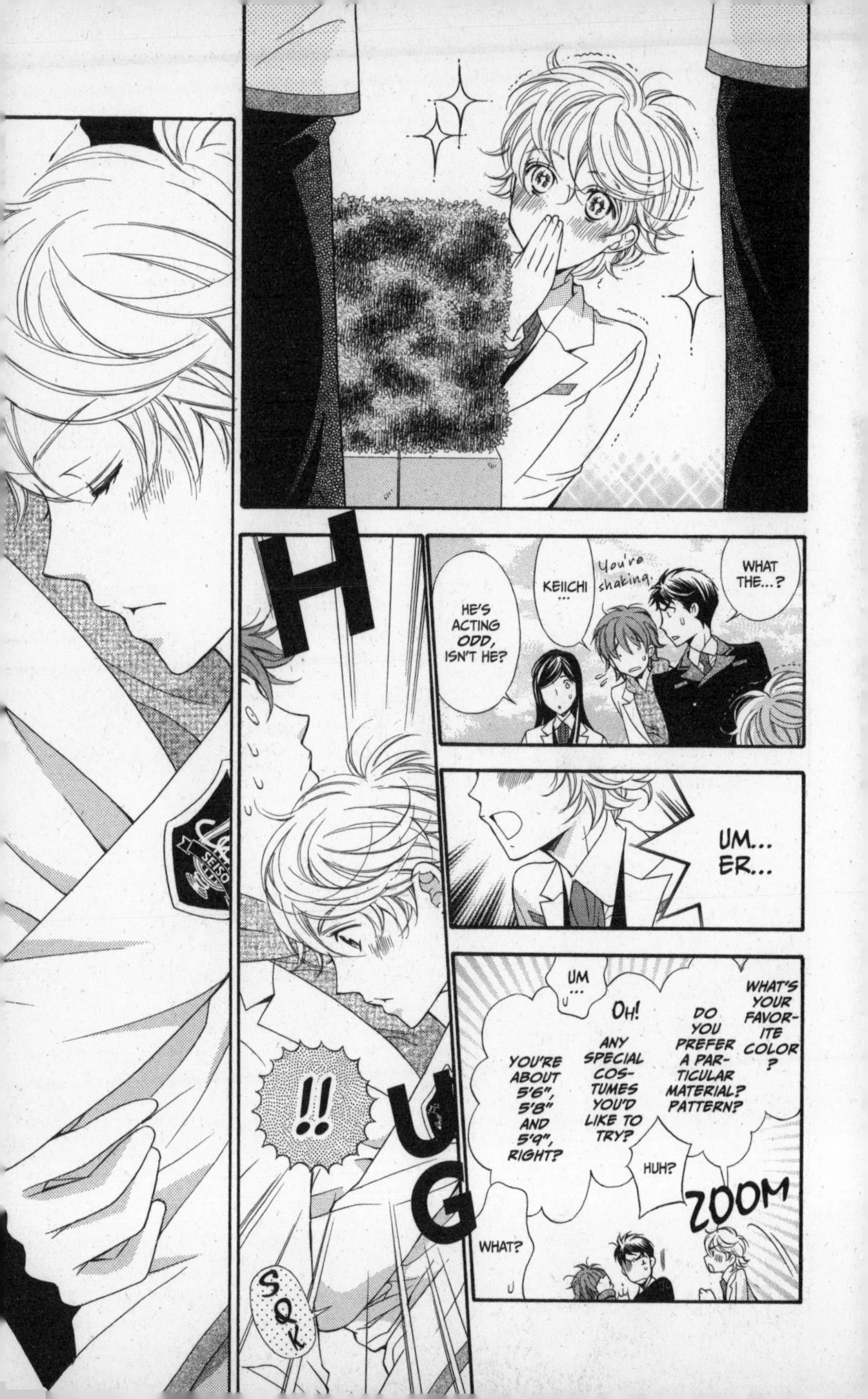
WHAT THE...?
You're shaking.
KEIICHI ...
HE'S ACTING ODD, ISN'T HE?
UM... ER...
WHAT'S YOUR FAVORITE COLOR?
DO YOU PREFER A PARTICULAR MATERIAL? PATTERN?
OH!
ANY SPECIAL COSTUMES YOU'D LIKE TO TRY?
UM ...
YOU'RE ABOUT 5'6", 5'8" AND 5'9", RIGHT?
ZOOM
HUH?
WHAT?
HUG
!!
SQK

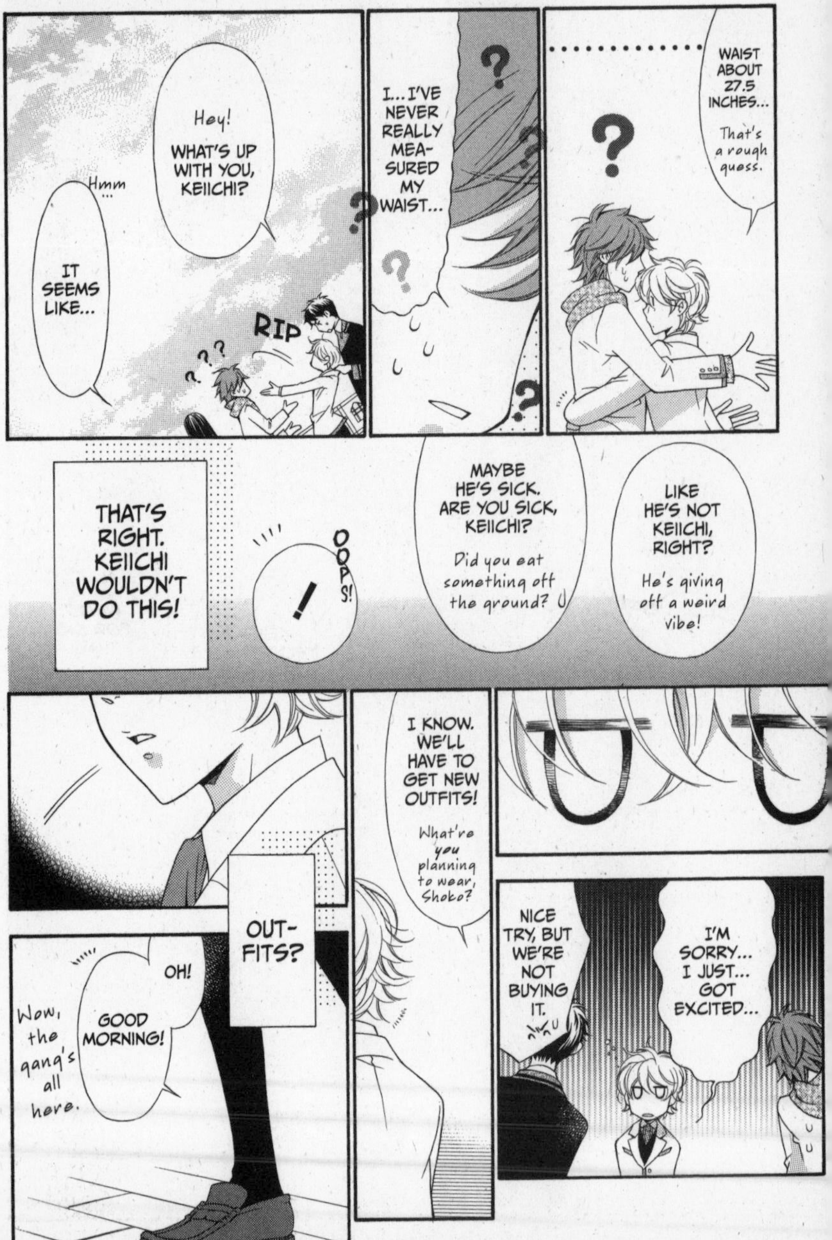

....
WAIST ABOUT 27.5 INCHES... That's a rough guess.
I... I'VE NEVER REALLY MEA-SURED MY WAIST...
Hey! WHAT'S UP WITH YOU, KEIICHI?
Hmm... IT SEEMS LIKE...
RIP
LIKE HE'S NOT KEIICHI, RIGHT? He's giving off a weird vibe!
MAYBE HE'S SICK. ARE YOU SICK, KEIICHI? Did you eat something off the ground?
OOPS!
!
THAT'S RIGHT. KEIICHI WOULDN'T DO THIS!
I'M SORRY... I JUST... GOT EXCITED...
NICE TRY, BUT WE'RE NOT BUYING IT.
I KNOW. WE'LL HAVE TO GET NEW OUTFITS! What're you planning to wear, Shoko?
OUT-FITS?
OH! GOOD MORNING!
Wow, the gang's all here.

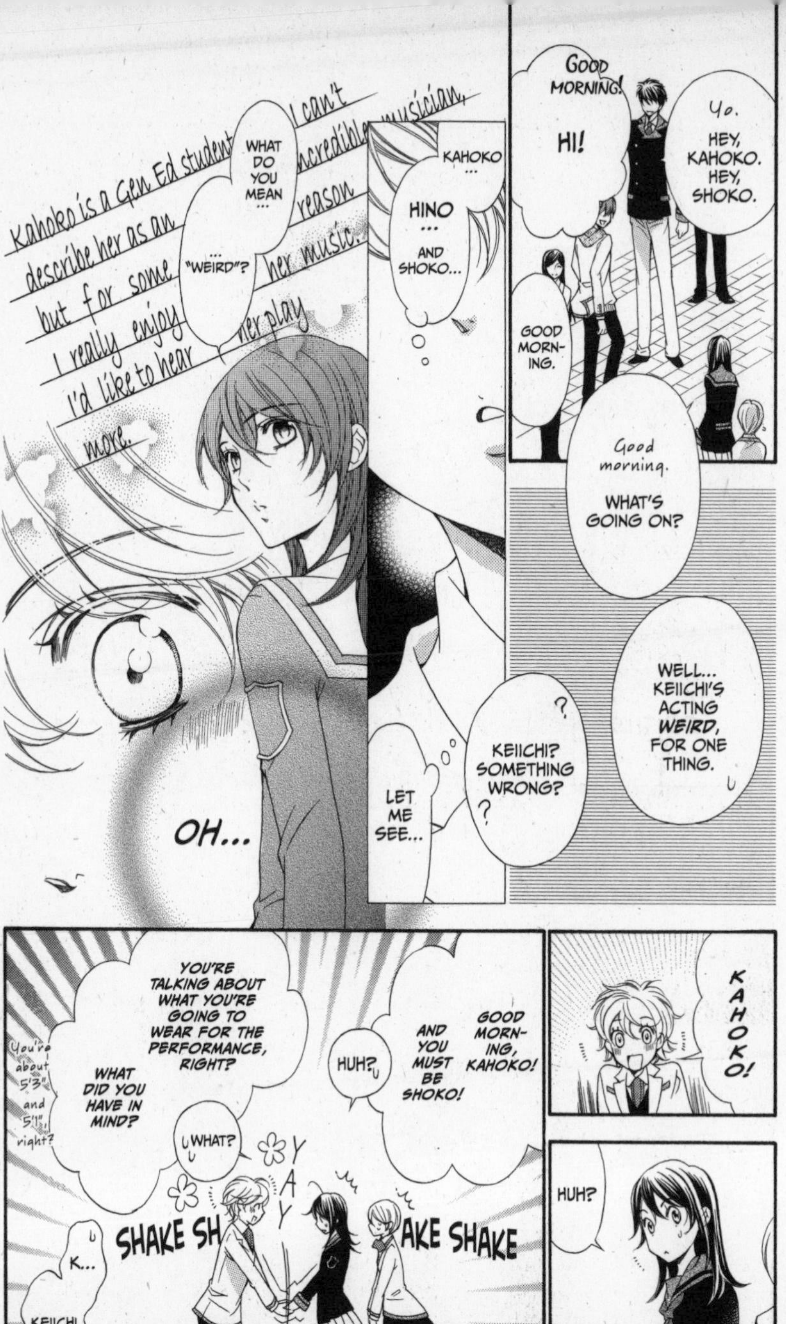
Yo.
HEY, KAHOKO. HEY, SHOKO.
GOOD MORNING!
HI!
GOOD MORNING.
Good morning.
WHAT'S GOING ON?
WELL... KEIICHI'S ACTING WEIRD, FOR ONE THING.
? KEIICHI? SOMETHING WRONG? ?
KAHOKO...
HINO... AND SHOKO...
LET ME SEE...
WHAT DO YOU MEAN...
... "WEIRD"?
Kahoko is a Gen Ed student. I can't describe her as an incredible musician, but for some reason I really enjoy her music. I'd like to hear her play more.
OH...
KAHOKO!
HUH?
GOOD MORNING, KAHOKO!
AND YOU MUST BE SHOKO!
HUH?
YOU'RE TALKING ABOUT WHAT YOU'RE GOING TO WEAR FOR THE PERFORMANCE, RIGHT?
WHAT DID YOU HAVE IN MIND?
WHAT?
YAY
SHAKE SHAKE SHAKE
You're about 5'3" and 5'1", right?
K...
KEIICHI?

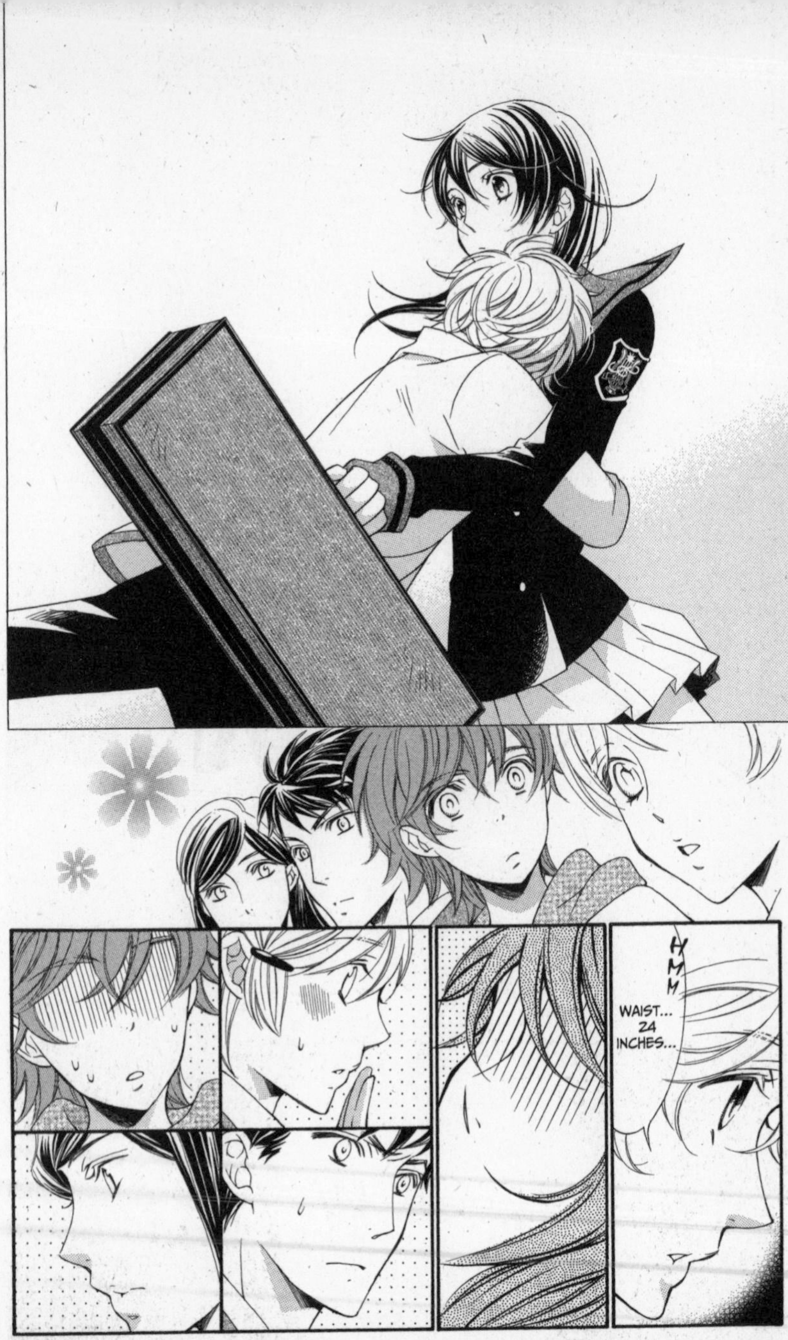
HMM
WAIST... 24 INCHES...

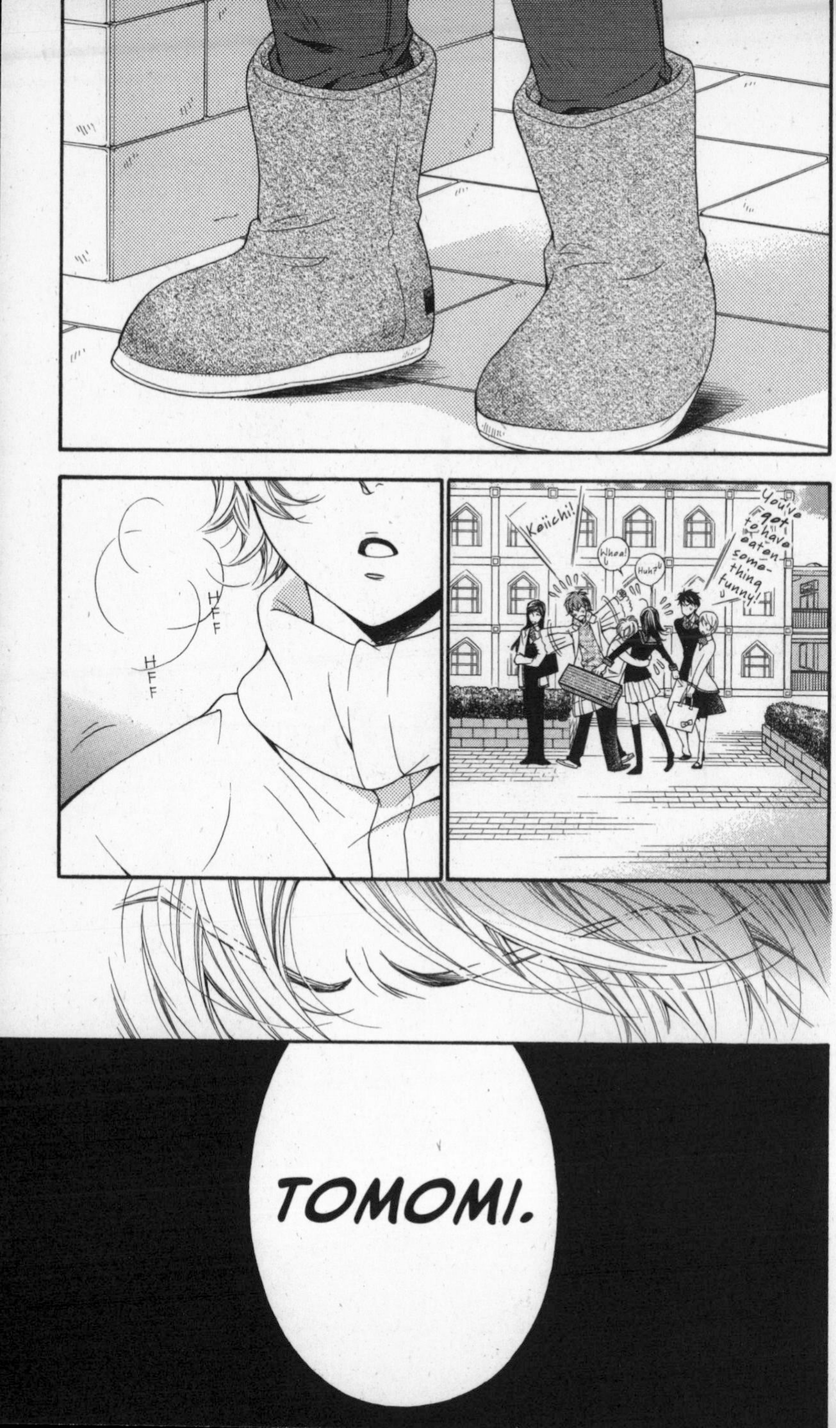
You've got to have eaten something funny!
Keiichi!
Whoa!
Huh?
HFF
HFF
TOMOMI.

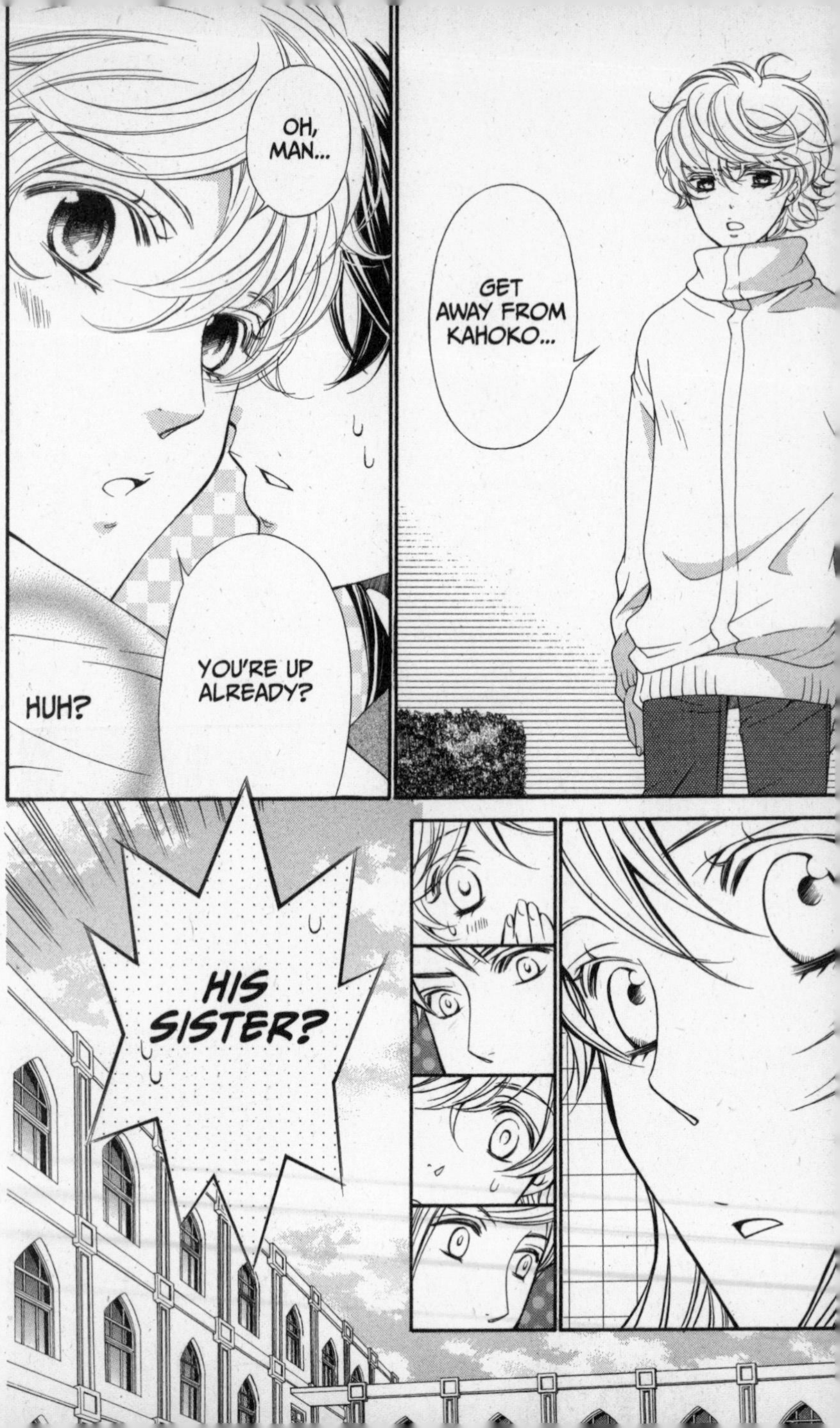
GET AWAY FROM KAHOKO...
OH, MAN...
YOU'RE UP ALREADY?
HUH?
HIS SISTER?

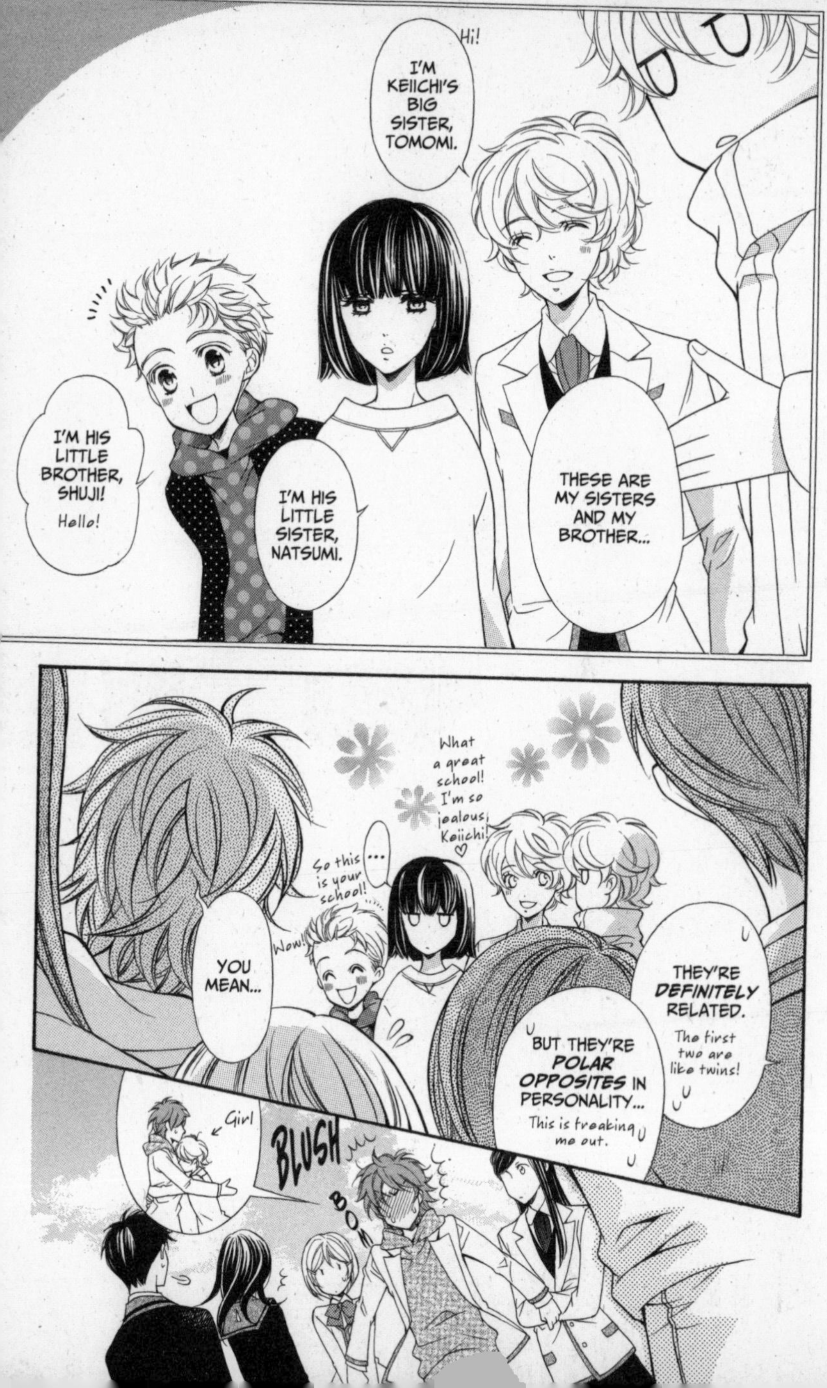
THESE ARE MY SISTERS AND MY BROTHER...
Hi!
I'M KEIICHI'S BIG SISTER, TOMOMI.
I'M HIS LITTLE SISTER, NATSUMI.
I'M HIS LITTLE BROTHER, SHUJI!
Hello!
THEY'RE *DEFINITELY* RELATED.
The first two are like twins!
BUT THEY'RE *POLAR OPPOSITES* IN PERSONALITY...
This is freaking me out.
What a great school! I'm so jealous, Keiichi ♡
...
So this is your school!
Wow!
YOU MEAN...
Girl
BLUSH
BOM

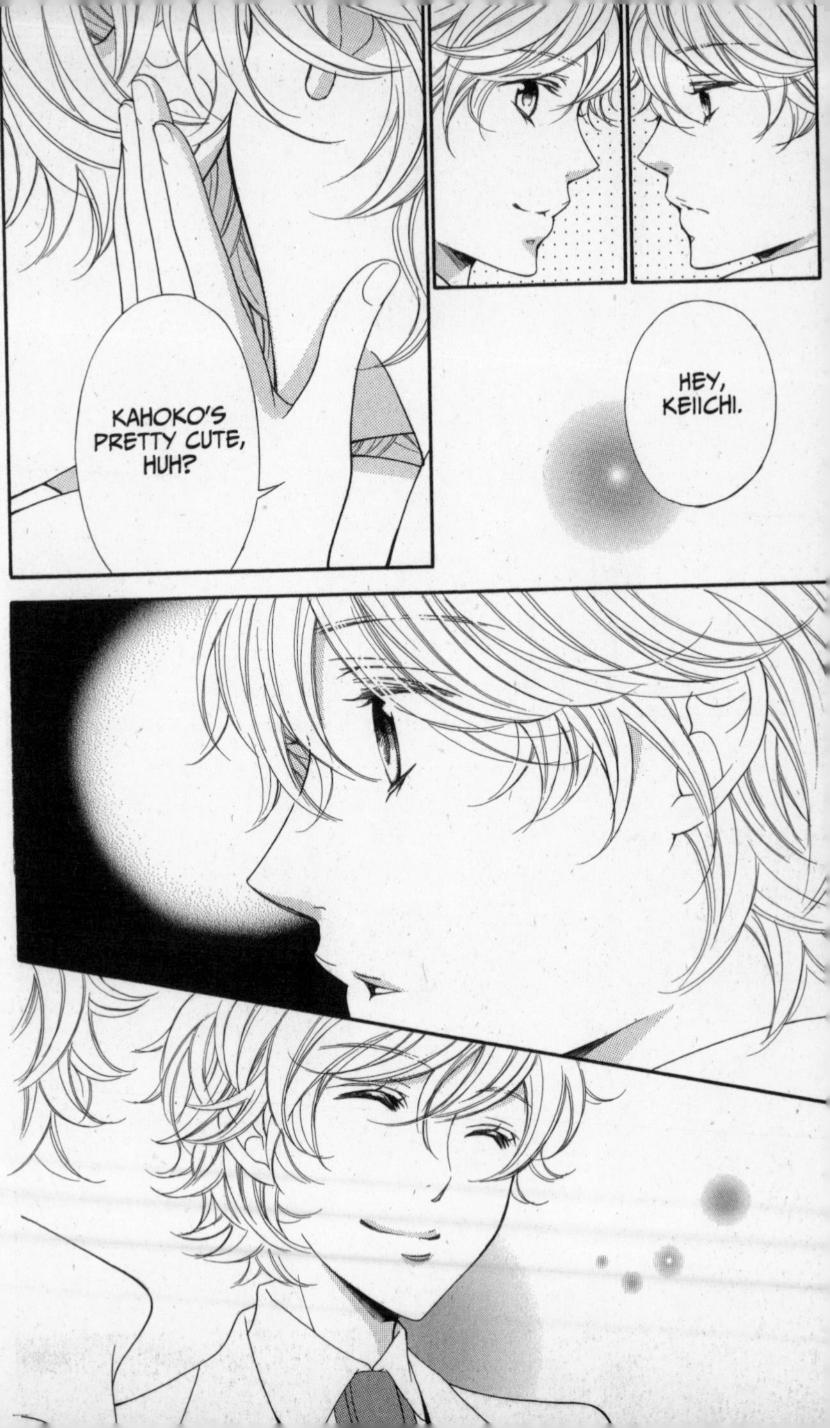
HEY, KEIICHI.
KAHOKO'S PRETTY CUTE, HUH?

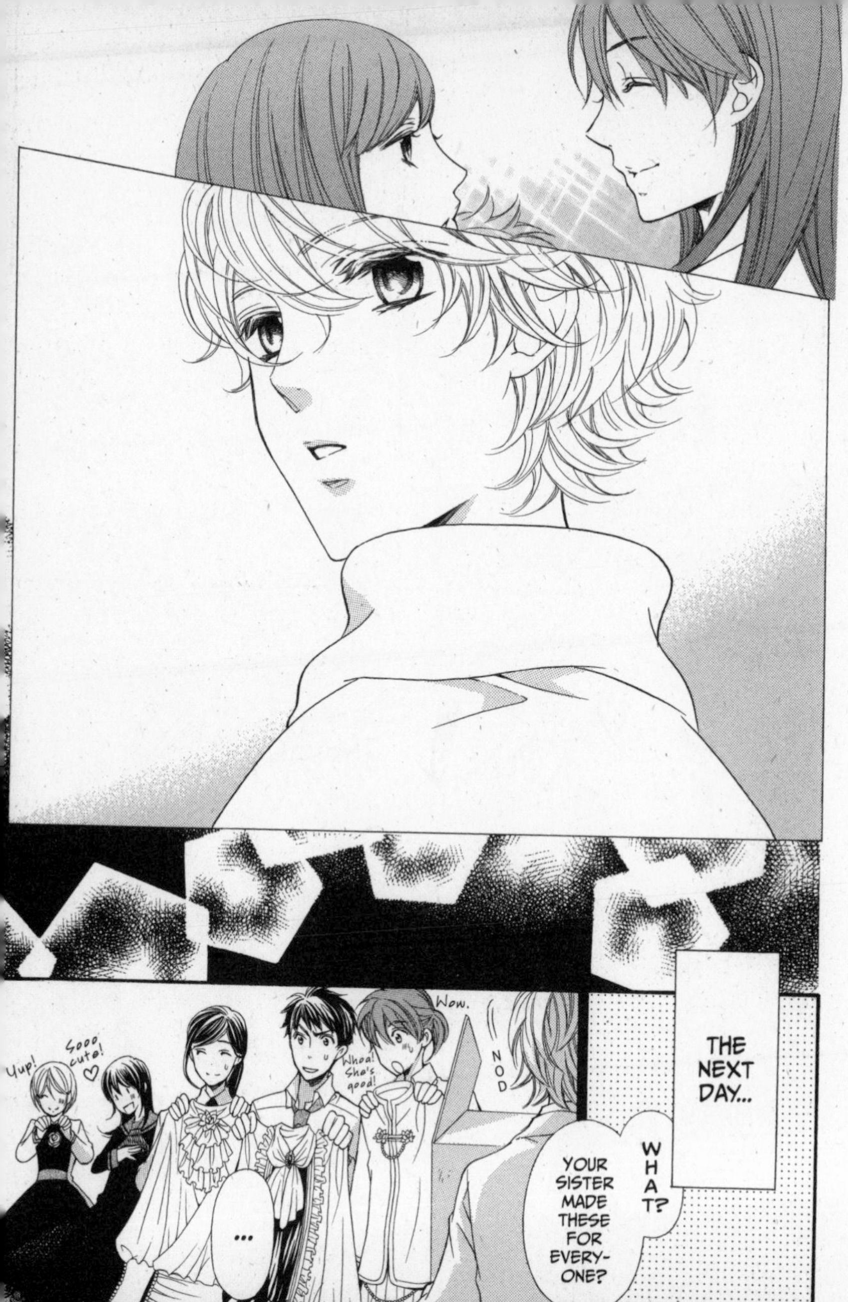
THE NEXT DAY...
WHAT?
YOUR SISTER MADE THESE FOR EVERY-ONE?
NOD
Wow.
Whoa! She's good!
...
Sooo cute! ♡
Yup!

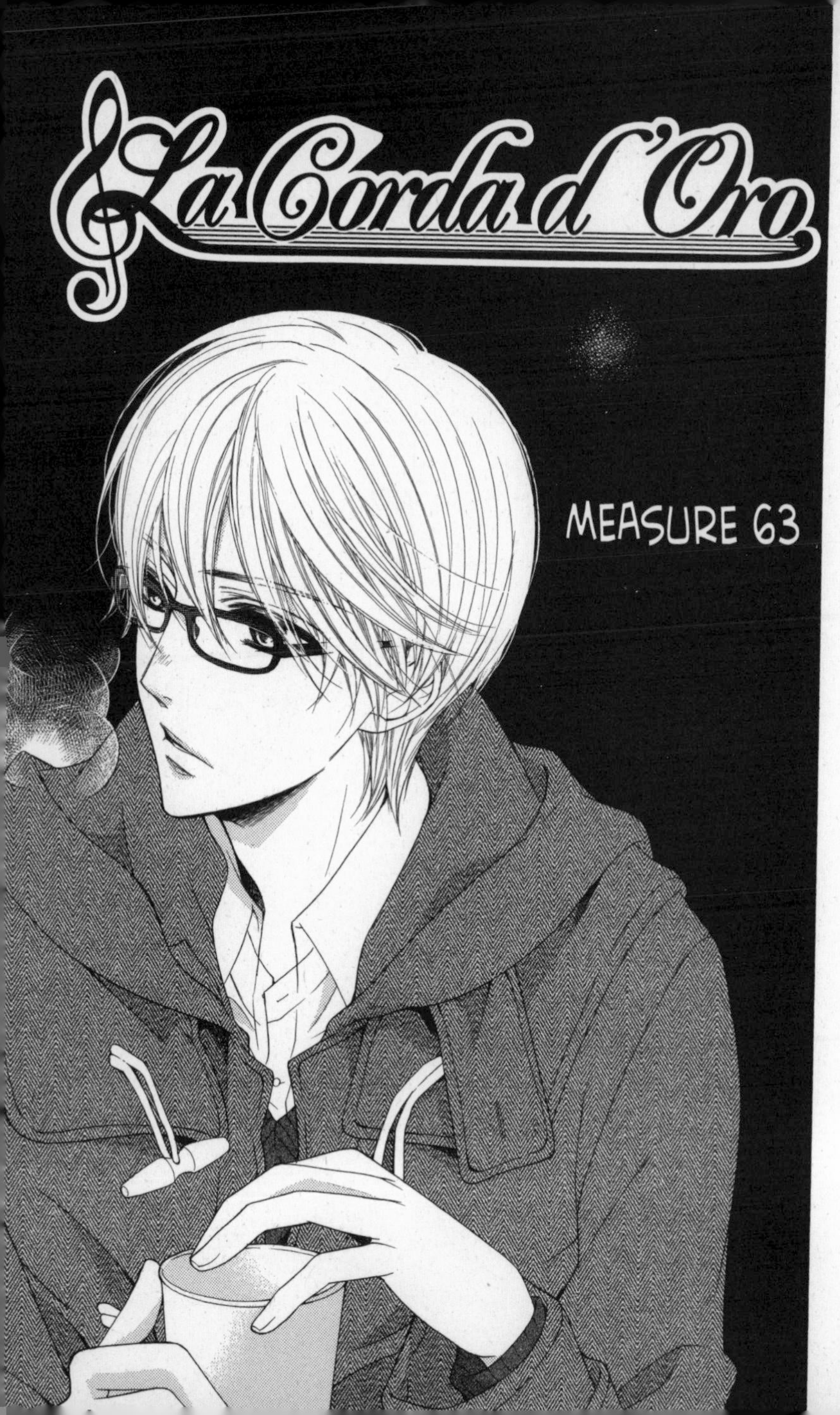
La Corda d'Oro
MEASURE 63

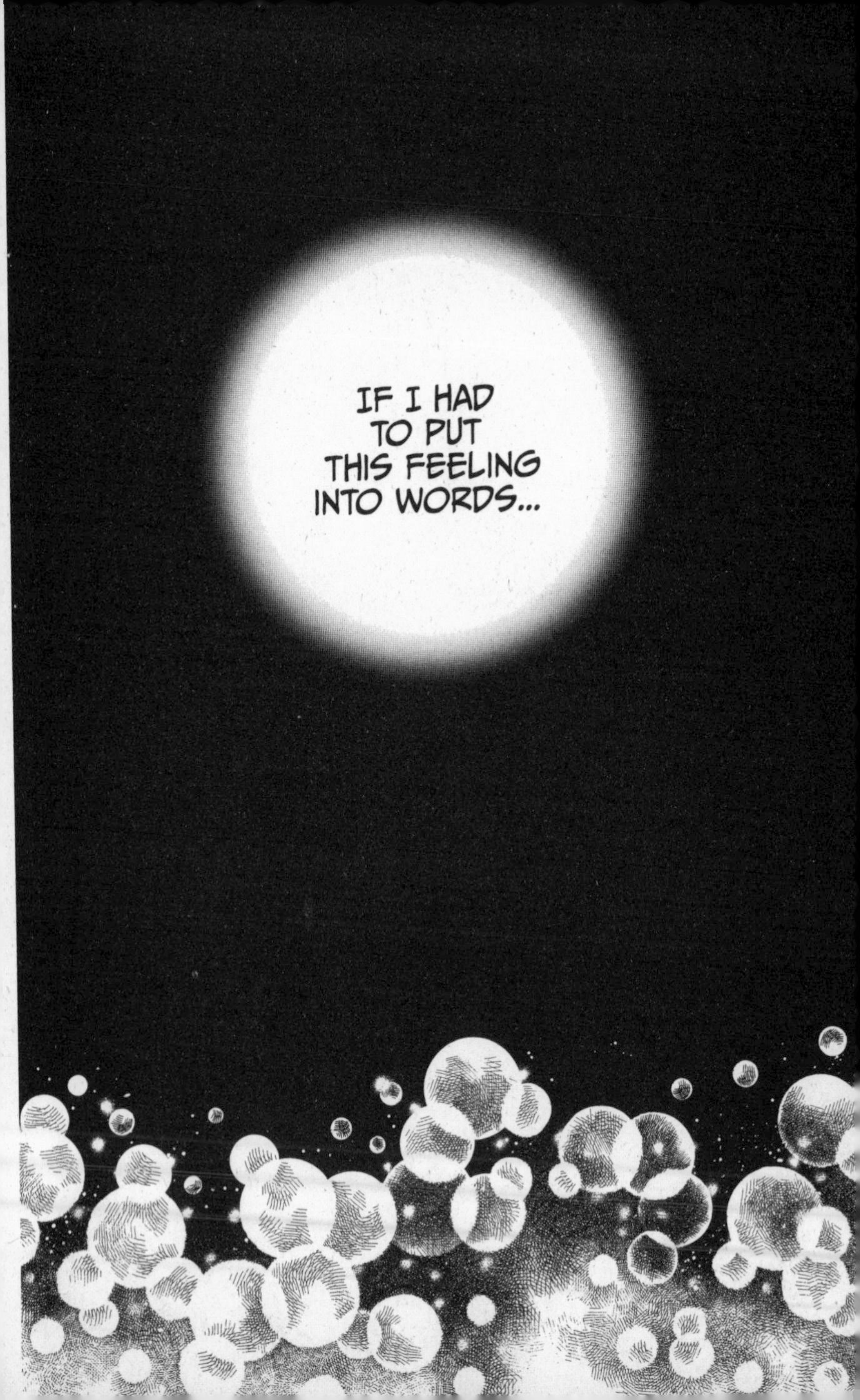
IF I HAD TO PUT THIS FEELING INTO WORDS...

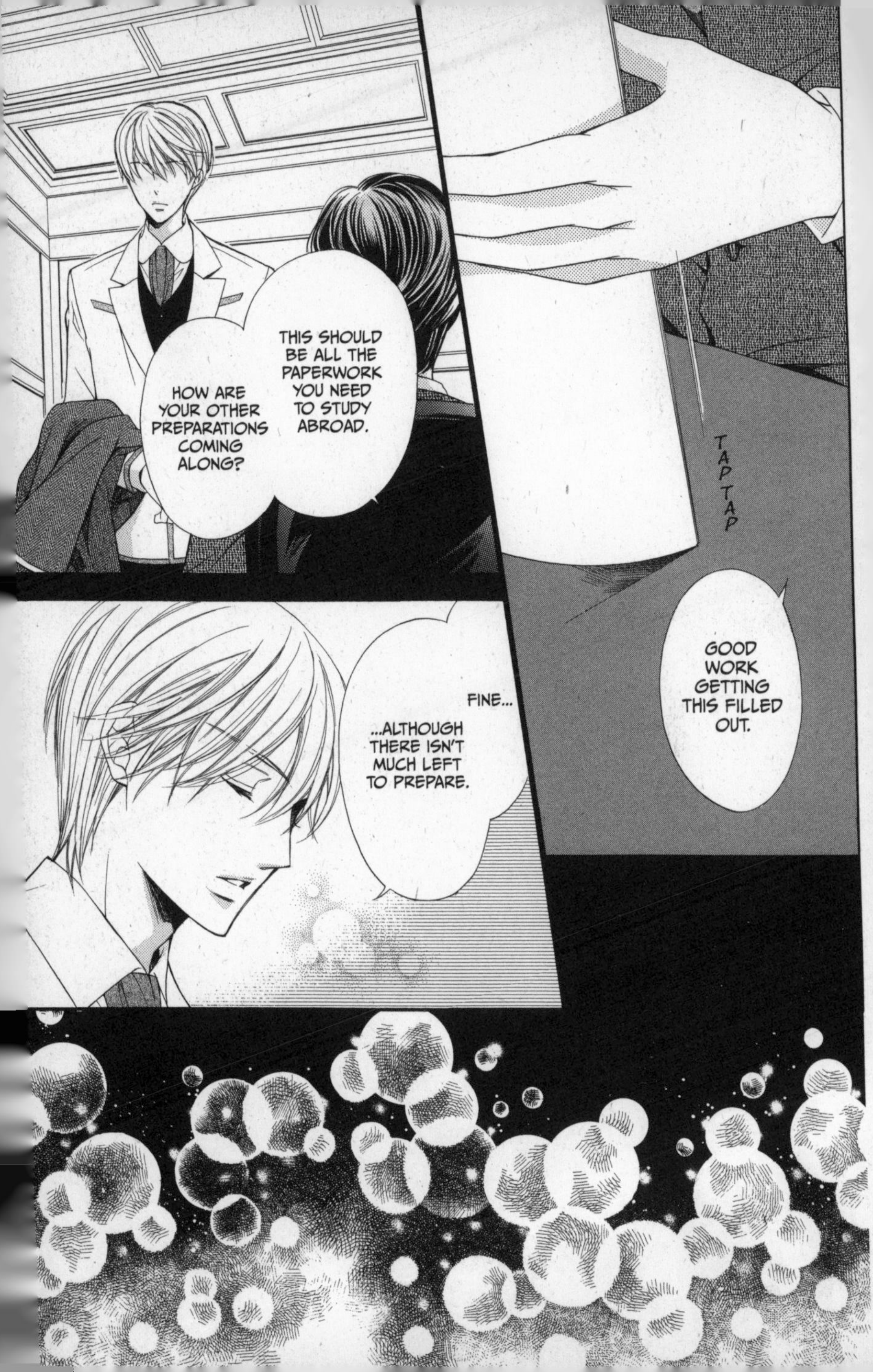
TAP TAP
GOOD WORK GETTING THIS FILLED OUT.
THIS SHOULD BE ALL THE PAPERWORK YOU NEED TO STUDY ABROAD.
HOW ARE YOUR OTHER PREPARATIONS COMING ALONG?
FINE...
...ALTHOUGH THERE ISN'T MUCH LEFT TO PREPARE.

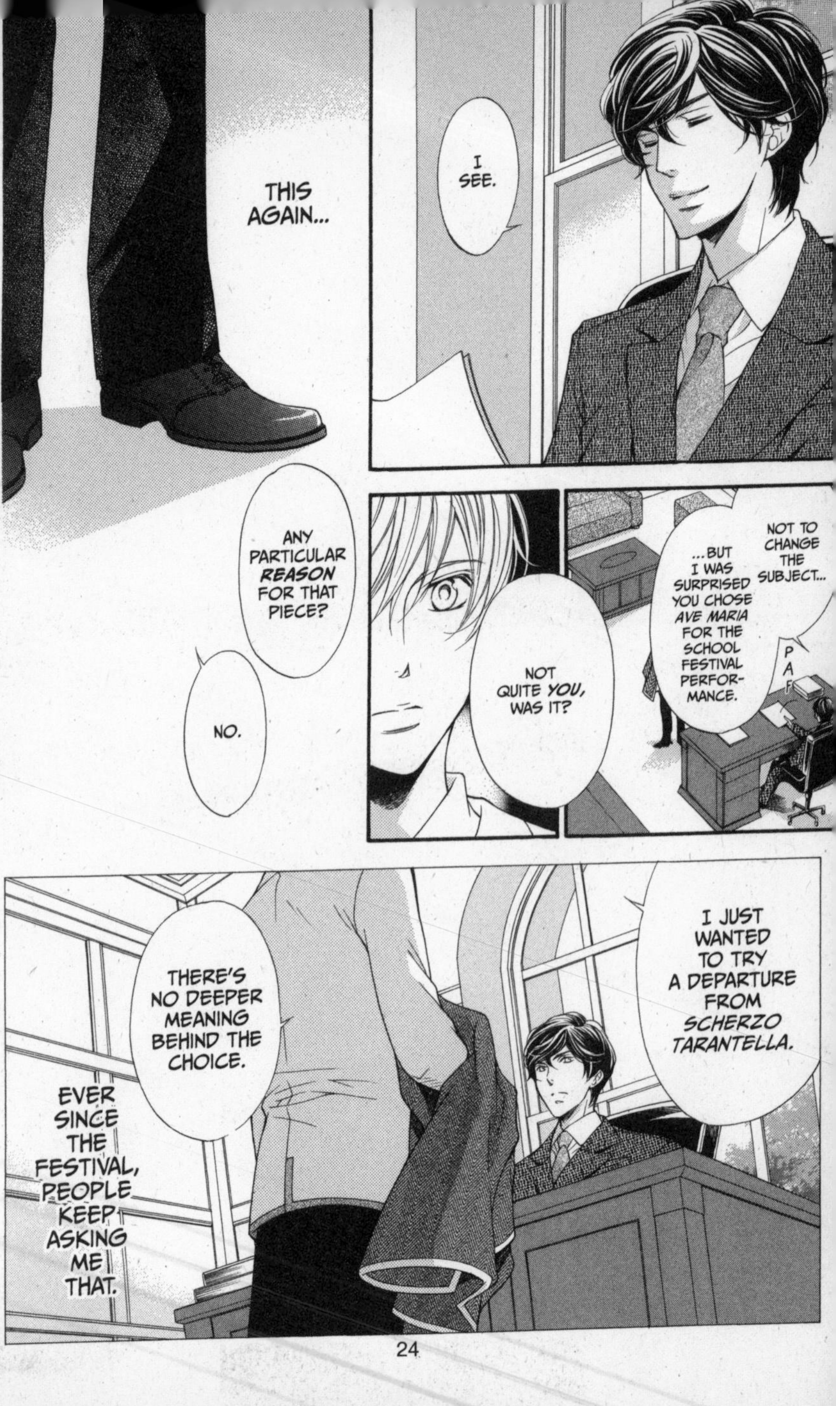

I SEE.
THIS AGAIN...
NOT TO CHANGE THE SUBJECT...
...BUT I WAS SURPRISED YOU CHOSE *AVE MARIA* FOR THE SCHOOL FESTIVAL PERFORMANCE.
PAF
NOT QUITE *YOU*, WAS IT?
ANY PARTICULAR ***REASON*** FOR THAT PIECE?
NO.
I JUST WANTED TO TRY A DEPARTURE FROM *SCHERZO TARANTELLA.*
THERE'S NO DEEPER MEANING BEHIND THE CHOICE.
EVER SINCE THE FESTIVAL, PEOPLE KEEP ASKING ME THAT.

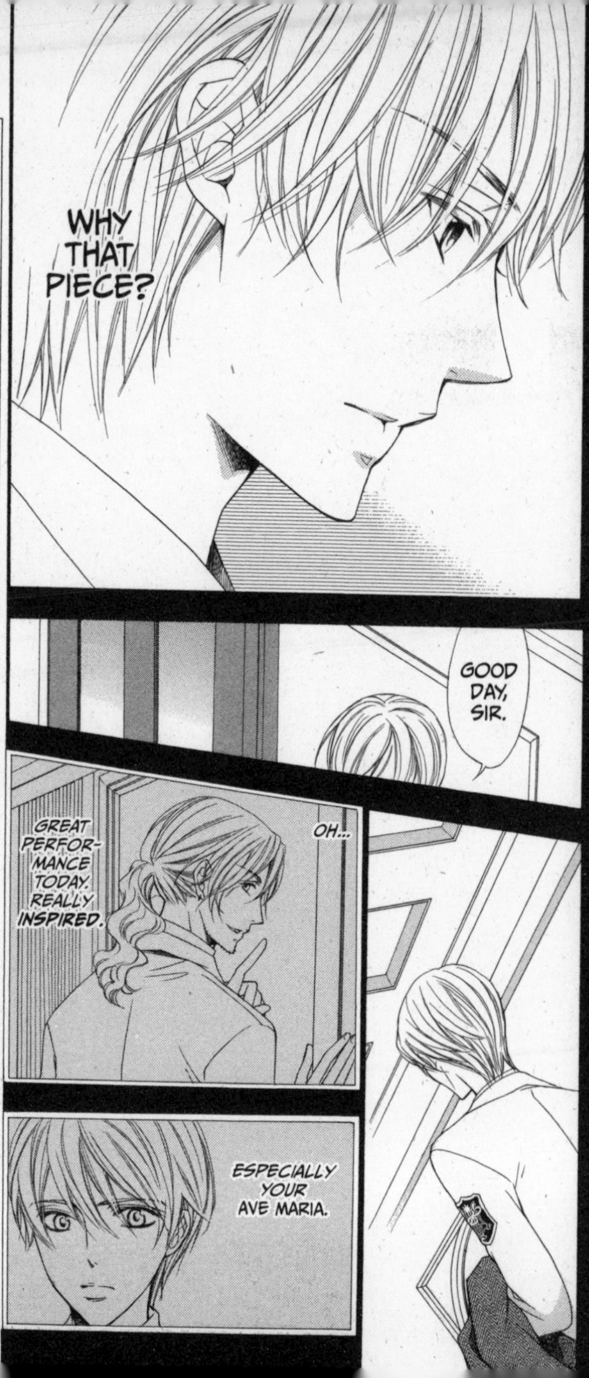
WHY THAT PIECE?
GOOD DAY, SIR.
OH...
GREAT PERFORMANCE TODAY. REALLY INSPIRED.
ESPECIALLY YOUR AVE MARIA.

Hello! It feels like so long since volume 14... (I'm sorry!) But here we are again at last!

This is the first time I've started a volume with a side story, but I thought it fit with the School Festival arc in volume 14.

Personally, I like Keiichi's sister. Her carefree attitude really speaks to me.

Well, I hope you enjoy the book!

Yuki Kure

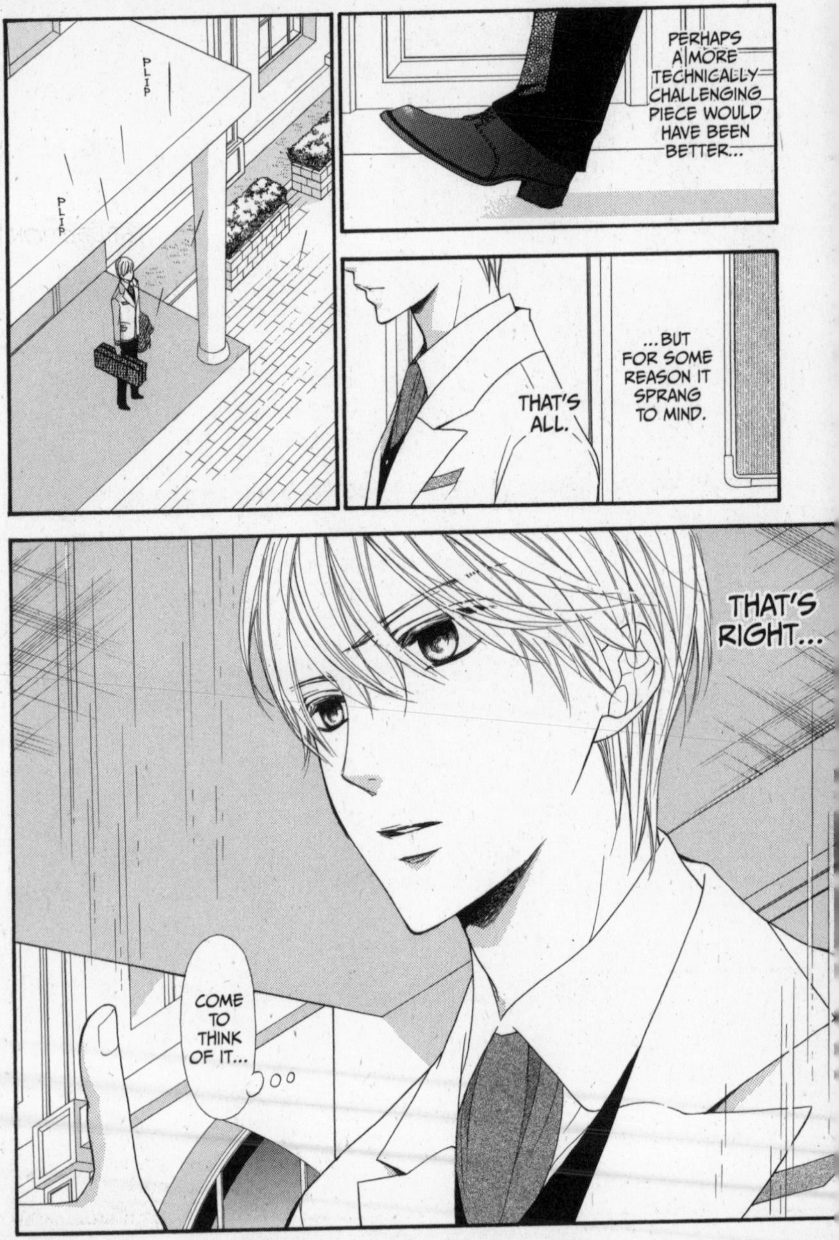
PERHAPS A MORE TECHNICALLY CHALLENGING PIECE WOULD HAVE BEEN BETTER...
...BUT FOR SOME REASON IT SPRANG TO MIND.
THAT'S ALL.
PLIP
PLIP
THAT'S RIGHT...
COME TO THINK OF IT...

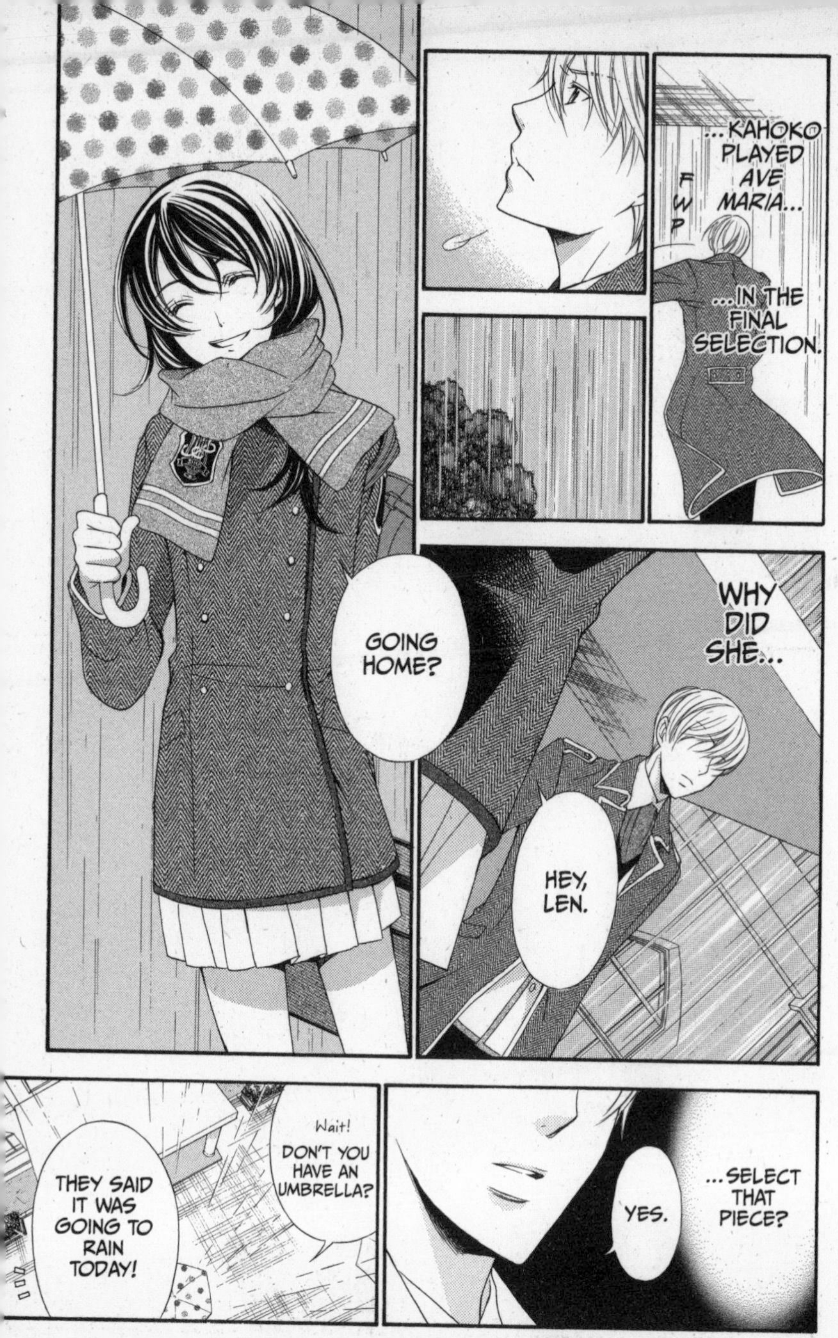
...KAHOKO PLAYED AVE MARIA...
FWP
...IN THE FINAL SELECTION.
WHY DID SHE...
HEY, LEN.
GOING HOME?
...SELECT THAT PIECE?
YES.
Wait!
DON'T YOU HAVE AN UMBRELLA?
THEY SAID IT WAS GOING TO RAIN TODAY!

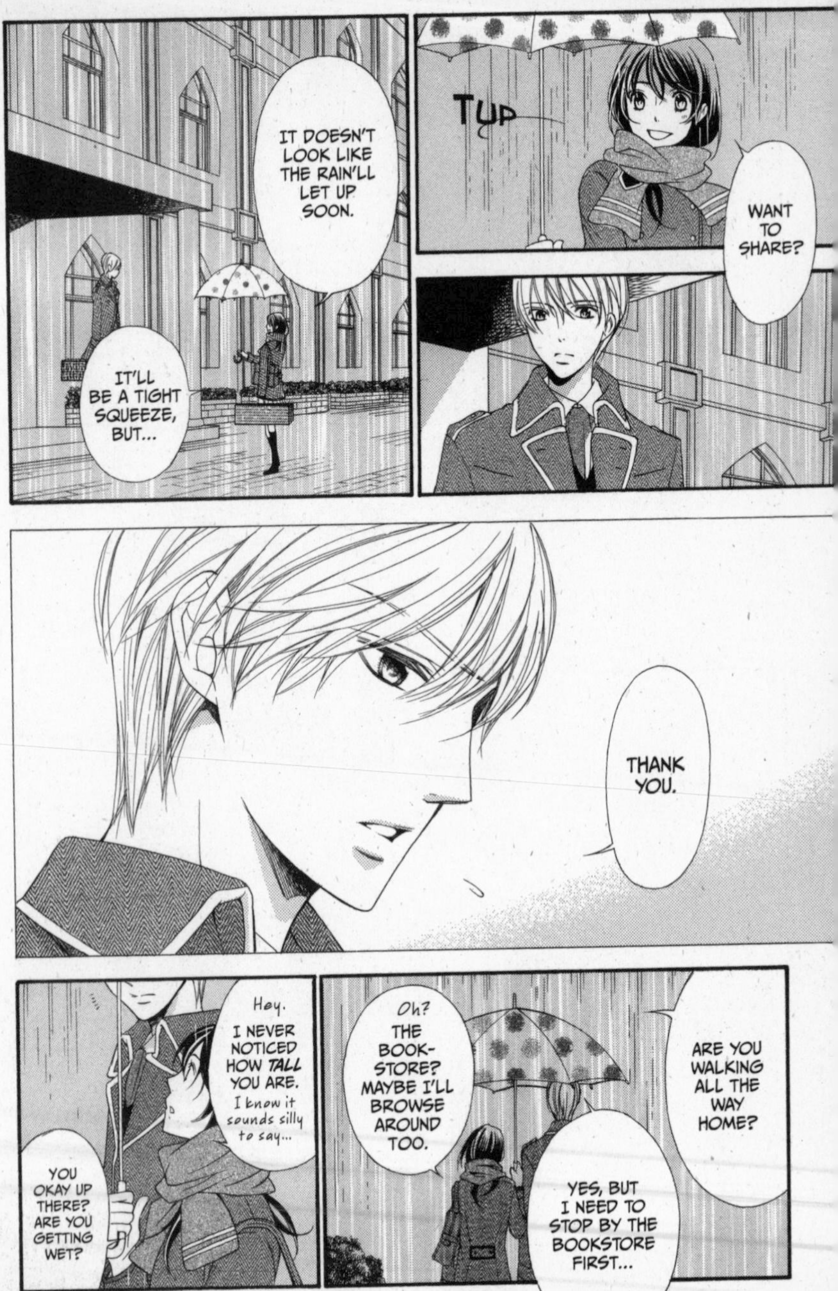
TUP
WANT TO SHARE?
IT DOESN'T LOOK LIKE THE RAIN'LL LET UP SOON.
IT'LL BE A TIGHT SQUEEZE, BUT...
THANK YOU.
ARE YOU WALKING ALL THE WAY HOME?
YES, BUT I NEED TO STOP BY THE BOOKSTORE FIRST...
Oh? THE BOOK-STORE? MAYBE I'LL BROWSE AROUND TOO.
Hey. I NEVER NOTICED HOW *TALL* YOU ARE. I know it sounds silly to say...
YOU OKAY UP THERE? ARE YOU GETTING WET?

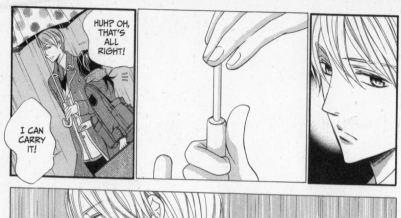

HUH? OH, THAT'S ALL RIGHT!

I CAN CARRY IT!

THANKS, LEN.

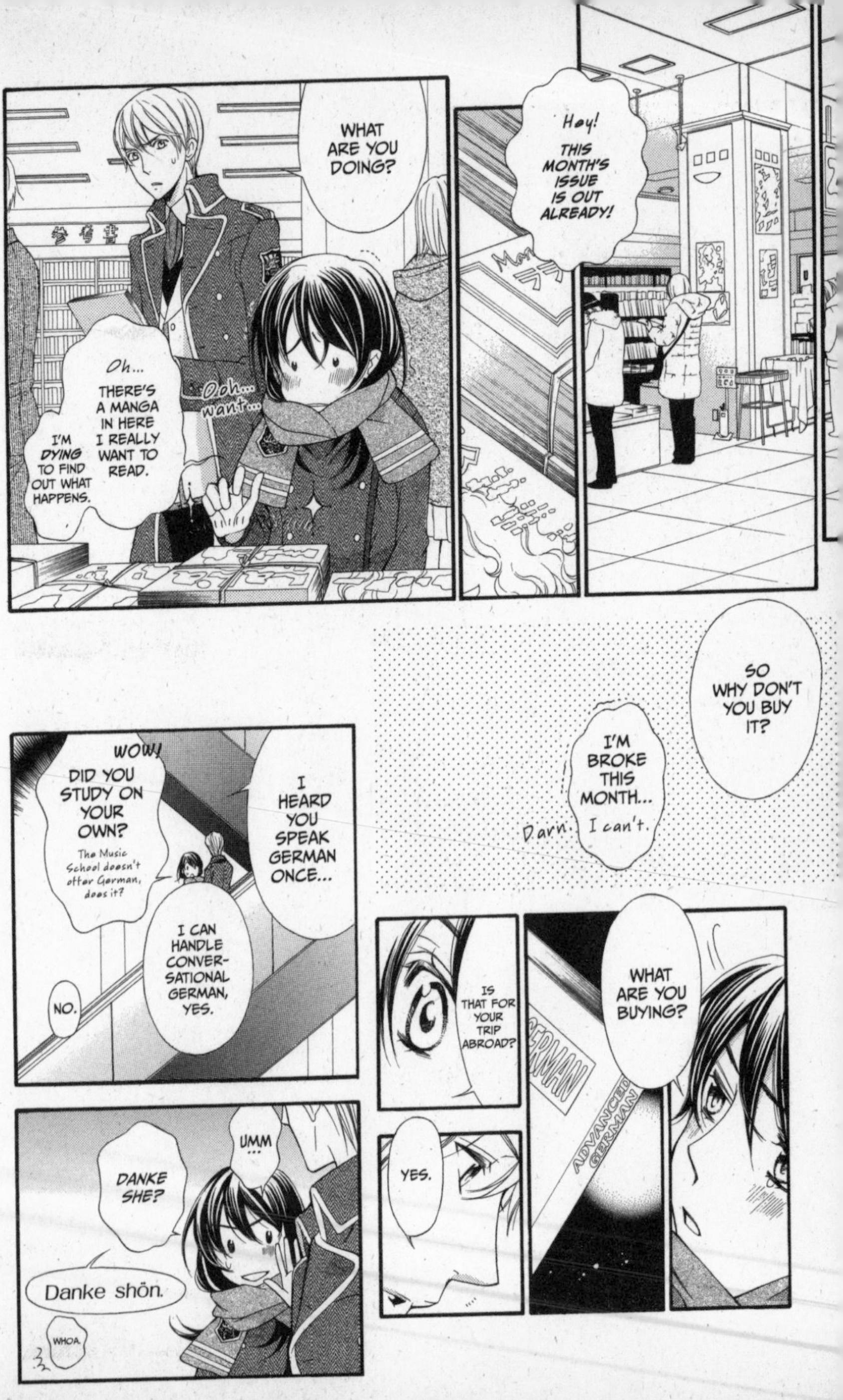

Hey!
THIS MONTH'S ISSUE IS OUT ALREADY!
WHAT ARE YOU DOING?
Ooh... want...
Oh...
THERE'S A MANGA IN HERE I REALLY WANT TO READ.
I'M DYING TO FIND OUT WHAT HAPPENS.
SO WHY DON'T YOU BUY IT?
I'M BROKE THIS MONTH...
I can't.
Darn.
WHAT ARE YOU BUYING?
ADVANCED GERMAN
GERMAN
IS THAT FOR YOUR TRIP ABROAD?
YES.
I HEARD YOU SPEAK GERMAN ONCE...
WOW! DID YOU STUDY ON YOUR OWN?
The Music School doesn't offer German, does it?
I CAN HANDLE CONVERSATIONAL GERMAN, YES.
NO.
UMM...
DANKE SHE?
Danke shön.
WHOA.

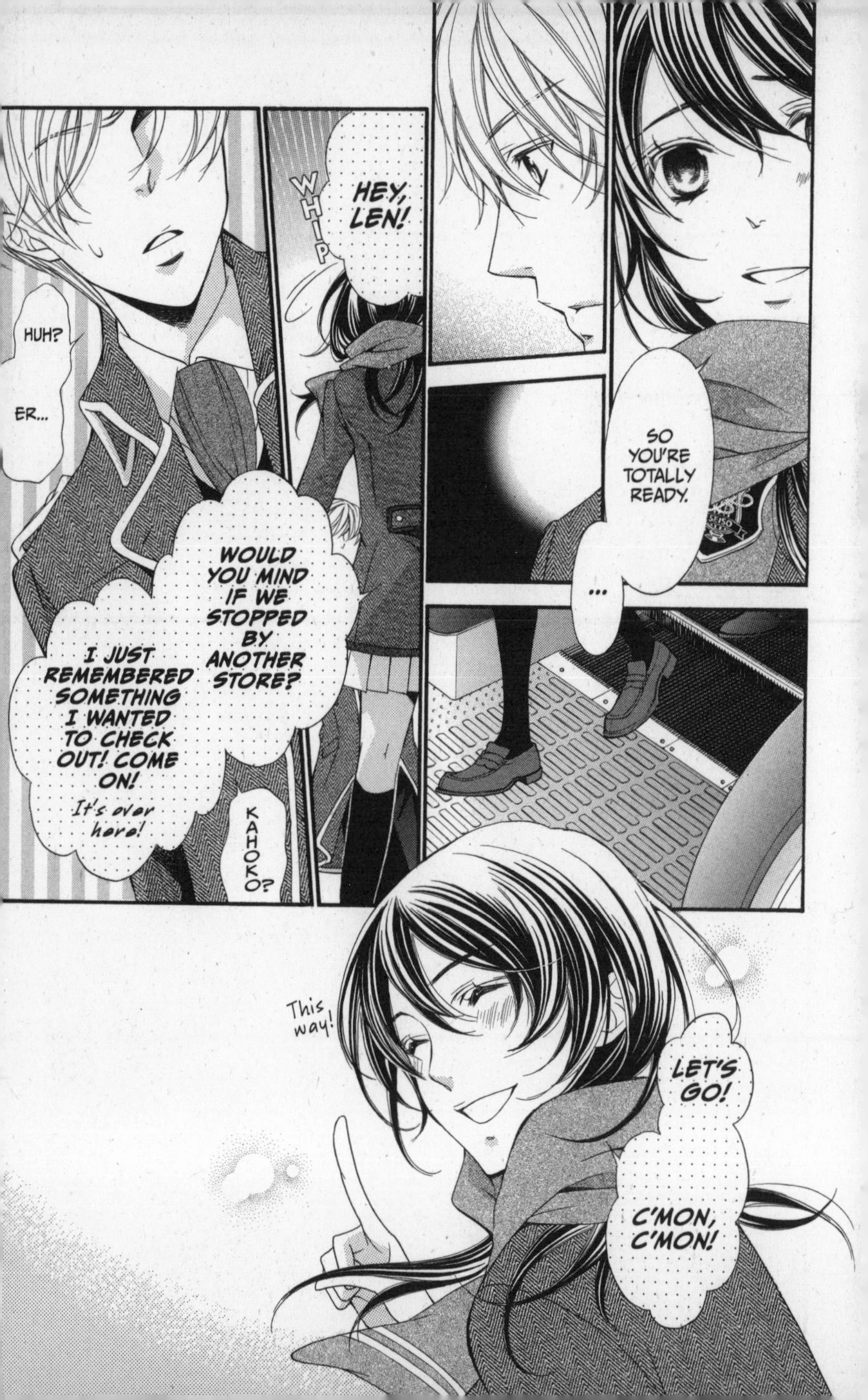
SO YOU'RE TOTALLY READY.
...
HEY, LEN!
WHIP
WOULD YOU MIND IF WE STOPPED BY ANOTHER STORE?
KAHOKO?
HUH?
ER...
I JUST REMEMBERED SOMETHING I WANTED TO CHECK OUT! COME ON!
It's over here!
LET'S GO!
C'MON, C'MON!
This way!

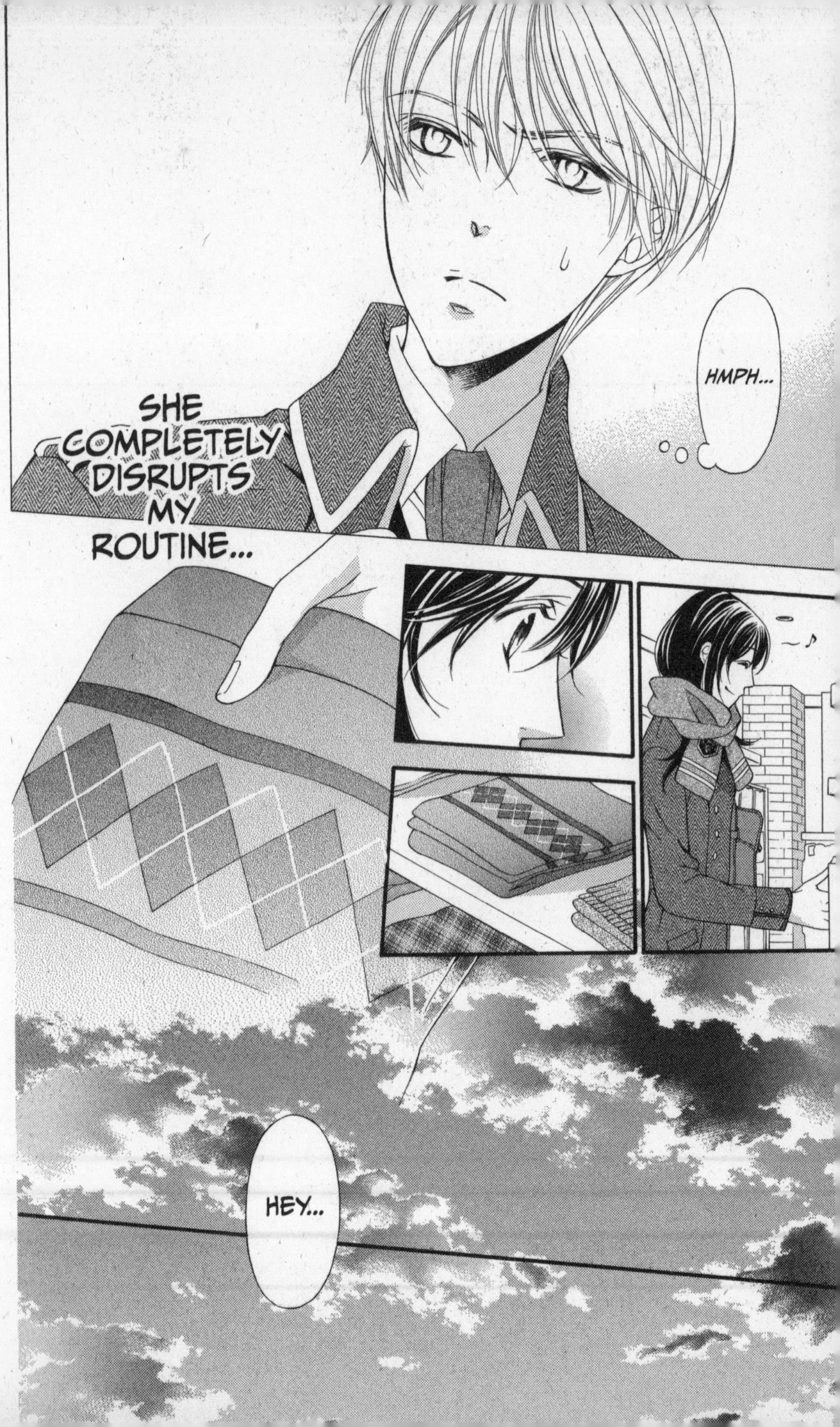
HMPH...
SHE COMPLETELY DISRUPTS MY ROUTINE...
~♪
HEY...

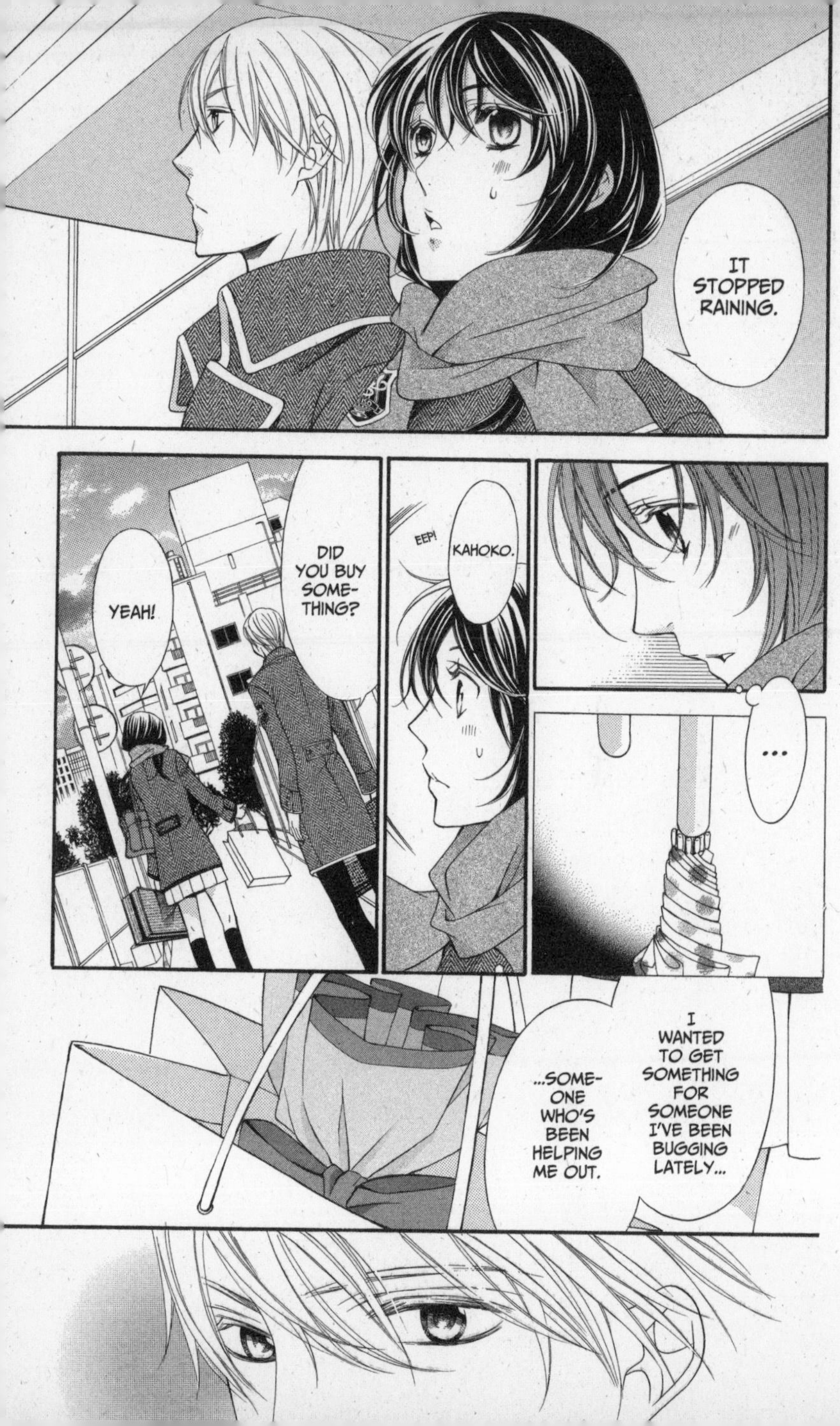
IT STOPPED RAINING.
...
KAHOKO.
EEP!
DID YOU BUY SOME-THING?
YEAH!
I WANTED TO GET SOMETHING FOR SOMEONE I'VE BEEN BUGGING LATELY...
...SOME-ONE WHO'S BEEN HELPING ME OUT.

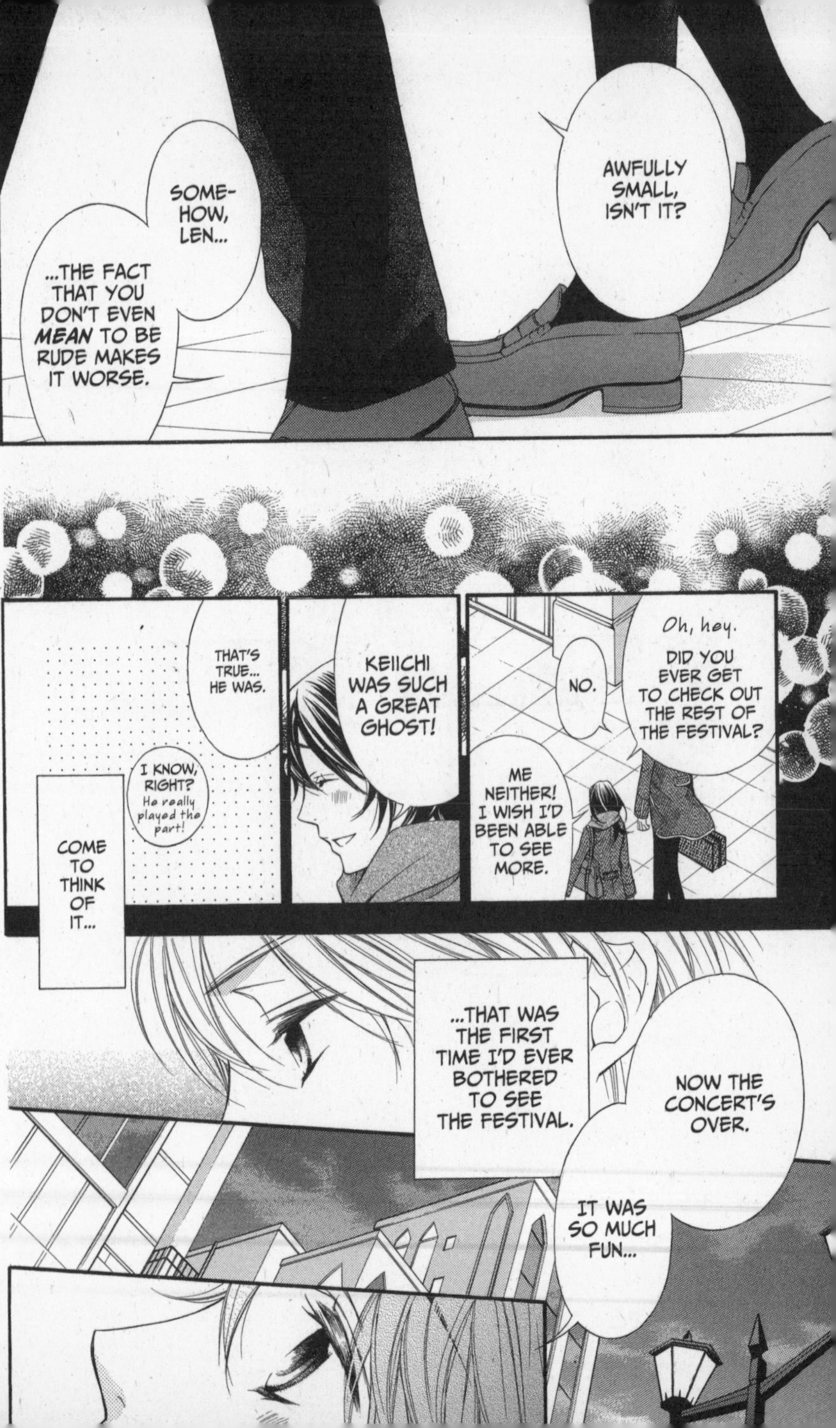
AWFULLY SMALL, ISN'T IT?
SOME-HOW, LEN...
...THE FACT THAT YOU DON'T EVEN *MEAN* TO BE RUDE MAKES IT WORSE.
Oh, hey. DID YOU EVER GET TO CHECK OUT THE REST OF THE FESTIVAL?
NO.
ME NEITHER! I WISH I'D BEEN ABLE TO SEE MORE.
KEIICHI WAS SUCH A GREAT GHOST!
THAT'S TRUE... HE WAS.
I KNOW, RIGHT? He really played the part!
COME TO THINK OF IT...
...THAT WAS THE FIRST TIME I'D EVER BOTHERED TO SEE THE FESTIVAL.
NOW THE CONCERT'S OVER.
IT WAS SO MUCH FUN...

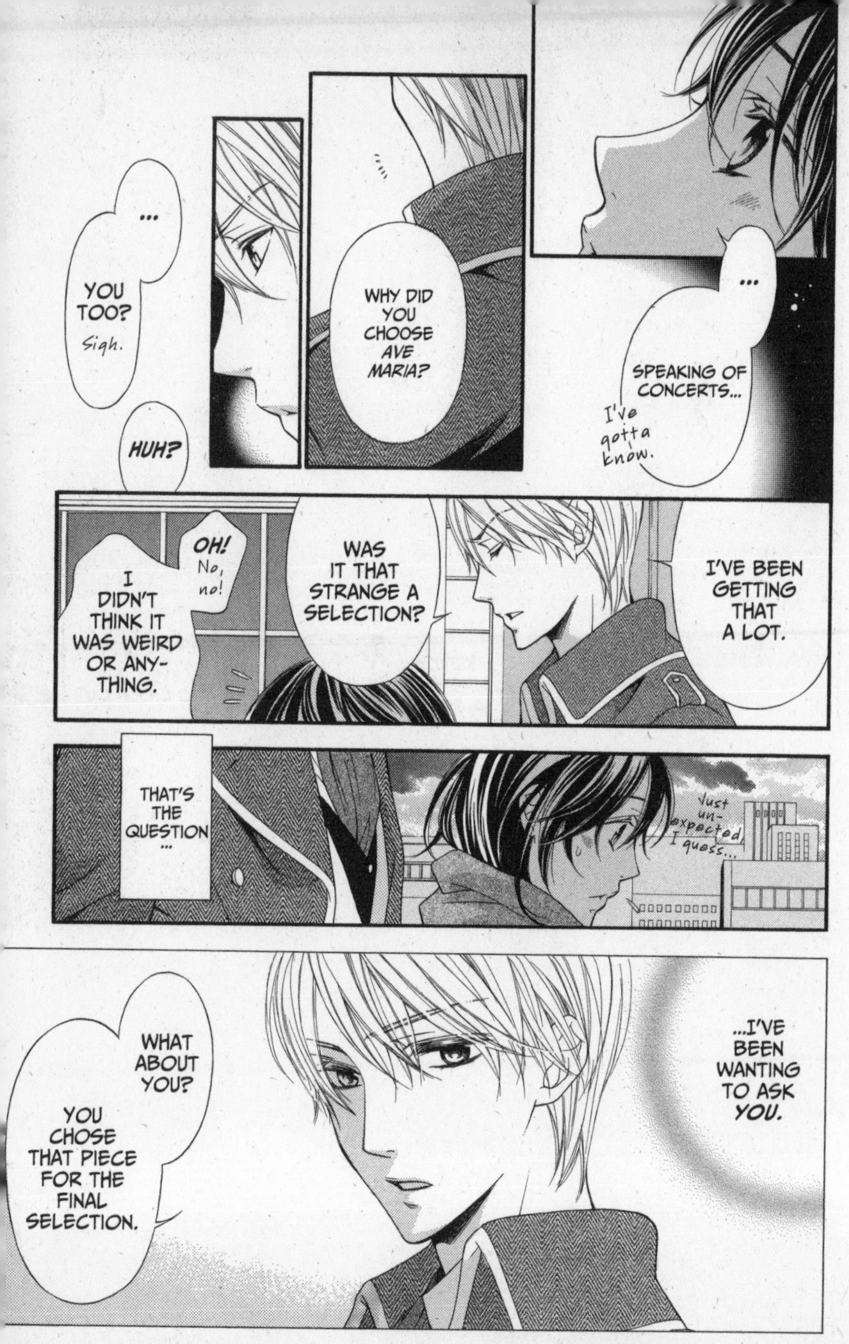
...
SPEAKING OF CONCERTS...
I've gotta know.
WHY DID YOU CHOOSE AVE MARIA?
...
YOU TOO?
Sigh.
HUH?
I'VE BEEN GETTING THAT A LOT.
WAS IT THAT STRANGE A SELECTION?
OH!
No, no!
I DIDN'T THINK IT WAS WEIRD OR ANYTHING.
Just unexpected I guess...
THAT'S THE QUESTION...
...I'VE BEEN WANTING TO ASK YOU.
WHAT ABOUT YOU?
YOU CHOSE THAT PIECE FOR THE FINAL SELECTION.

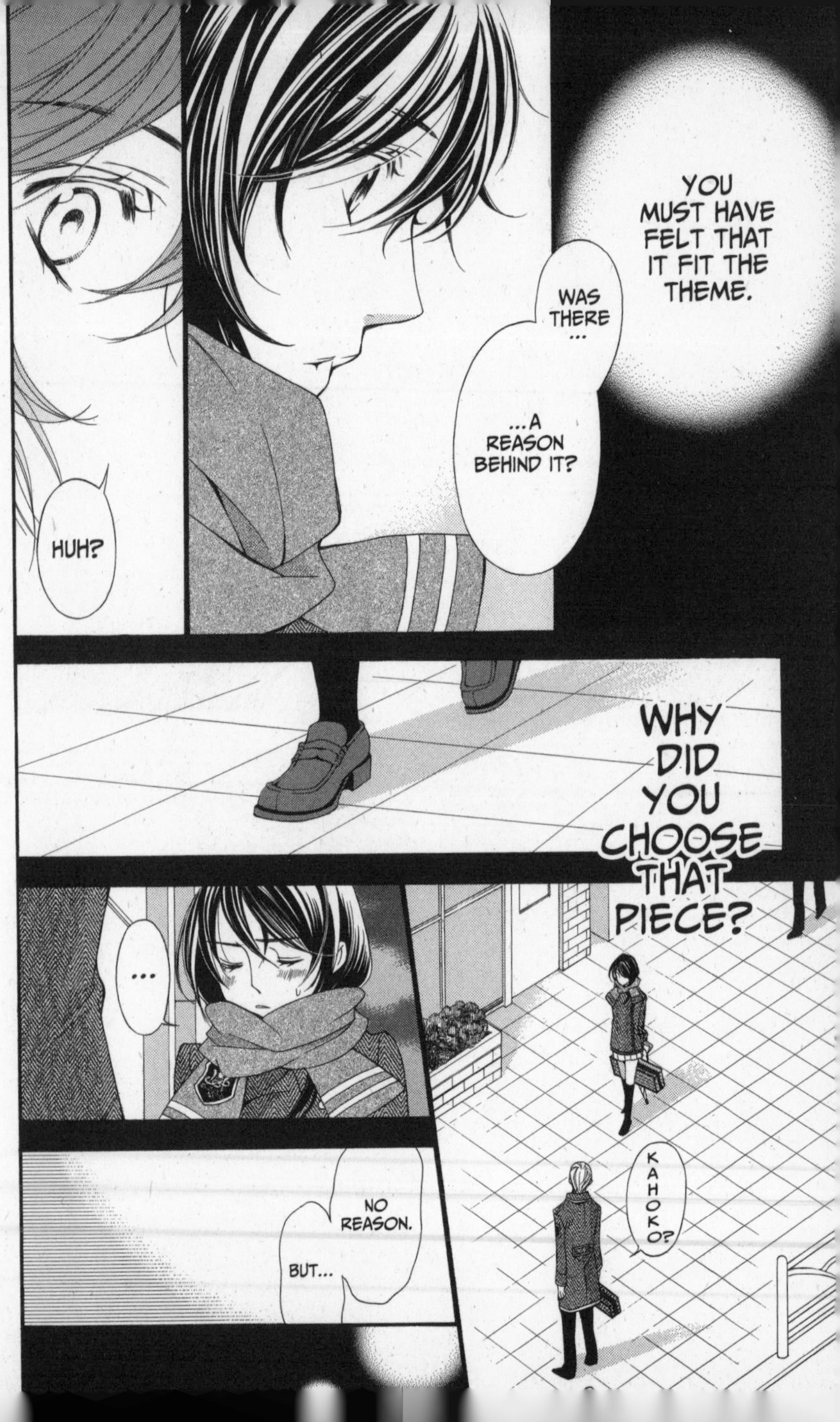
YOU MUST HAVE FELT THAT IT FIT THE THEME.
WAS THERE ...
...A REASON BEHIND IT?
HUH?
WHY DID YOU CHOOSE THAT PIECE?
KAHOKO?
...
NO REASON.
BUT...

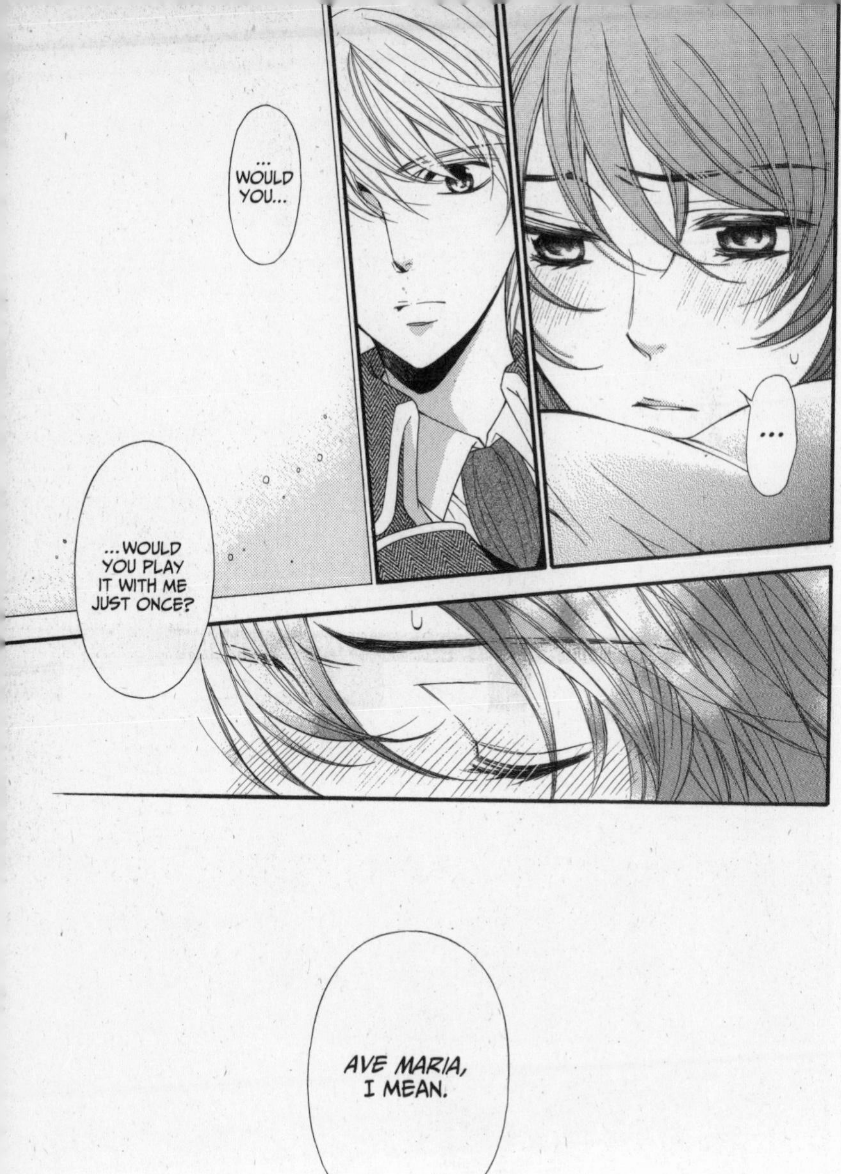
...
...WOULD YOU...
...WOULD YOU PLAY IT WITH ME JUST ONCE?
AVE MARIA, I MEAN.

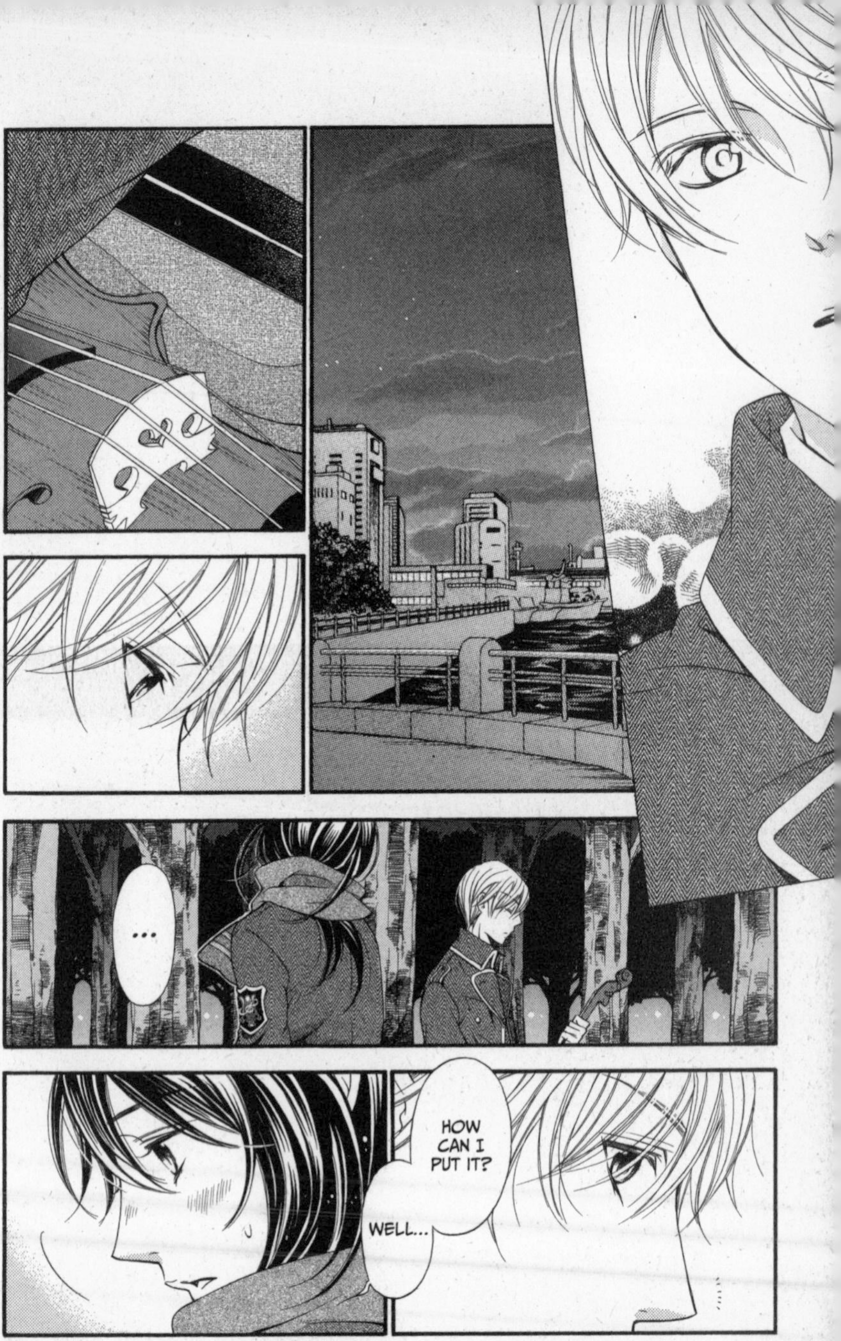
...
HOW CAN I PUT IT?
WELL...

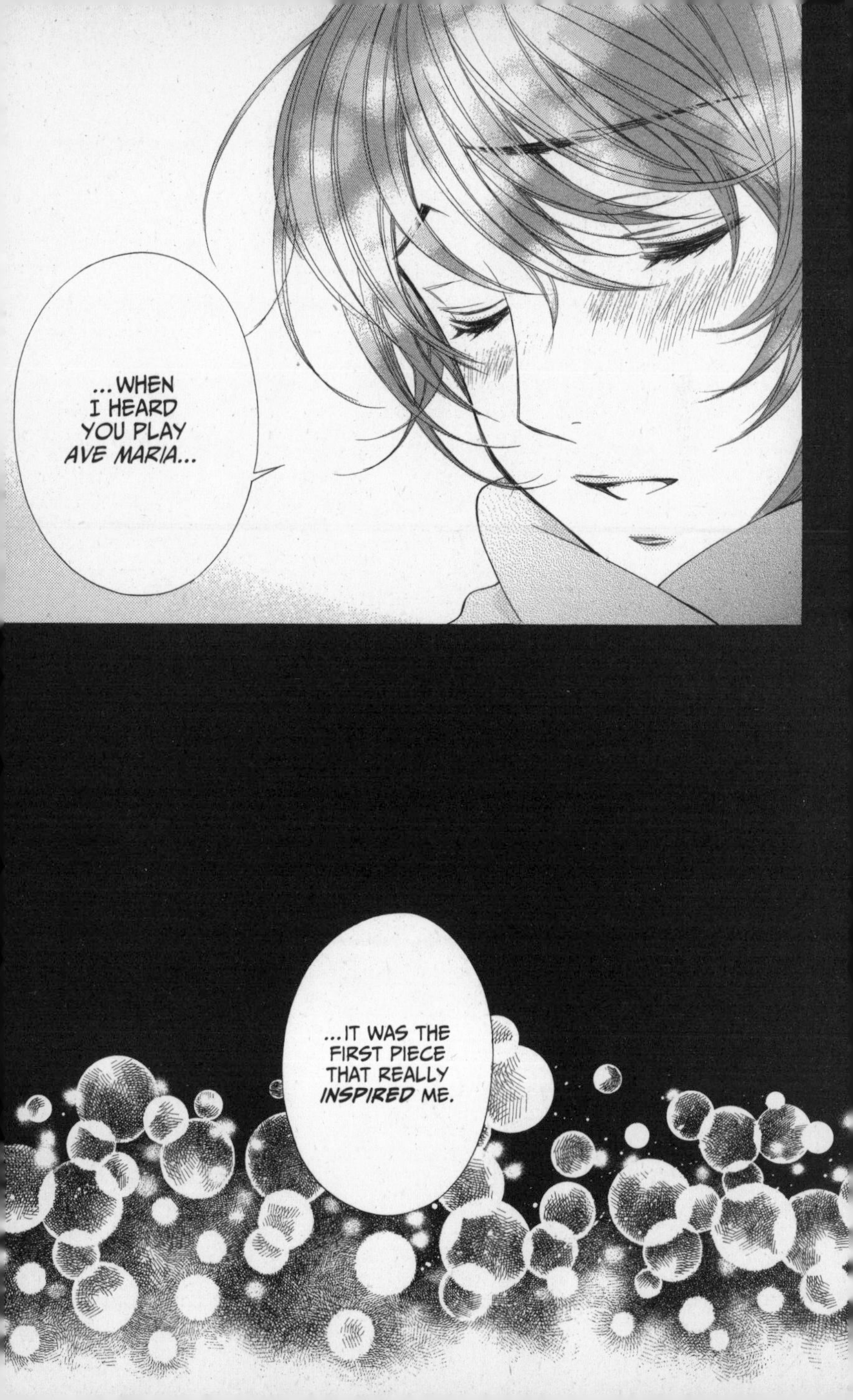
...WHEN I HEARD YOU PLAY *AVE MARIA*...
...IT WAS THE FIRST PIECE THAT REALLY *INSPIRED* ME.

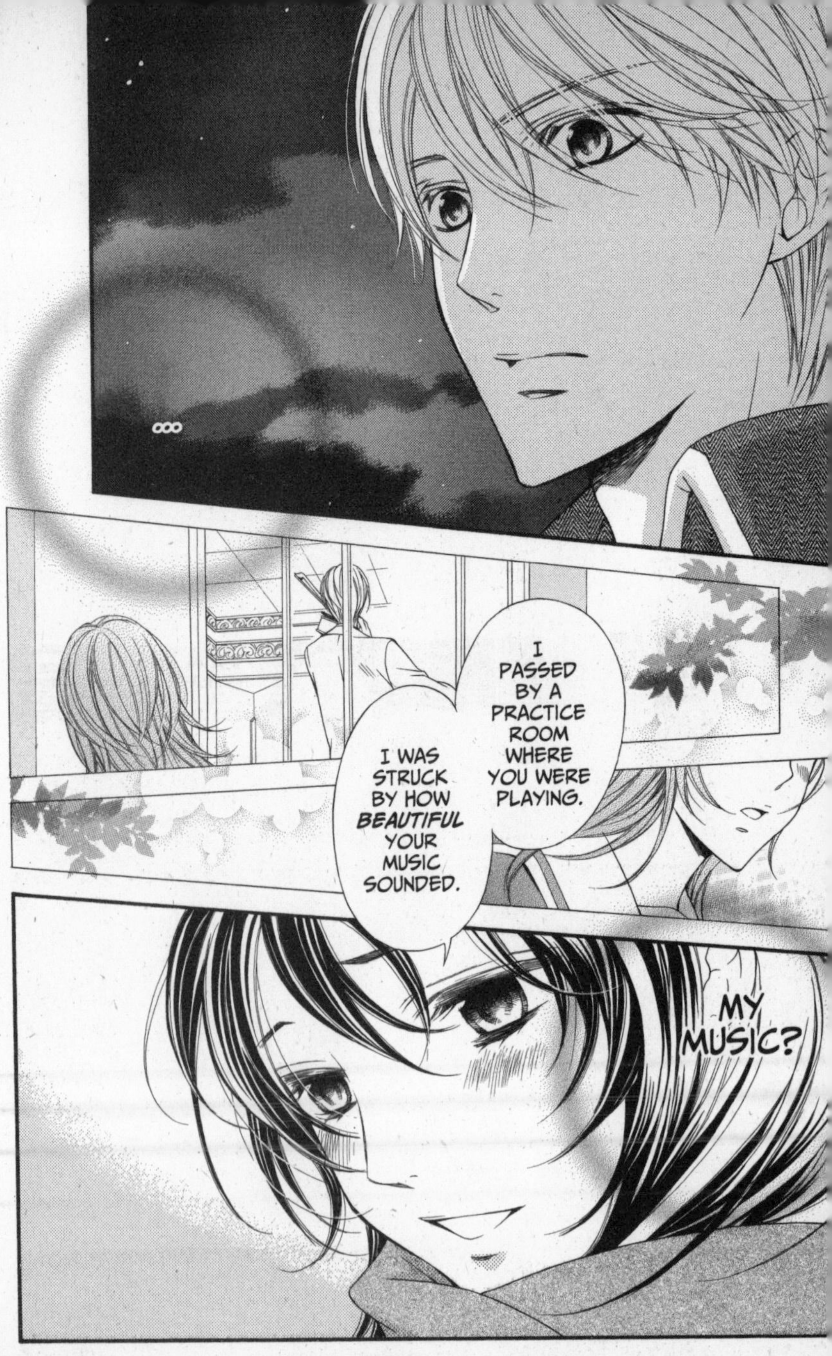
...
I PASSED BY A PRACTICE ROOM WHERE YOU WERE PLAYING.
I WAS STRUCK BY HOW *BEAUTIFUL* YOUR MUSIC SOUNDED.
MY MUSIC?

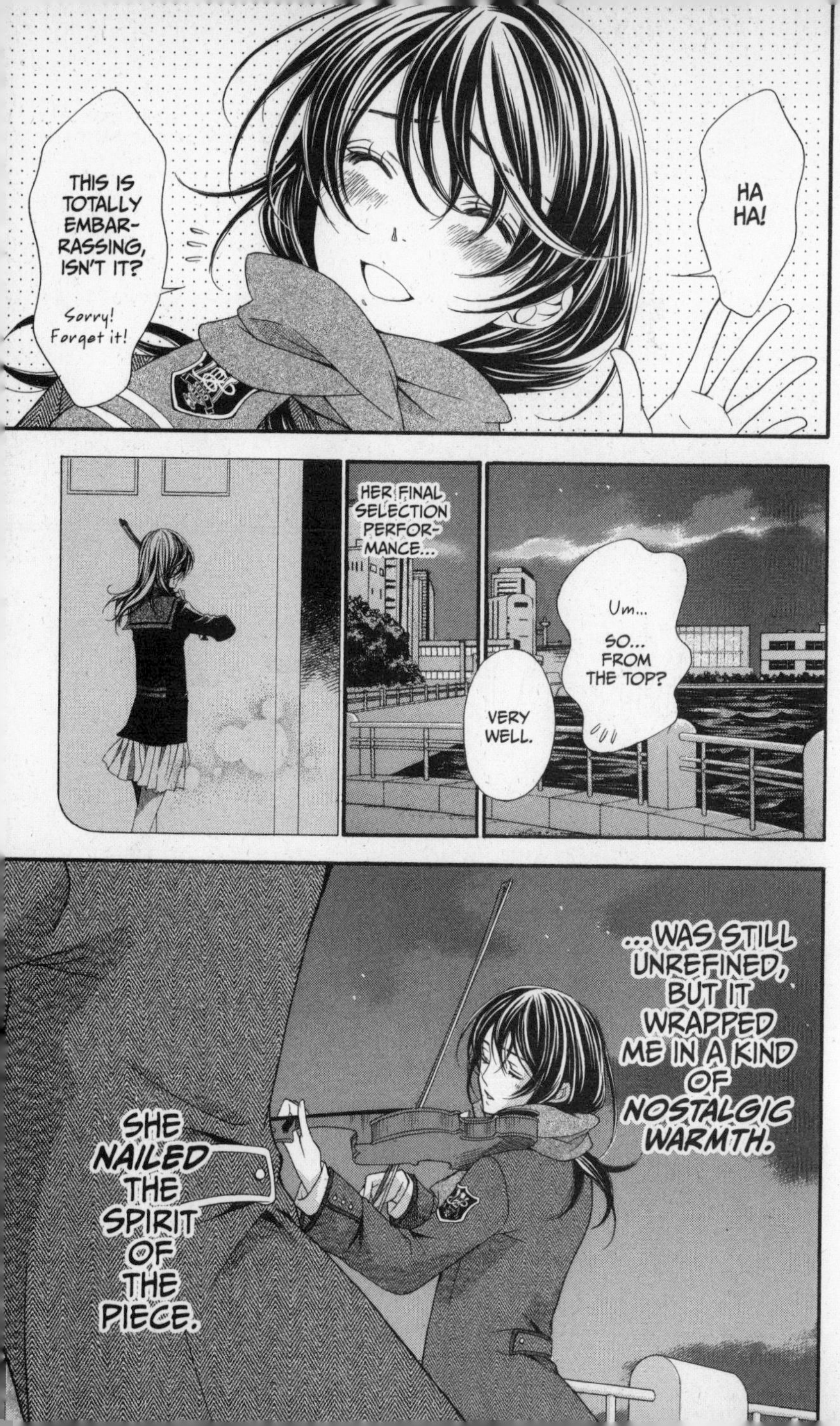
HA HA!
THIS IS TOTALLY EMBARRASSING, ISN'T IT?
Sorry! Forget it!
Um...
SO... FROM THE TOP?
VERY WELL.
HER FINAL SELECTION PERFORMANCE...
...WAS STILL UNREFINED, BUT IT WRAPPED ME IN A KIND OF NOSTALGIC WARMTH.
SHE NAILED THE SPIRIT OF THE PIECE.

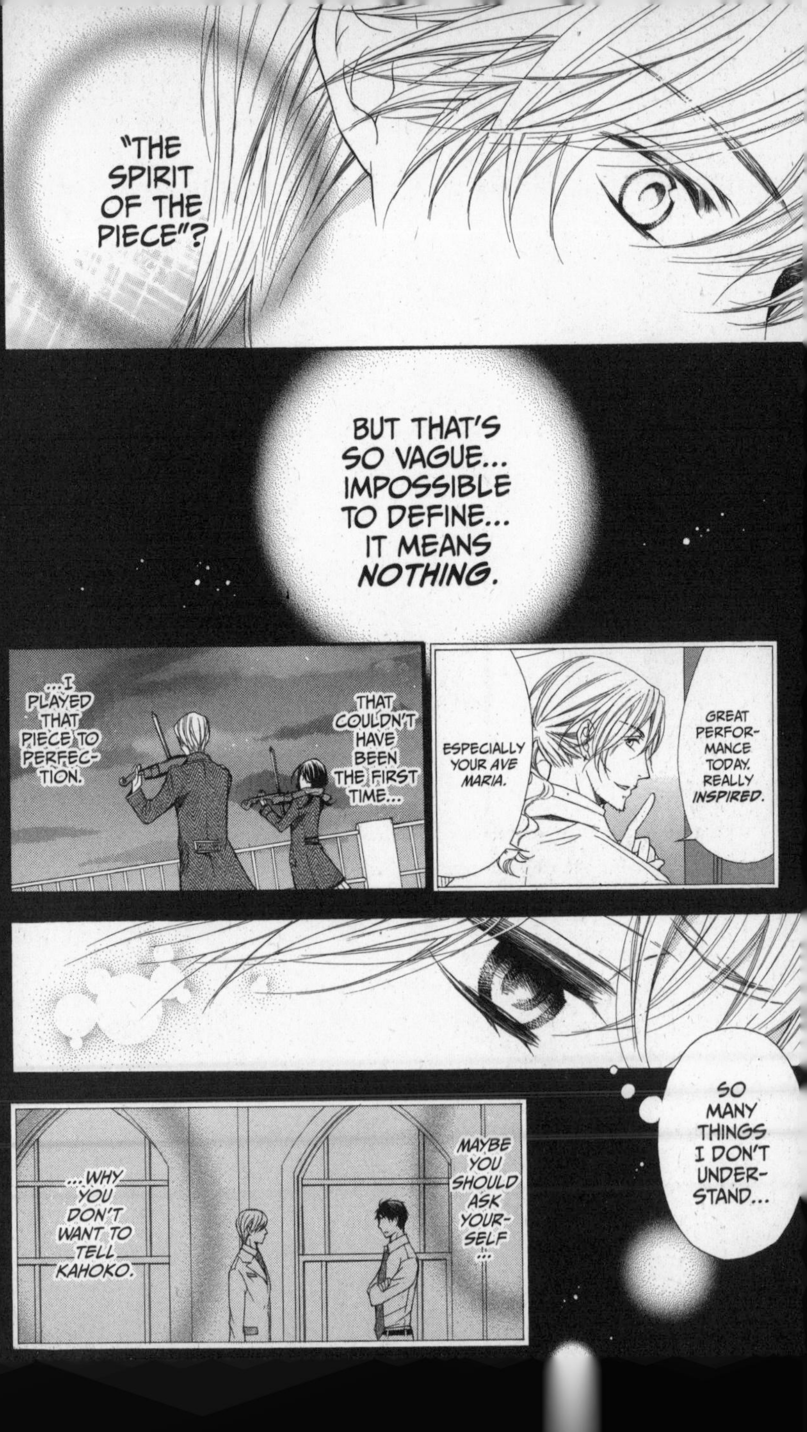
"THE SPIRIT OF THE PIECE"?
BUT THAT'S SO VAGUE... IMPOSSIBLE TO DEFINE... IT MEANS *NOTHING*.
GREAT PERFORMANCE TODAY. REALLY *INSPIRED*.
ESPECIALLY YOUR *AVE MARIA*.
THAT COULDN'T HAVE BEEN THE FIRST TIME...
...I PLAYED THAT PIECE TO PERFECTION.
SO MANY THINGS I DON'T UNDERSTAND...
MAYBE YOU SHOULD ASK YOURSELF...
...WHY YOU DON'T WANT TO TELL KAHOKO.

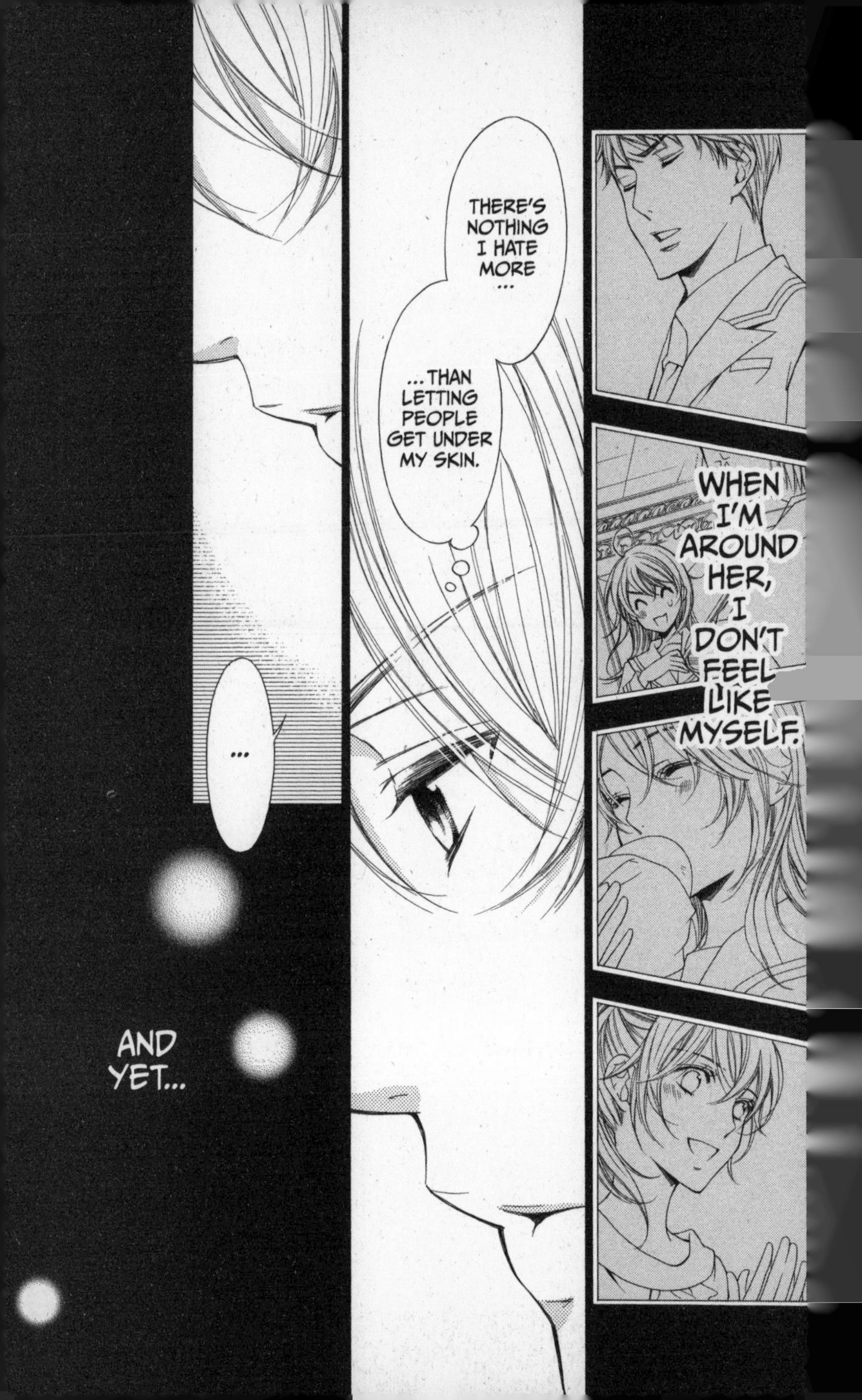
WHEN I'M AROUND HER, I DON'T FEEL LIKE MYSELF.
THERE'S NOTHING I HATE MORE ...
...THAN LETTING PEOPLE GET UNDER MY SKIN.
...
AND YET...

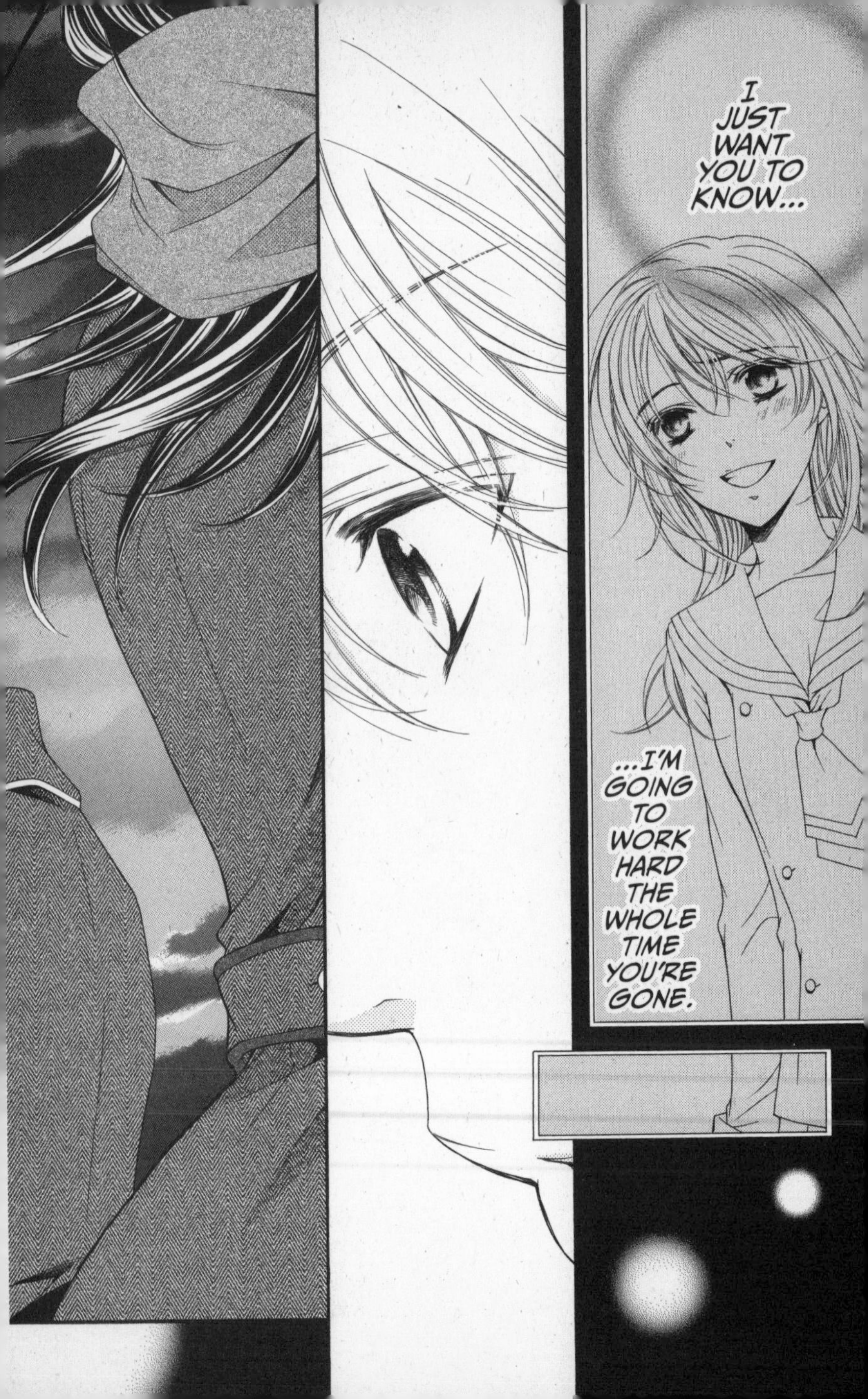
I JUST WANT YOU TO KNOW...
...I'M GOING TO WORK HARD THE WHOLE TIME YOU'RE GONE.

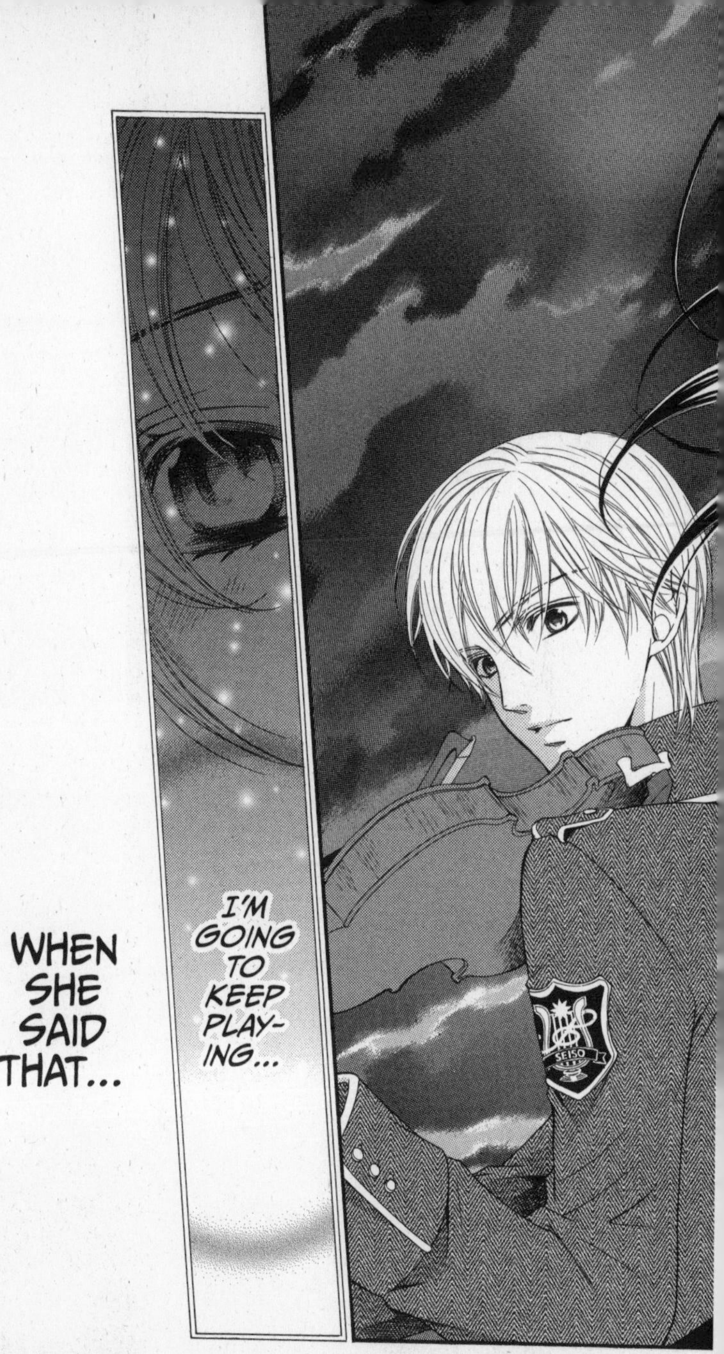
I'M GOING TO KEEP PLAYING...
WHEN SHE SAID THAT...

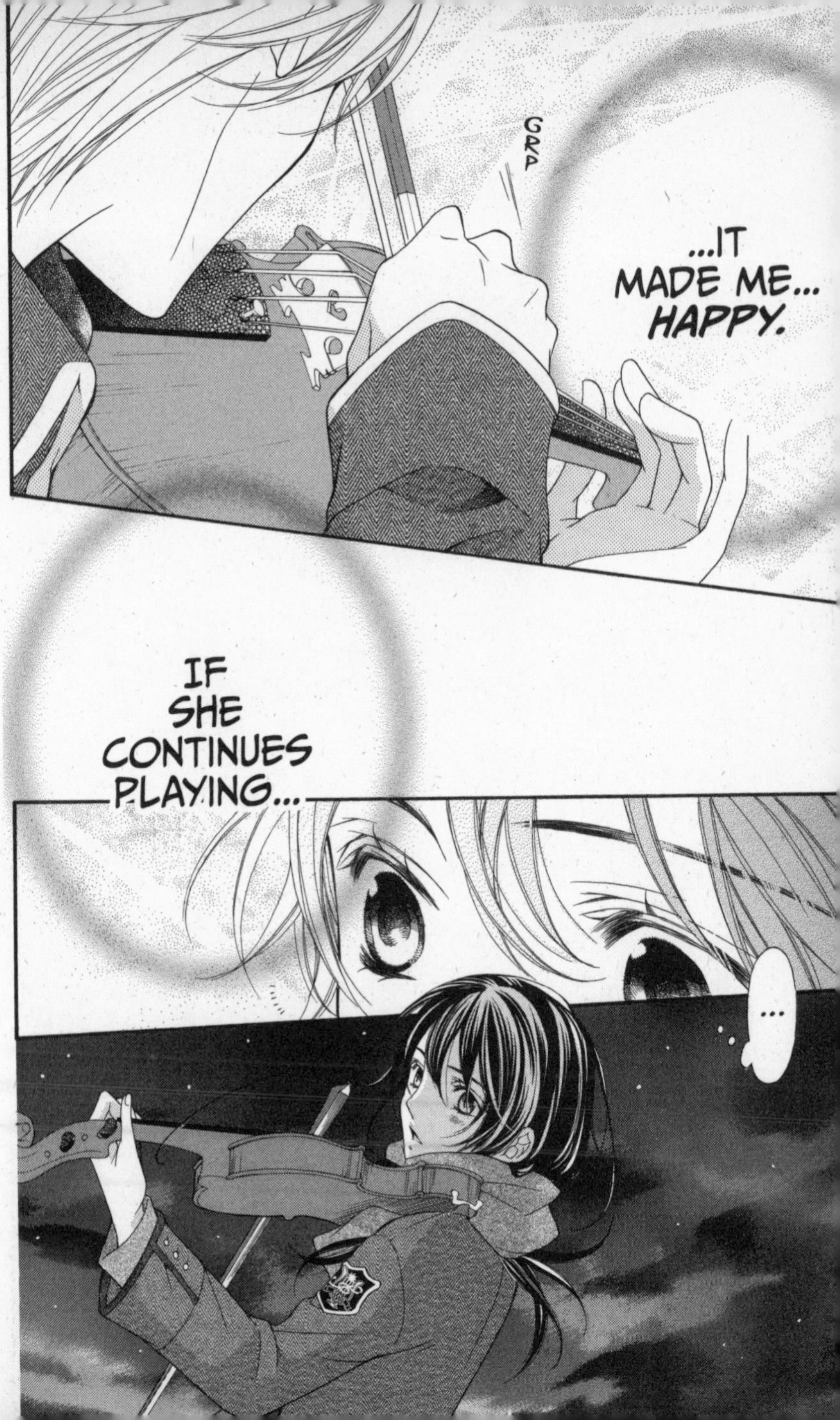
GRP
...IT MADE ME... HAPPY.
IF SHE CONTINUES PLAYING...
...

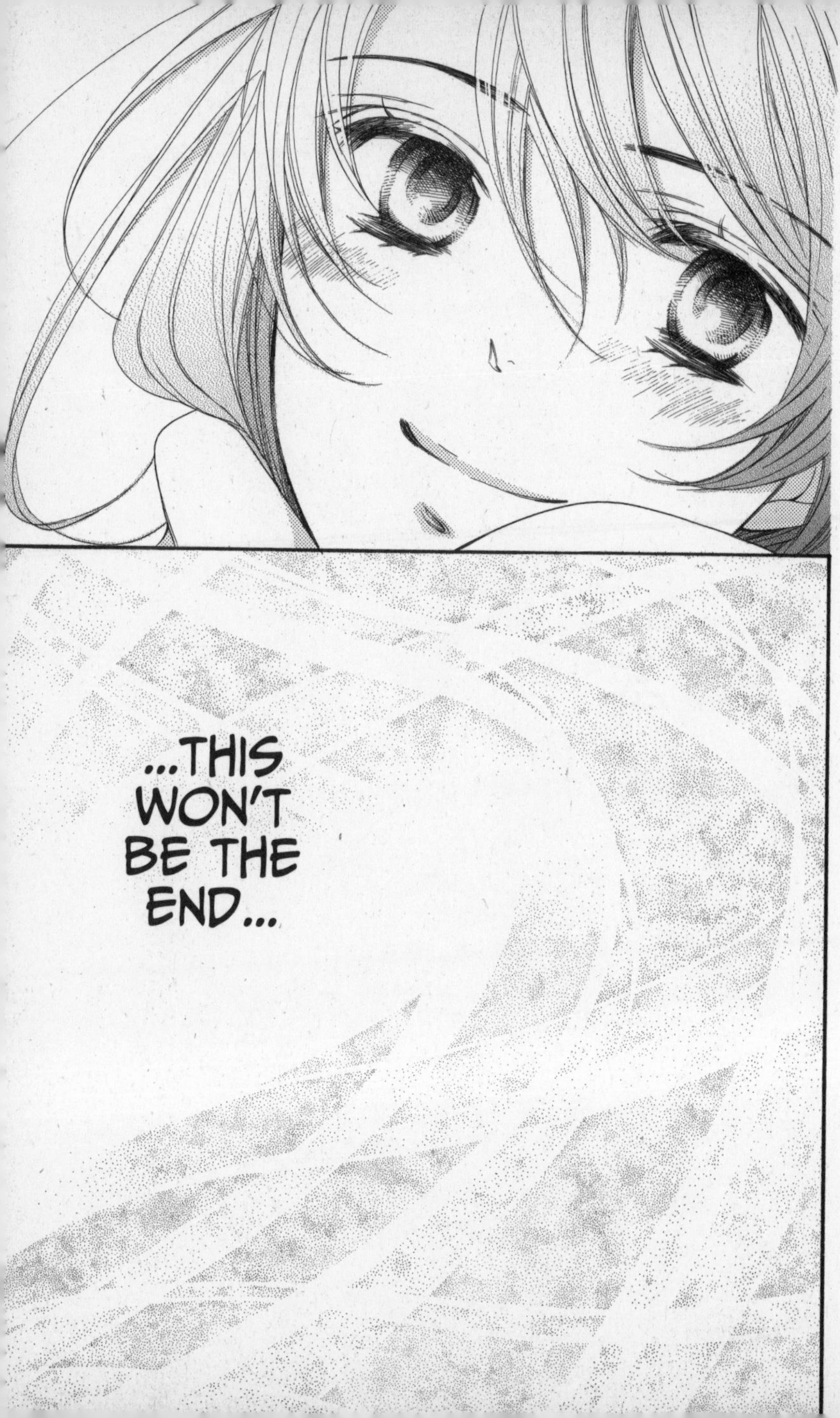
...THIS WON'T BE THE END...

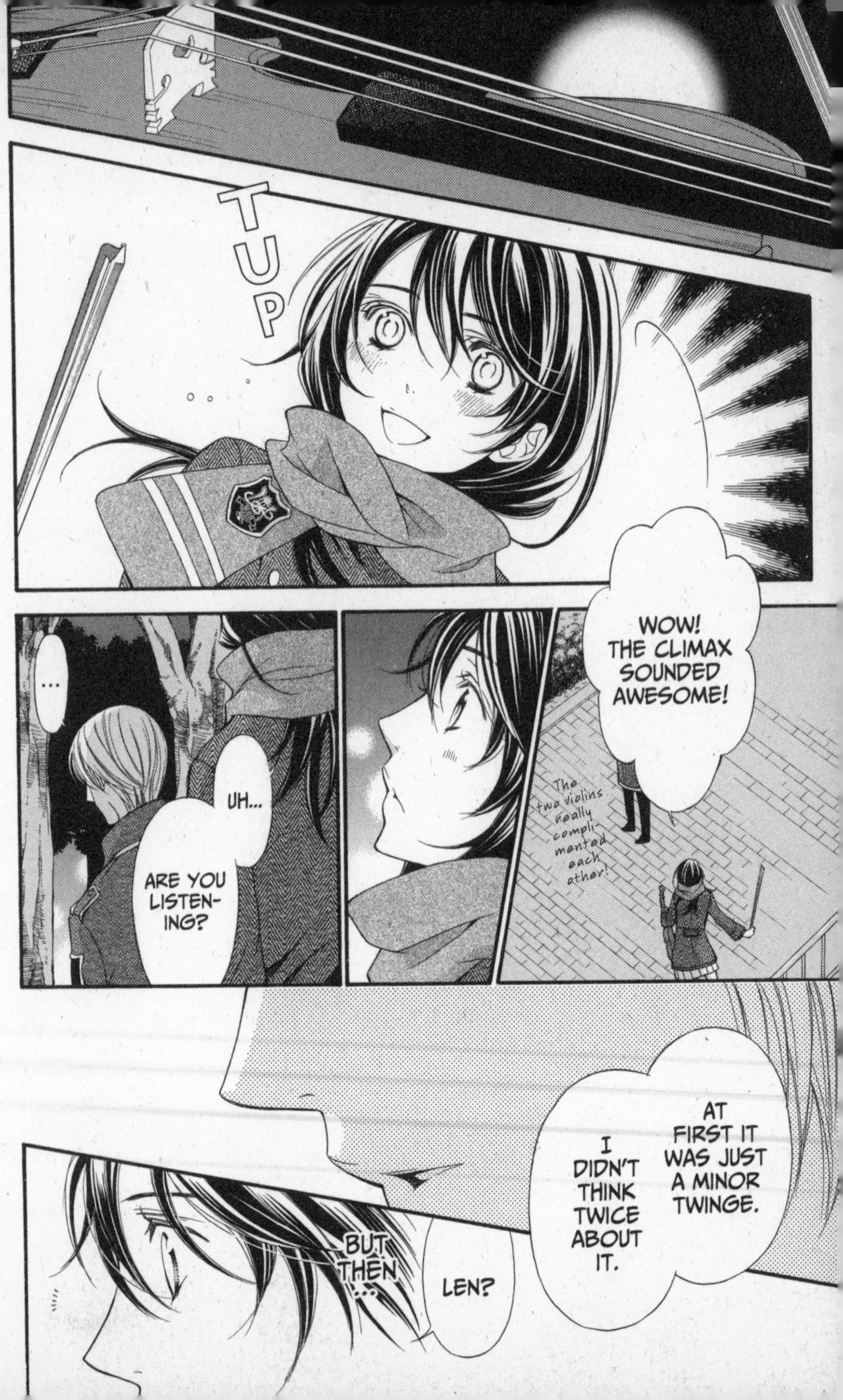
TUP
WOW! THE CLIMAX SOUNDED AWESOME!
The two violins really complimented each other!
...
UH...
ARE YOU LISTENING?
AT FIRST IT WAS JUST A MINOR TWINGE.
I DIDN'T THINK TWICE ABOUT IT.
BUT THEN...
LEN?

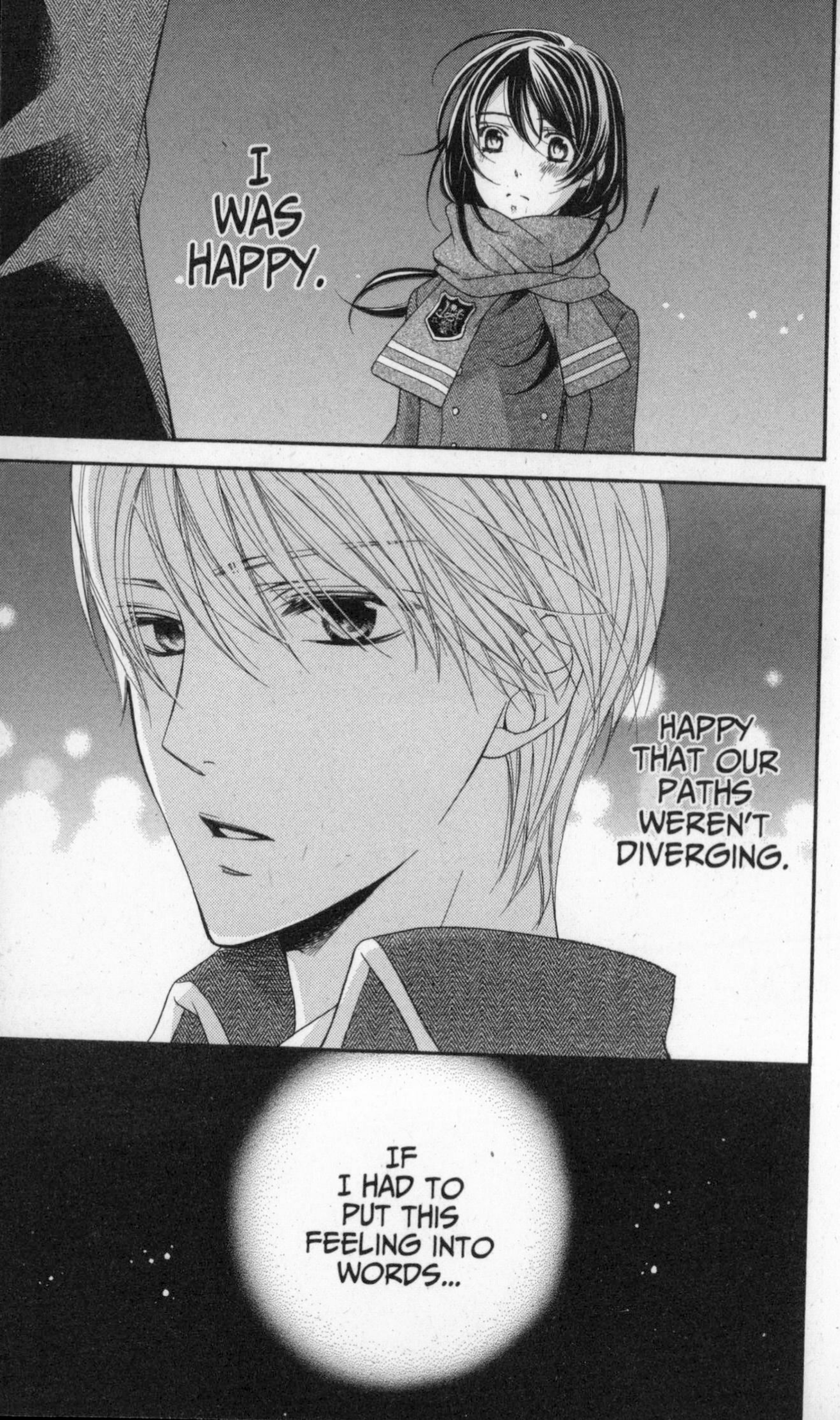
I WAS HAPPY.
HAPPY THAT OUR PATHS WEREN'T DIVERGING.
IF I HAD TO PUT THIS FEELING INTO WORDS...

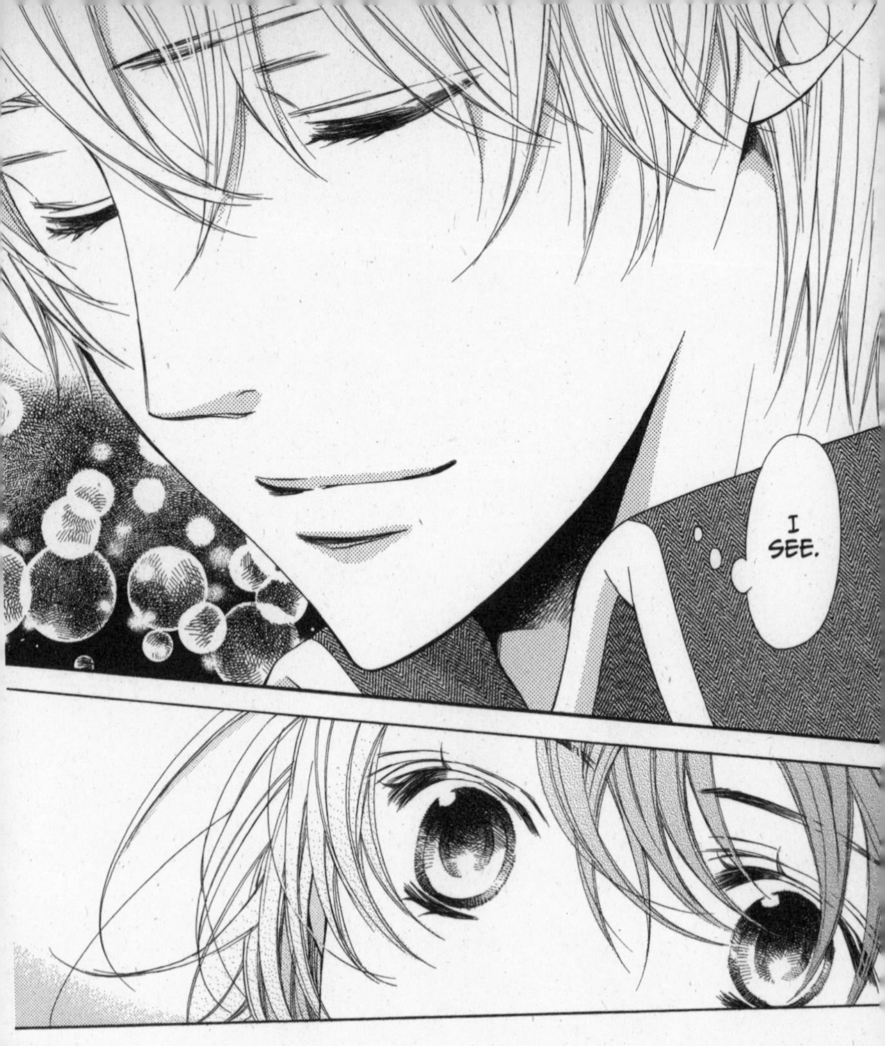
I SEE.

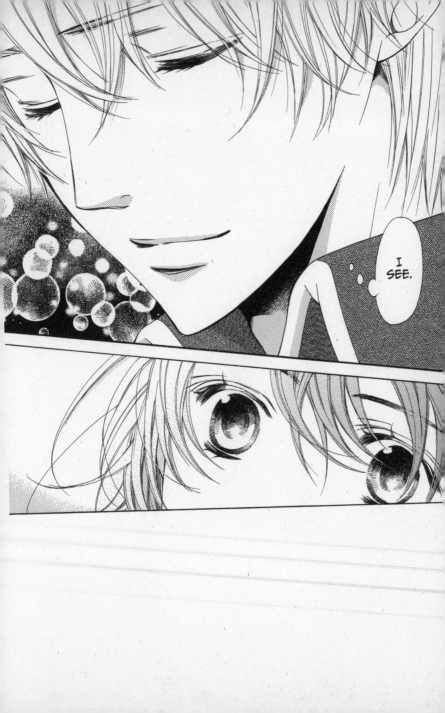

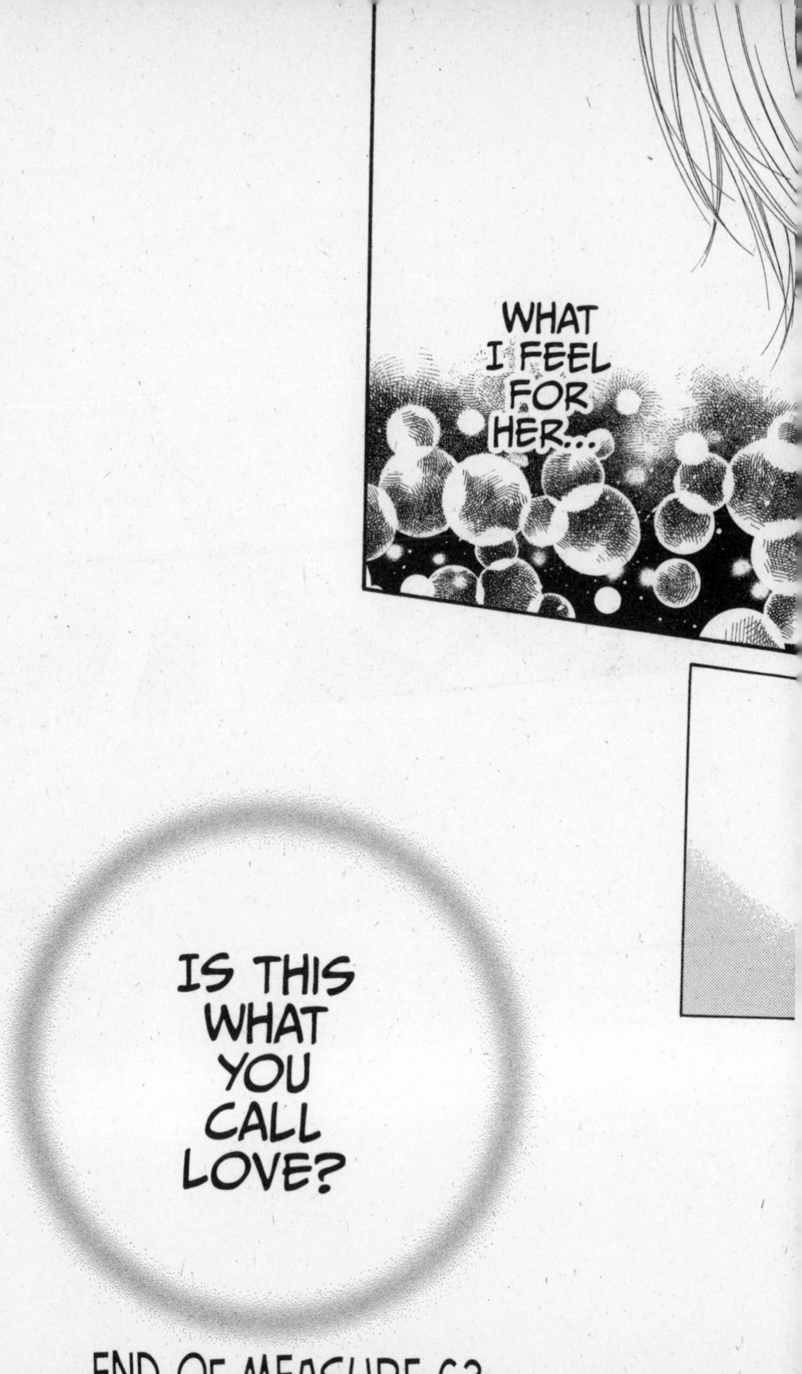
WHAT I FEEL FOR HER...
IS THIS WHAT YOU CALL LOVE?

END OF MEASURE 63

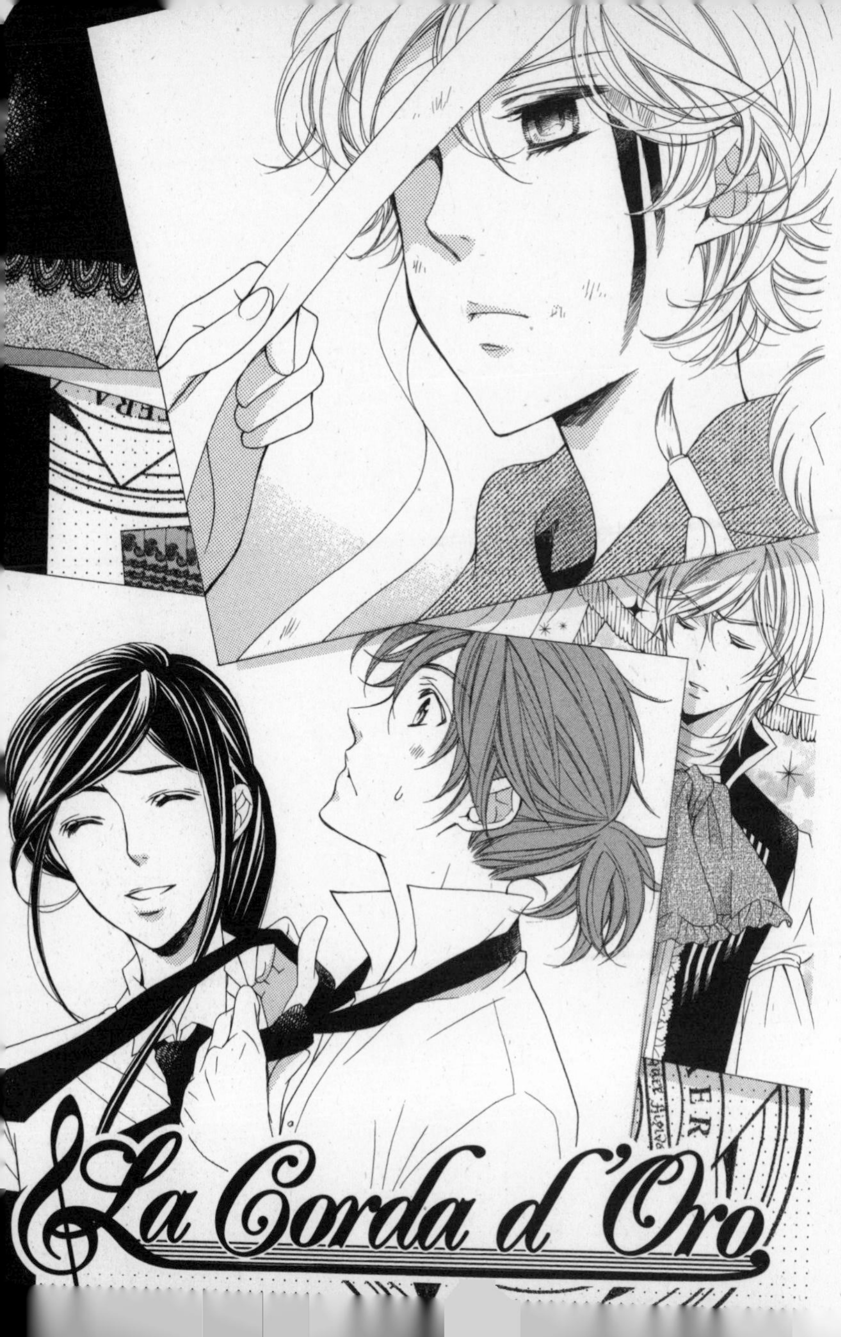
La Corda d'Oro

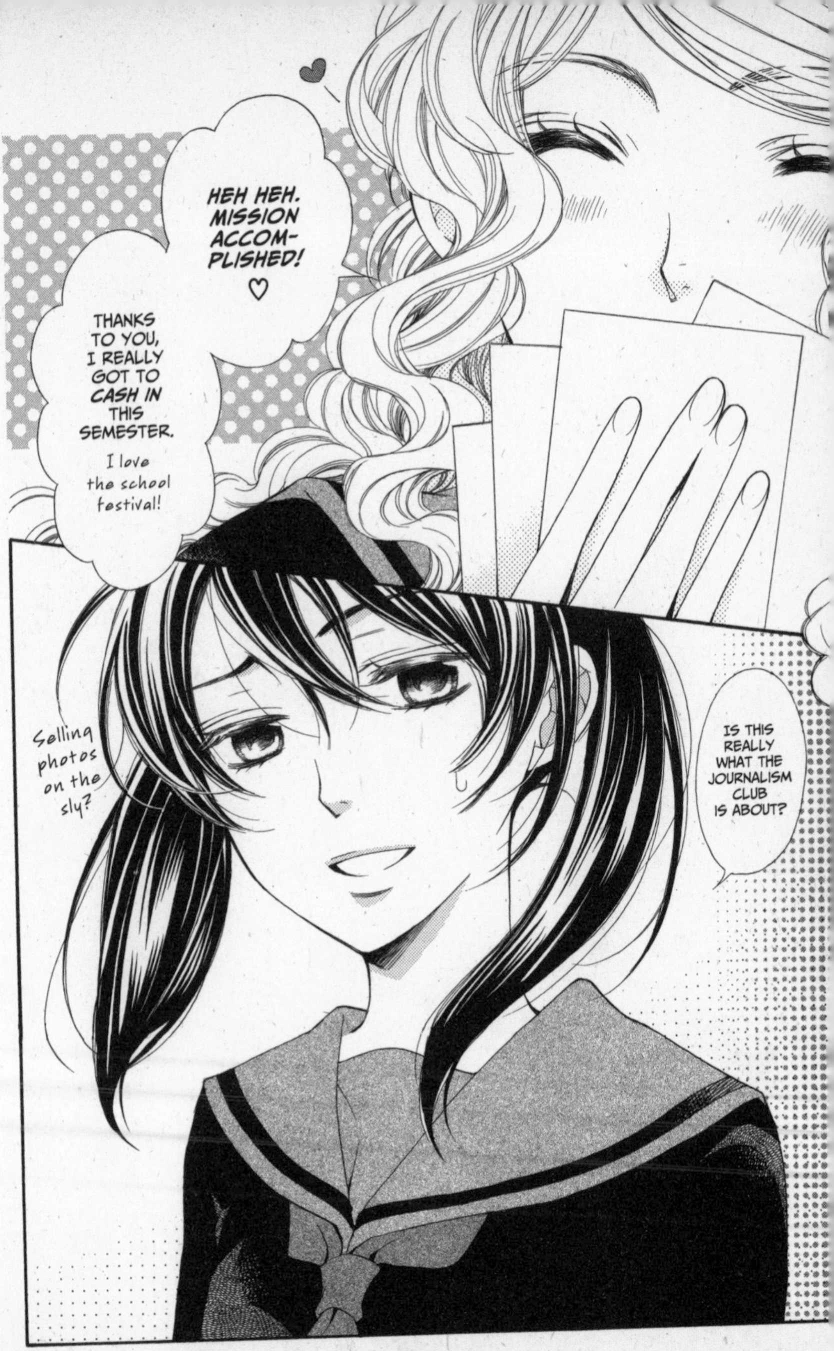
HEH HEH. MISSION ACCOMPLISHED! ♡
THANKS TO YOU, I REALLY GOT TO CASH IN THIS SEMESTER.
I love the school festival!
IS THIS REALLY WHAT THE JOURNALISM CLUB IS ABOUT?
Selling photos on the sly?

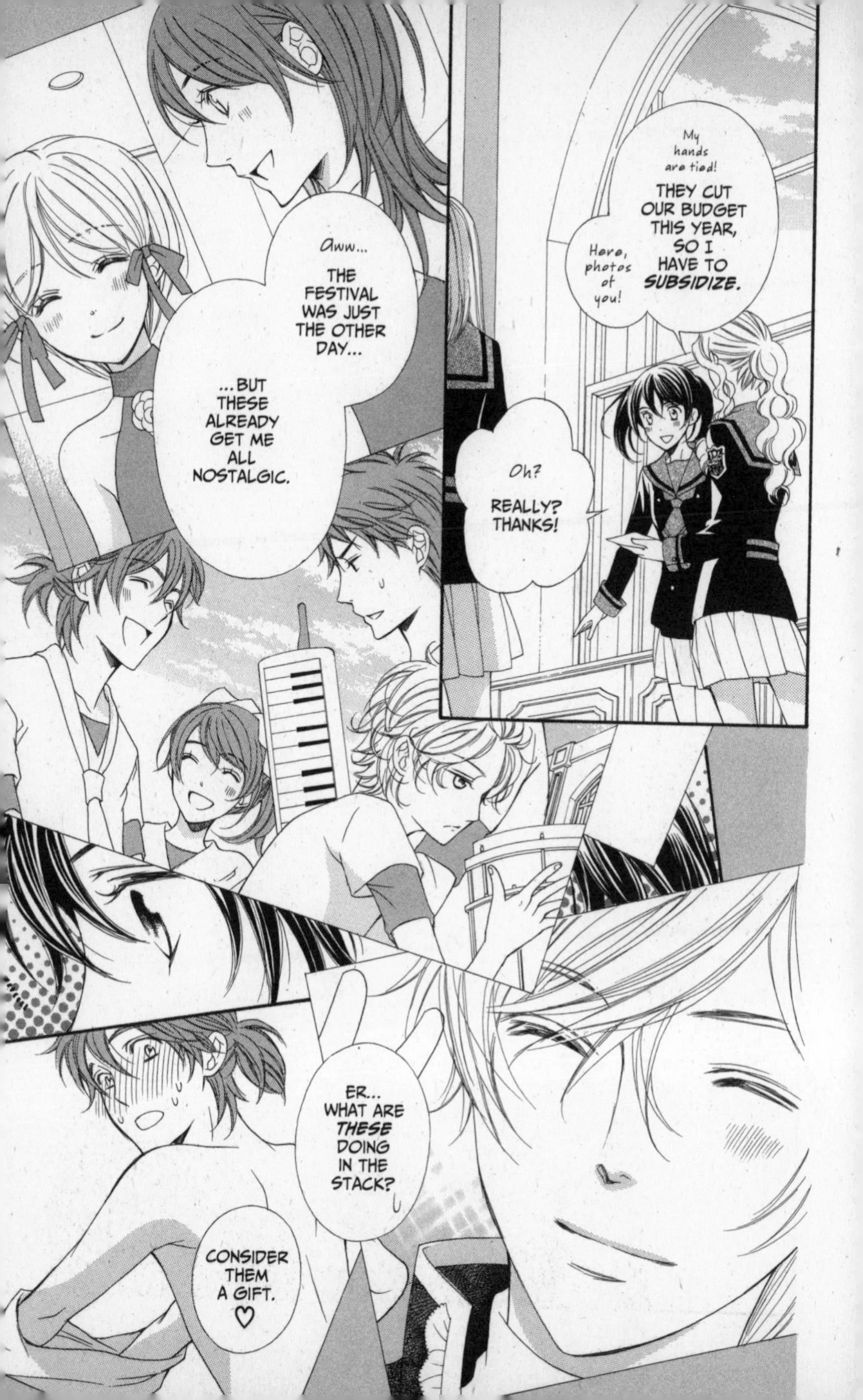
My hands are tied! THEY CUT OUR BUDGET THIS YEAR, SO I HAVE TO SUBSIDIZE.
Here, photos of you!
Oh? REALLY? THANKS!
Aww... THE FESTIVAL WAS JUST THE OTHER DAY... ...BUT THESE ALREADY GET ME ALL NOSTALGIC.
ER... WHAT ARE THESE DOING IN THE STACK?
CONSIDER THEM A GIFT. ♡

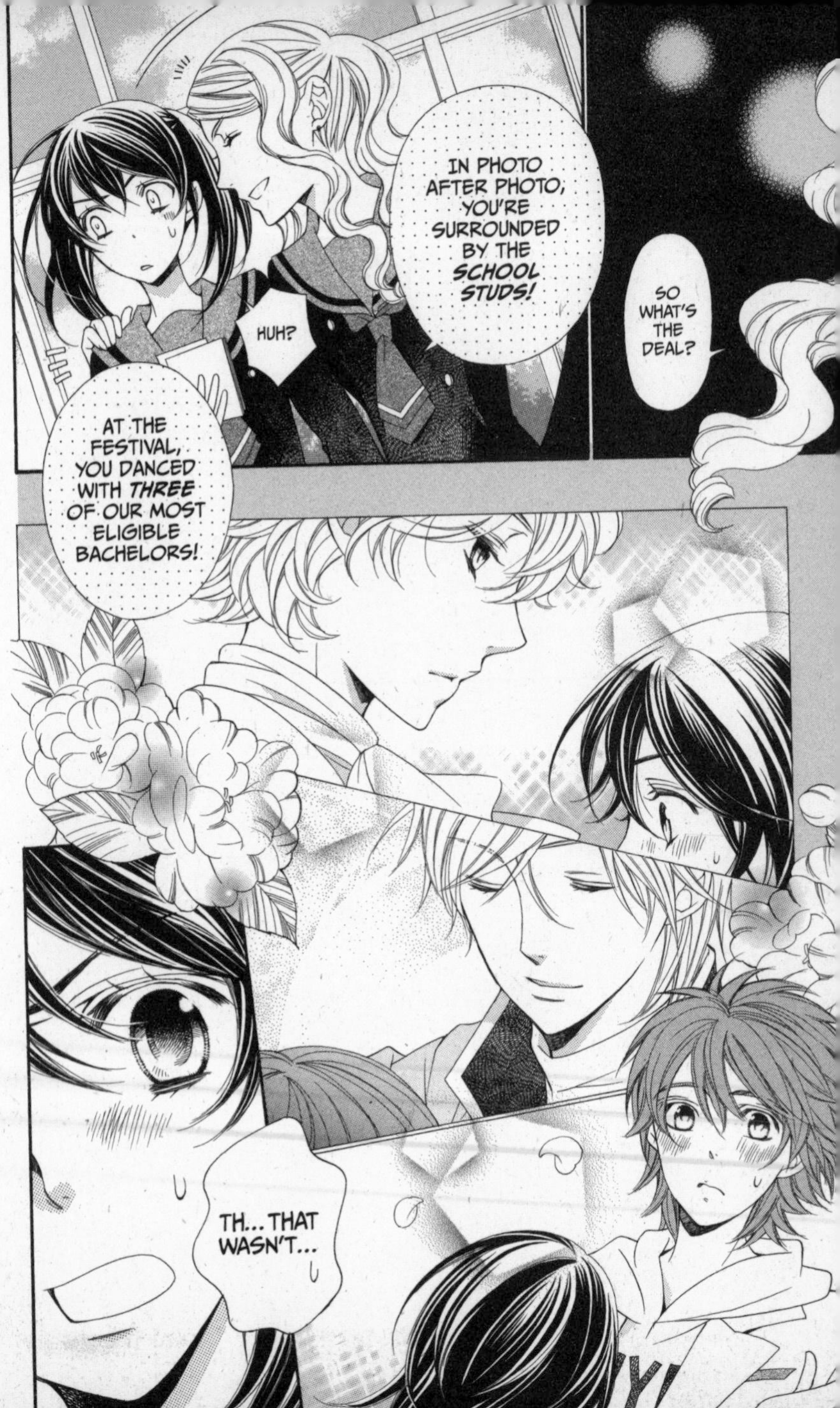
SO WHAT'S THE DEAL?
IN PHOTO AFTER PHOTO, YOU'RE SURROUNDED BY THE *SCHOOL STUDS!*
HUH?
AT THE FESTIVAL, YOU DANCED WITH *THREE* OF OUR MOST ELIGIBLE BACHELORS!
TH... THAT WASN'T...

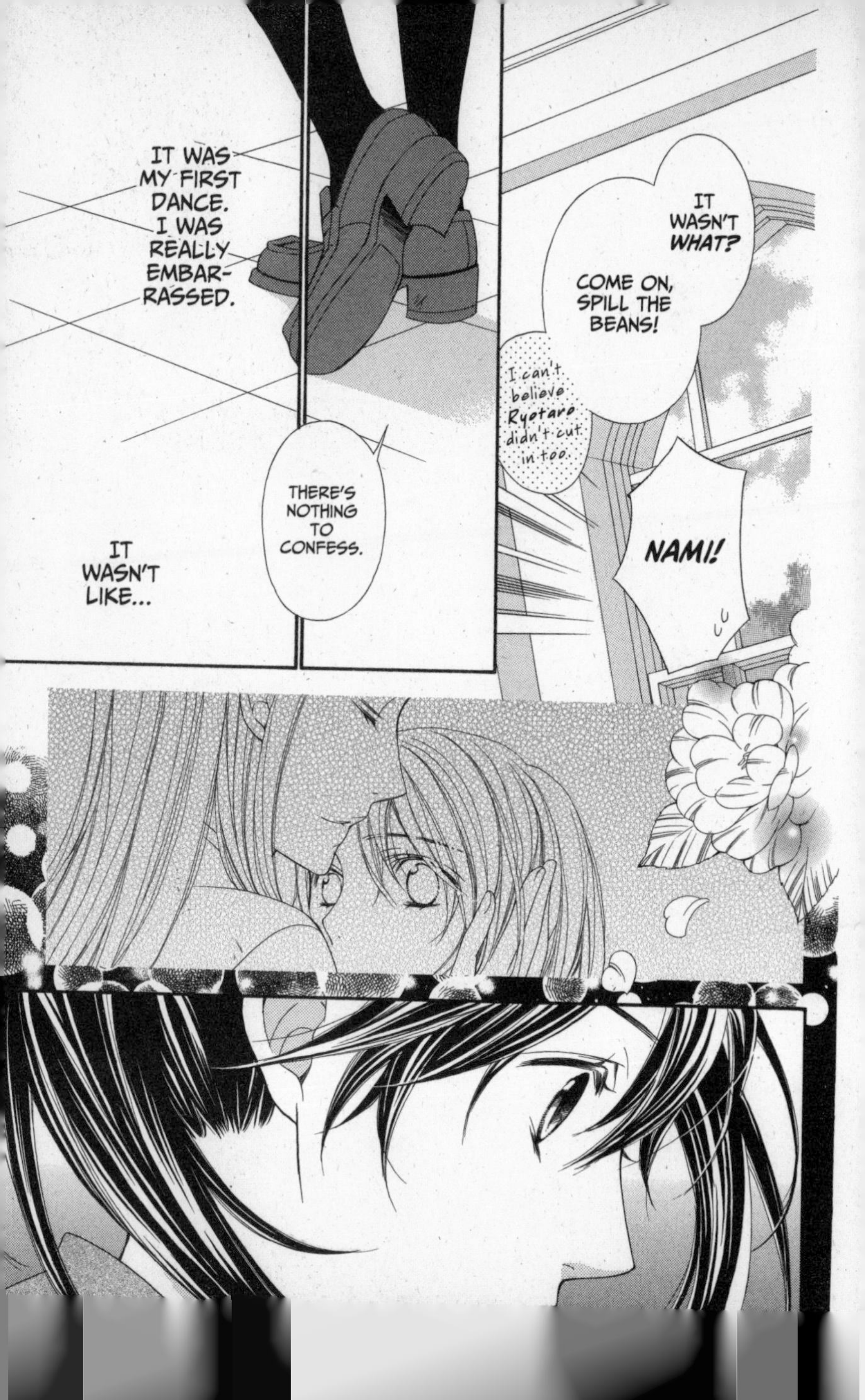
IT WASN'T WHAT?
COME ON, SPILL THE BEANS!
I can't believe Ryotaro didn't cut in too.
NAMI!
THERE'S NOTHING TO CONFESS.
IT WAS MY FIRST DANCE. I WAS REALLY EMBARRASSED.
IT WASN'T LIKE...

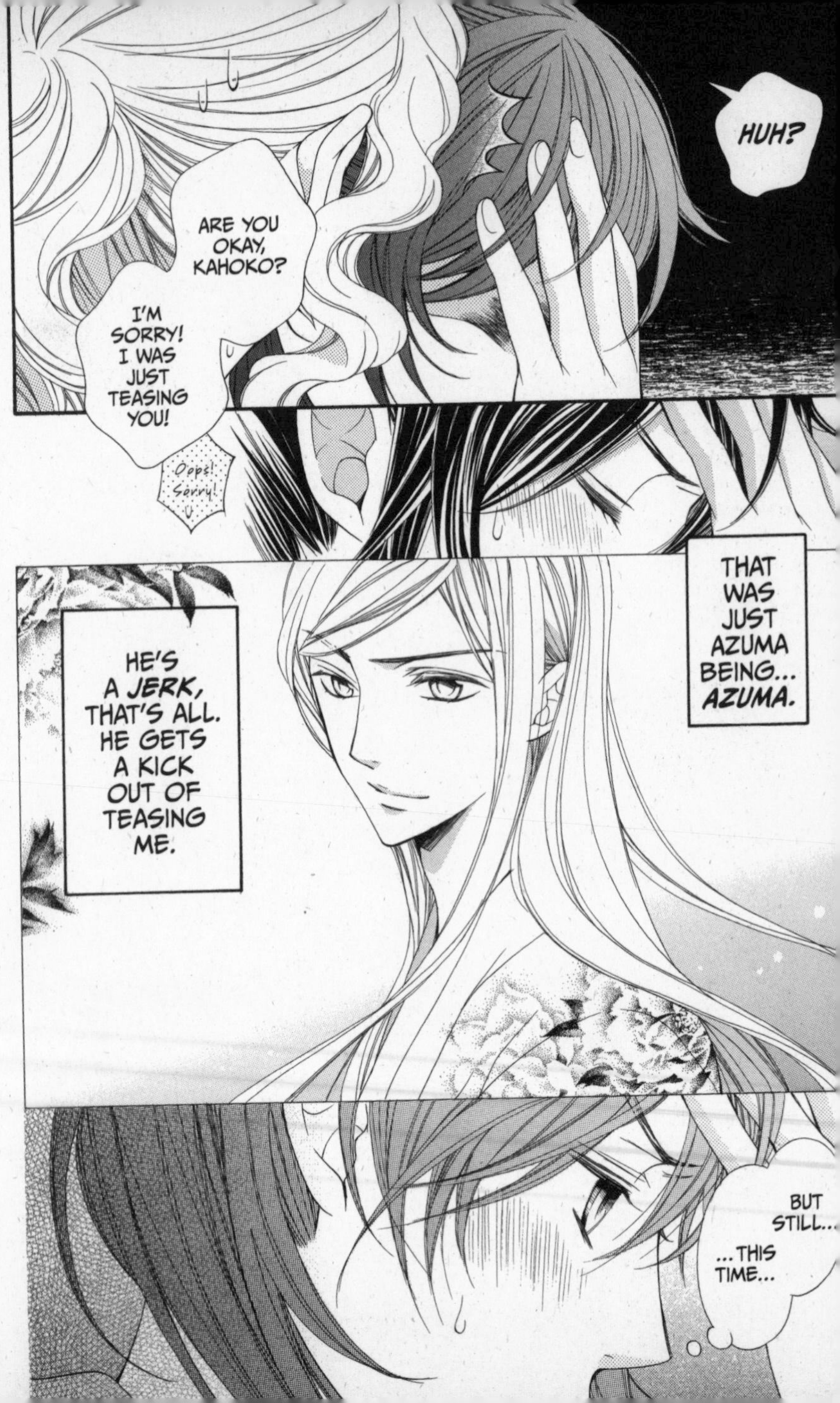
HUH?
ARE YOU OKAY, KAHOKO?
I'M SORRY! I WAS JUST TEASING YOU!
Oops! Sorry!
THAT WAS JUST AZUMA BEING... *AZUMA*.
HE'S A *JERK*, THAT'S ALL. HE GETS A KICK OUT OF TEASING ME.
BUT STILL...
...THIS TIME...

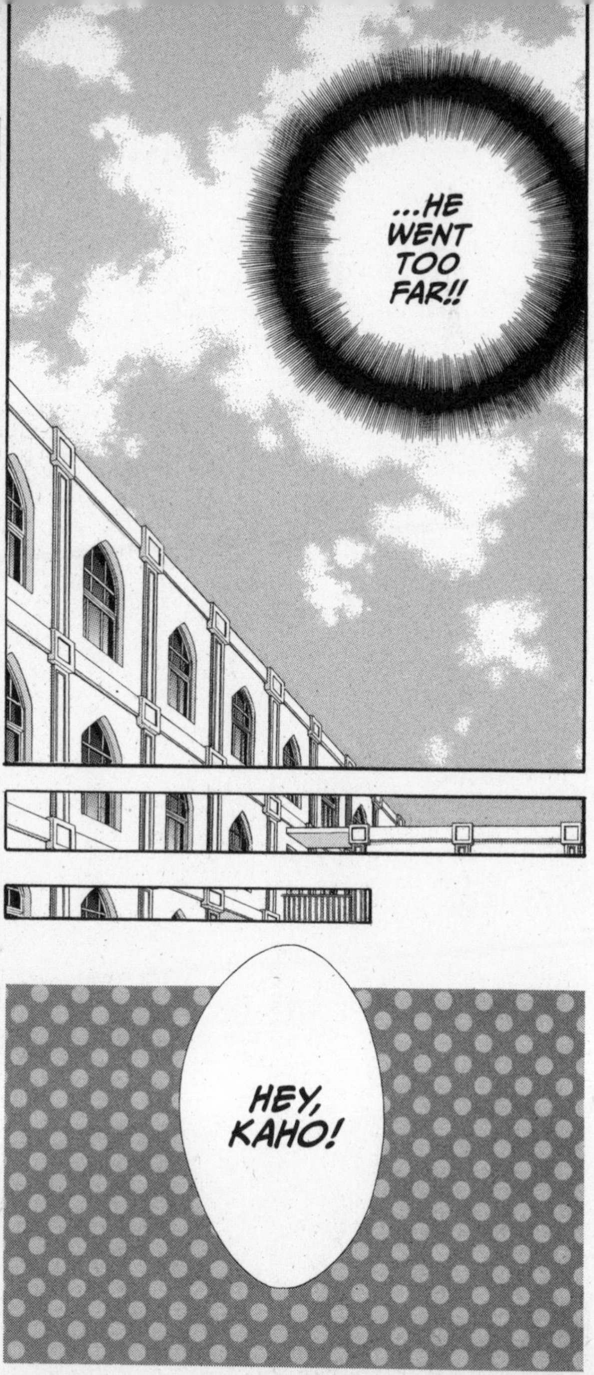
...HE WENT TOO FAR!!
HEY, KAHO!

For the title page of Measure 63, I drew Len in black-framed glasses. I have to admit he seems more like the delicate, frameless type, though. Incidentally, the title my editor came up with for that illustration was, "Breathlessly Close"... ♡

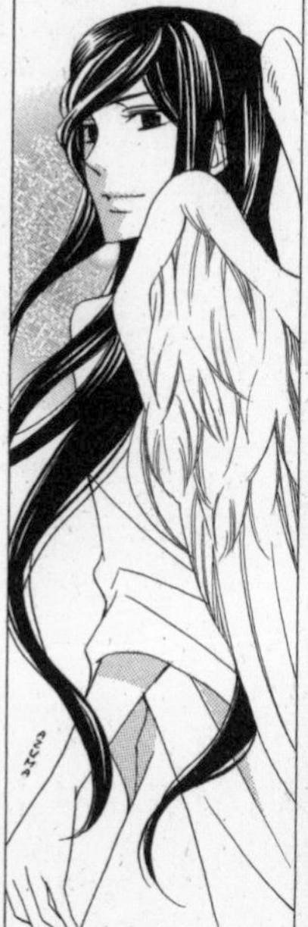

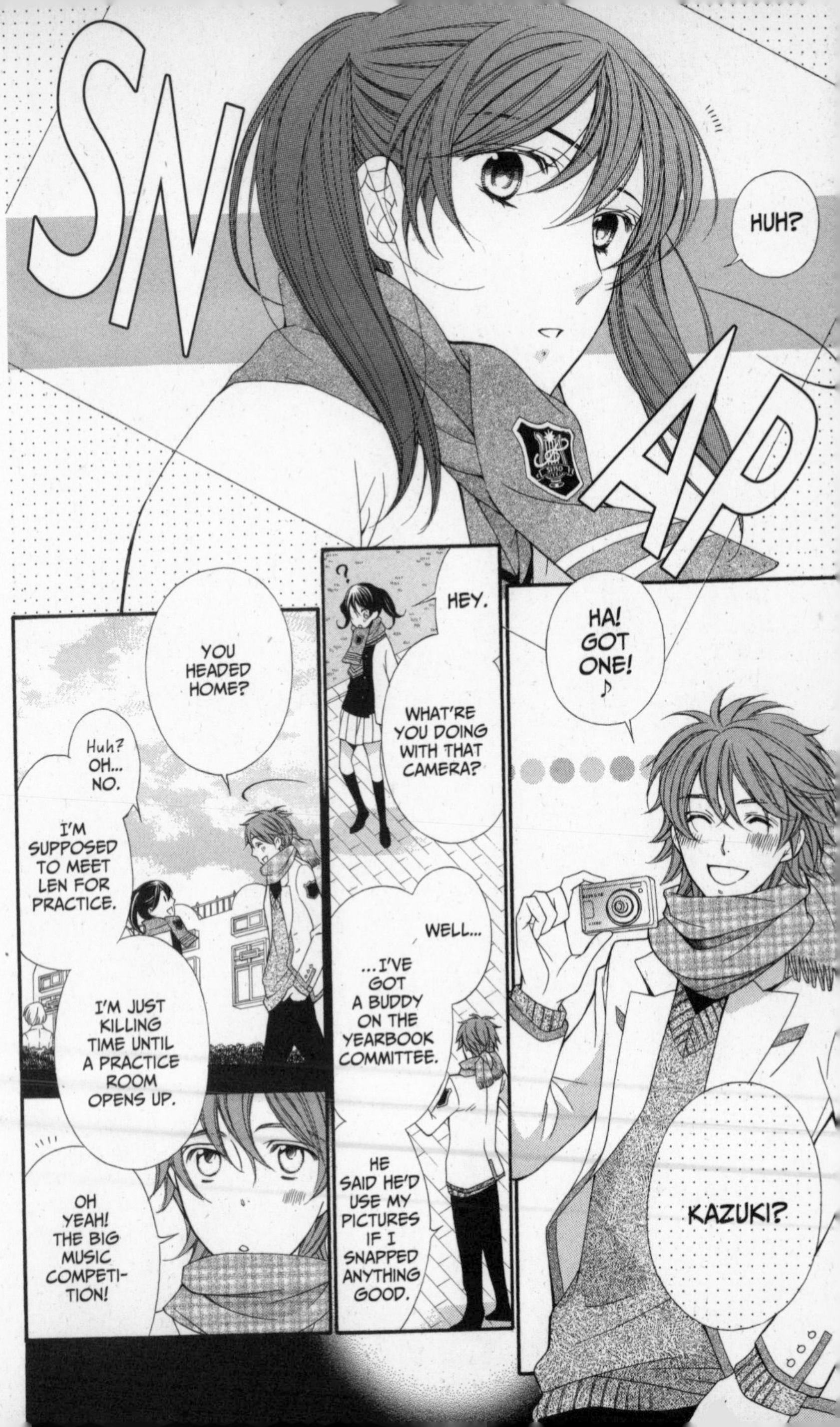
SNAP
HUH?
HA! GOT ONE! ♪
KAZUKI?
HEY.
WHAT'RE YOU DOING WITH THAT CAMERA?
WELL...
...I'VE GOT A BUDDY ON THE YEARBOOK COMMITTEE.
HE SAID HE'D USE MY PICTURES IF I SNAPPED ANYTHING GOOD.
YOU HEADED HOME?
Huh? OH... NO.
I'M SUPPOSED TO MEET LEN FOR PRACTICE.
I'M JUST KILLING TIME UNTIL A PRACTICE ROOM OPENS UP.
OH YEAH! THE BIG MUSIC COMPETITION!

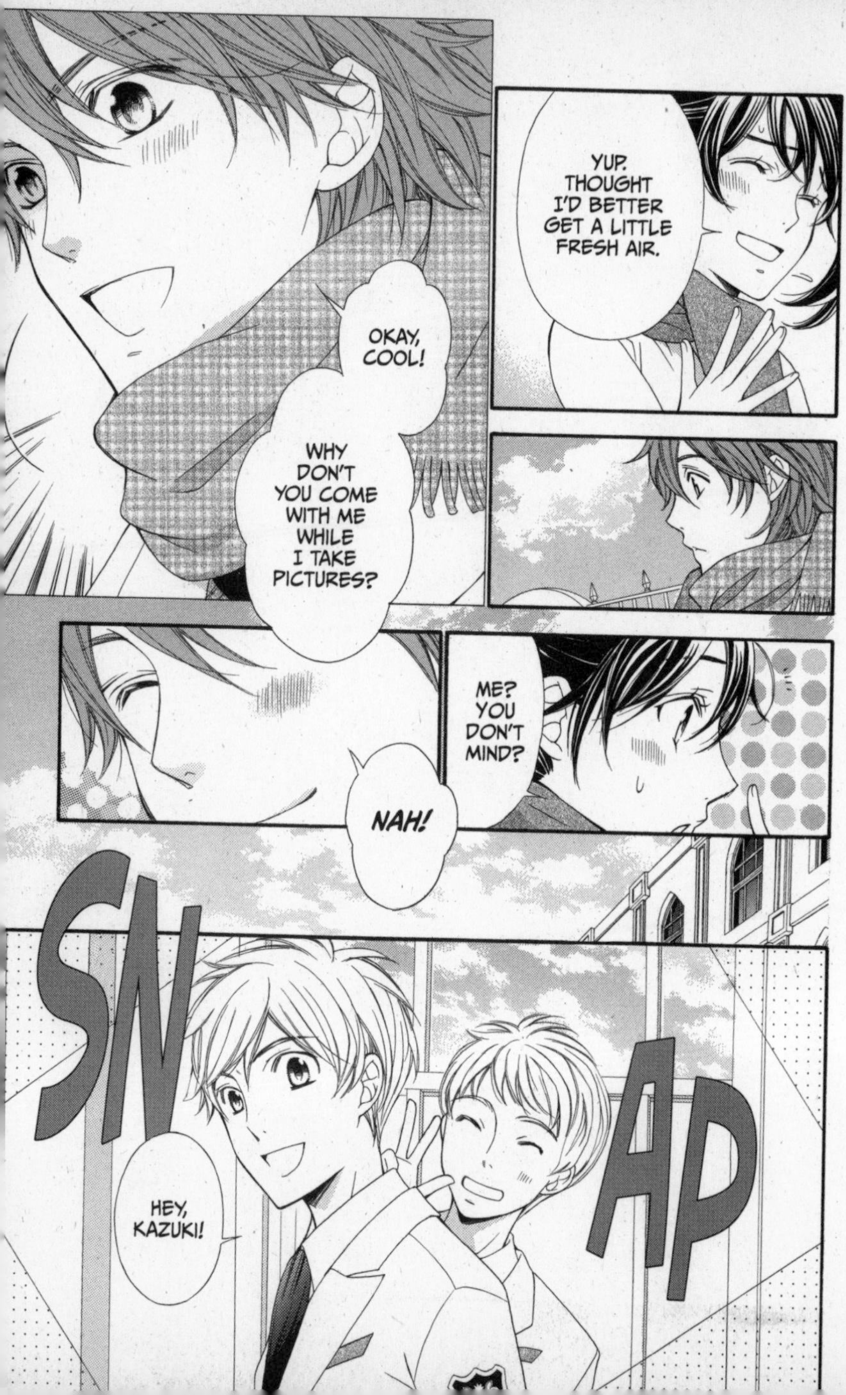
YUP. THOUGHT I'D BETTER GET A LITTLE FRESH AIR.
OKAY, COOL!
WHY DON'T YOU COME WITH ME WHILE I TAKE PICTURES?
ME? YOU DON'T MIND?
NAH!
SNAP
HEY, KAZUKI!

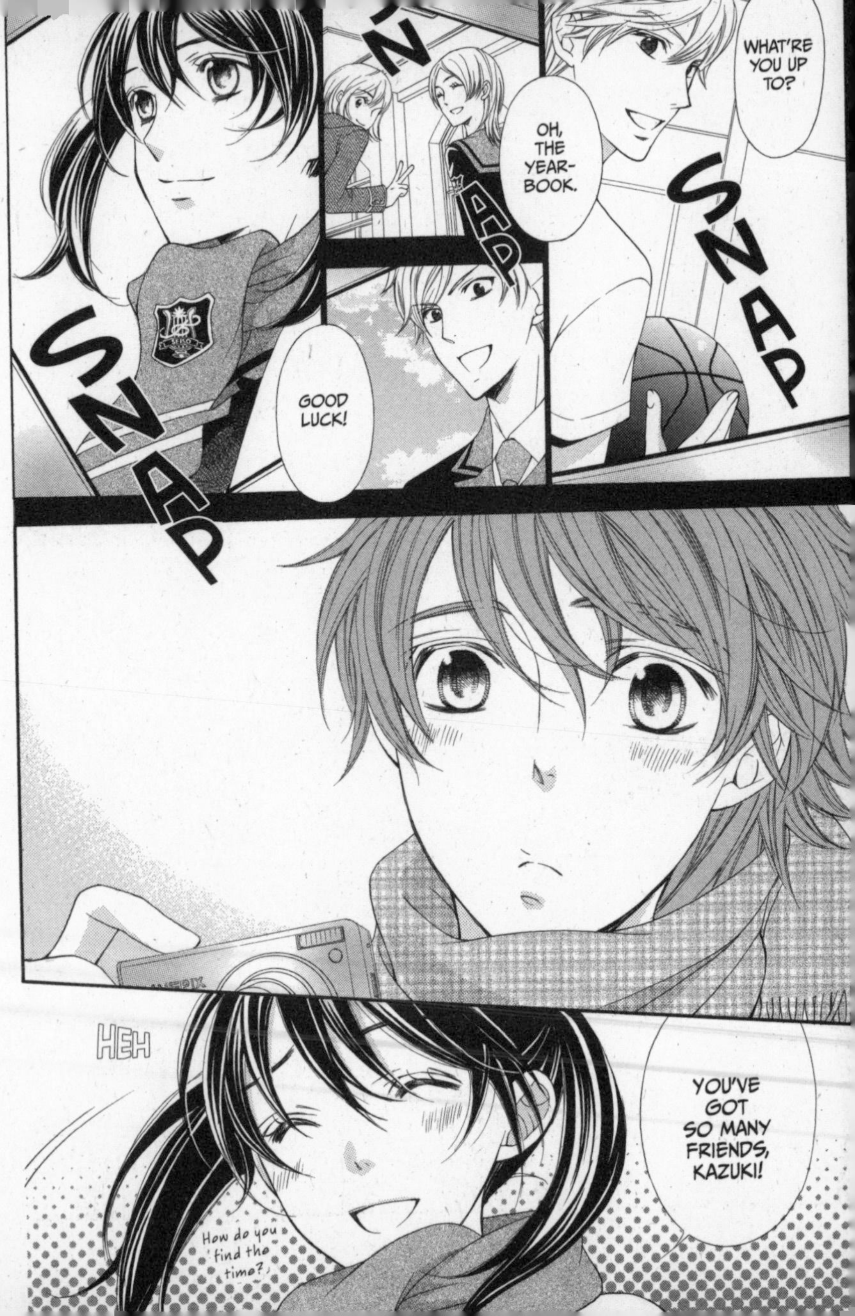
WHAT'RE YOU UP TO?
SNAP
OH, THE YEAR-BOOK.
GOOD LUCK!
SNAP
YOU'VE GOT SO MANY FRIENDS, KAZUKI!
HEH
How do you find the time?

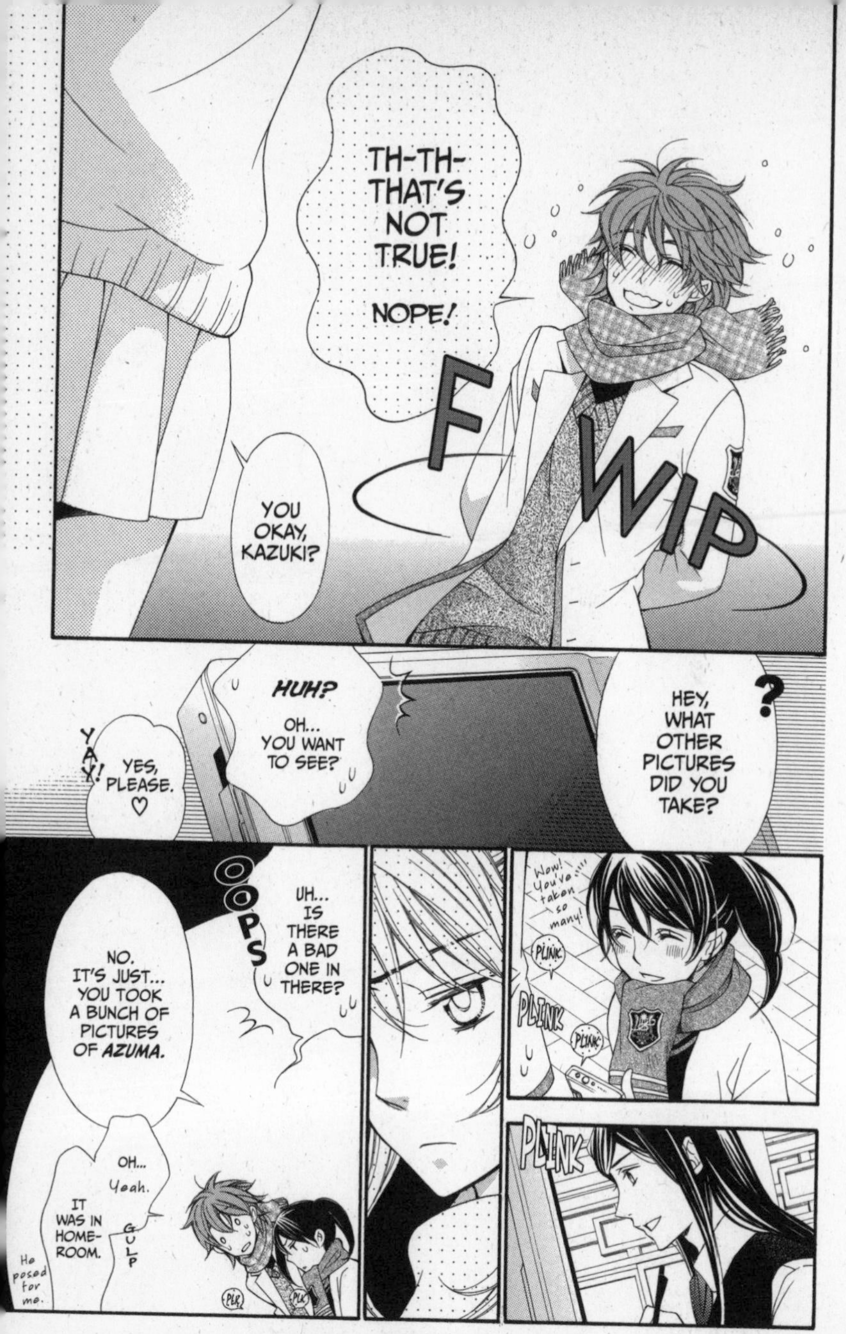
TH-TH-THAT'S NOT TRUE!
NOPE!
FWIP
YOU OKAY, KAZUKI?
HEY, WHAT OTHER PICTURES DID YOU TAKE?
?
HUH?
OH... YOU WANT TO SEE?
YAY!
YES, PLEASE. ♡
Wow! You've taken so many!
PLINK
PLINK
PLINK
PLINK
UH... IS THERE A BAD ONE IN THERE?
OOPS
NO. IT'S JUST... YOU TOOK A BUNCH OF PICTURES OF AZUMA.
OH...
Yeah.
IT WAS IN HOME-ROOM.
GULP
He posed for me.
PLK
PLK

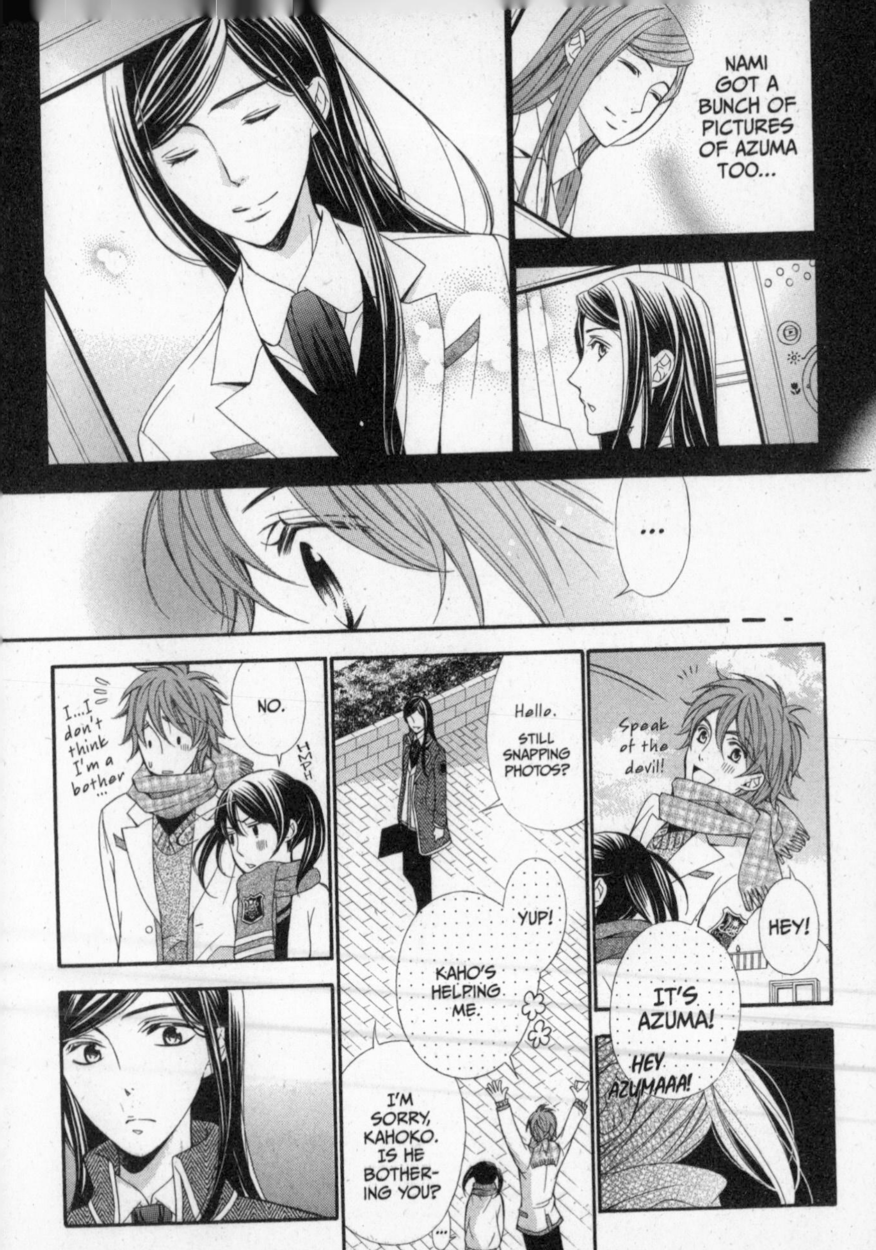
NAMI GOT A BUNCH OF PICTURES OF AZUMA TOO...
...
Speak of the devil!
HEY!
IT'S AZUMA!
HEY AZUMAAA!
Hello. STILL SNAPPING PHOTOS?
YUP! KAHO'S HELPING ME.
I'M SORRY, KAHOKO. IS HE BOTHERING YOU?
...
NO.
HMPH
I...I don't think I'm a bother...

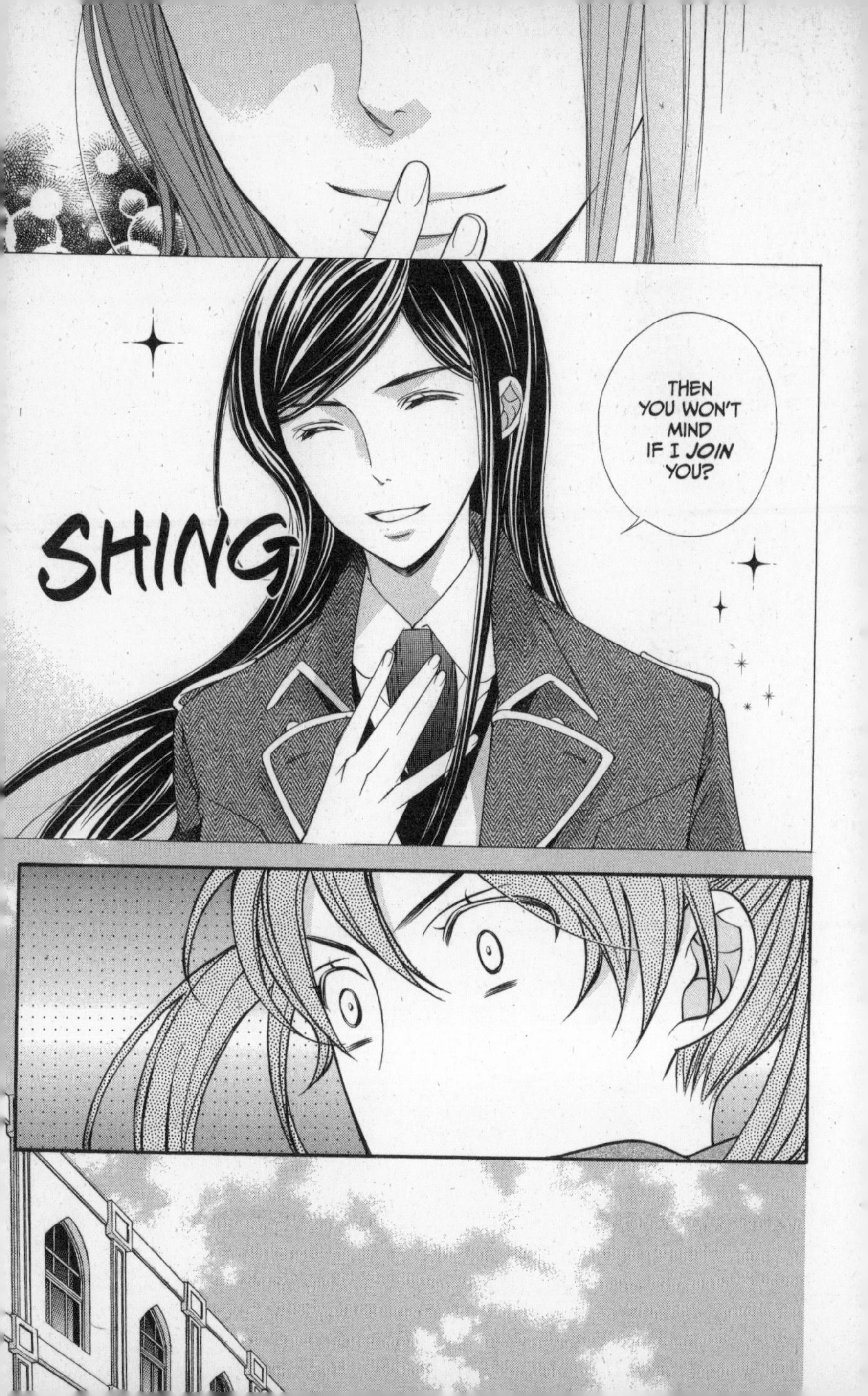
THEN YOU WON'T MIND IF I *JOIN* YOU?
SHING

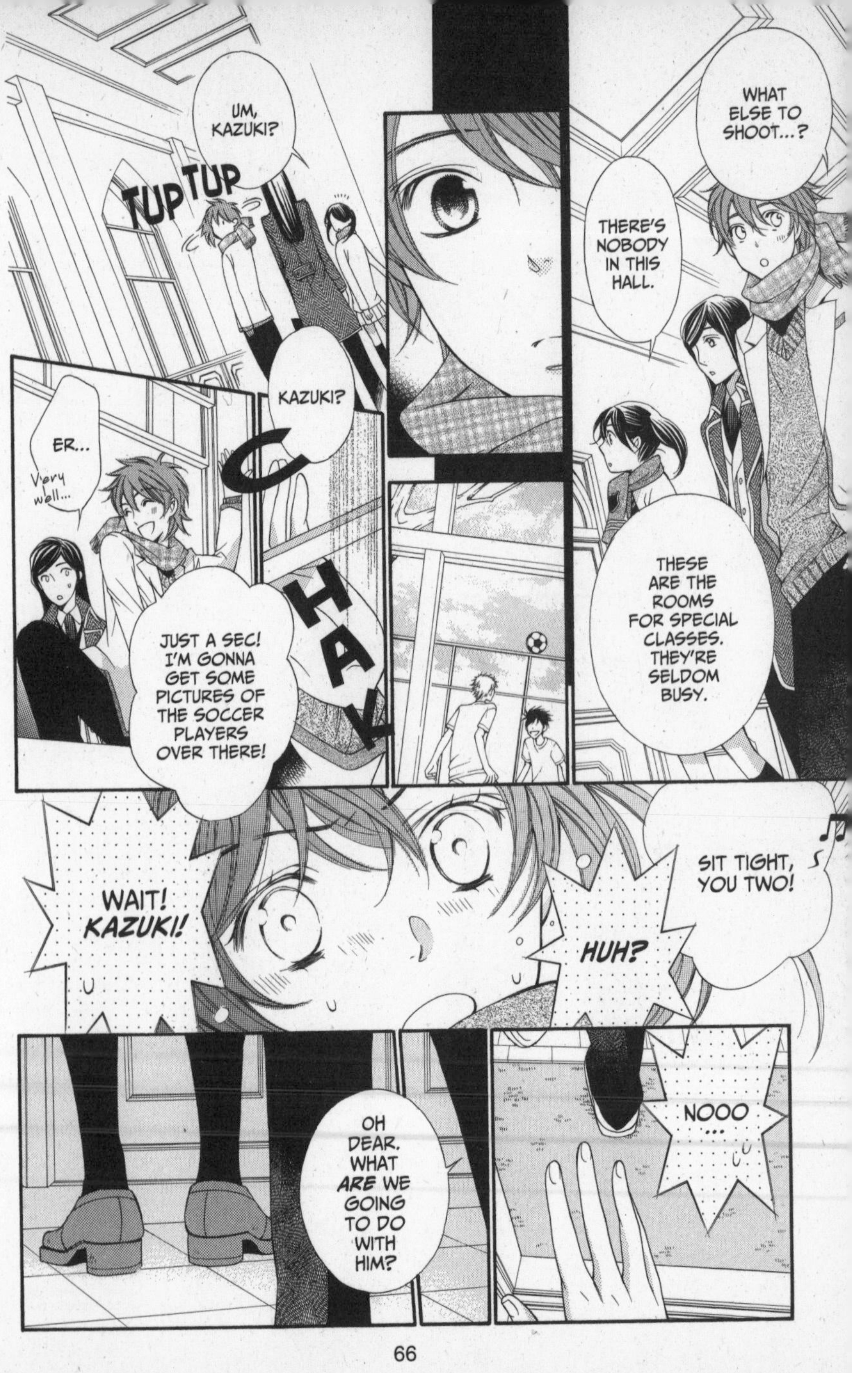
WHAT ELSE TO SHOOT...?
THERE'S NOBODY IN THIS HALL.
THESE ARE THE ROOMS FOR SPECIAL CLASSES. THEY'RE SELDOM BUSY.
UM, KAZUKI?
TUP TUP
KAZUKI?
CHAK
ER...
Very well...
JUST A SEC! I'M GONNA GET SOME PICTURES OF THE SOCCER PLAYERS OVER THERE!
SIT TIGHT, YOU TWO!
HUH?
WAIT! KAZUKI!
NOOO...
OH DEAR. WHAT ARE WE GOING TO DO WITH HIM?

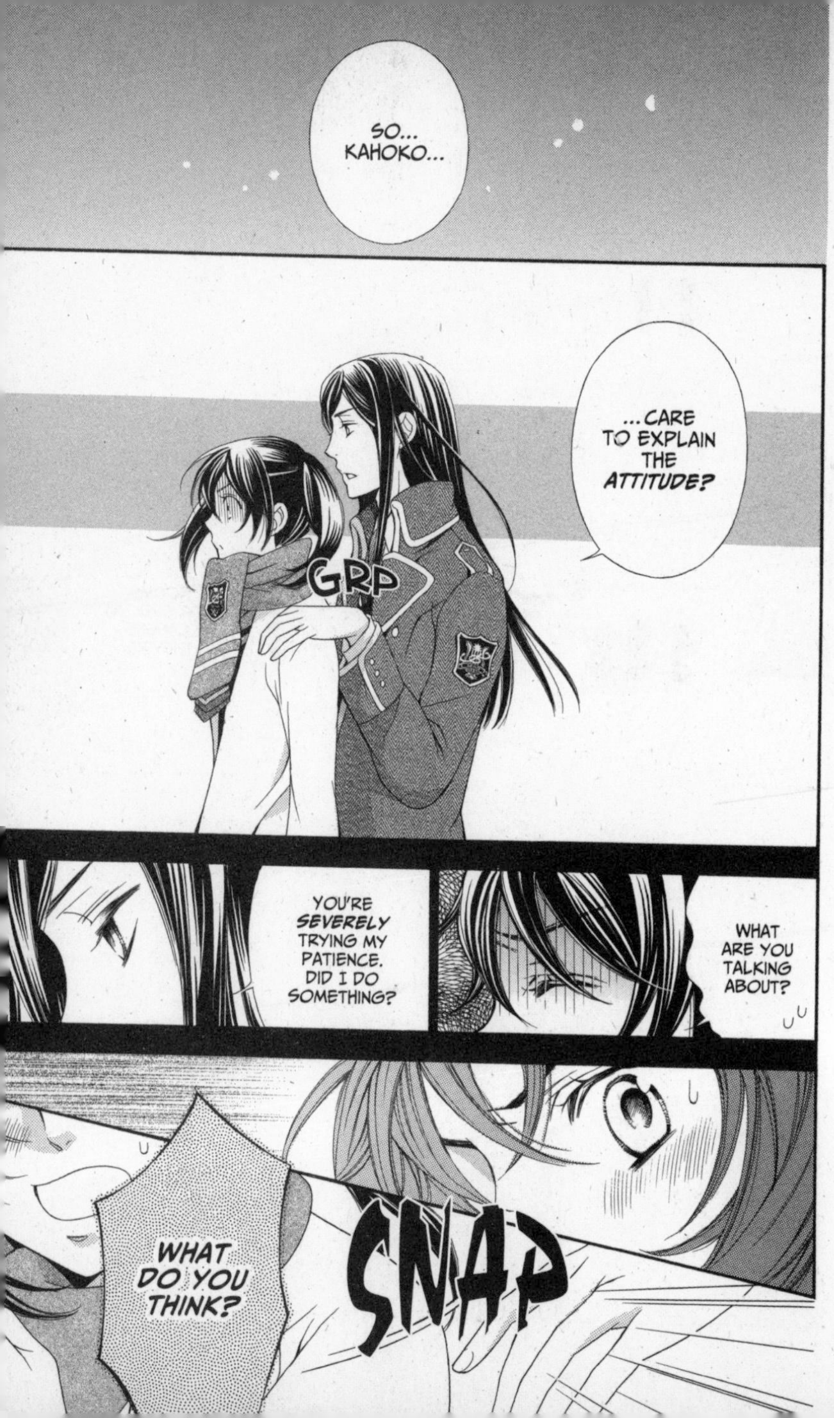
SO... KAHOKO...
...CARE TO EXPLAIN THE ATTITUDE?
GRP
WHAT ARE YOU TALKING ABOUT?
YOU'RE SEVERELY TRYING MY PATIENCE. DID I DO SOMETHING?
SNAP
WHAT DO YOU THINK?

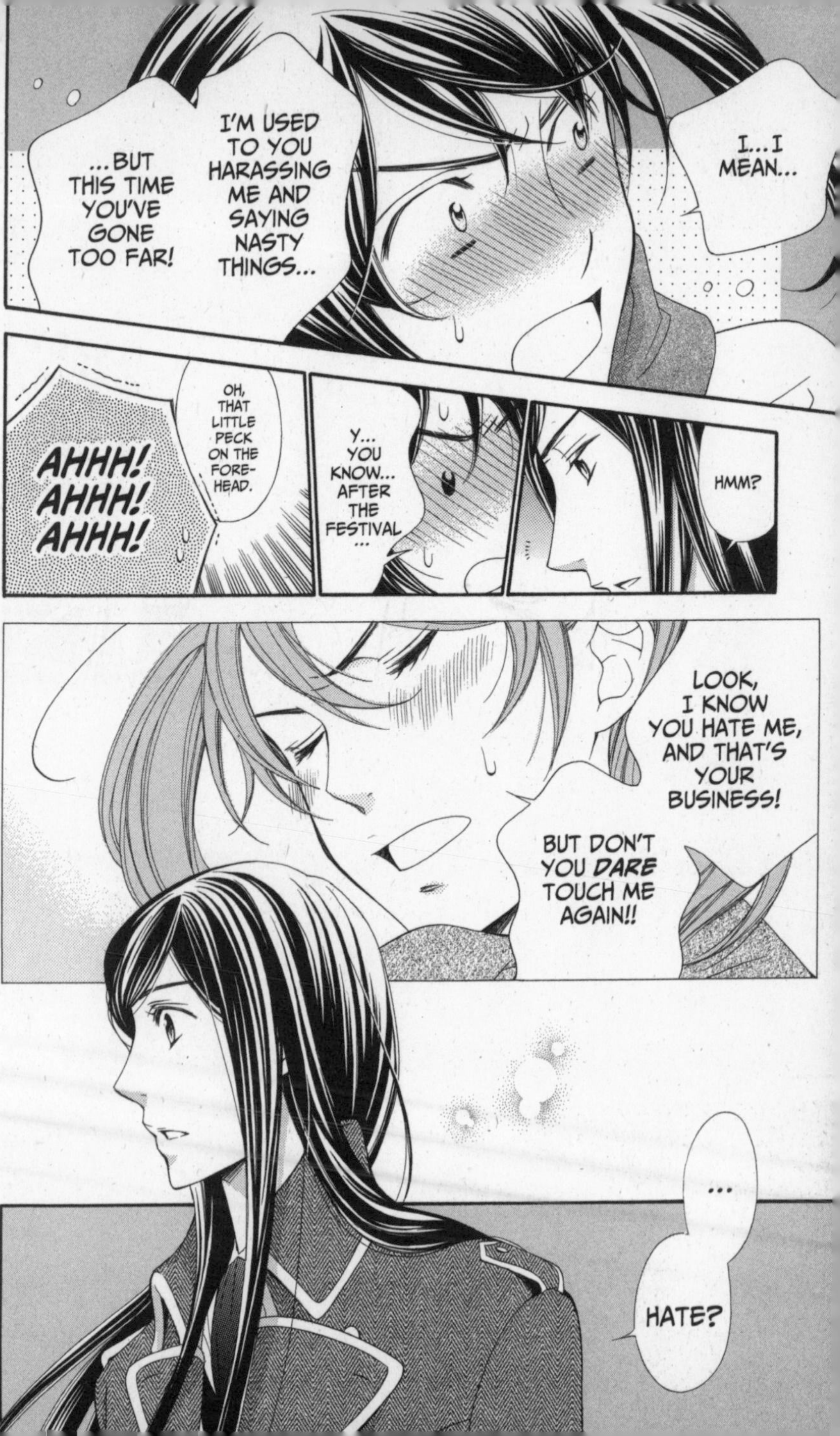
I...I MEAN...
I'M USED TO YOU HARASSING ME AND SAYING NASTY THINGS...
...BUT THIS TIME YOU'VE GONE TOO FAR!
HMM?
Y... YOU KNOW... AFTER THE FESTIVAL ...
OH, THAT LITTLE PECK ON THE FORE-HEAD.
AHHH! AHHH! AHHH!
LOOK, I KNOW YOU HATE ME, AND THAT'S YOUR BUSINESS!
BUT DON'T YOU DARE TOUCH ME AGAIN!!
...
HATE?

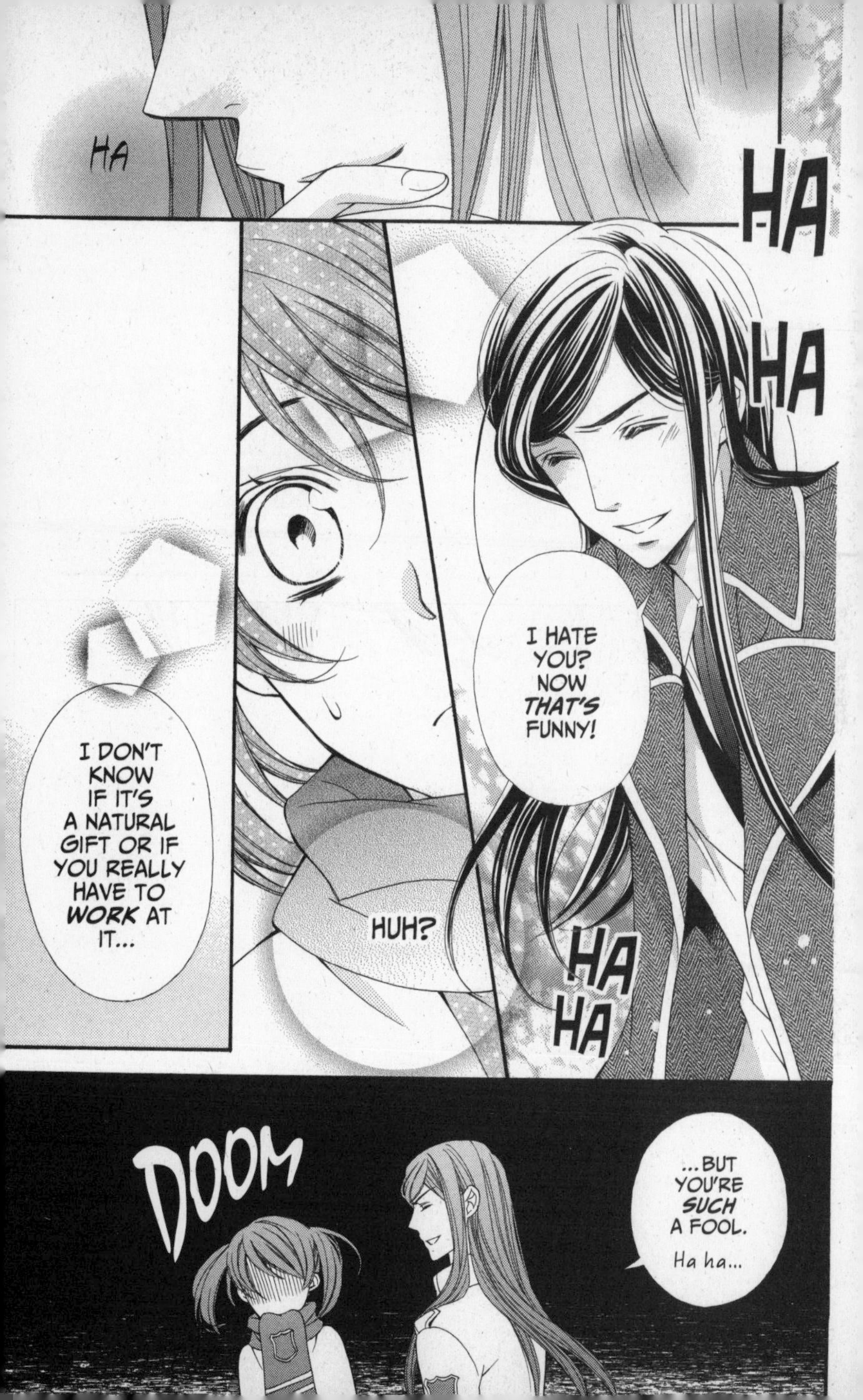
HA
HA
HA
I HATE YOU? NOW *THAT'S* FUNNY!
HA HA
HUH?
I DON'T KNOW IF IT'S A NATURAL GIFT OR IF YOU REALLY HAVE TO **WORK** AT IT...
...BUT YOU'RE *SUCH* A FOOL.
Ha ha...
DOOM

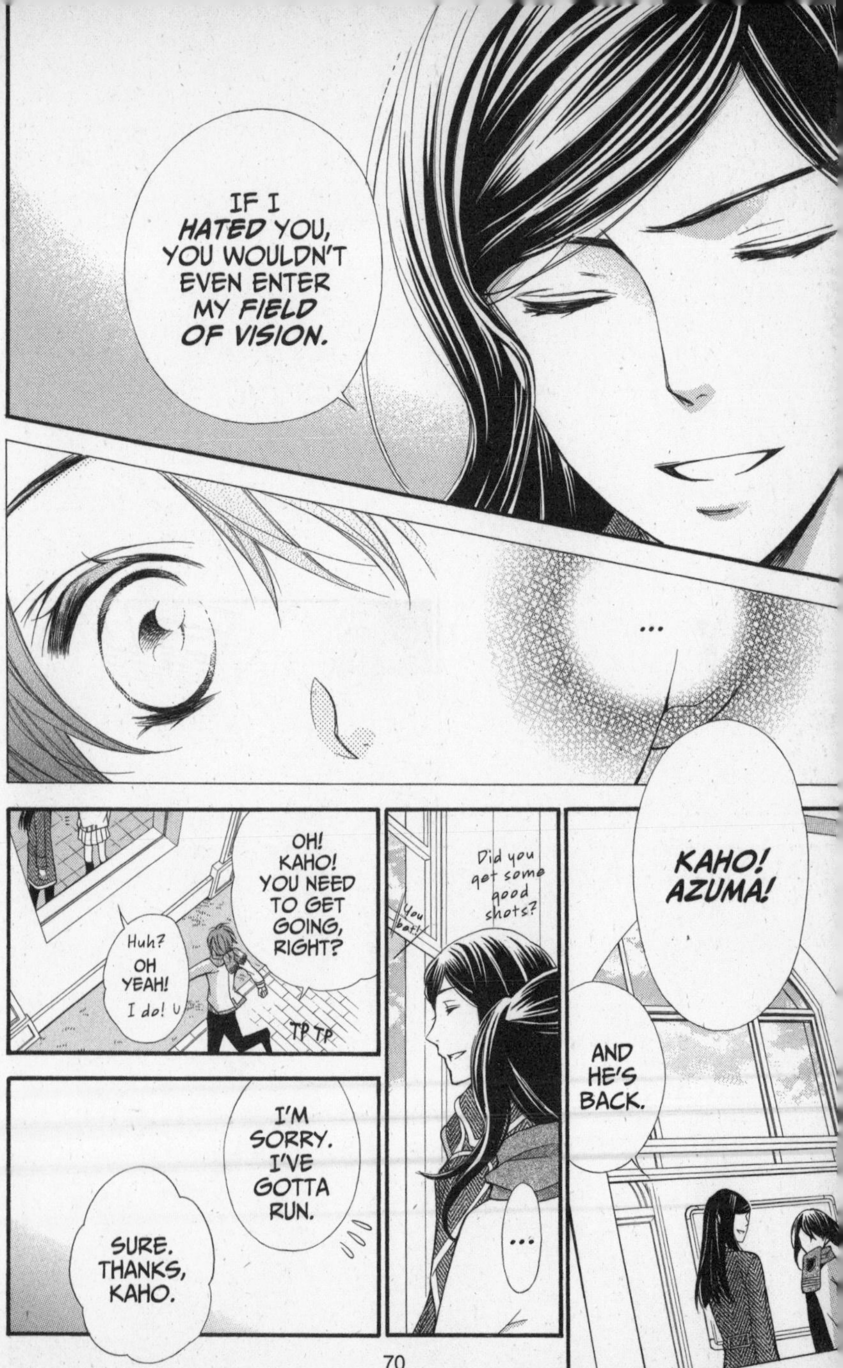
IF I HATED YOU, YOU WOULDN'T EVEN ENTER MY FIELD OF VISION.
...
KAHO! AZUMA!
AND HE'S BACK.
Did you get some good shots?
You bet!
...
OH! KAHO! YOU NEED TO GET GOING, RIGHT?
Huh? OH YEAH! I do!
TP TP
I'M SORRY. I'VE GOTTA RUN.
SURE. THANKS, KAHO.

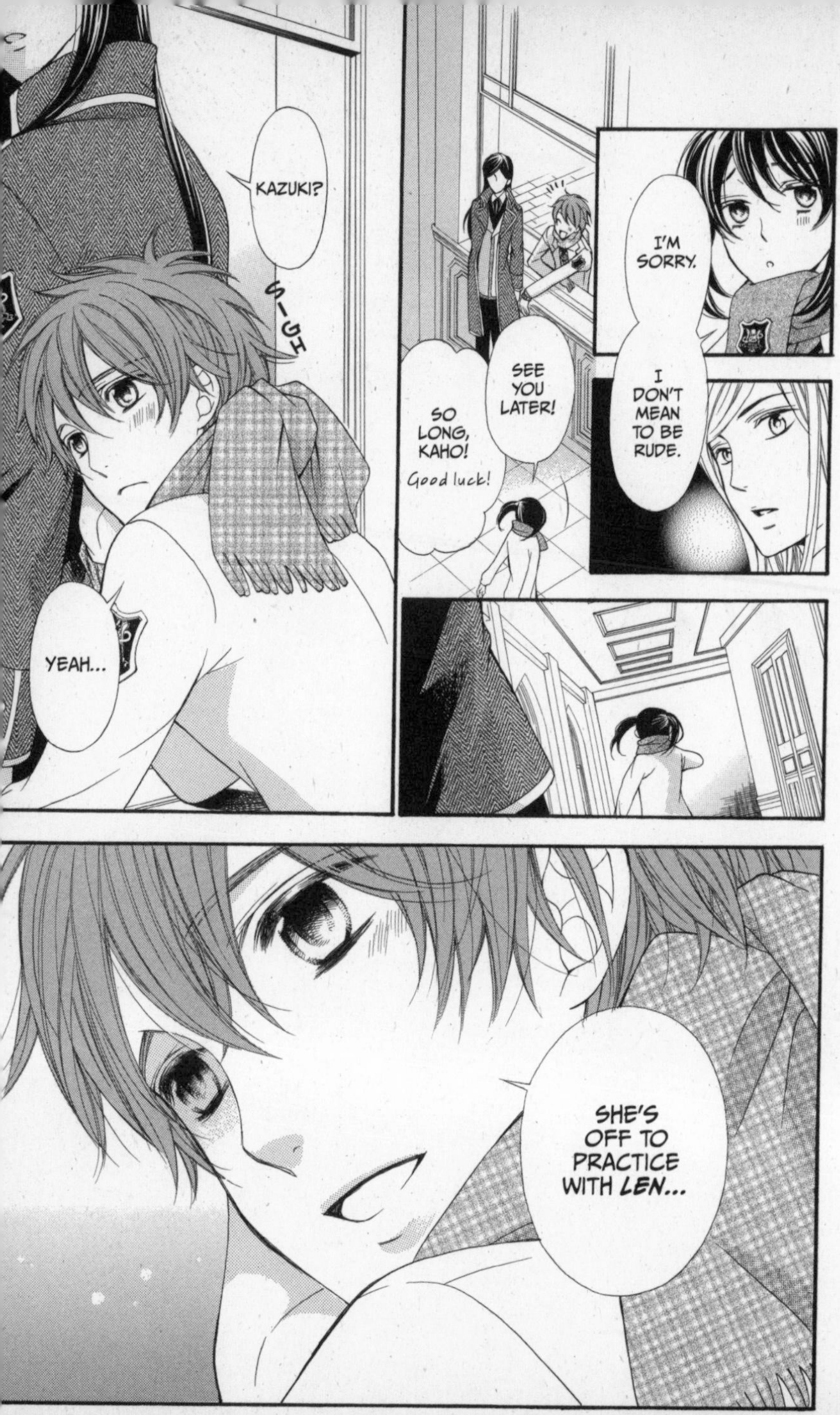
I'M SORRY.
I DON'T MEAN TO BE RUDE.
SEE YOU LATER!
SO LONG, KAHO!
Good luck!
KAZUKI?
SIGH
YEAH...
SHE'S OFF TO PRACTICE WITH *LEN*...

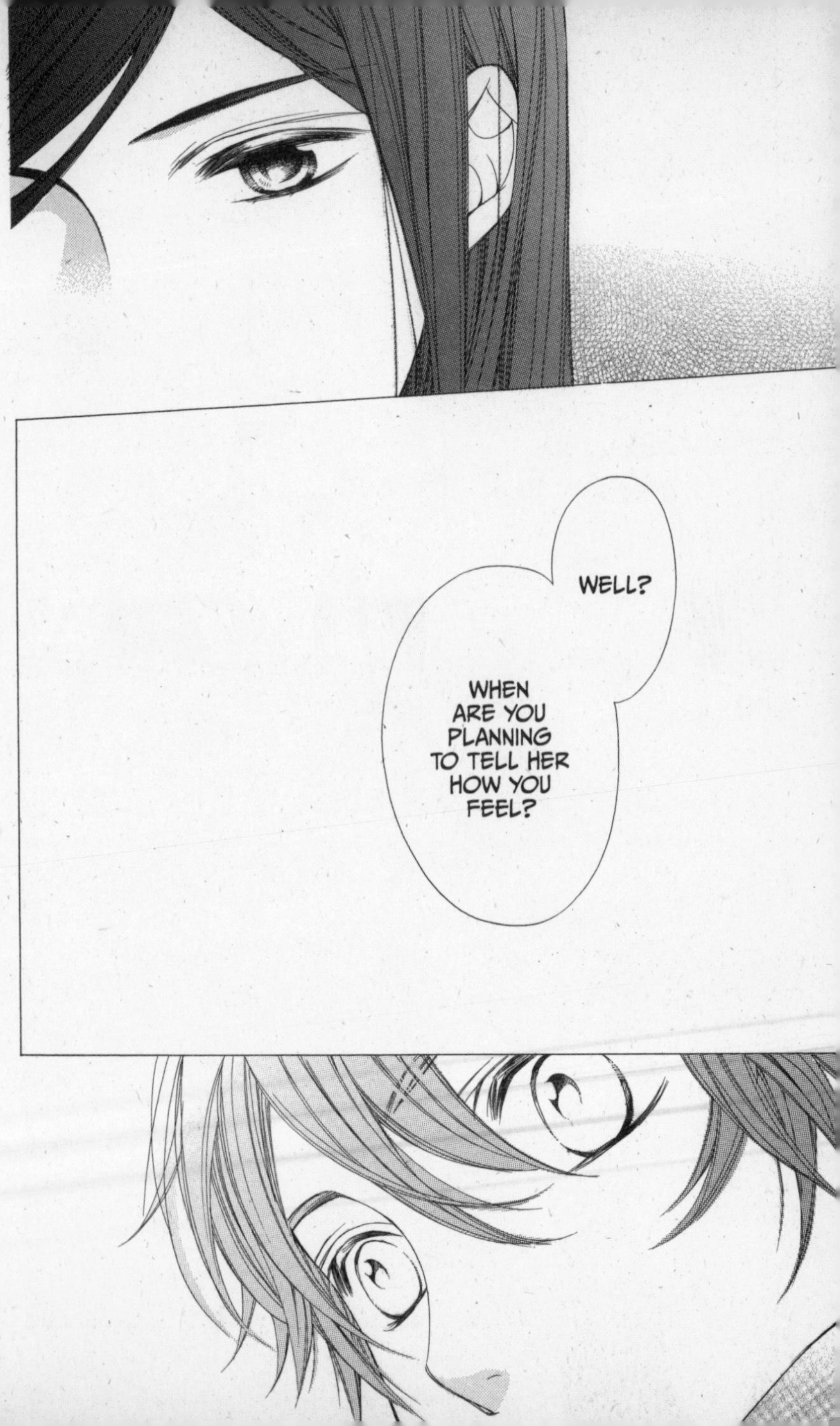
WELL?
WHEN ARE YOU PLANNING TO TELL HER HOW YOU FEEL?

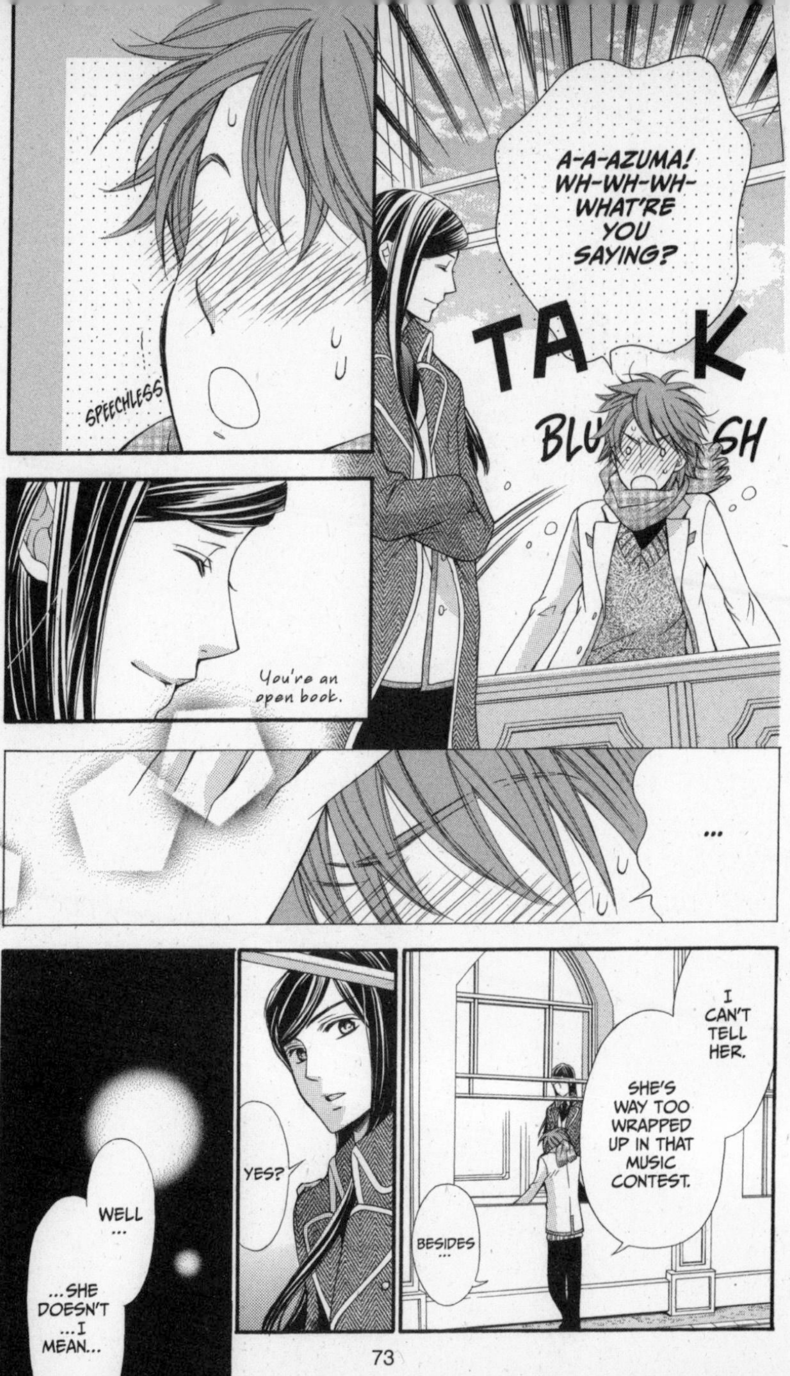
A-A-AZUMA! WH-WH-WH-WHAT'RE YOU SAYING?
TAK
BLUSH
SPEECHLESS
You're an open book.
...
I CAN'T TELL HER.
SHE'S WAY TOO WRAPPED UP IN THAT MUSIC CONTEST.
BESIDES...
YES?
WELL...
...SHE DOESN'T ...I MEAN...

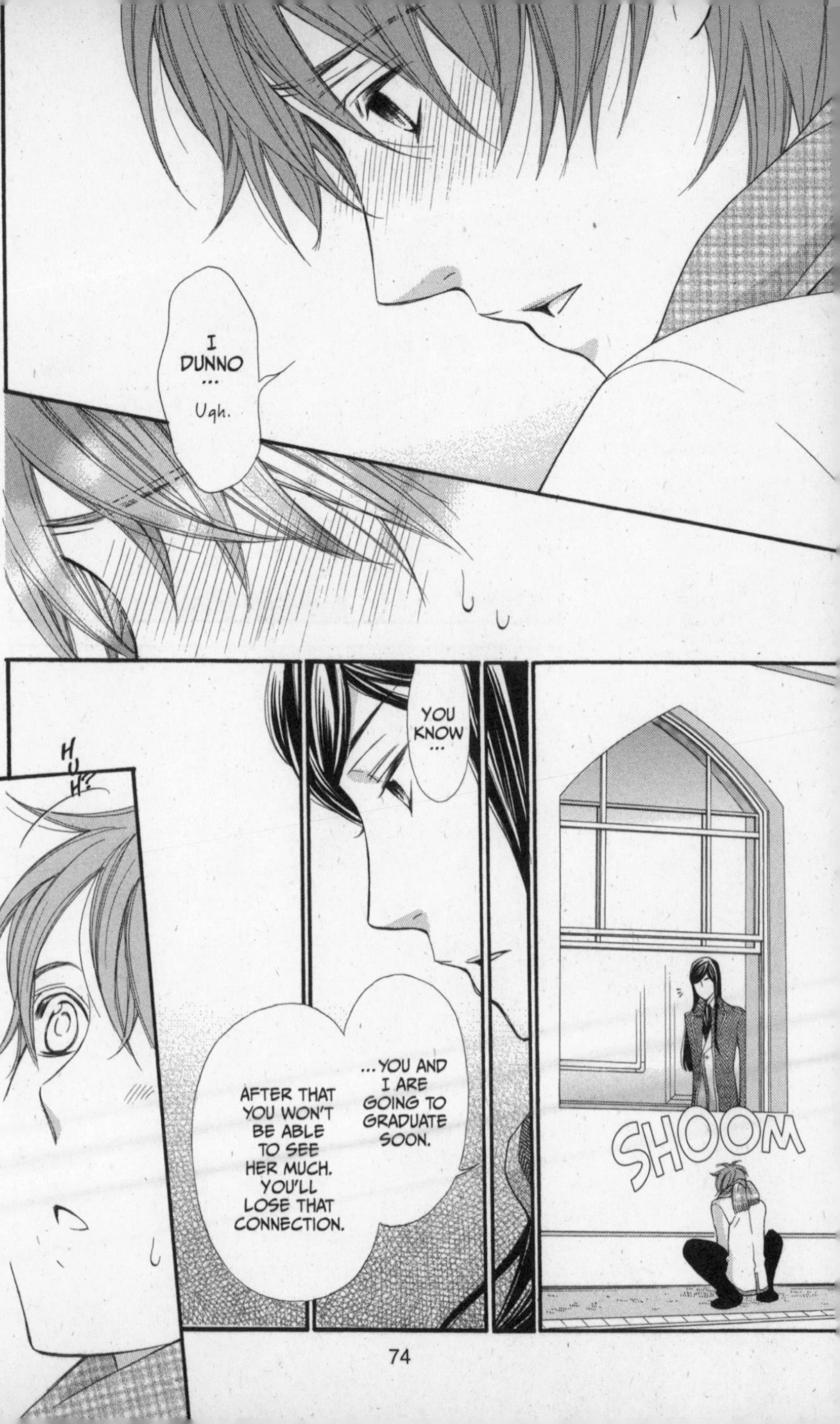
I DUNNO... Ugh.
SHOOM
YOU KNOW...
...YOU AND I ARE GOING TO GRADUATE SOON.
AFTER THAT YOU WON'T BE ABLE TO SEE HER MUCH. YOU'LL LOSE THAT CONNECTION.
HUH?

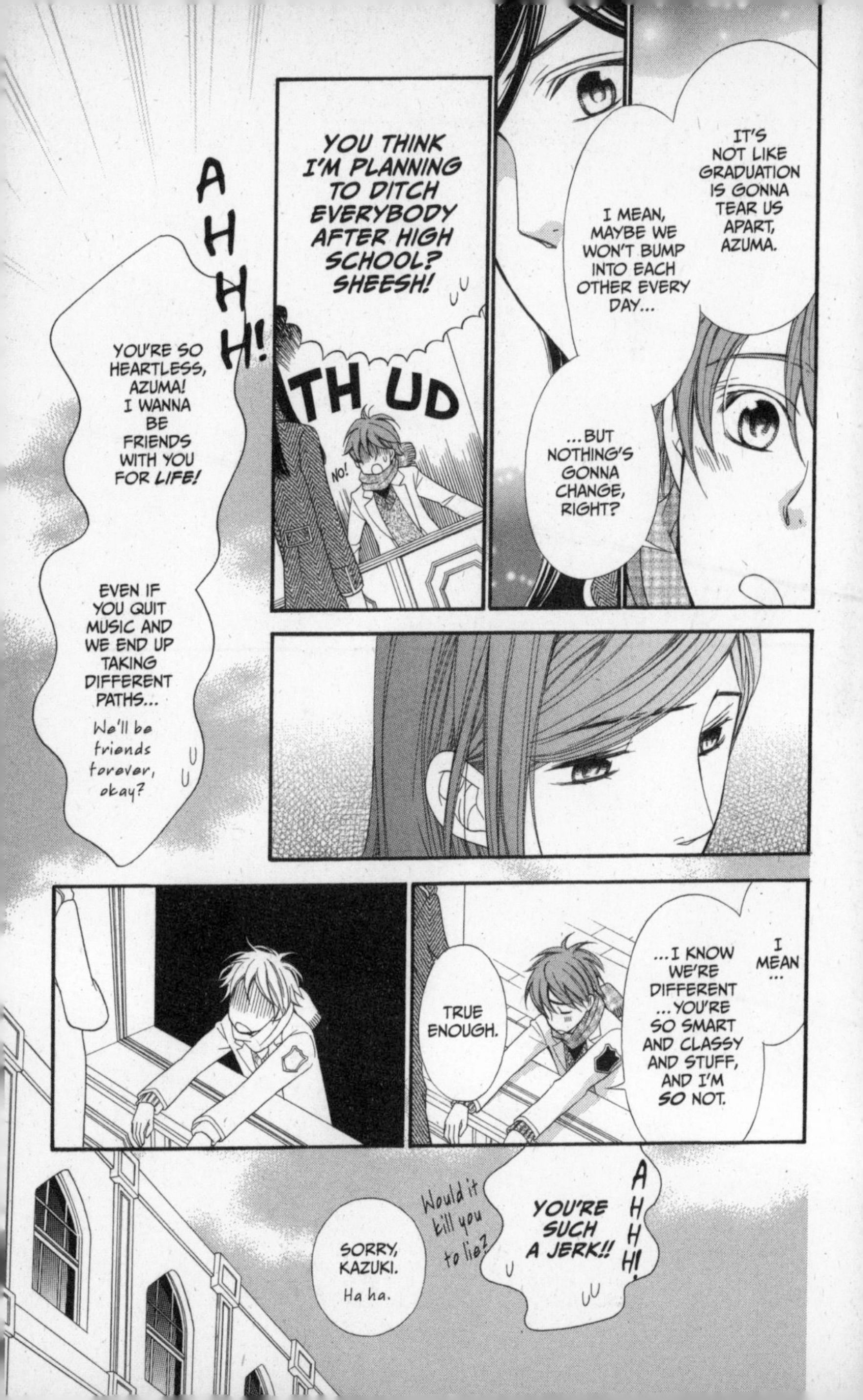
IT'S NOT LIKE GRADUATION IS GONNA TEAR US APART, AZUMA.
I MEAN, MAYBE WE WON'T BUMP INTO EACH OTHER EVERY DAY...
...BUT NOTHING'S GONNA CHANGE, RIGHT?
YOU THINK I'M PLANNING TO DITCH EVERYBODY AFTER HIGH SCHOOL? SHEESH!
THUD
NO!
AHHH!
YOU'RE SO HEARTLESS, AZUMA! I WANNA BE FRIENDS WITH YOU FOR *LIFE!*
EVEN IF YOU QUIT MUSIC AND WE END UP TAKING DIFFERENT PATHS...
We'll be friends forever, okay?
I MEAN...
...I KNOW WE'RE DIFFERENT ...YOU'RE SO SMART AND CLASSY AND STUFF, AND I'M *SO* NOT.
TRUE ENOUGH.
AHHH!
YOU'RE SUCH A JERK!!
Would it kill you to lie?
SORRY, KAZUKI.
Ha ha.

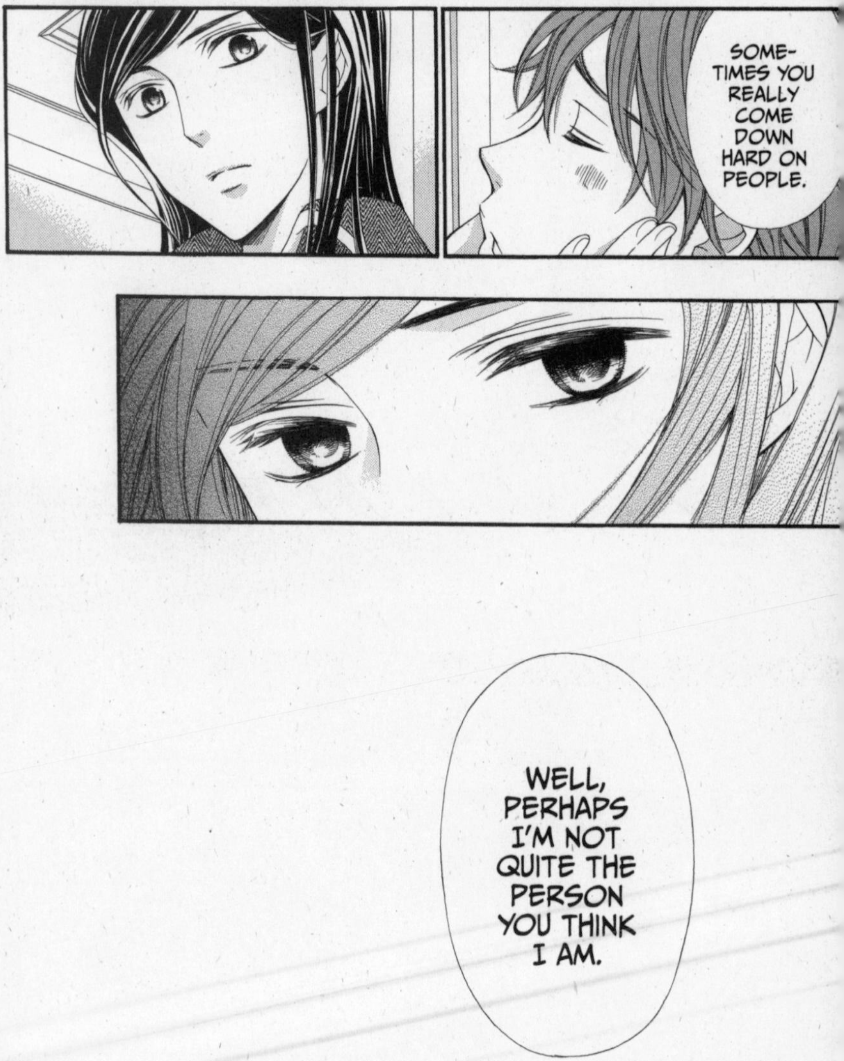
SOME-TIMES YOU REALLY COME DOWN HARD ON PEOPLE.
WELL, PERHAPS I'M NOT QUITE THE PERSON YOU THINK I AM.

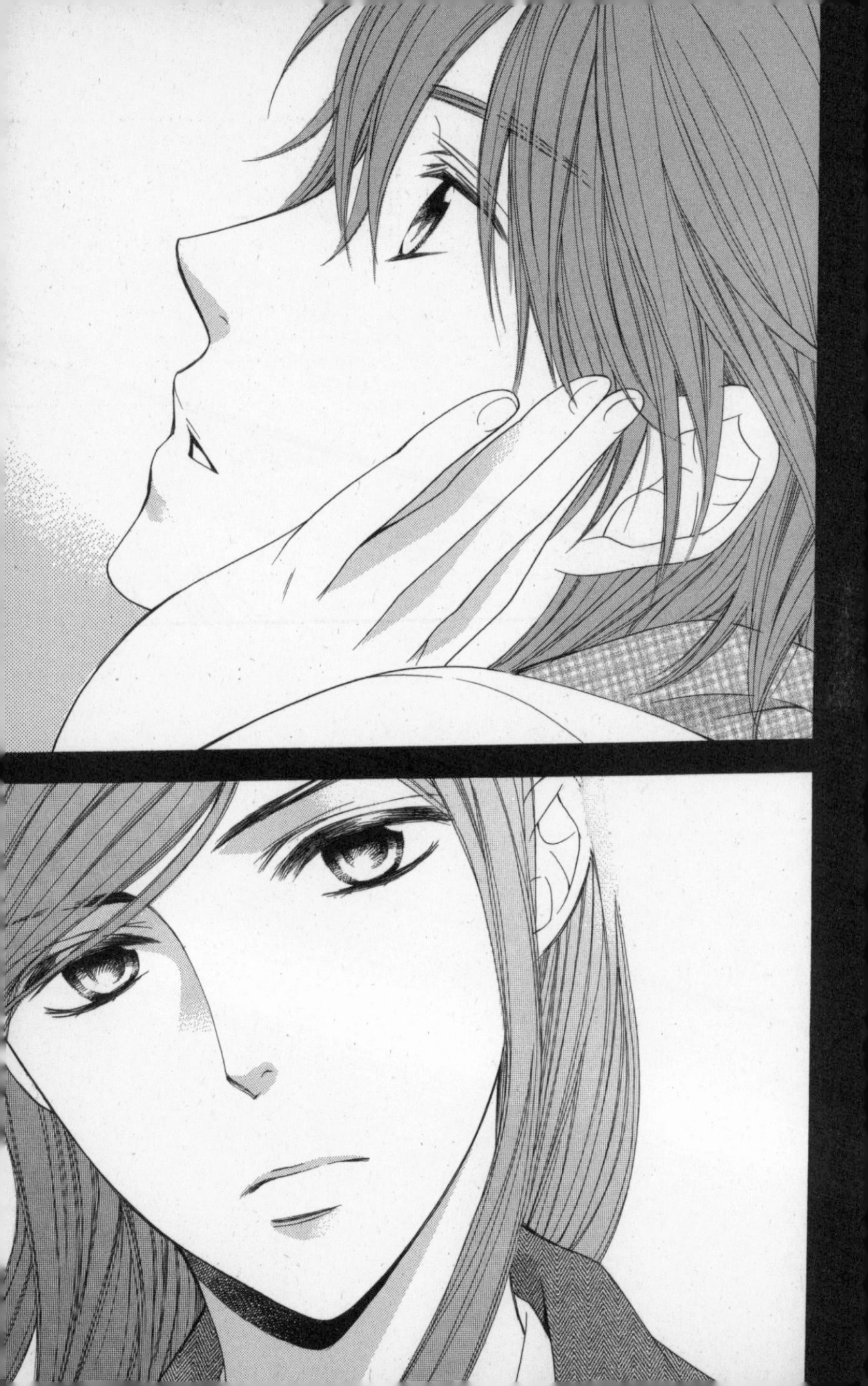

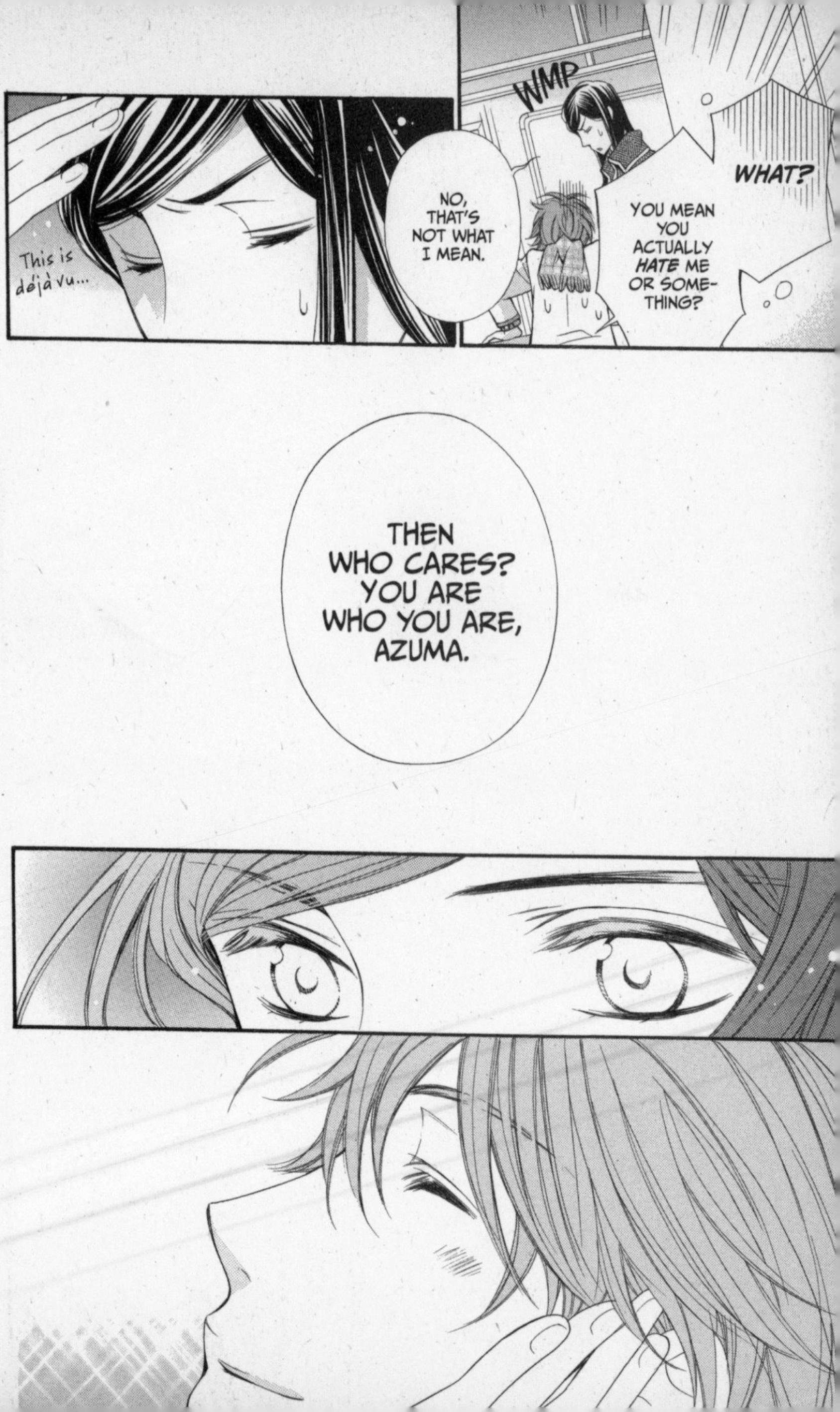
WHAT?
YOU MEAN YOU ACTUALLY *HATE* ME OR SOME-THING?
WMP
NO, THAT'S NOT WHAT I MEAN.
This is déjà vu...
THEN WHO CARES? YOU ARE WHO YOU ARE, AZUMA.

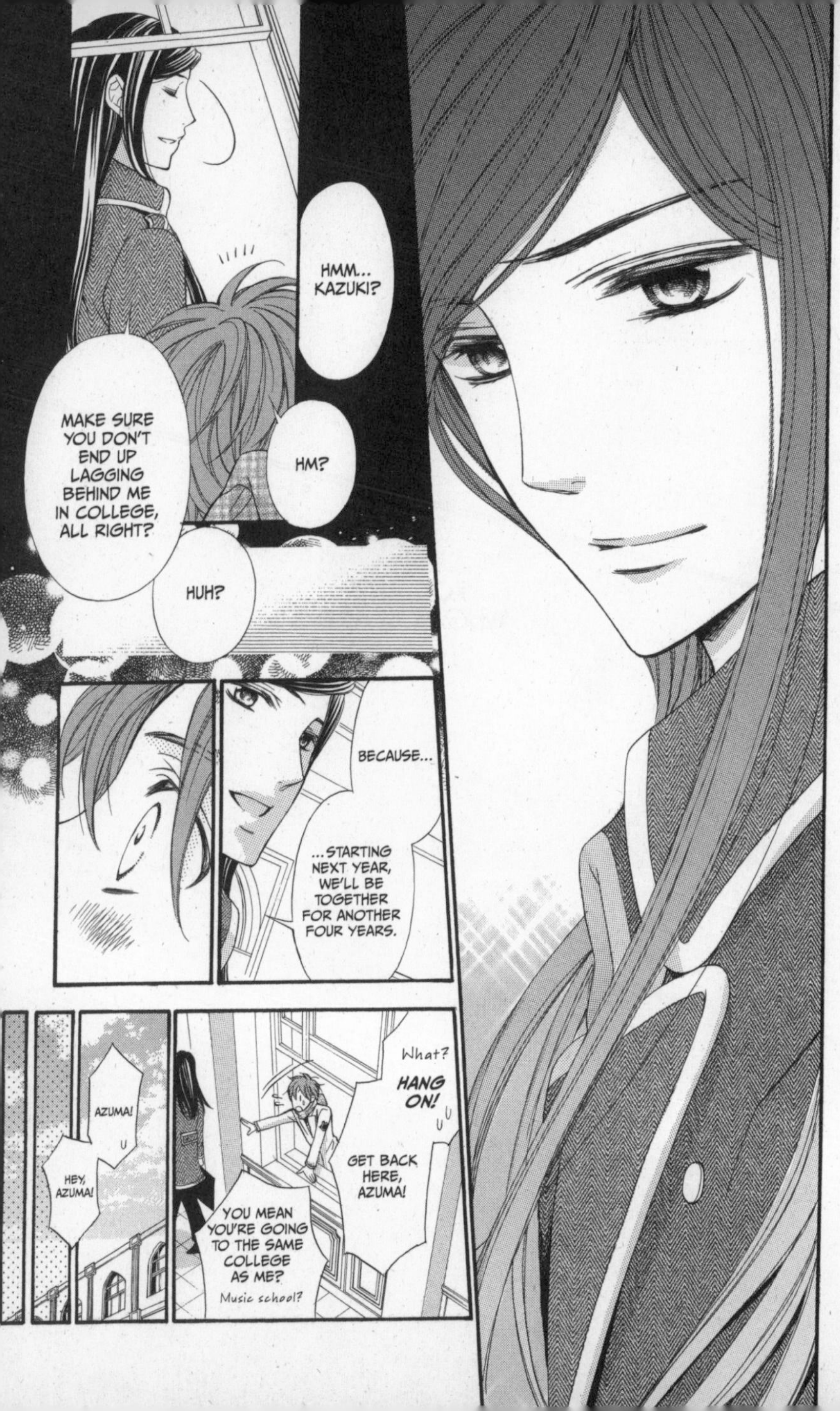
HMM.. KAZUKI?
HM?
MAKE SURE YOU DON'T END UP LAGGING BEHIND ME IN COLLEGE, ALL RIGHT?
HUH?
BECAUSE...
...STARTING NEXT YEAR, WE'LL BE TOGETHER FOR ANOTHER FOUR YEARS.
What?
HANG ON!
GET BACK HERE, AZUMA!
YOU MEAN YOU'RE GOING TO THE SAME COLLEGE AS ME?
Music school?
AZUMA!
HEY, AZUMA!

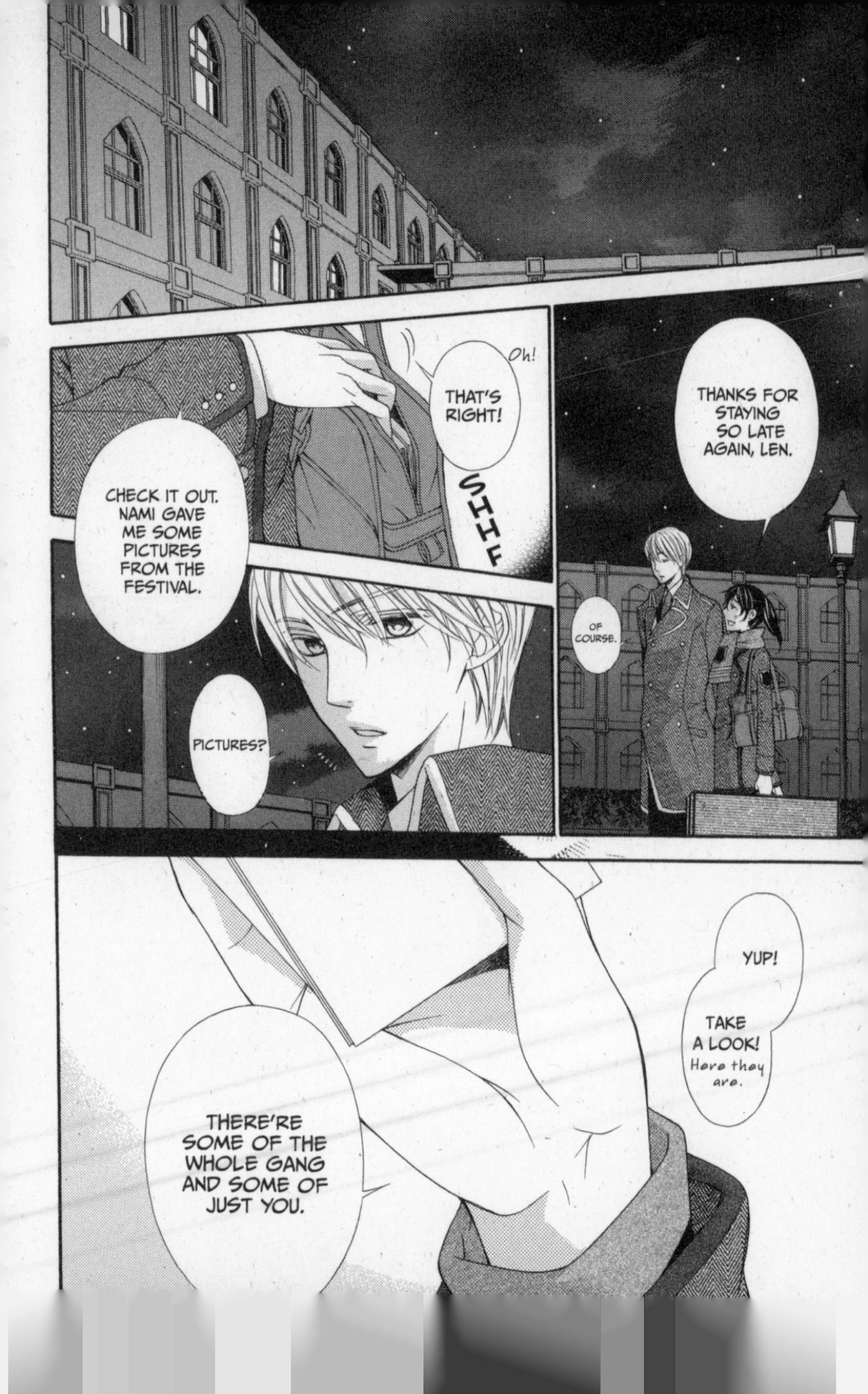
THANKS FOR STAYING SO LATE AGAIN, LEN.
OF COURSE.
Oh!
THAT'S RIGHT!
SHHF
CHECK IT OUT. NAMI GAVE ME SOME PICTURES FROM THE FESTIVAL.
PICTURES?
YUP!
TAKE A LOOK!
Here they are.
THERE'RE SOME OF THE WHOLE GANG AND SOME OF JUST YOU.

YOU TOOK A BUNCH OF PICTURES OF **AZUMA.**

YEAH. IT WAS IN HOME-ROOM.

OH YEAH...

I KNOW WHAT MADE ME FEEL WEIRD.

IN KAZUKI'S PICTURES, AZUMA LOOKS SO... *GENTLE.*

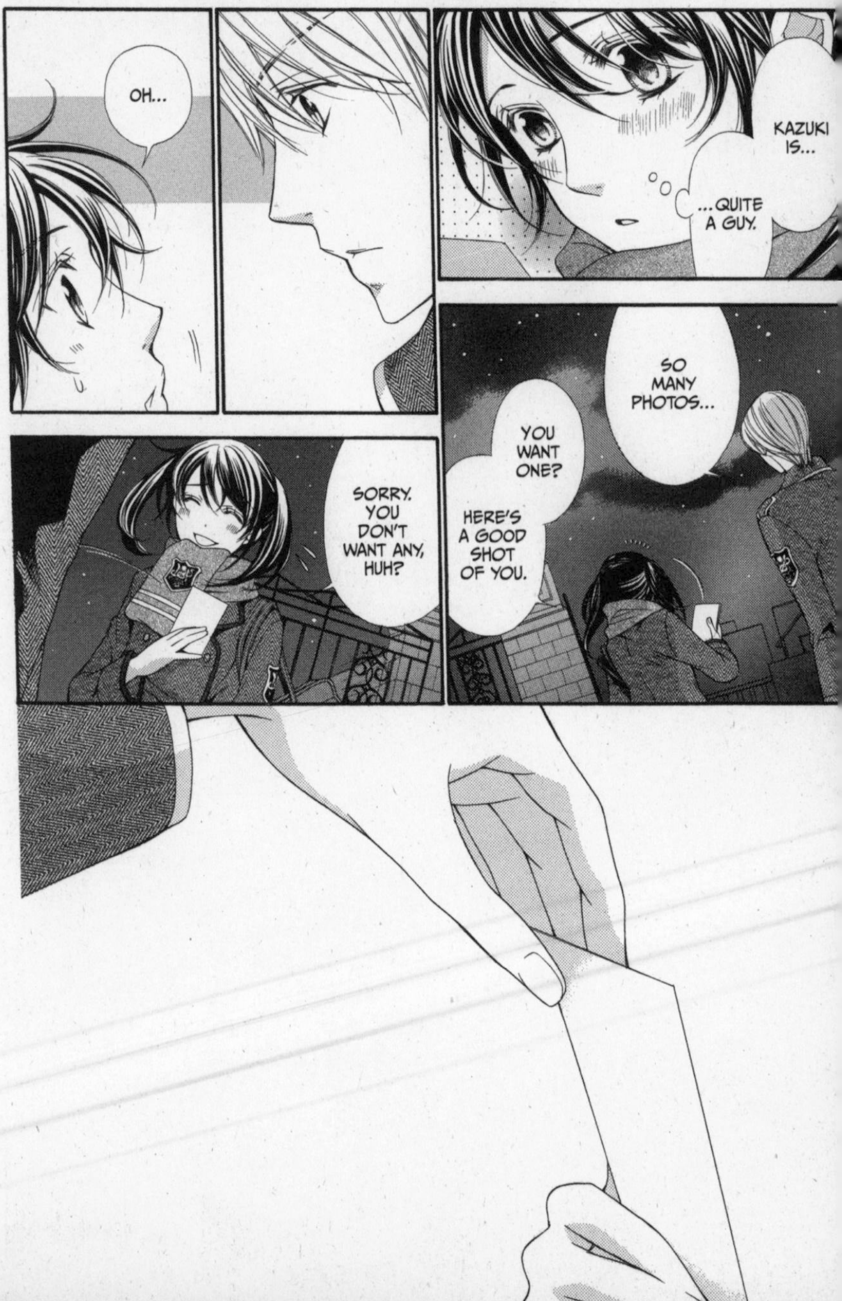
KAZUKI IS...
...QUITE A GUY.
OH...
SO MANY PHOTOS...
YOU WANT ONE?
HERE'S A GOOD SHOT OF YOU.
SORRY. YOU DON'T WANT ANY, HUH?

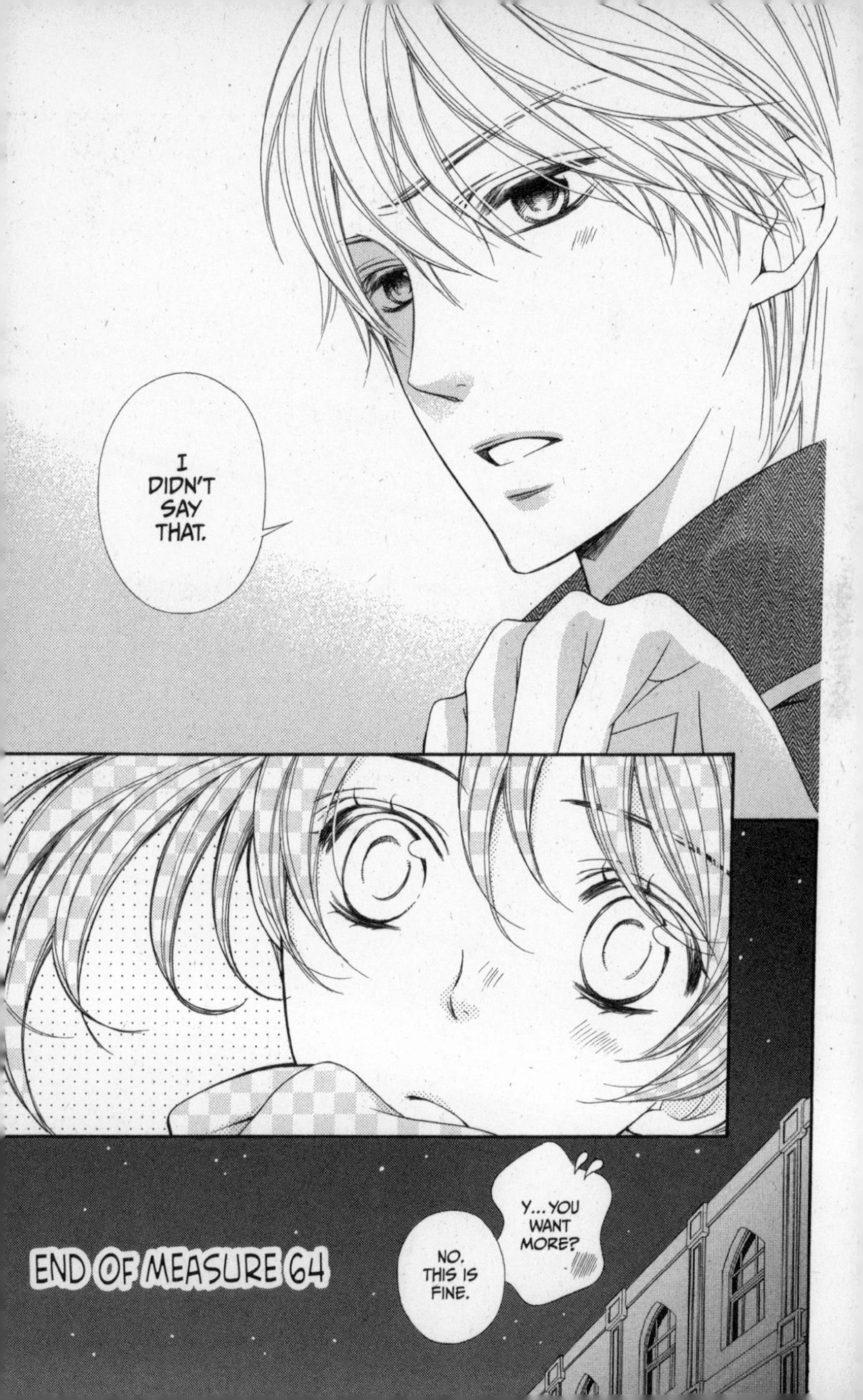
I DIDN'T SAY THAT.
Y... YOU WANT MORE?
NO. THIS IS FINE.
END OF MEASURE 64

La Corda d'Oro

MEASURE 65

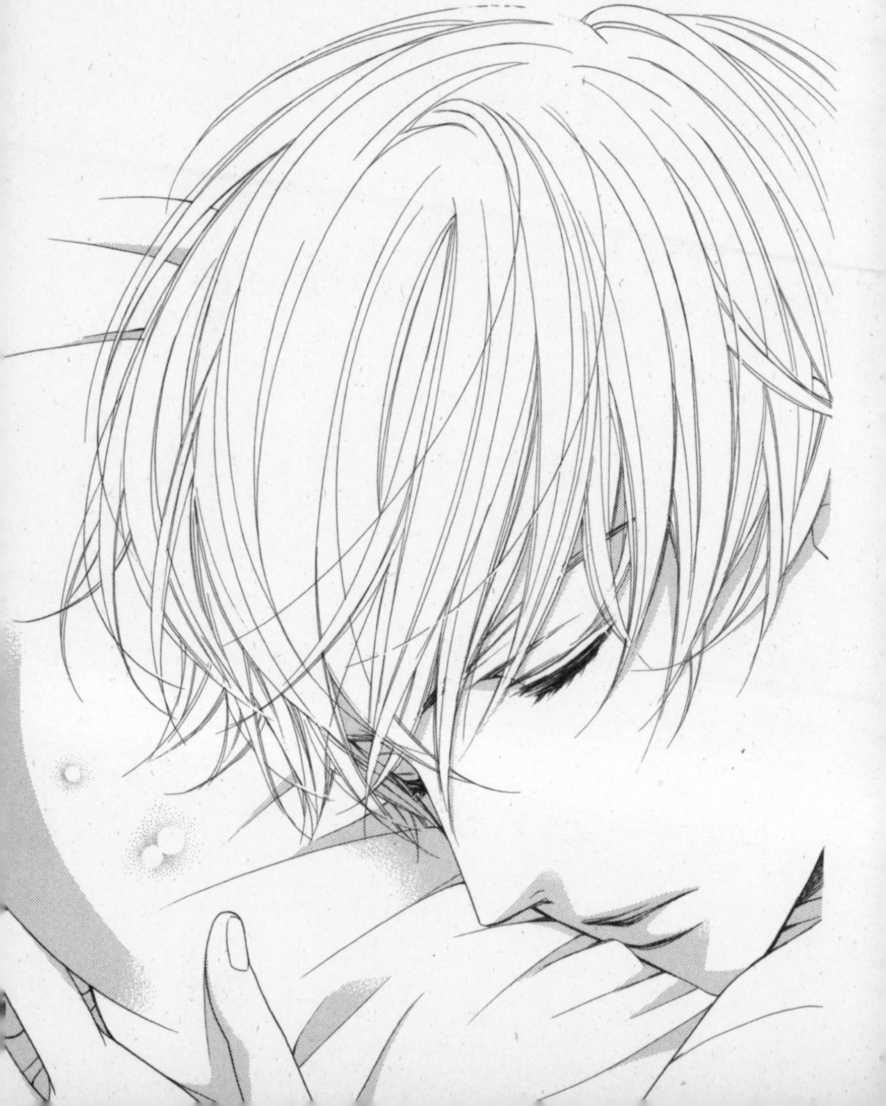

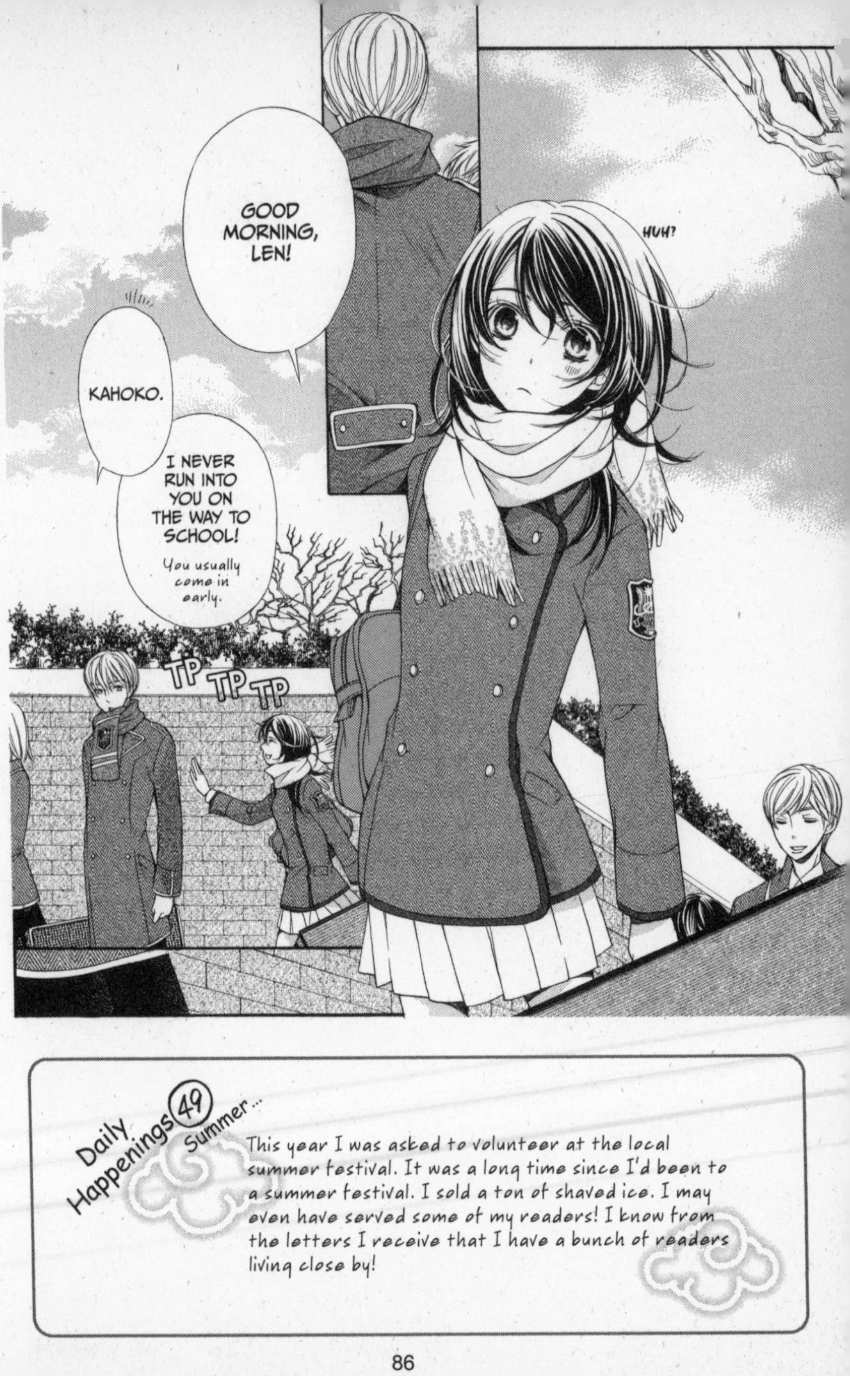
HUH?
GOOD MORNING, LEN!
KAHOKO.
I NEVER RUN INTO YOU ON THE WAY TO SCHOOL!
You usually come in early.
TP TP TP

Daily Happenings (49) Summer...

This year I was asked to volunteer at the local summer festival. It was a long time since I'd been to a summer festival. I sold a ton of shaved ice. I may even have served some of my readers! I know from the letters I receive that I have a bunch of readers living close by!

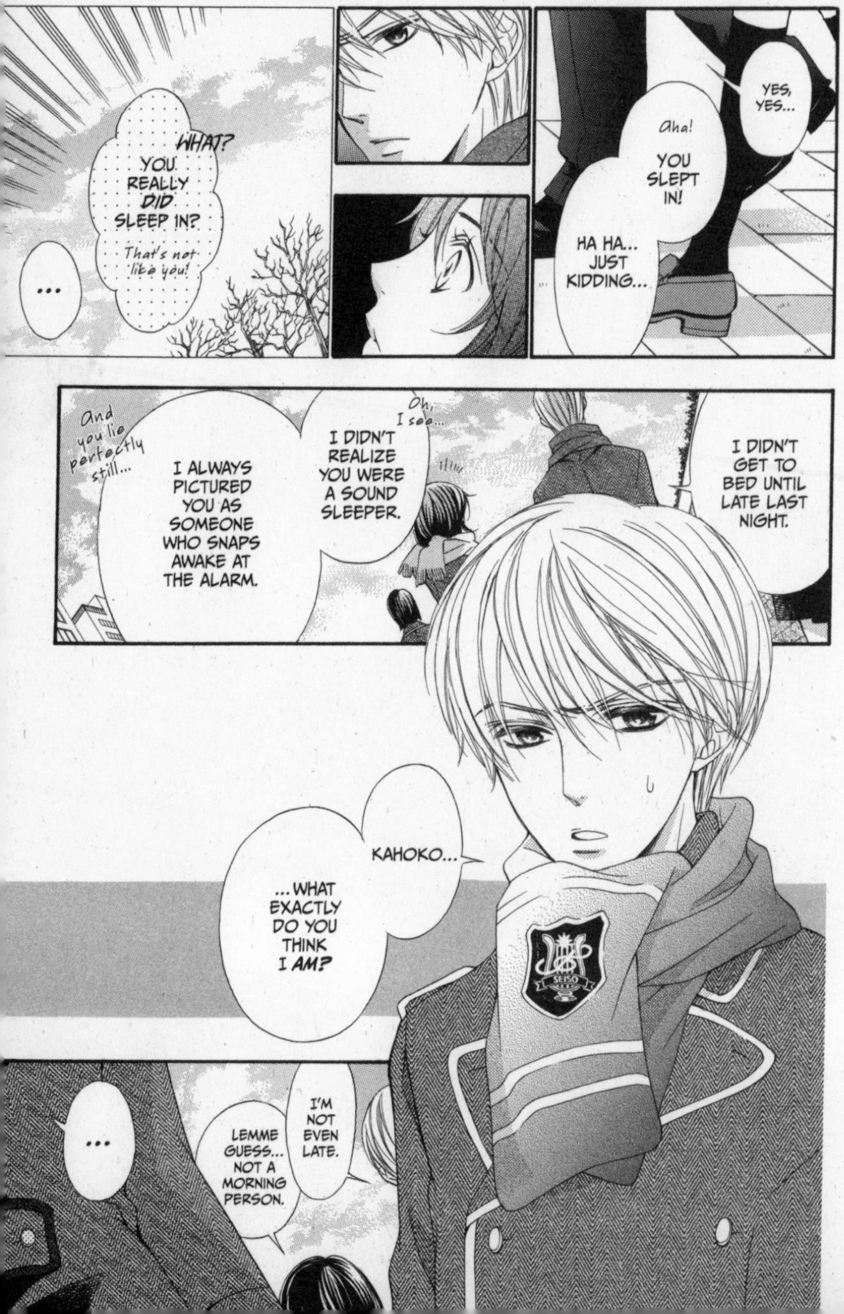
YES, YES...
Aha! YOU SLEPT IN!
HA HA... JUST KIDDING...
WHAT? YOU REALLY DID SLEEP IN? That's not like you!
...
I DIDN'T GET TO BED UNTIL LATE LAST NIGHT.
Oh, I see...
I DIDN'T REALIZE YOU WERE A SOUND SLEEPER.
I ALWAYS PICTURED YOU AS SOMEONE WHO SNAPS AWAKE AT THE ALARM.
And you lie perfectly still...
KAHOKO... ...WHAT EXACTLY DO YOU THINK I AM?
SEISO
I'M NOT EVEN LATE.
LEMME GUESS... NOT A MORNING PERSON.
...

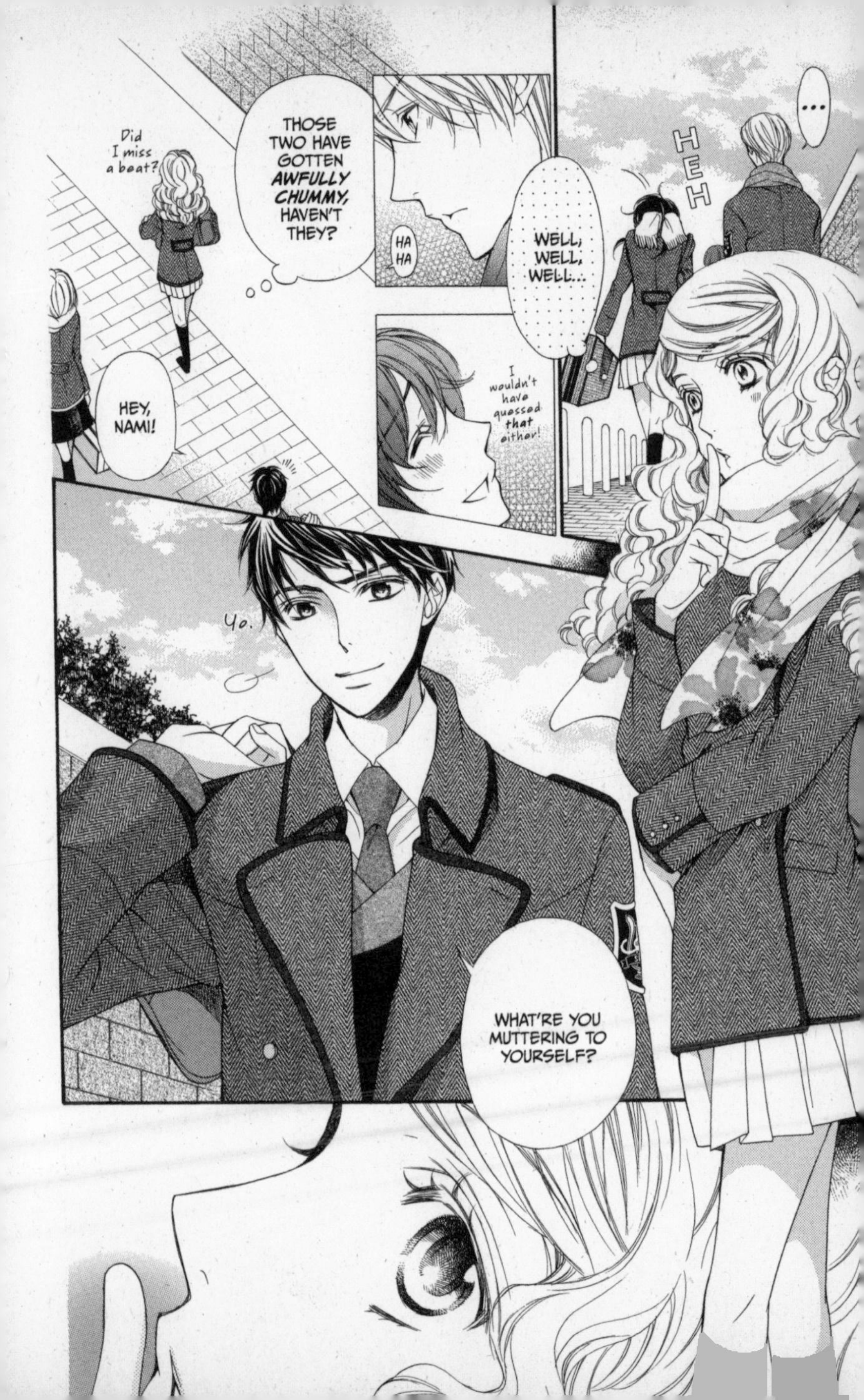
...
HEH
WELL, WELL, WELL...
HA HA
THOSE TWO HAVE GOTTEN AWFULLY CHUMMY, HAVEN'T THEY?
I wouldn't have guessed that either!
Did I miss a beat?
HEY, NAMI!
Yo.
WHAT'RE YOU MUTTERING TO YOURSELF?

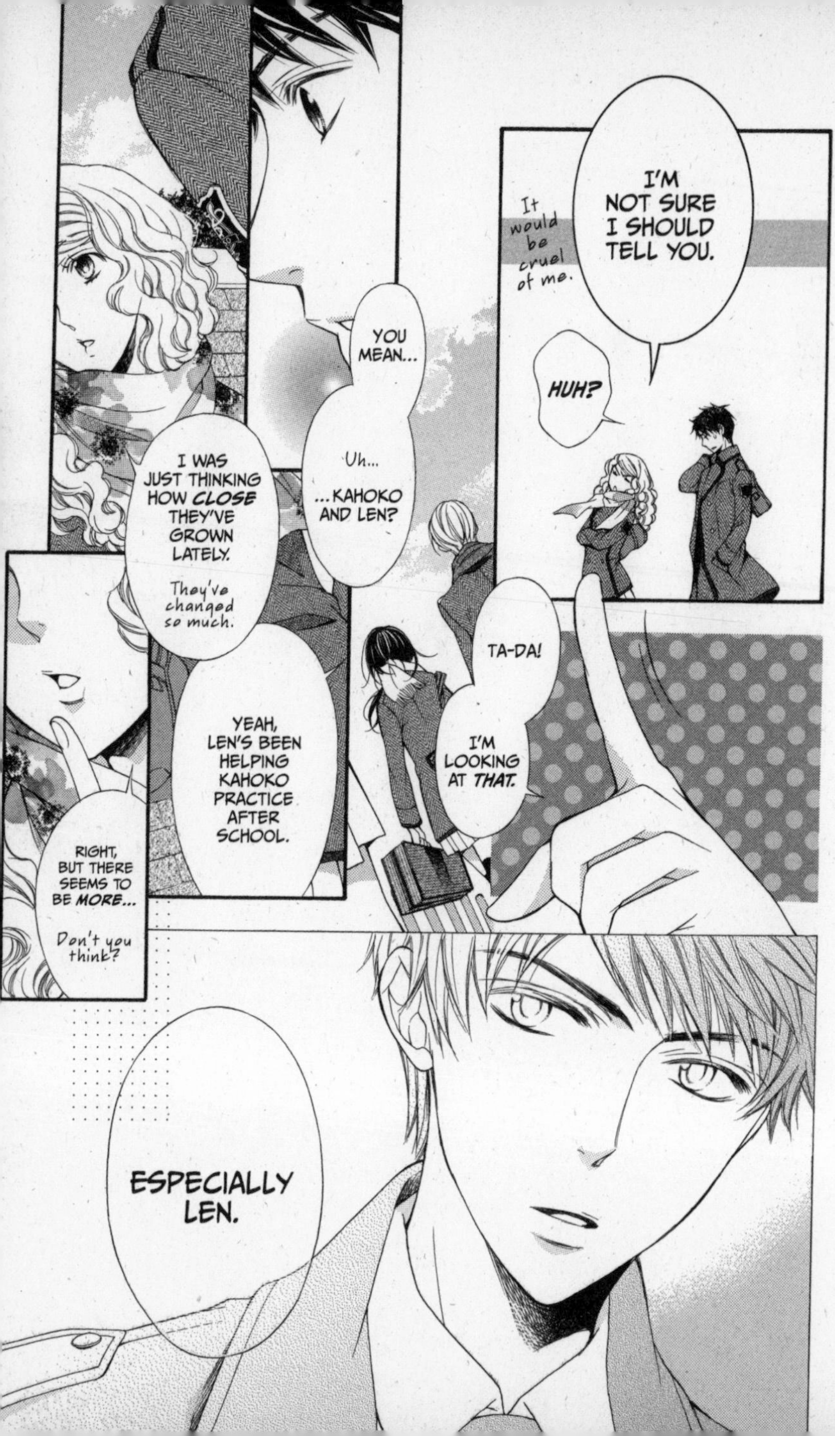
I'M NOT SURE I SHOULD TELL YOU.
It would be cruel of me.
HUH?
TA-DA!
I'M LOOKING AT THAT.
YOU MEAN...
Uh...
...KAHOKO AND LEN?
I WAS JUST THINKING HOW CLOSE THEY'VE GROWN LATELY.
They've changed so much.
YEAH, LEN'S BEEN HELPING KAHOKO PRACTICE AFTER SCHOOL.
RIGHT, BUT THERE SEEMS TO BE MORE...
Don't you think?
ESPECIALLY LEN.

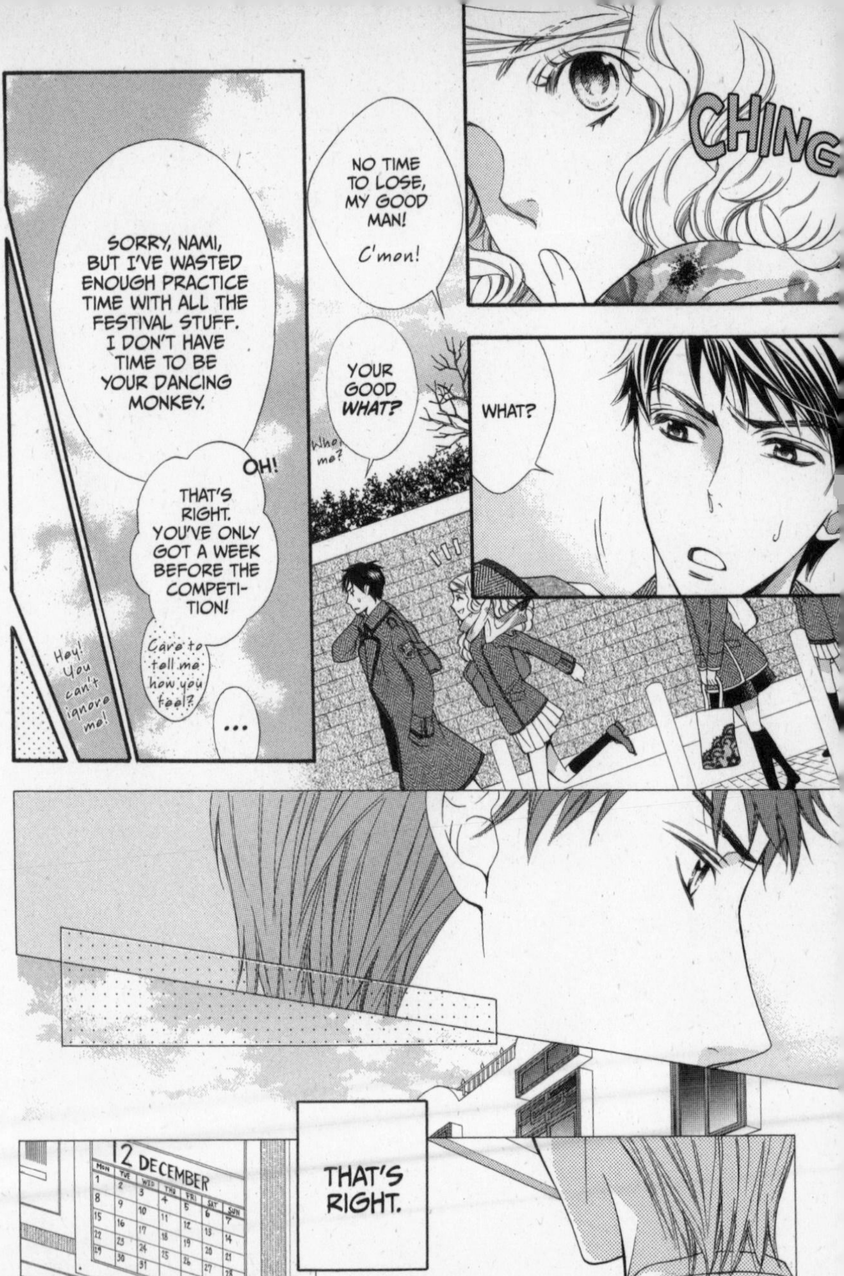
CHING
NO TIME TO LOSE, MY GOOD MAN!
C'mon!
WHAT?
YOUR GOOD WHAT?
Who, me?
SORRY, NAMI, BUT I'VE WASTED ENOUGH PRACTICE TIME WITH ALL THE FESTIVAL STUFF. I DON'T HAVE TIME TO BE YOUR DANCING MONKEY.
OH!
THAT'S RIGHT. YOU'VE ONLY GOT A WEEK BEFORE THE COMPETITION!
Care to tell me how you feel?
...
Hey! You can't ignore me!
THAT'S RIGHT.
12 DECEMBER

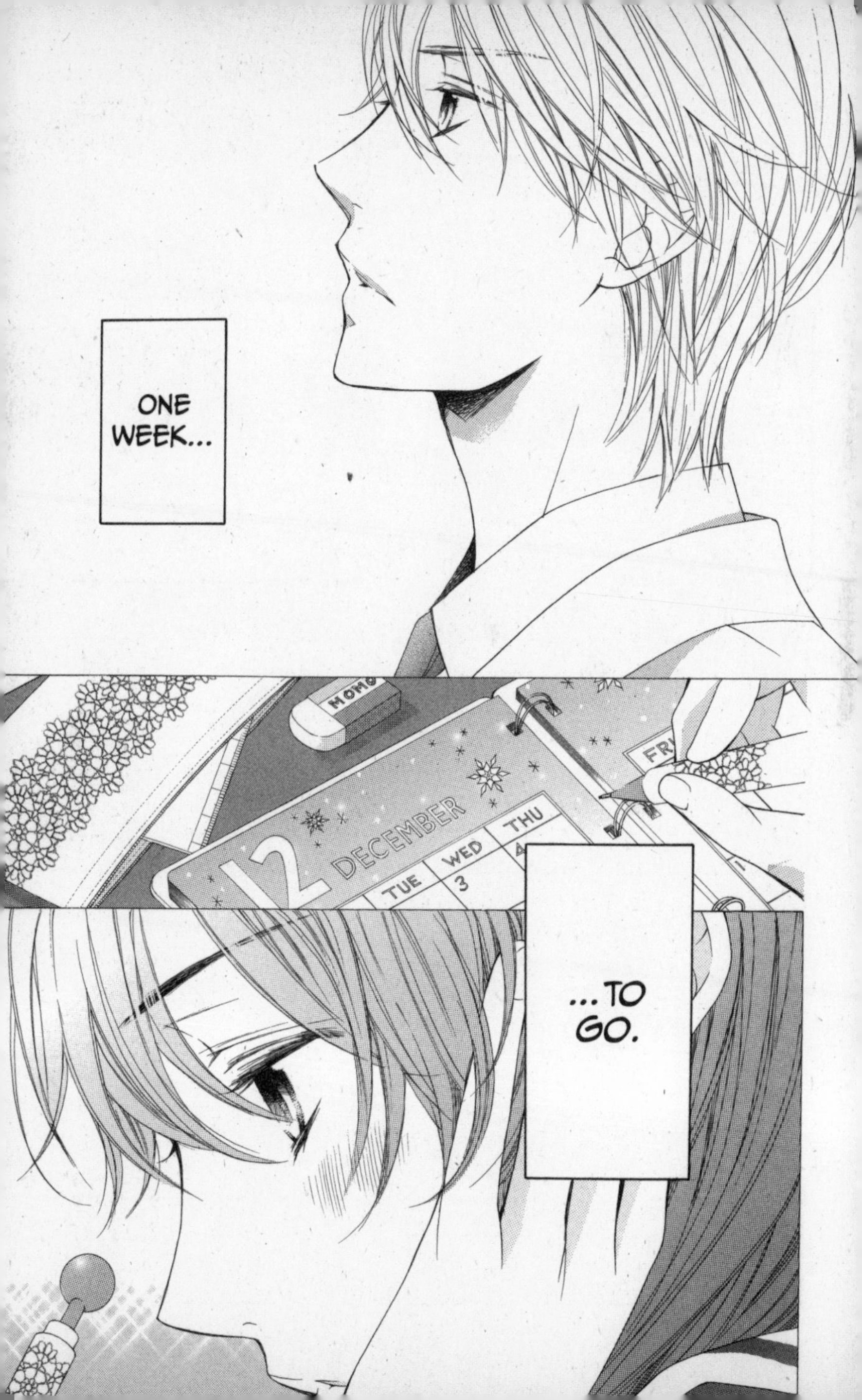
ONE WEEK...
12 DECEMBER
TUE
WED
THU
3
...TO GO.

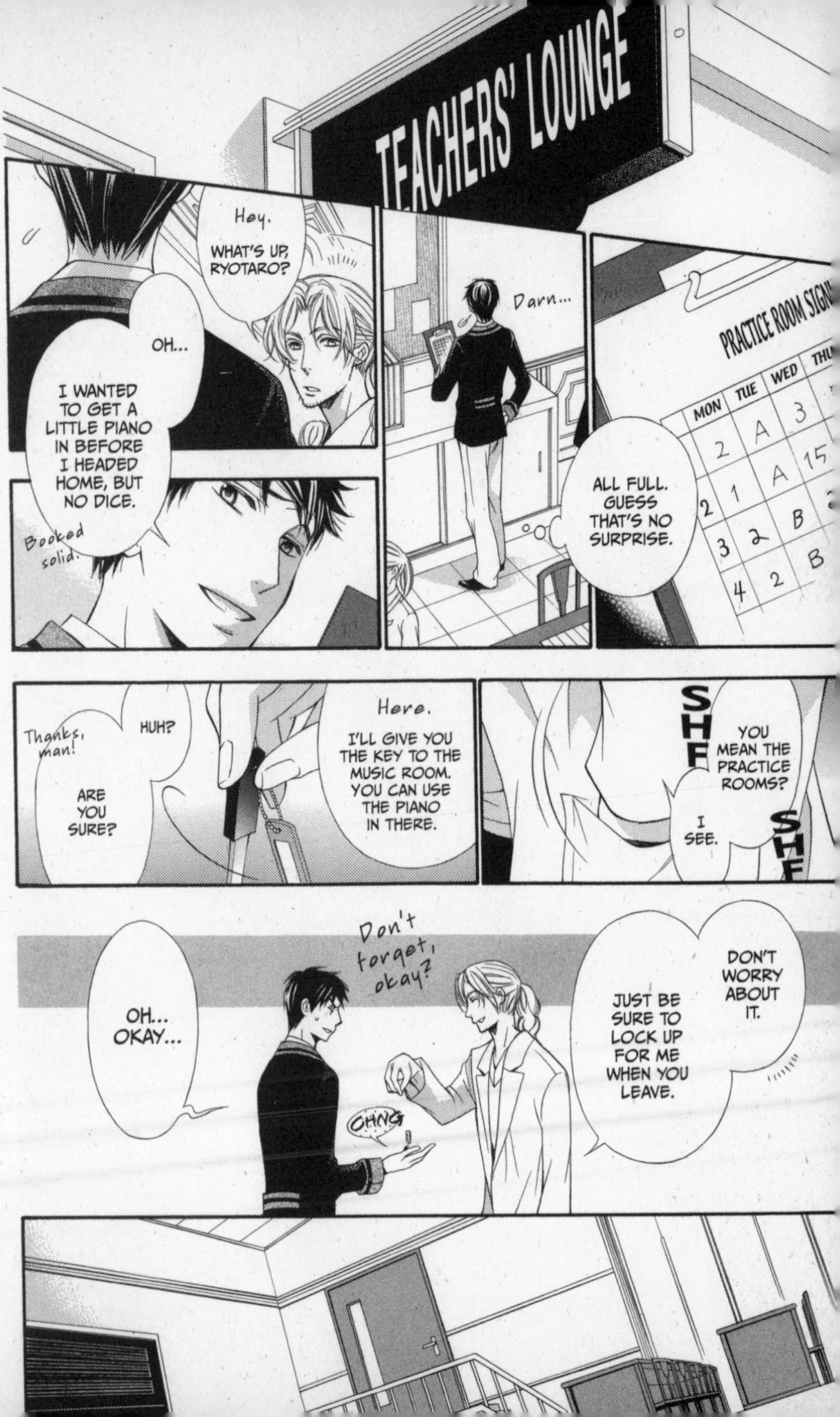
TEACHERS' LOUNGE
PRACTICE ROOM SIGN
MON TUE WED THU
ALL FULL. GUESS THAT'S NO SURPRISE.
Darn...
Hey.
WHAT'S UP, RYOTARO?
OH...
I WANTED TO GET A LITTLE PIANO IN BEFORE I HEADED HOME, BUT NO DICE.
Booked solid.
SHF
YOU MEAN THE PRACTICE ROOMS?
I SEE.
SHF
Here.
I'LL GIVE YOU THE KEY TO THE MUSIC ROOM. YOU CAN USE THE PIANO IN THERE.
HUH?
ARE YOU SURE?
Thanks, man!
DON'T WORRY ABOUT IT.
JUST BE SURE TO LOCK UP FOR ME WHEN YOU LEAVE.
Don't forget, okay?
CHING
OH... OKAY...

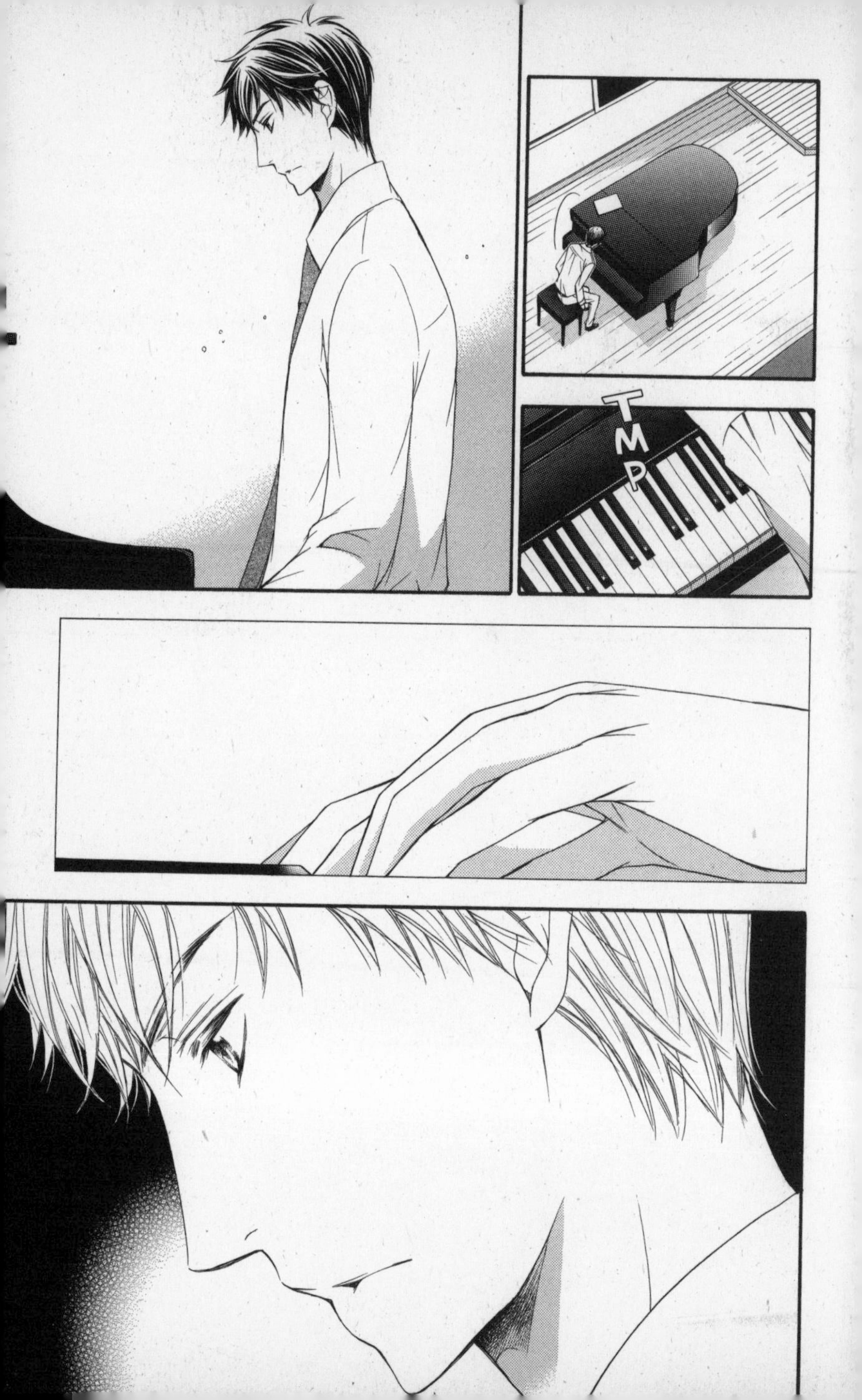
TMP

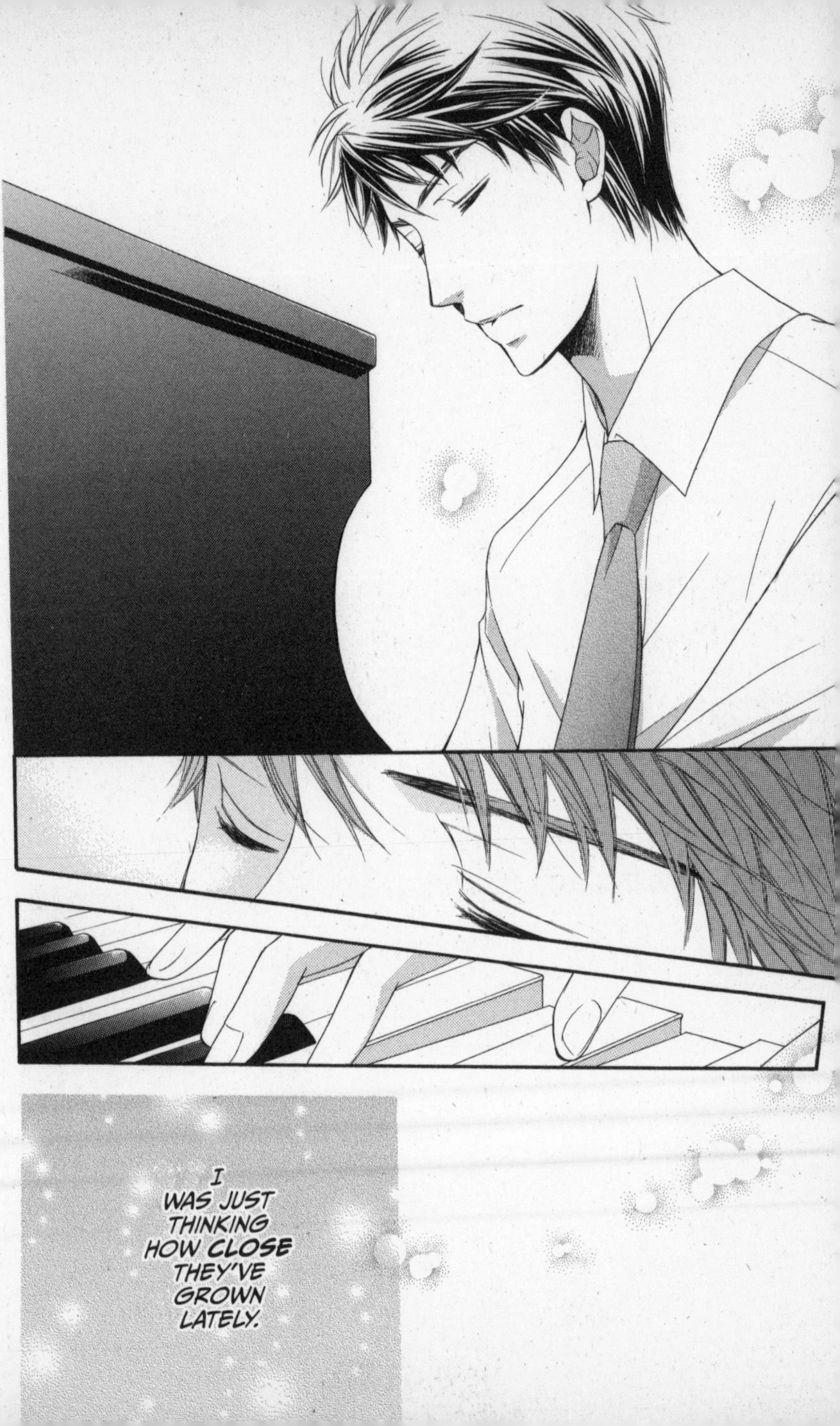
I WAS JUST THINKING HOW CLOSE THEY'VE GROWN LATELY.

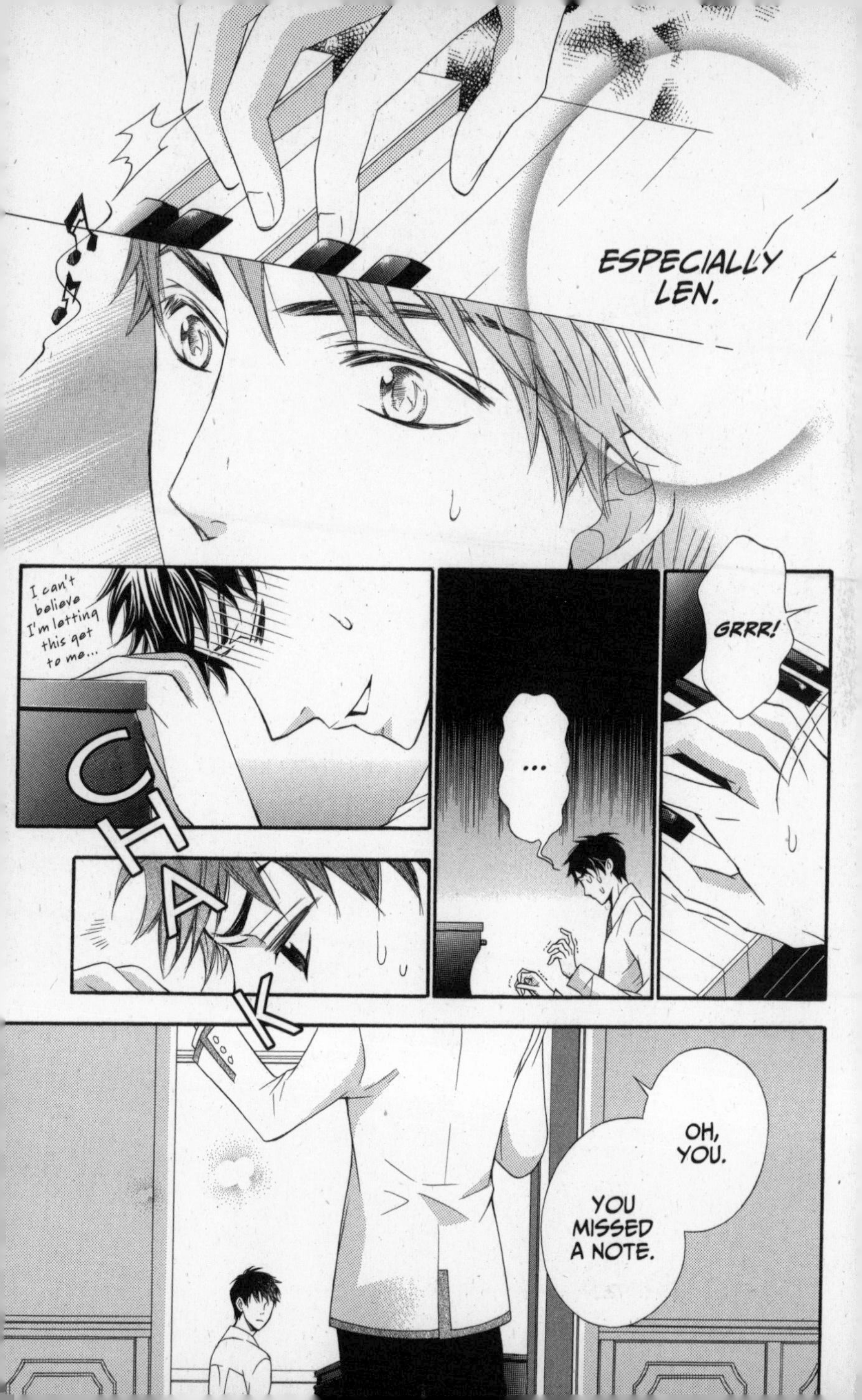
ESPECIALLY LEN.
GRRR!
...
I can't believe I'm letting this get to me...
CHAK
OH, YOU.
YOU MISSED A NOTE.

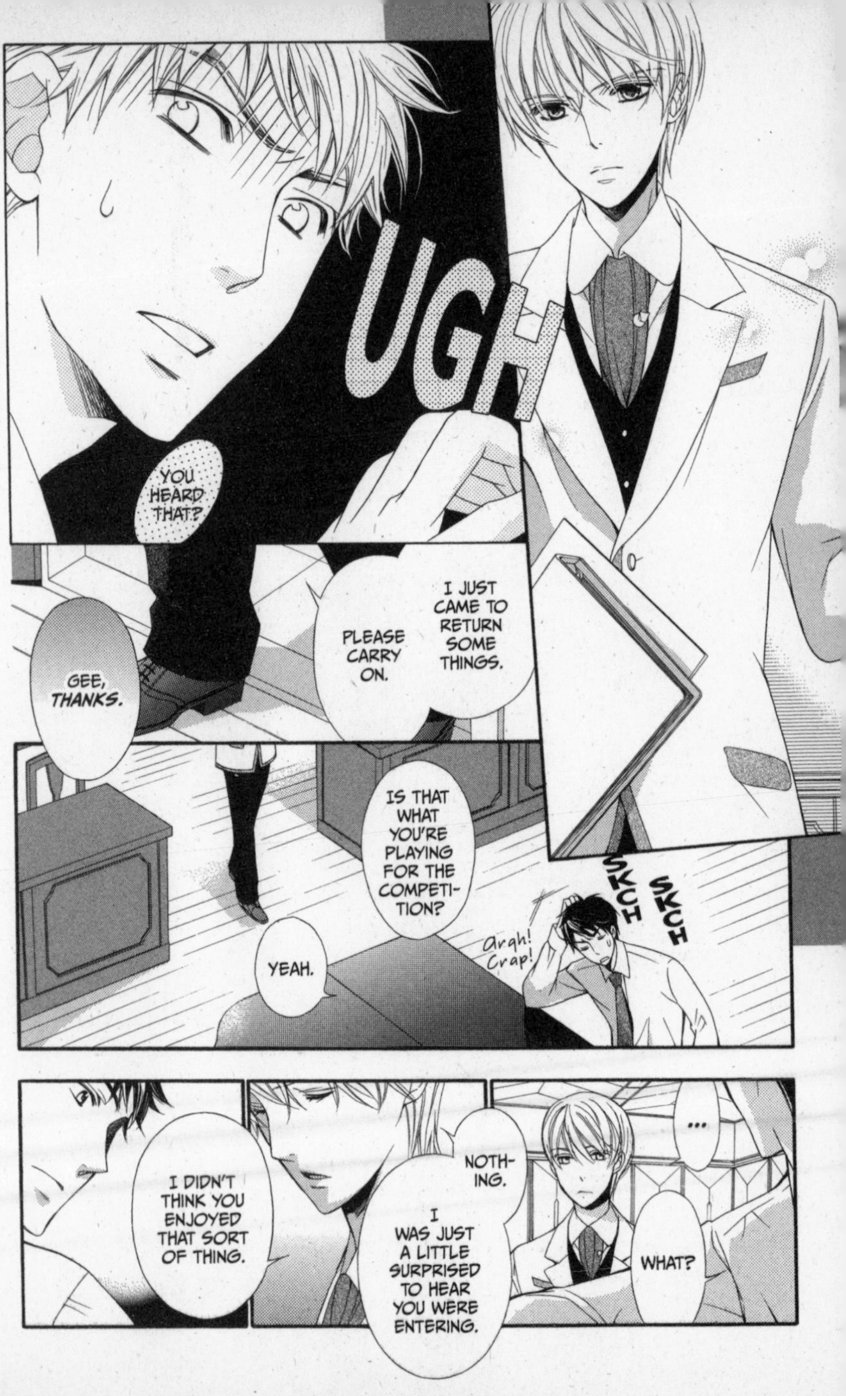
UGH
YOU HEARD THAT?
I JUST CAME TO RETURN SOME THINGS.
PLEASE CARRY ON.
GEE, THANKS.
SKCH SKCH
Argh! Crap!
IS THAT WHAT YOU'RE PLAYING FOR THE COMPETITION?
YEAH.
...
WHAT?
NOTHING.
I WAS JUST A LITTLE SURPRISED TO HEAR YOU WERE ENTERING.
I DIDN'T THINK YOU ENJOYED THAT SORT OF THING.

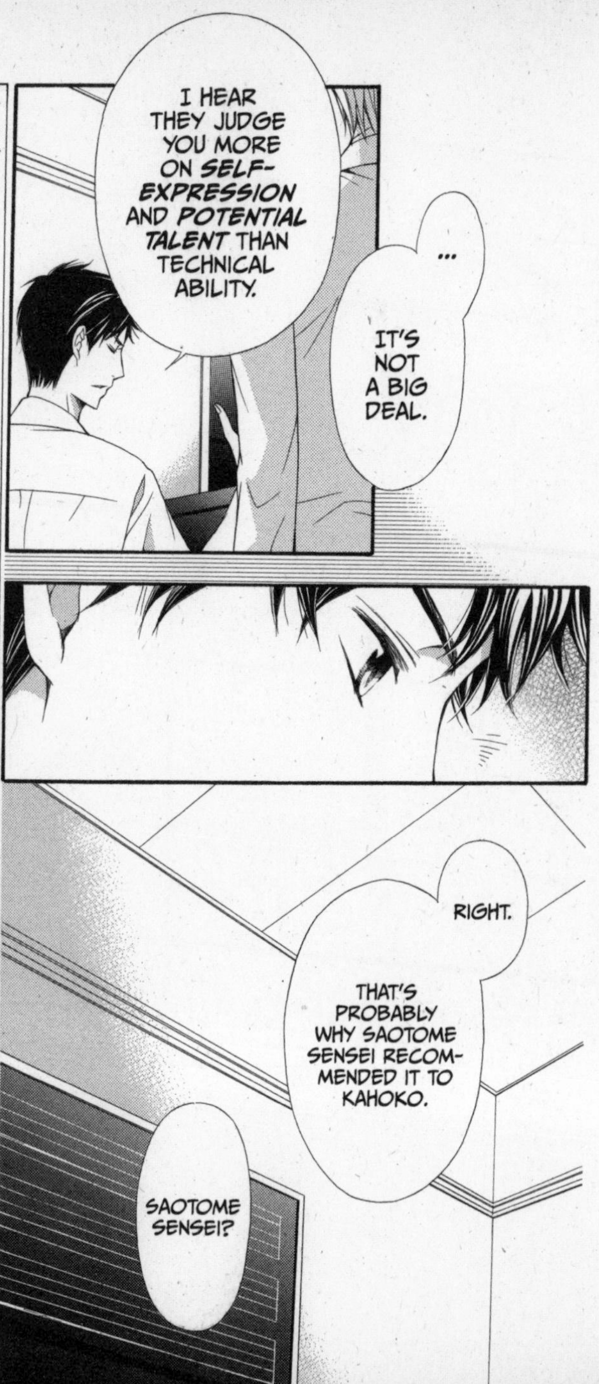
I HEAR THEY JUDGE YOU MORE ON *SELF-EXPRESSION* AND *POTENTIAL TALENT* THAN TECHNICAL ABILITY.
...
IT'S NOT A BIG DEAL.
RIGHT.
THAT'S PROBABLY WHY SAOTOME SENSEI RECOM-MENDED IT TO KAHOKO.
SAOTOME SENSEI?

I don't have a theme to the bonus drawings this time. I'm sorry...Just a bunch of random costumes, really. I know Azuma on page 59 is pretty bizarre. Here's the lineup...

Angel
Pirate
Wolfman (Dog?)
Vampire

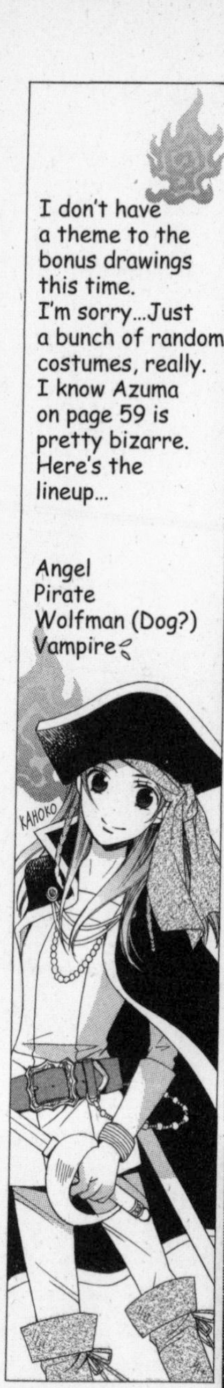
KAHOKO

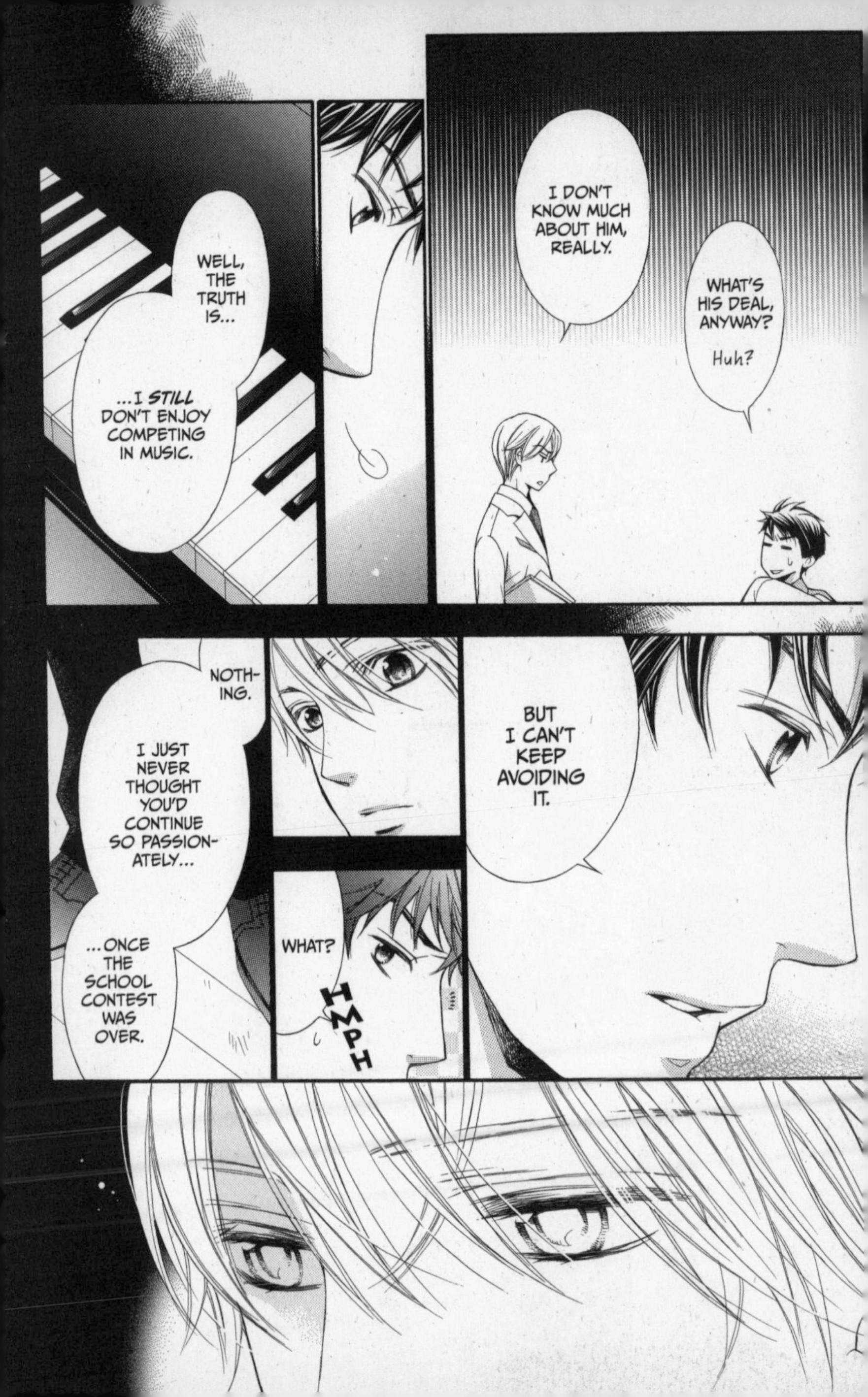
WHAT'S HIS DEAL, ANYWAY?
Huh?
I DON'T KNOW MUCH ABOUT HIM, REALLY.
WELL, THE TRUTH IS...
...I *STILL* DON'T ENJOY COMPETING IN MUSIC.
BUT I CAN'T KEEP AVOIDING IT.
WHAT?
HMPH
NOTH-ING.
I JUST NEVER THOUGHT YOU'D CONTINUE SO PASSION-ATELY...
...ONCE THE SCHOOL CONTEST WAS OVER.

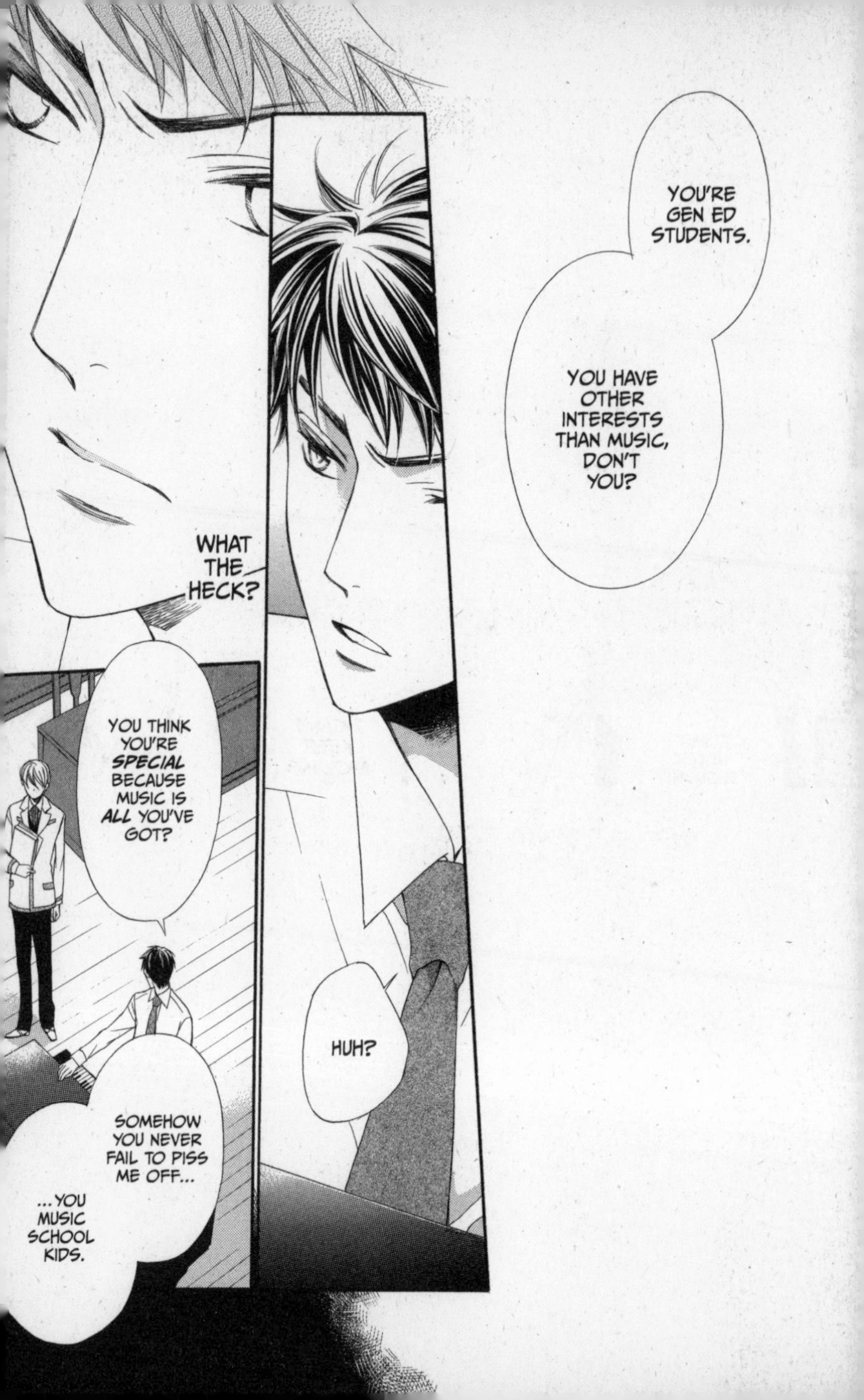
YOU'RE GEN ED STUDENTS.
YOU HAVE OTHER INTERESTS THAN MUSIC, DON'T YOU?
HUH?
WHAT THE HECK?
YOU THINK YOU'RE *SPECIAL* BECAUSE MUSIC IS *ALL* YOU'VE GOT?
SOMEHOW YOU NEVER FAIL TO PISS ME OFF...
...YOU MUSIC SCHOOL KIDS.

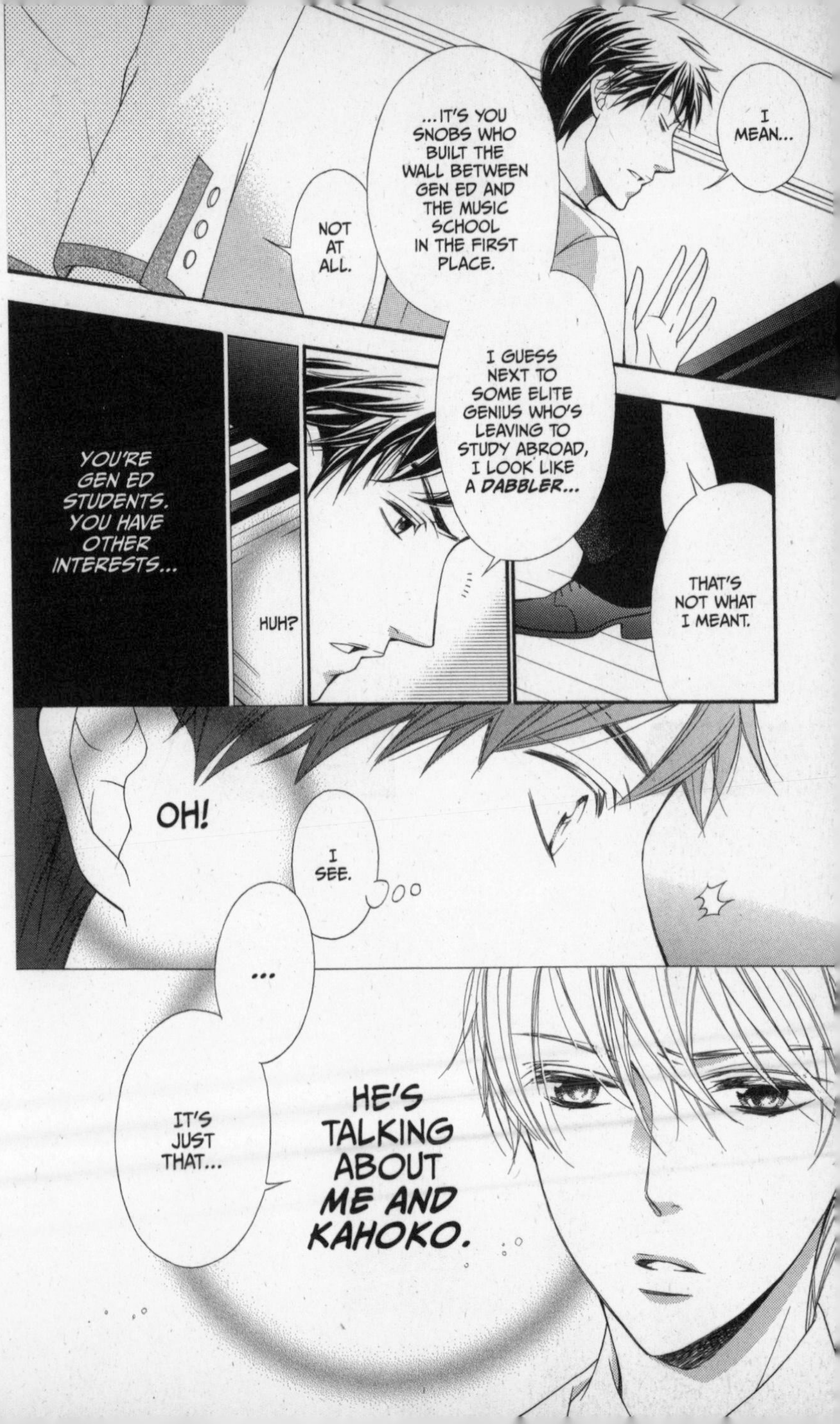
I MEAN...
NOT AT ALL.
...IT'S YOU SNOBS WHO BUILT THE WALL BETWEEN GEN ED AND THE MUSIC SCHOOL IN THE FIRST PLACE.
I GUESS NEXT TO SOME ELITE GENIUS WHO'S LEAVING TO STUDY ABROAD, I LOOK LIKE A *DABBLER*...
THAT'S NOT WHAT I MEANT.
HUH?
YOU'RE GEN ED STUDENTS. YOU HAVE OTHER INTERESTS...
OH!
I SEE.
...
IT'S JUST THAT...
HE'S TALKING ABOUT *ME AND KAHOKO.*

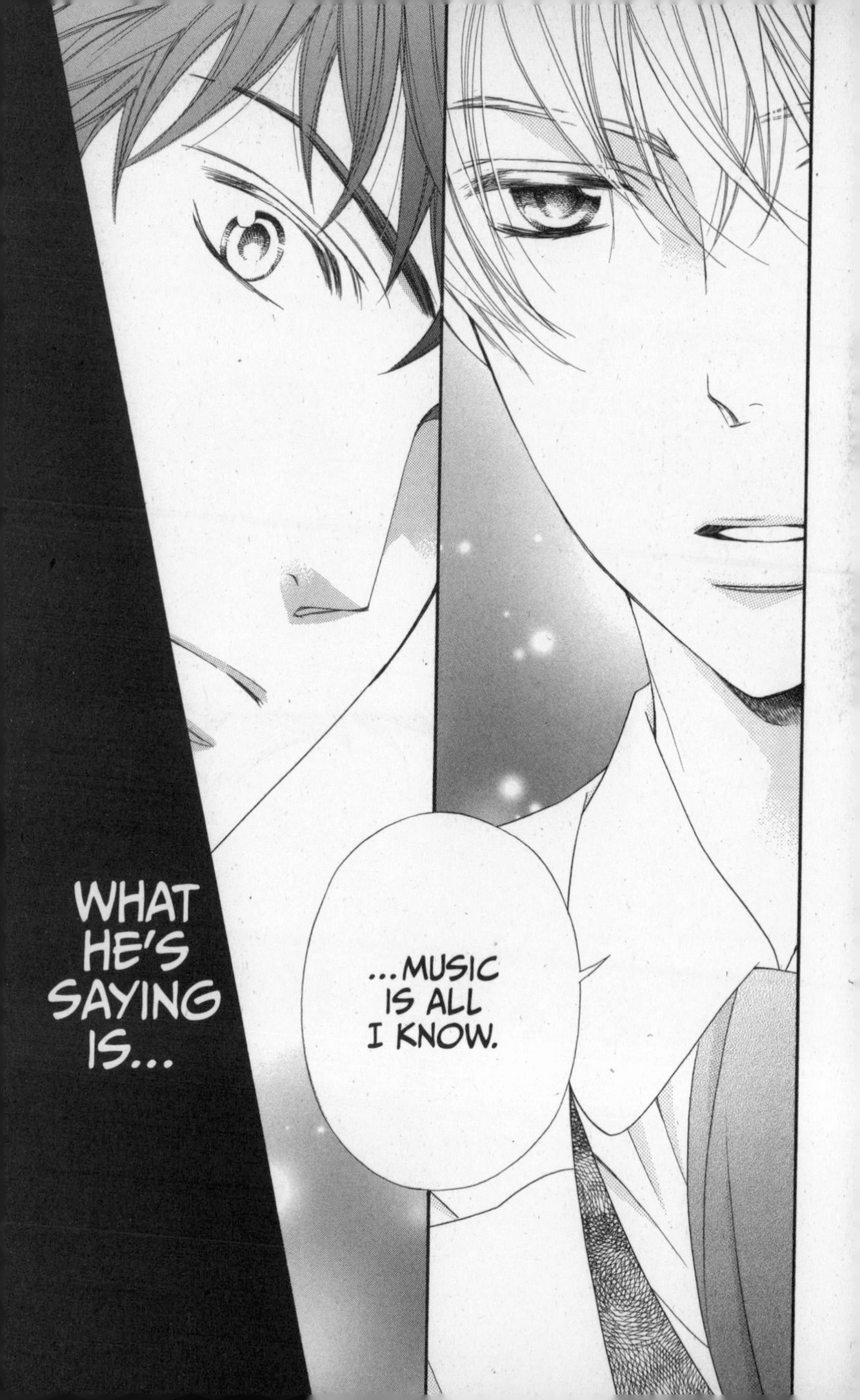
WHAT HE'S SAYING IS...
...MUSIC IS ALL I KNOW.

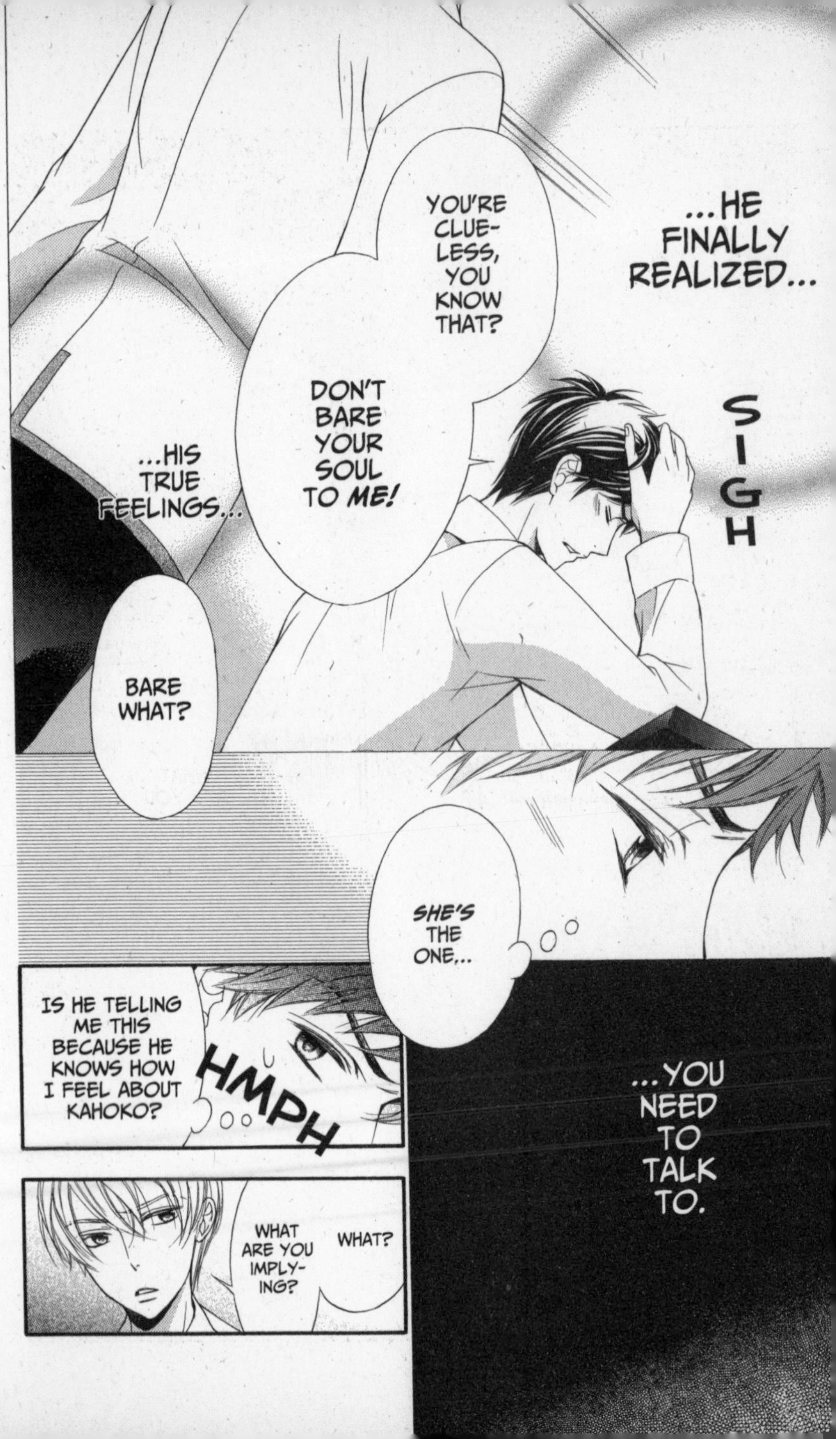
...HE FINALLY REALIZED...
SIGH
YOU'RE CLUELESS, YOU KNOW THAT?
DON'T BARE YOUR SOUL TO ME!
...HIS TRUE FEELINGS...
BARE WHAT?
SHE'S THE ONE...
...YOU NEED TO TALK TO.
IS HE TELLING ME THIS BECAUSE HE KNOWS HOW I FEEL ABOUT KAHOKO?
HMPH
WHAT?
WHAT ARE YOU IMPLYING?

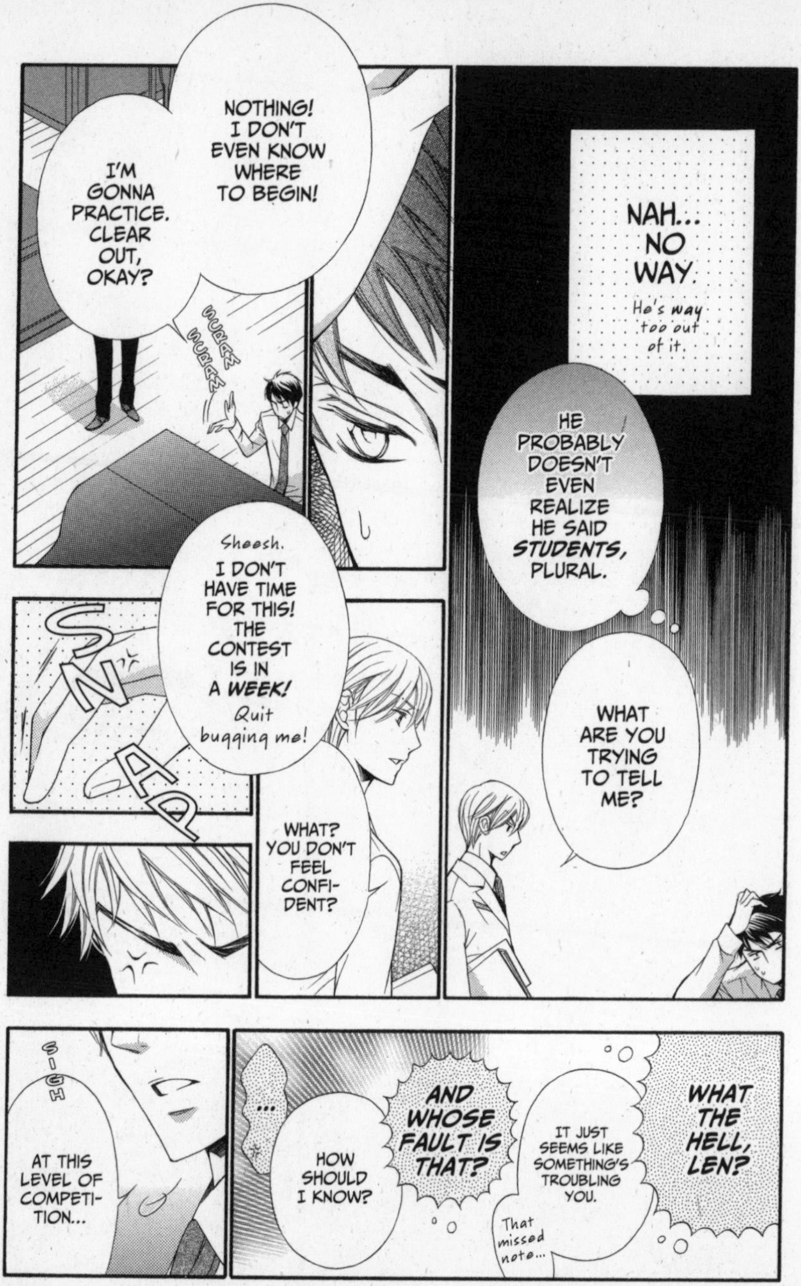
NAH... NO WAY.
He's way too out of it.
HE PROBABLY DOESN'T EVEN REALIZE HE SAID STUDENTS, PLURAL.
WHAT ARE YOU TRYING TO TELL ME?
NOTHING! I DON'T EVEN KNOW WHERE TO BEGIN!
I'M GONNA PRACTICE. CLEAR OUT, OKAY?
WHAT? YOU DON'T FEEL CONFI-DENT?
Sheesh. I DON'T HAVE TIME FOR THIS! THE CONTEST IS IN A WEEK! Quit bugging me!
SNAP
WHAT THE HELL, LEN?
IT JUST SEEMS LIKE SOMETHING'S TROUBLING YOU.
That missed note...
AND WHOSE FAULT IS THAT?
...
HOW SHOULD I KNOW?
SIGH
AT THIS LEVEL OF COMPETI-TION...

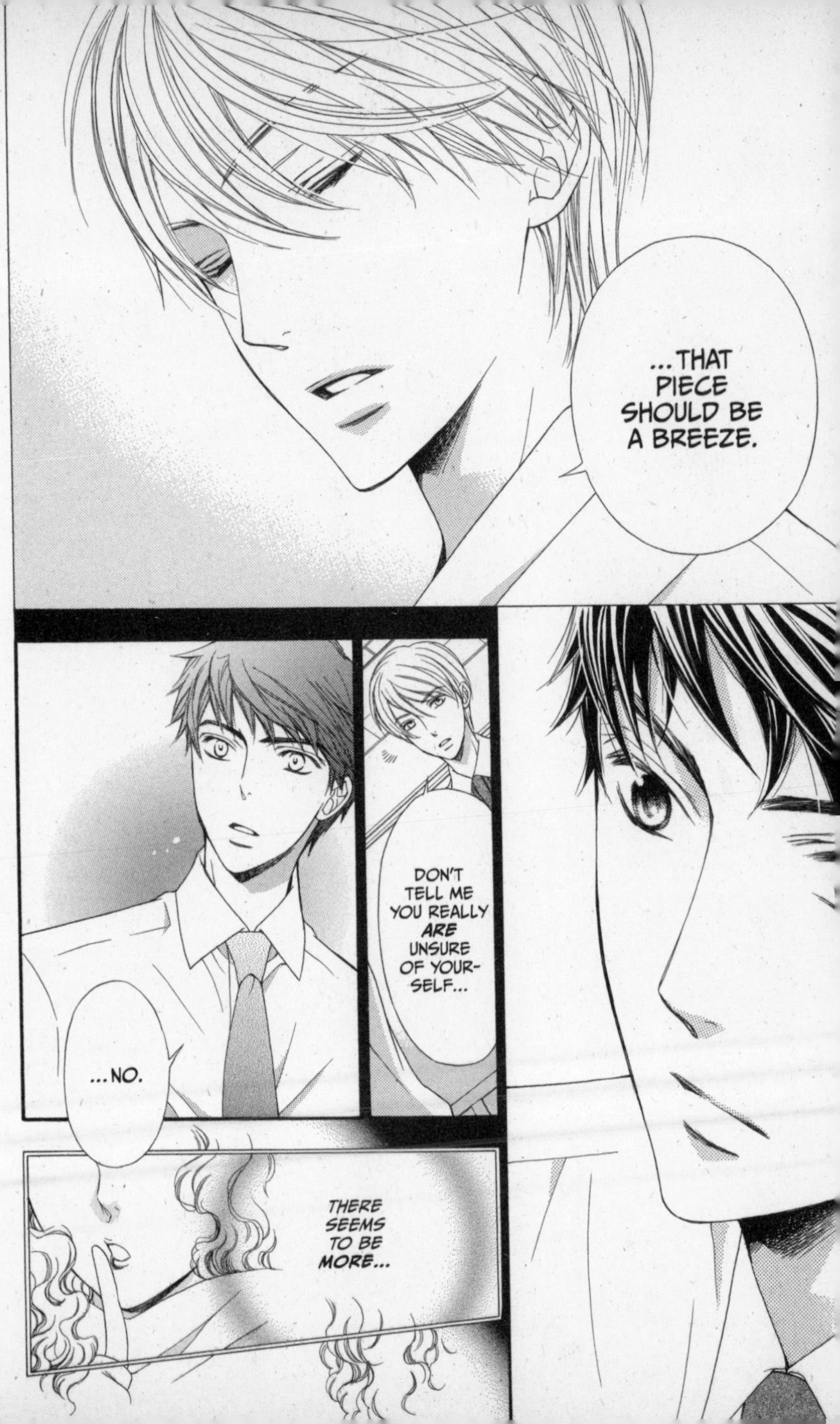
...THAT PIECE SHOULD BE A BREEZE.
DON'T TELL ME YOU REALLY *ARE* UNSURE OF YOURSELF...
...NO.
THERE SEEMS TO BE MORE...

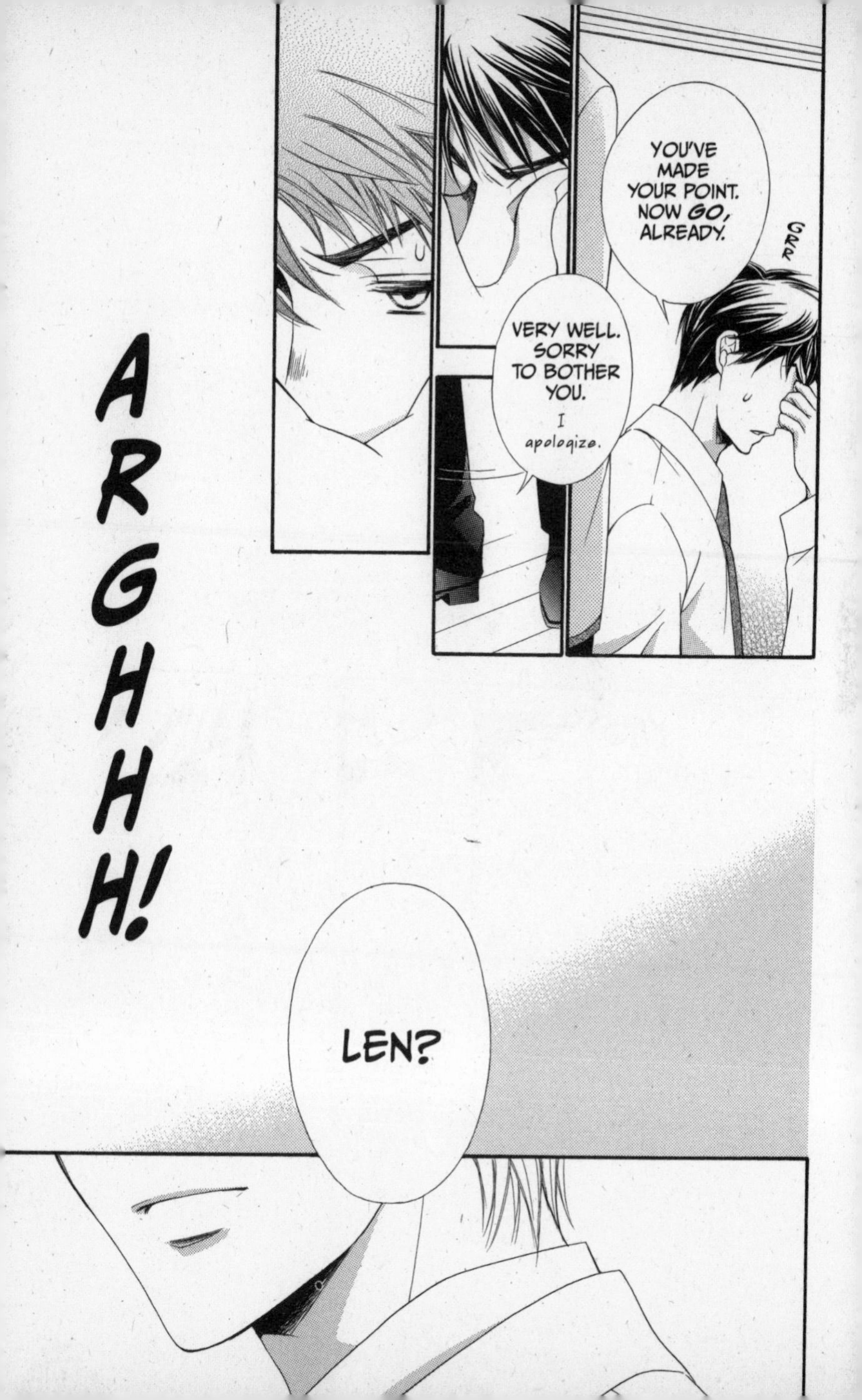
YOU'VE MADE YOUR POINT. NOW GO, ALREADY.
GRR
VERY WELL. SORRY TO BOTHER YOU.
I apologize.
ARGHHH!
LEN?

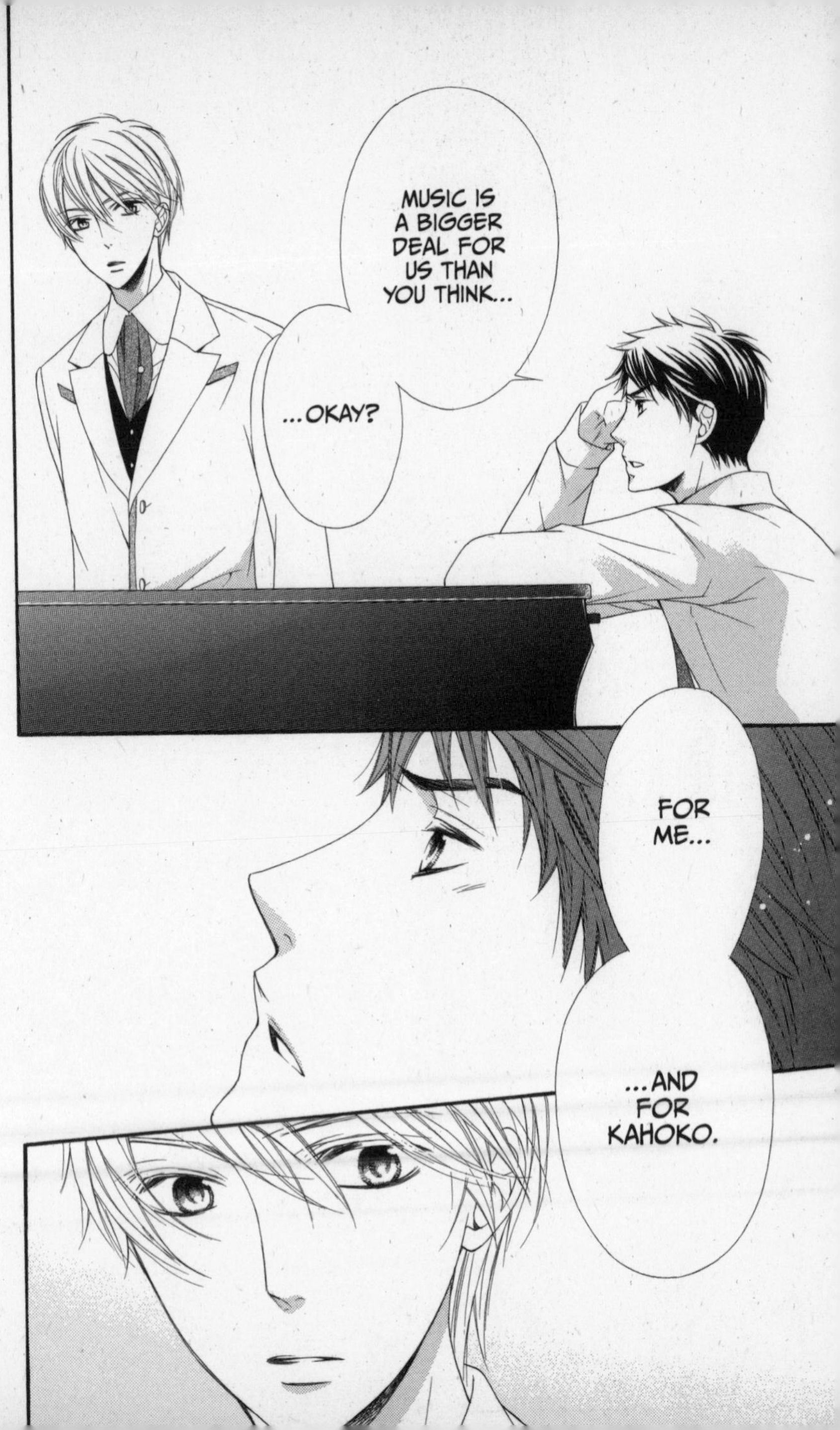
MUSIC IS A BIGGER DEAL FOR US THAN YOU THINK...
...OKAY?
FOR ME...
...AND FOR KAHOKO.

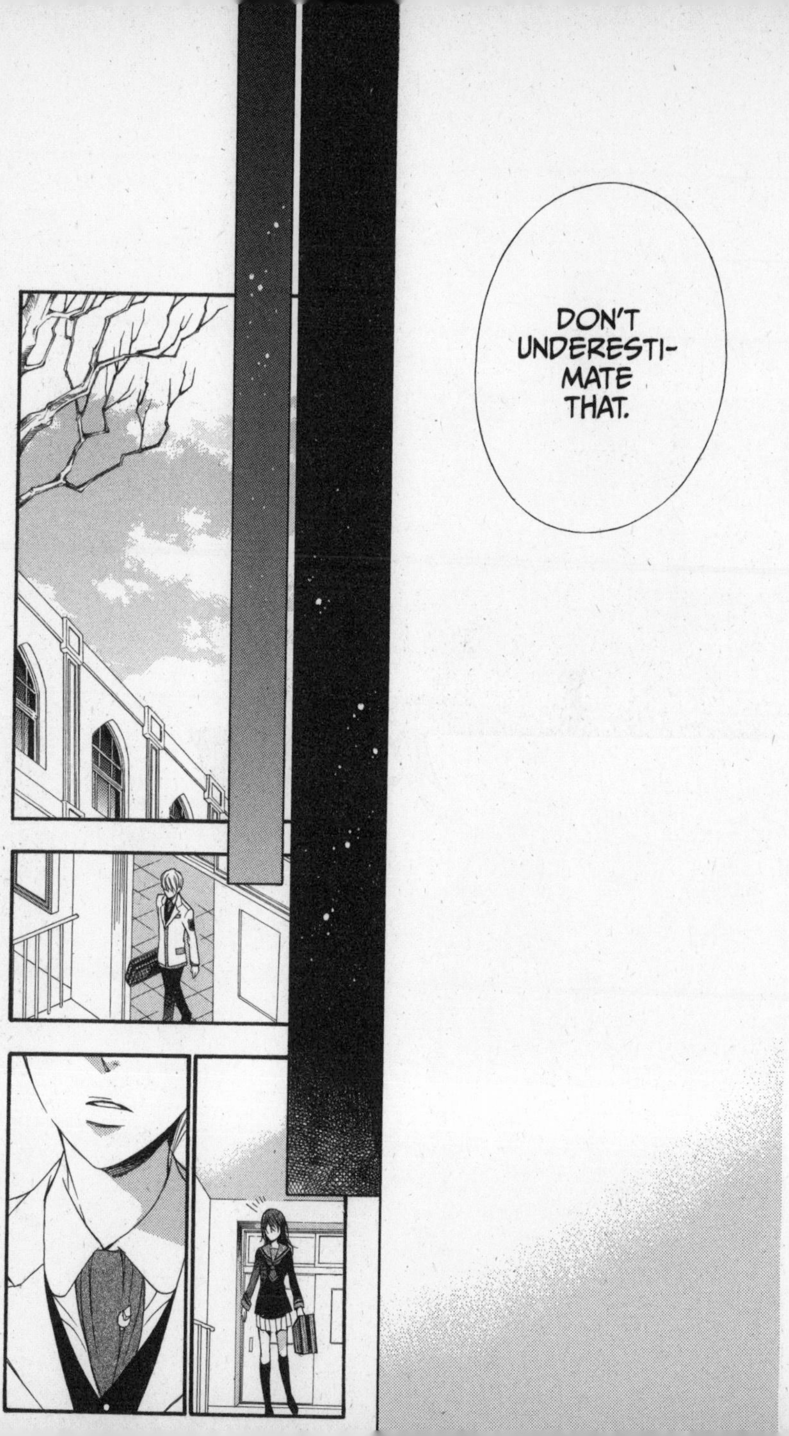
DON'T UNDERESTI- MATE THAT.

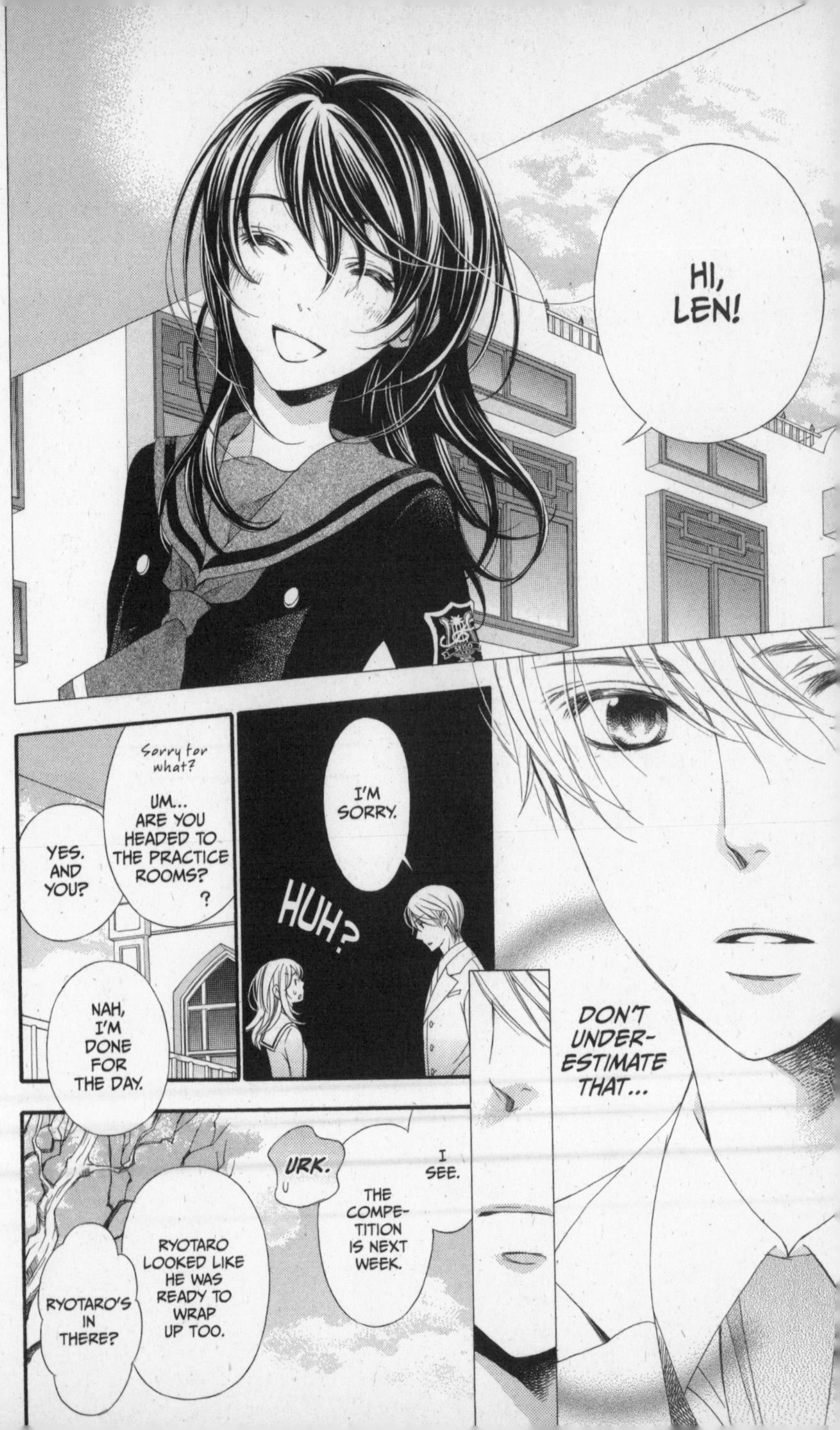
HI, LEN!
DON'T UNDER-ESTIMATE THAT...
I'M SORRY.
HUH?
Sorry for what?
UM... ARE YOU HEADED TO THE PRACTICE ROOMS?
?
YES. AND YOU?
NAH, I'M DONE FOR THE DAY.
I SEE.
URK.
THE COMPE-TITION IS NEXT WEEK.
RYOTARO LOOKED LIKE HE WAS READY TO WRAP UP TOO.
RYOTARO'S IN THERE?

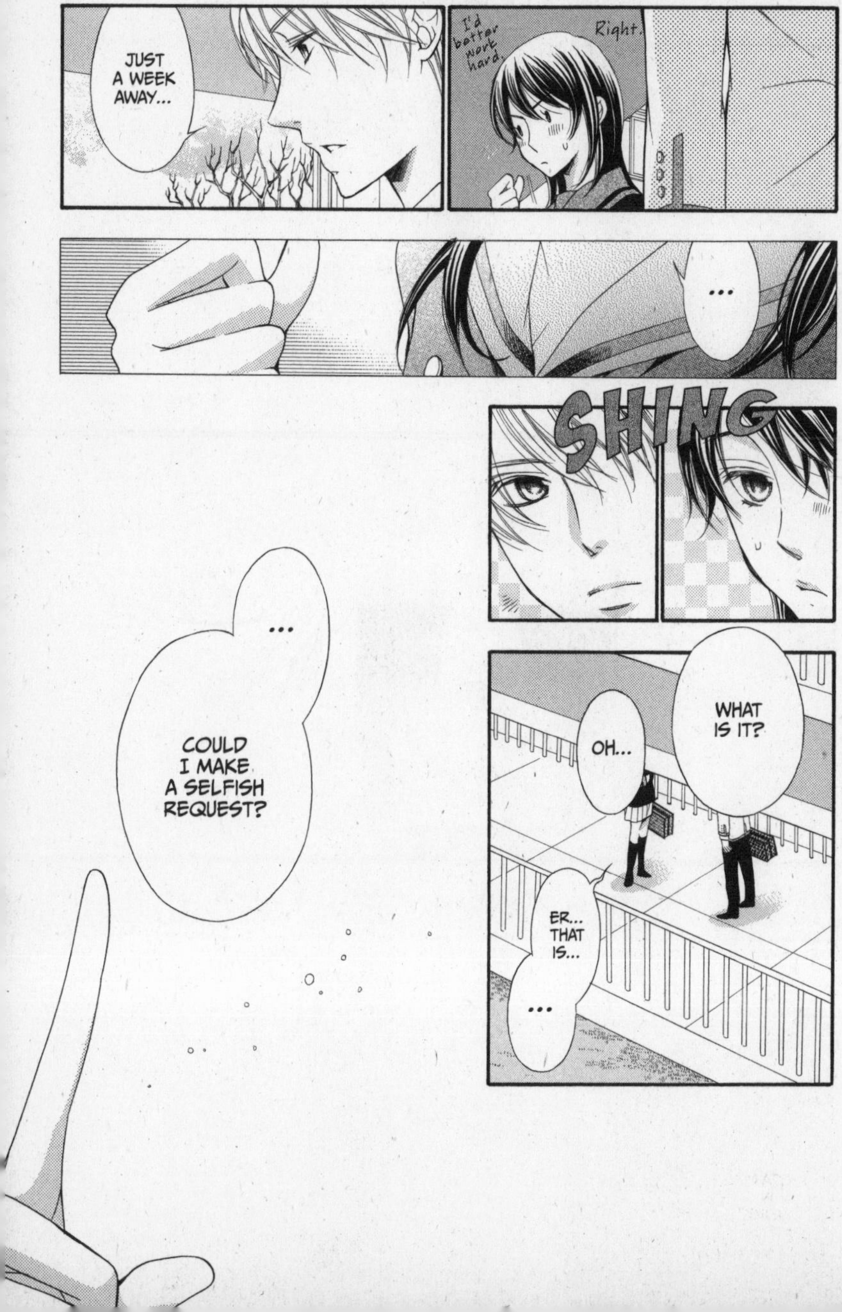
Right.
I'd better work hard.
JUST A WEEK AWAY...
...
SHING
WHAT IS IT?
OH...
ER... THAT IS...
...
...
COULD I MAKE A SELFISH REQUEST?

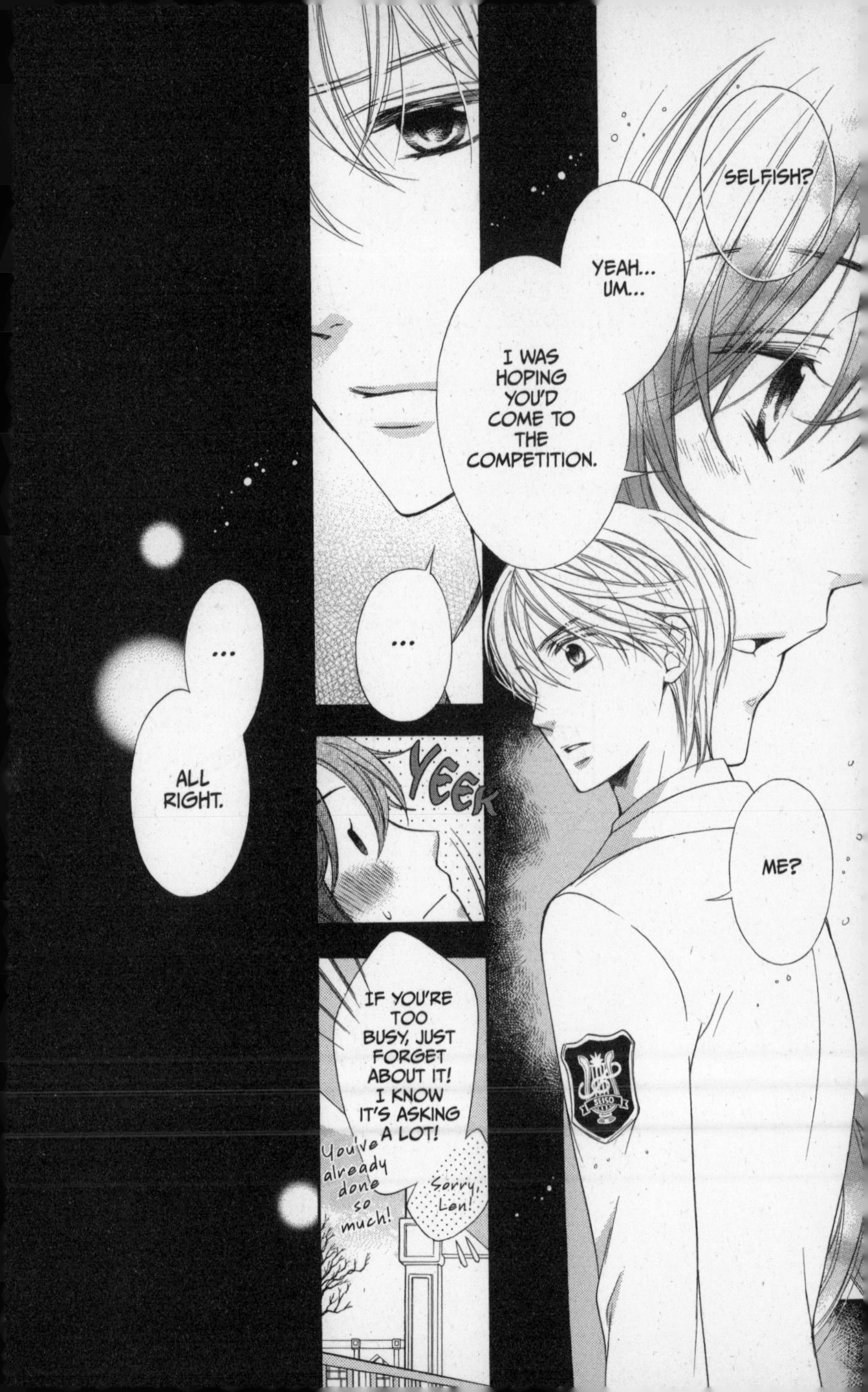
SELFISH?
ME?
YEAH... UM...
I WAS HOPING YOU'D COME TO THE COMPETITION.
...
YEEK
IF YOU'RE TOO BUSY, JUST FORGET ABOUT IT! I KNOW IT'S ASKING A LOT!
Sorry, Len!
You've already done so much!
...
ALL RIGHT.

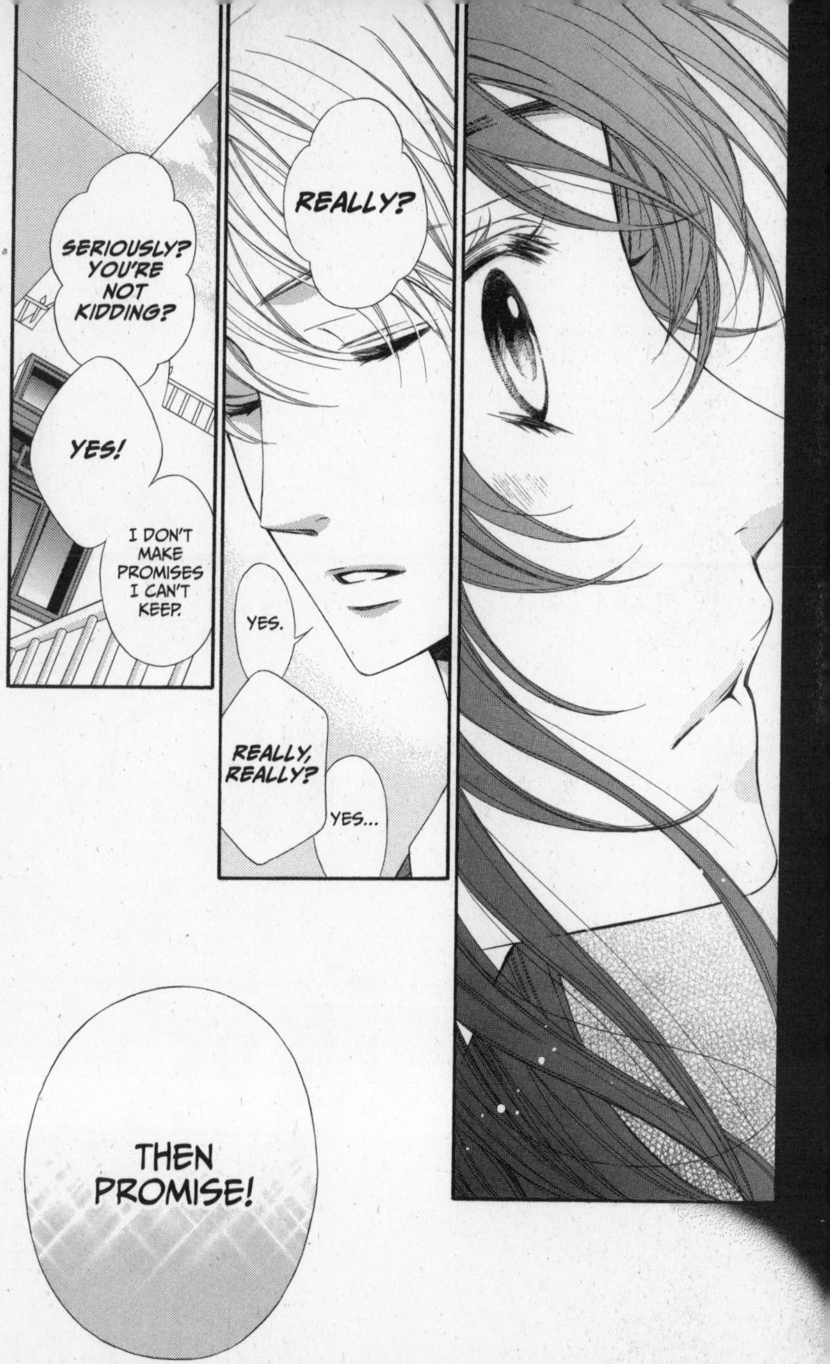
REALLY?
YES.
REALLY, REALLY?
YES...
SERIOUSLY? YOU'RE NOT KIDDING?
YES!
I DON'T MAKE PROMISES I CAN'T KEEP.
THEN PROMISE!

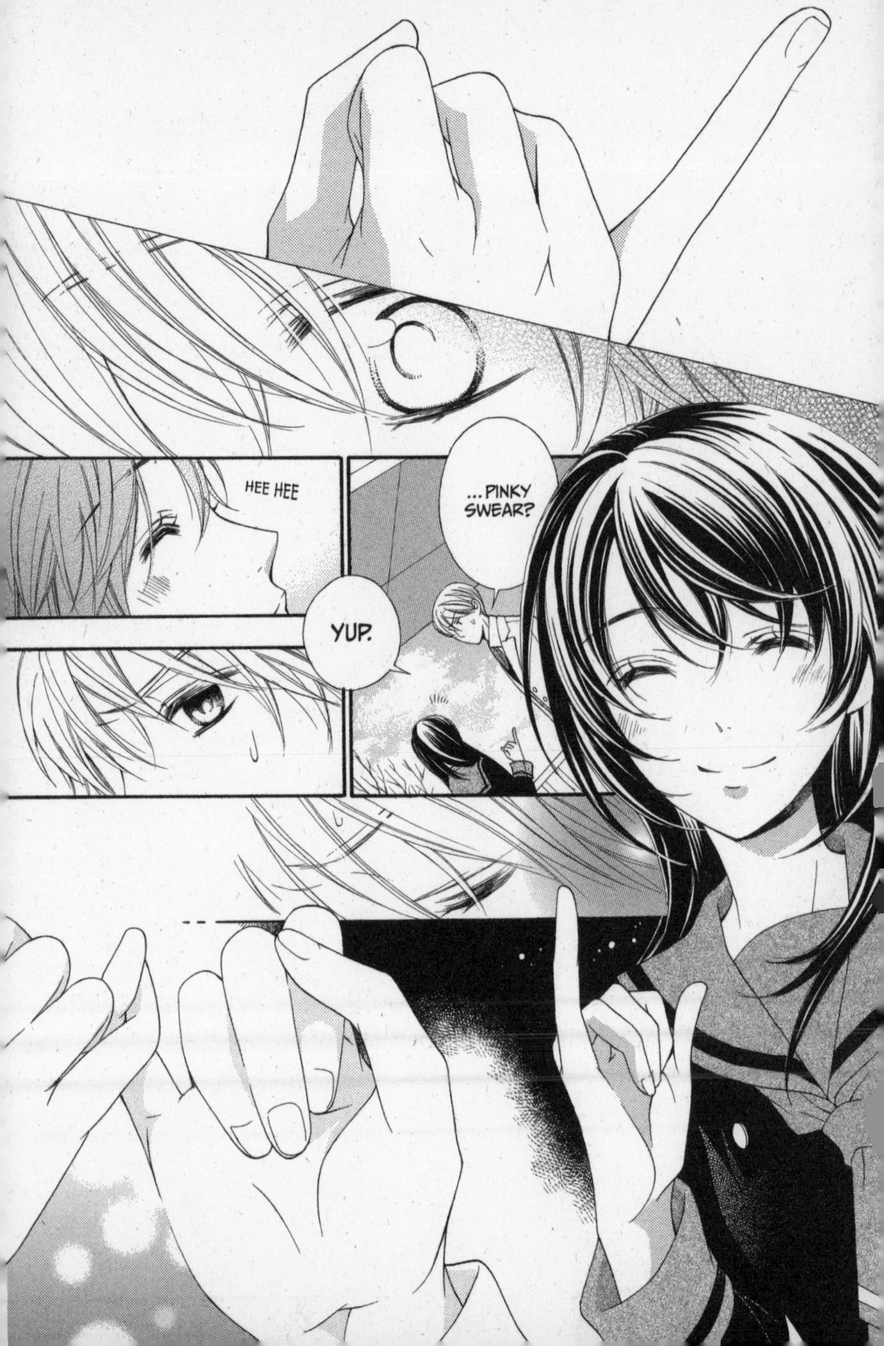
...PINKY SWEAR?
HEE HEE
YUP.

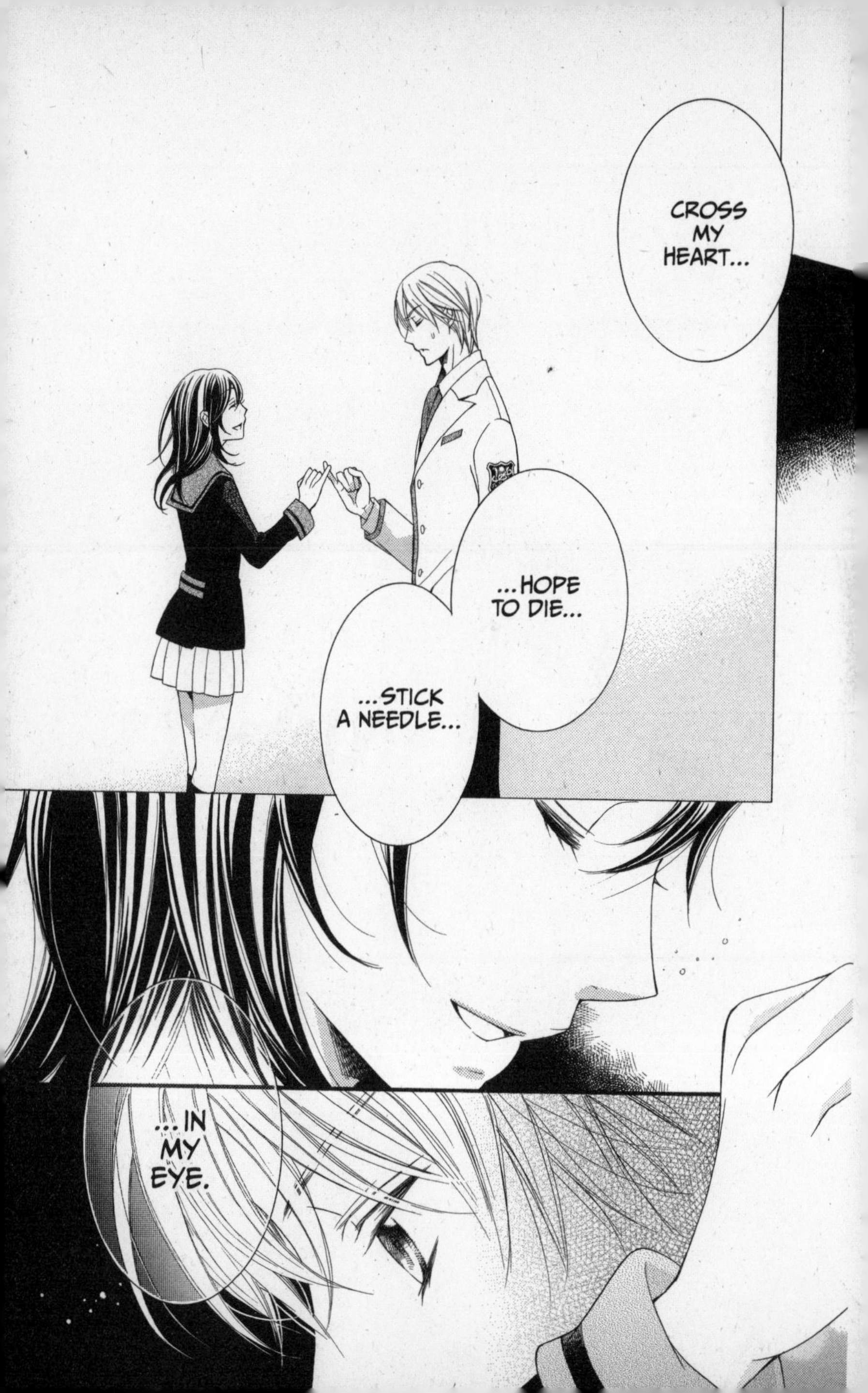
CROSS MY HEART...
...HOPE TO DIE...
...STICK A NEEDLE...
...IN MY EYE.

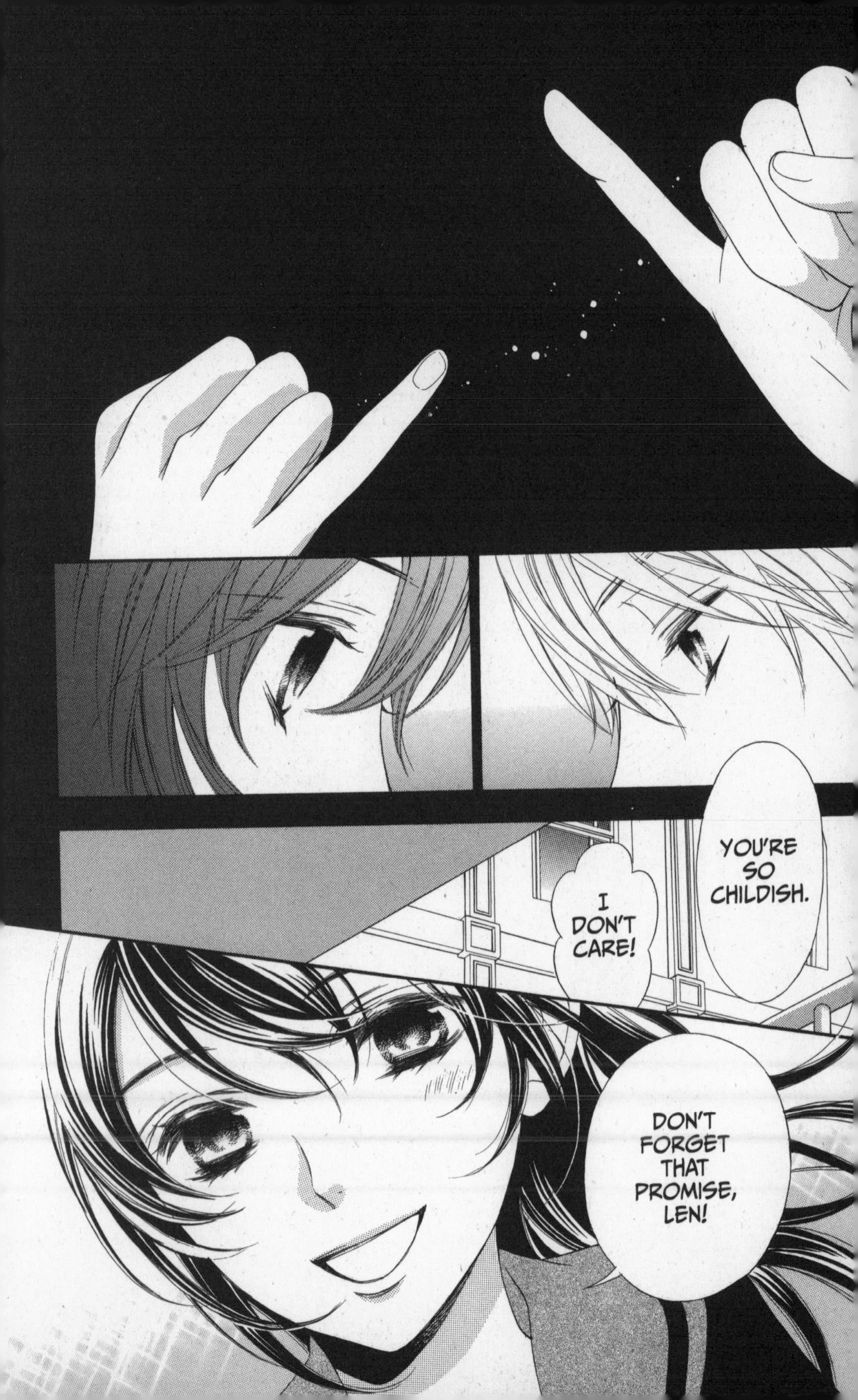
YOU'RE SO CHILDISH.
I DON'T CARE!
DON'T FORGET THAT PROMISE, LEN!

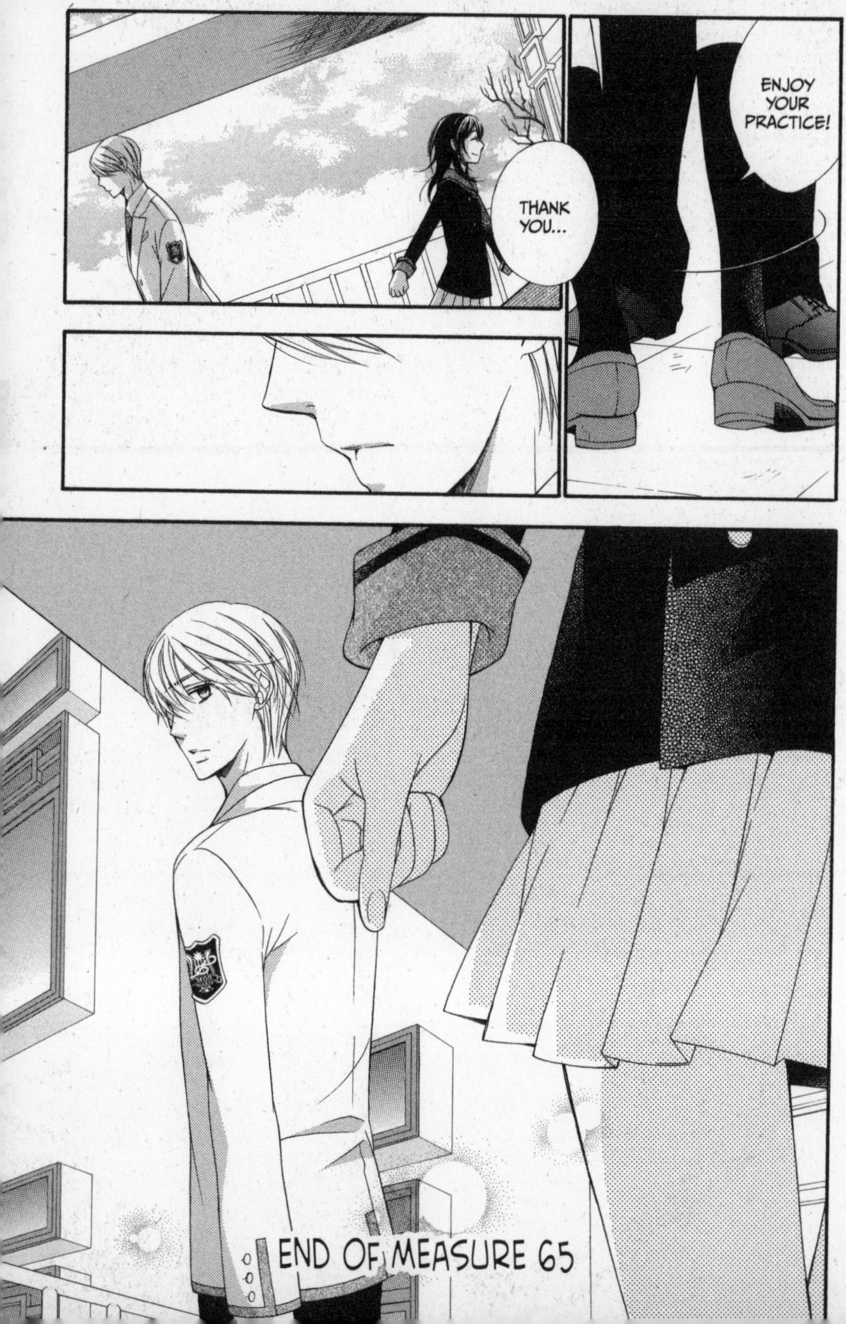
ENJOY YOUR PRACTICE!
THANK YOU...
END OF MEASURE 65

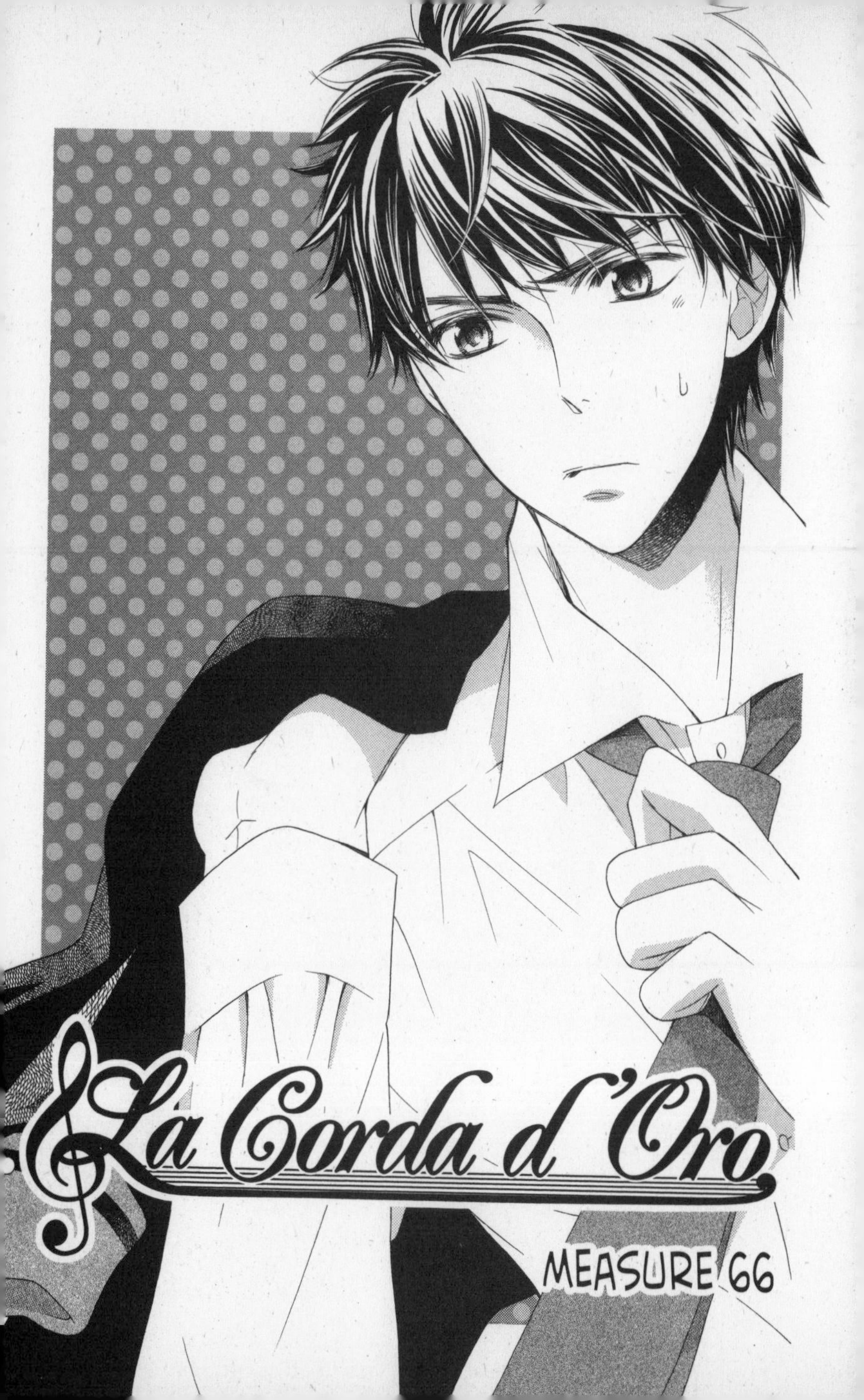
La Corda d'Oro
MEASURE 66

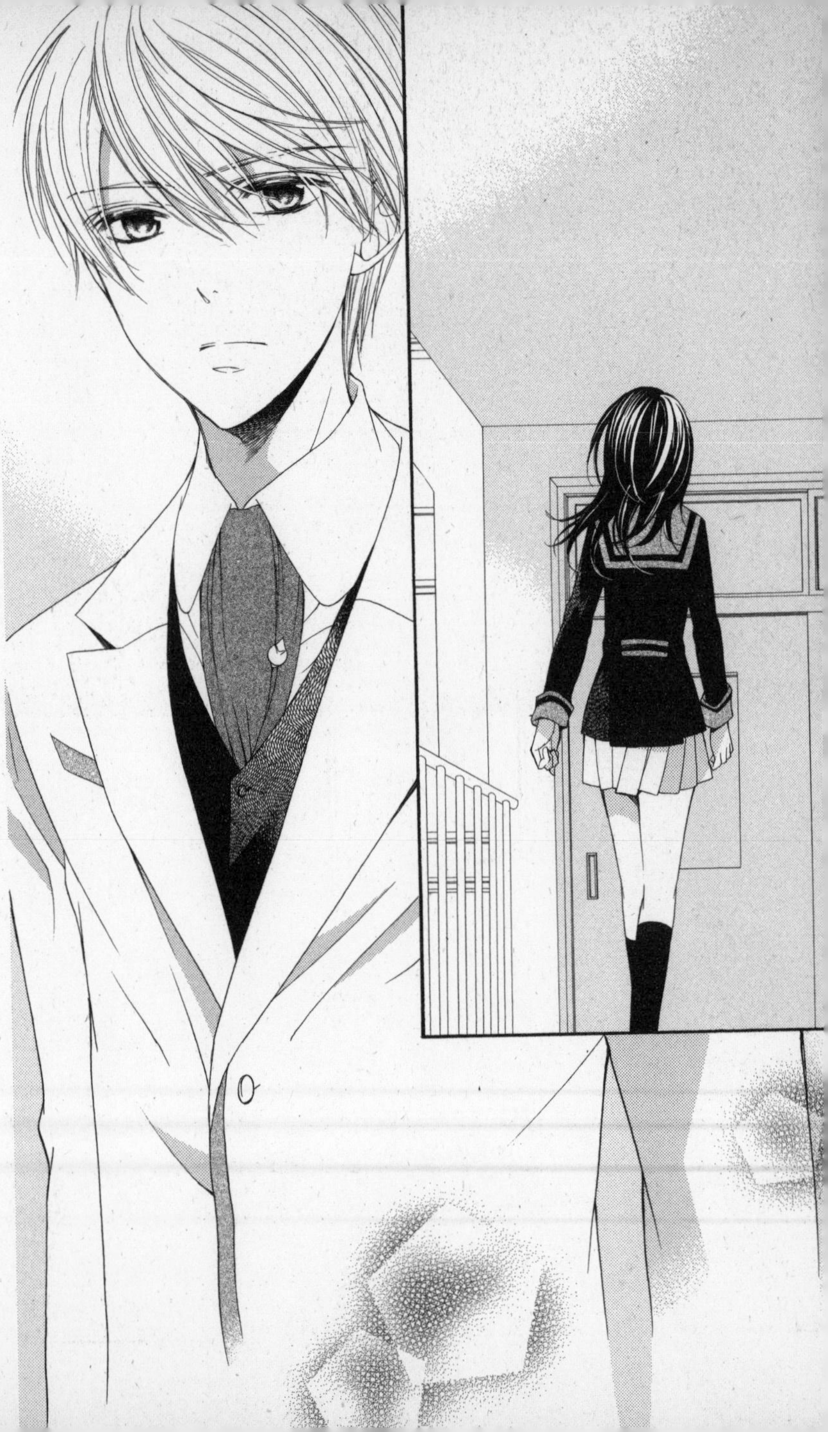

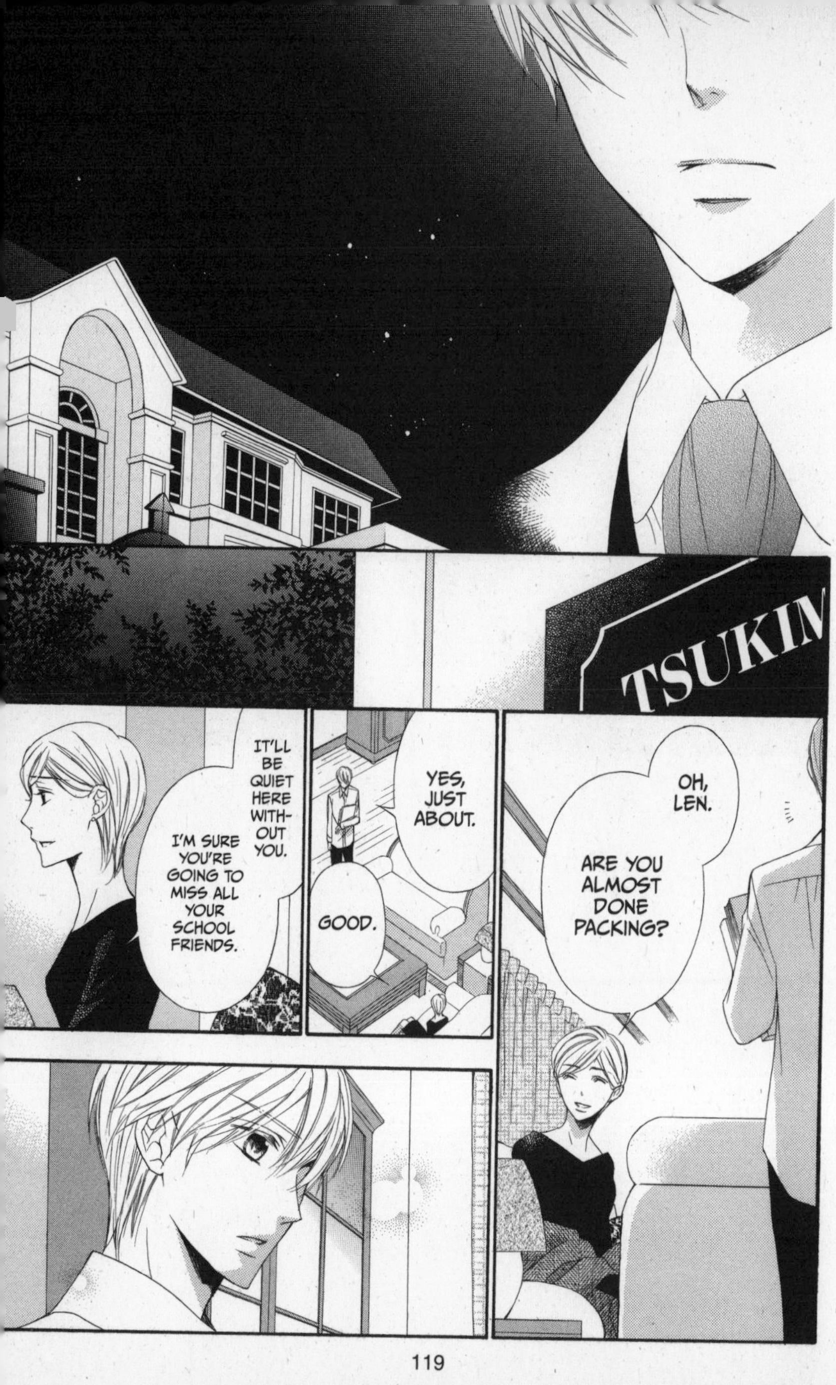
TSUKIM
OH, LEN.
ARE YOU ALMOST DONE PACKING?
YES, JUST ABOUT.
GOOD.
IT'LL BE QUIET HERE WITHOUT YOU.
I'M SURE YOU'RE GOING TO MISS ALL YOUR SCHOOL FRIENDS.

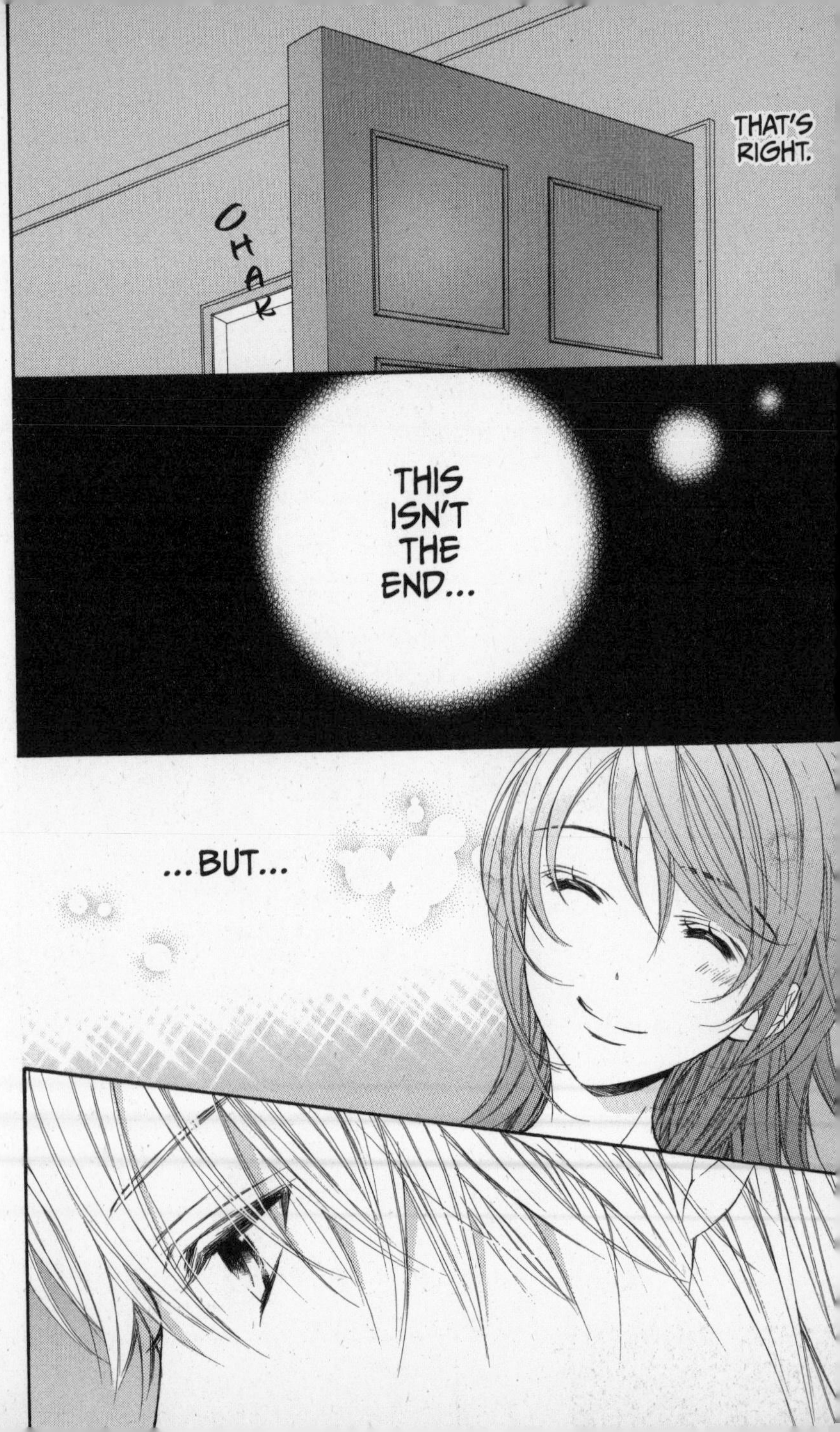
THAT'S RIGHT.
CHAK
THIS ISN'T THE END...
...BUT...

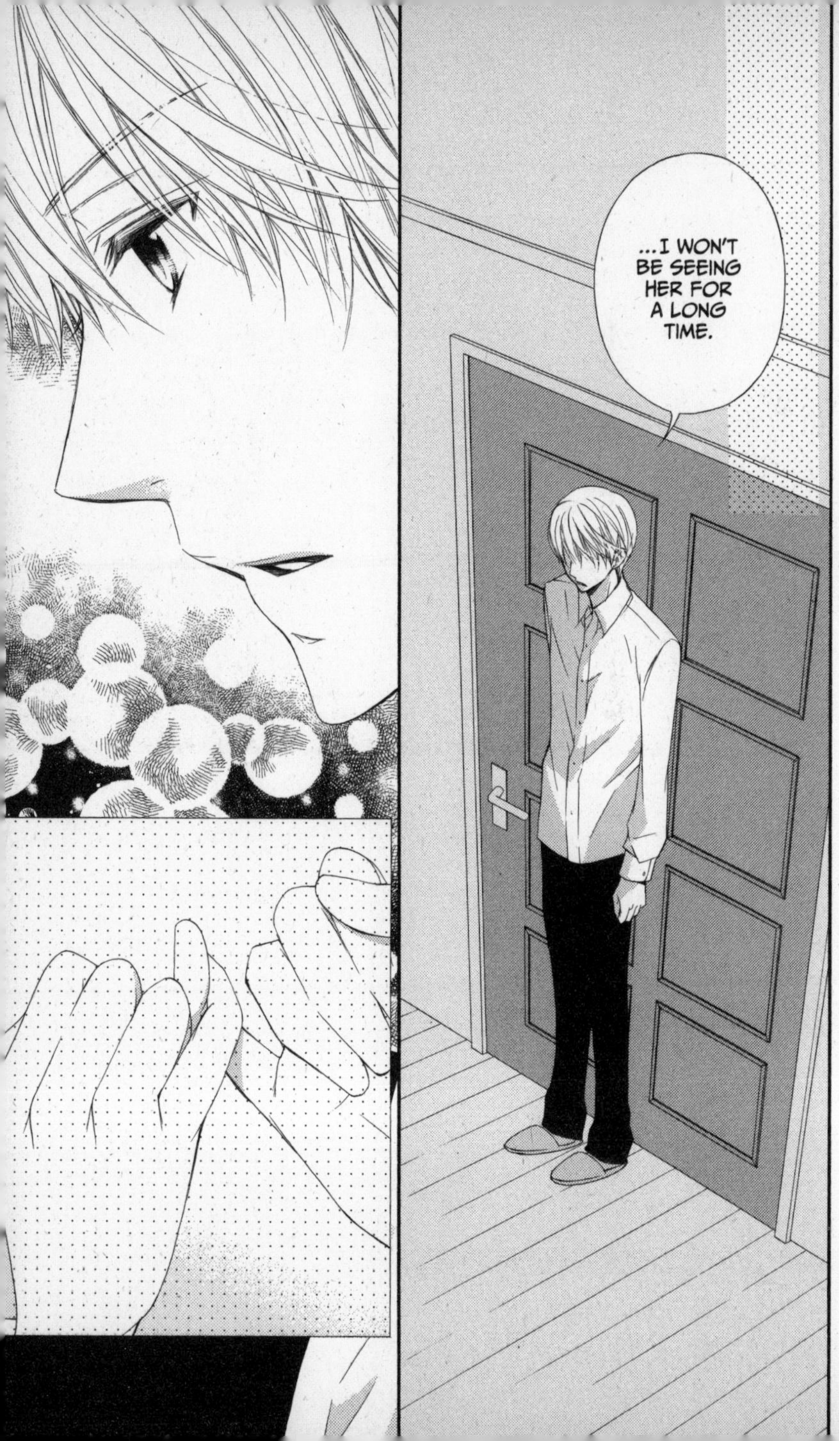
...I WON'T BE SEEING HER FOR A LONG TIME.

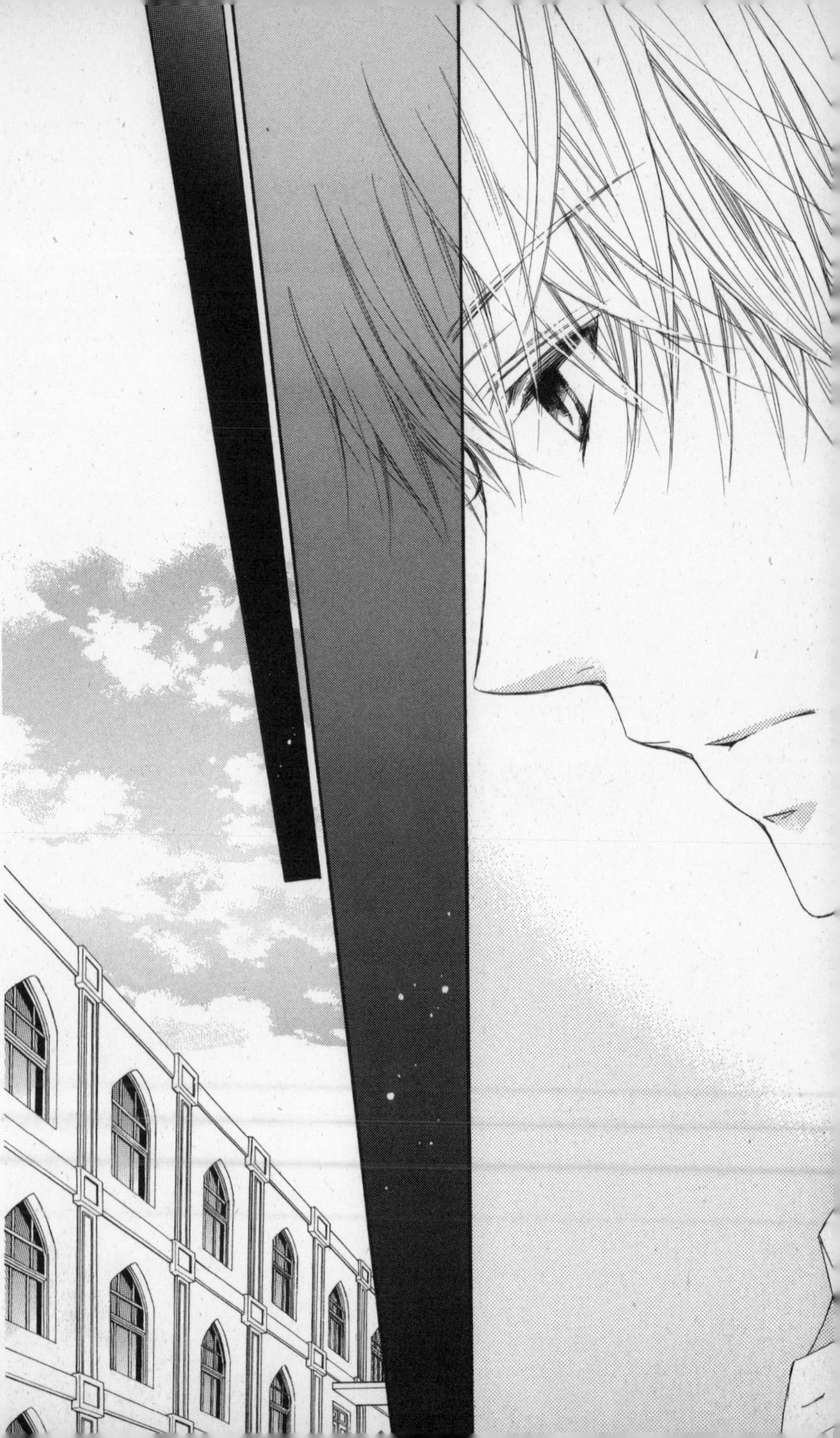

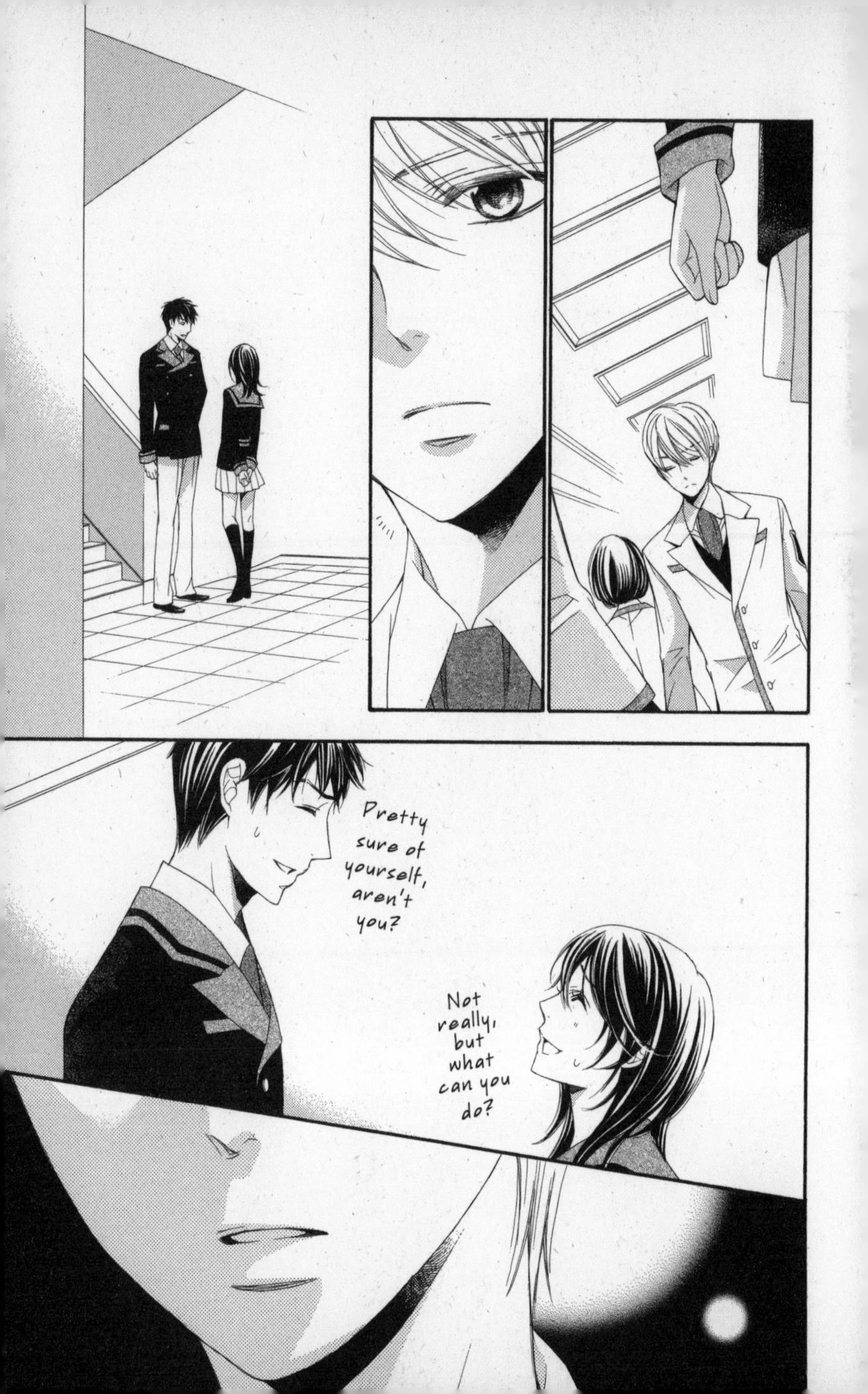
Pretty sure of yourself, aren't you?
Not really, but what can you do?

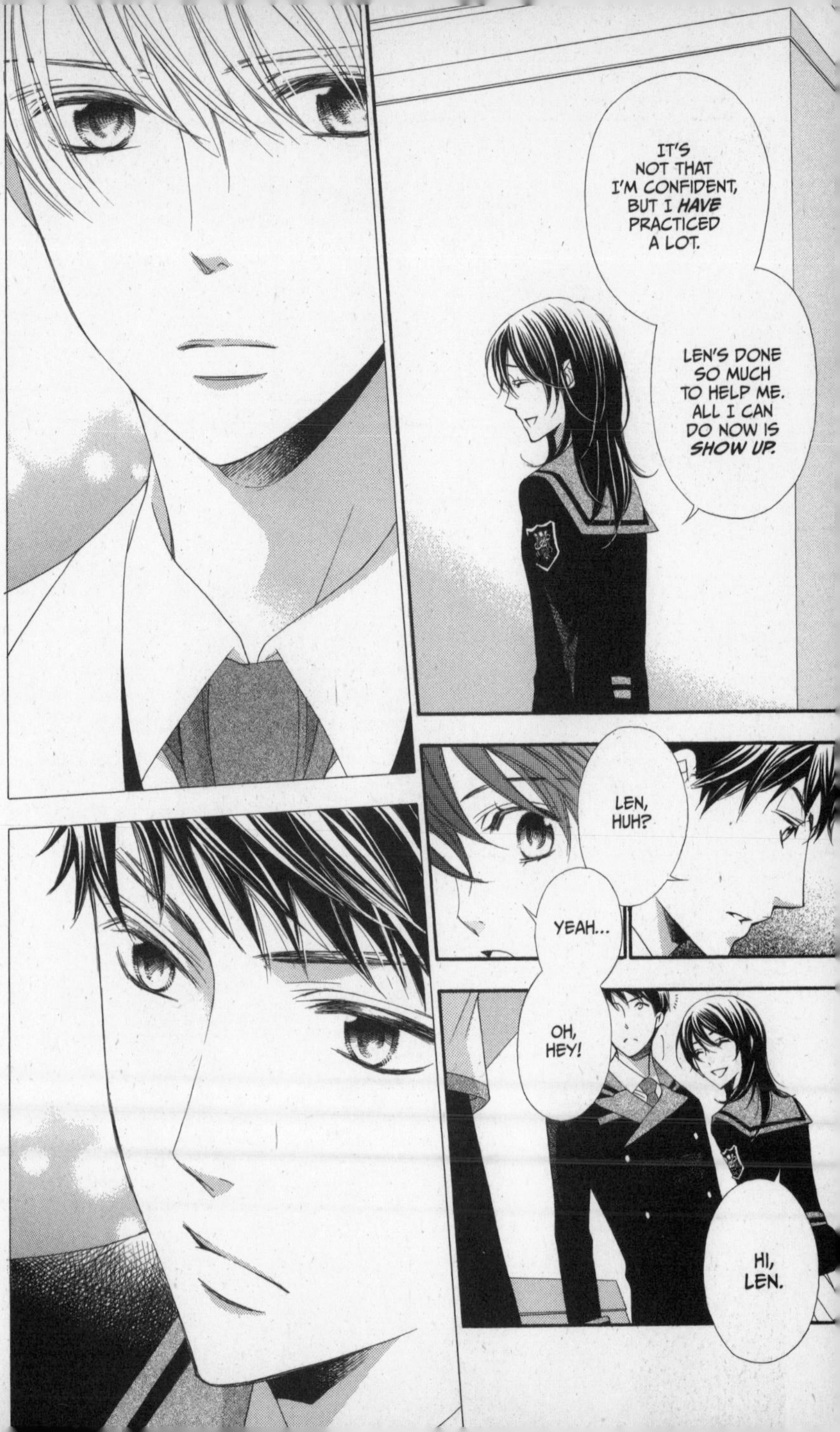
IT'S NOT THAT I'M CONFIDENT, BUT I *HAVE* PRACTICED A LOT.
LEN'S DONE SO MUCH TO HELP ME. ALL I CAN DO NOW IS *SHOW UP.*
LEN, HUH?
YEAH...
OH, HEY!
HI, LEN.

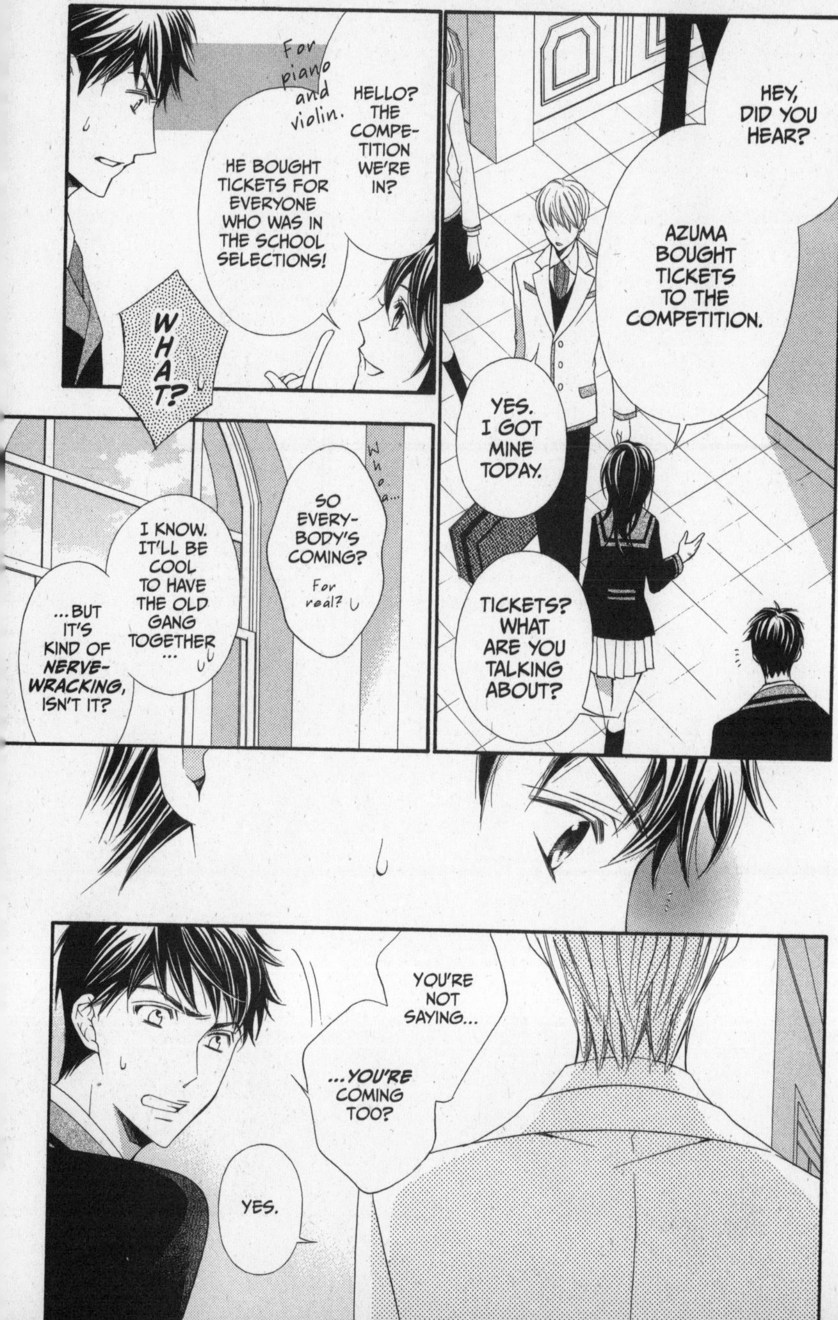
HEY, DID YOU HEAR?
AZUMA BOUGHT TICKETS TO THE COMPETITION.
YES. I GOT MINE TODAY.
TICKETS? WHAT ARE YOU TALKING ABOUT?
HELLO? THE COMPETITION WE'RE IN?
For piano and violin.
HE BOUGHT TICKETS FOR EVERYONE WHO WAS IN THE SCHOOL SELECTIONS!
WHAT?
Whoa...
SO EVERYBODY'S COMING?
For real?
I KNOW. IT'LL BE COOL TO HAVE THE OLD GANG TOGETHER...
...BUT IT'S KIND OF NERVE-WRACKING, ISN'T IT?
YOU'RE NOT SAYING...
...YOU'RE COMING TOO?
YES.

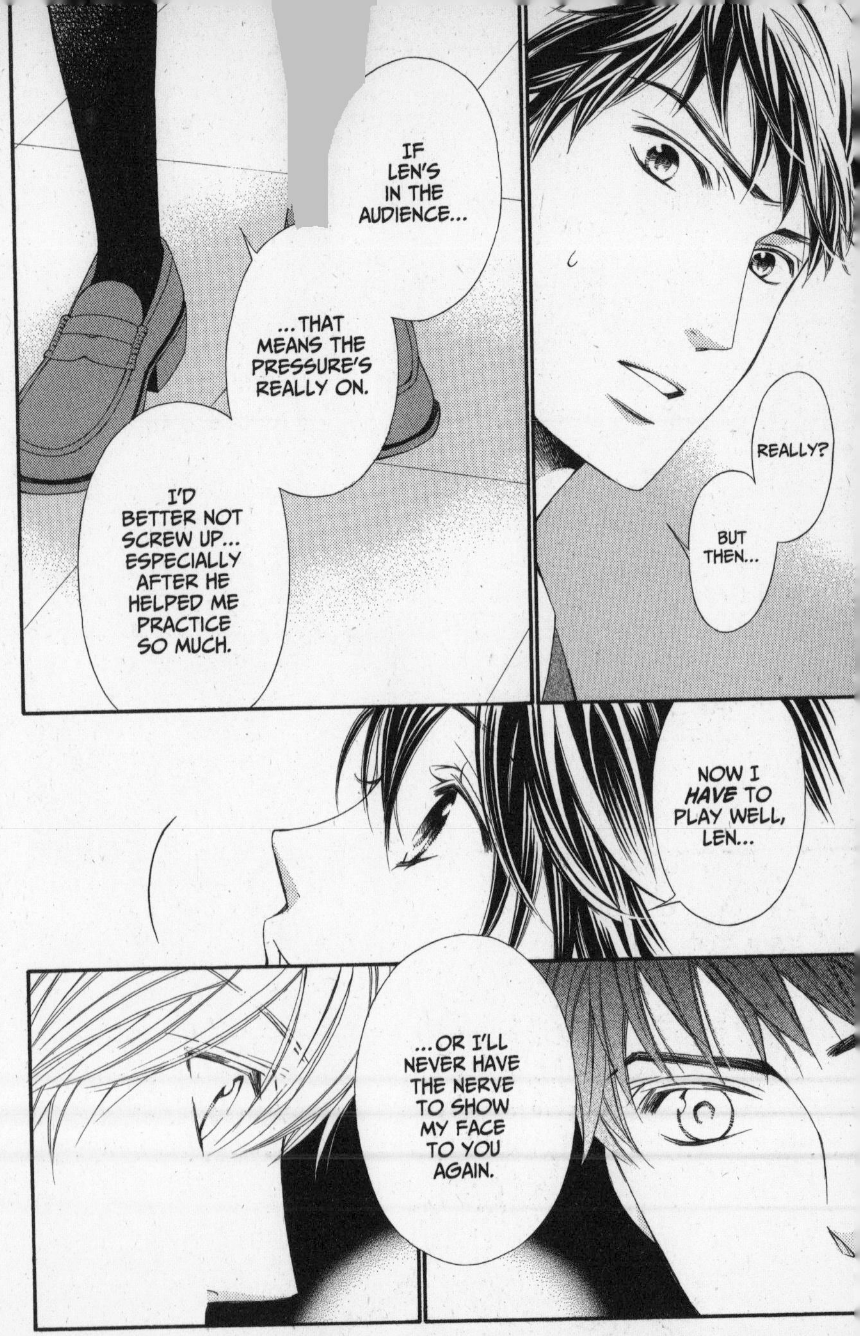
REALLY?
BUT THEN...
IF LEN'S IN THE AUDIENCE...
...THAT MEANS THE PRESSURE'S REALLY ON.
I'D BETTER NOT SCREW UP... ESPECIALLY AFTER HE HELPED ME PRACTICE SO MUCH.
NOW I *HAVE* TO PLAY WELL, LEN...
...OR I'LL NEVER HAVE THE NERVE TO SHOW MY FACE TO YOU AGAIN.

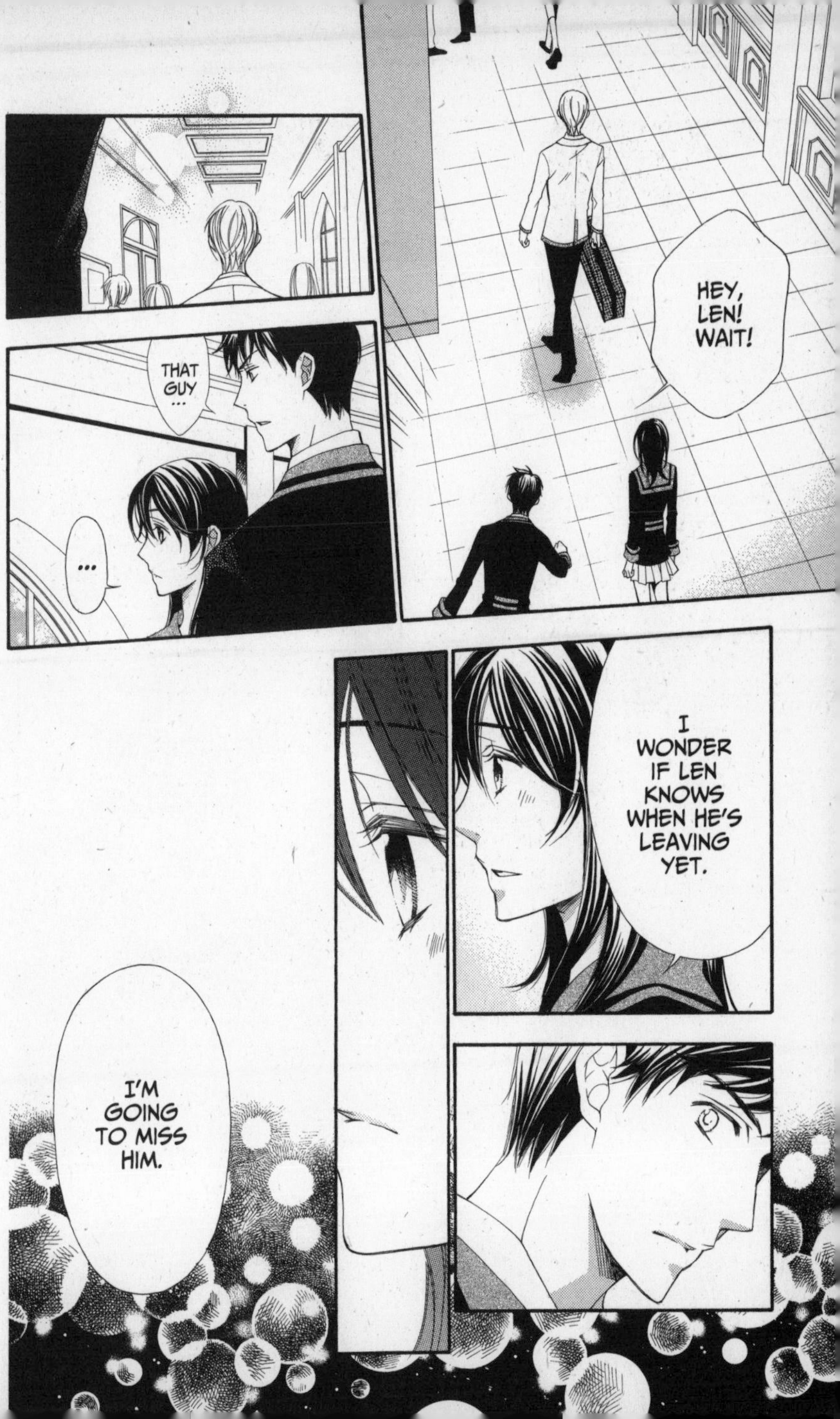
HEY, LEN! WAIT!
THAT GUY...
...
I WONDER IF LEN KNOWS WHEN HE'S LEAVING YET.
I'M GOING TO MISS HIM.

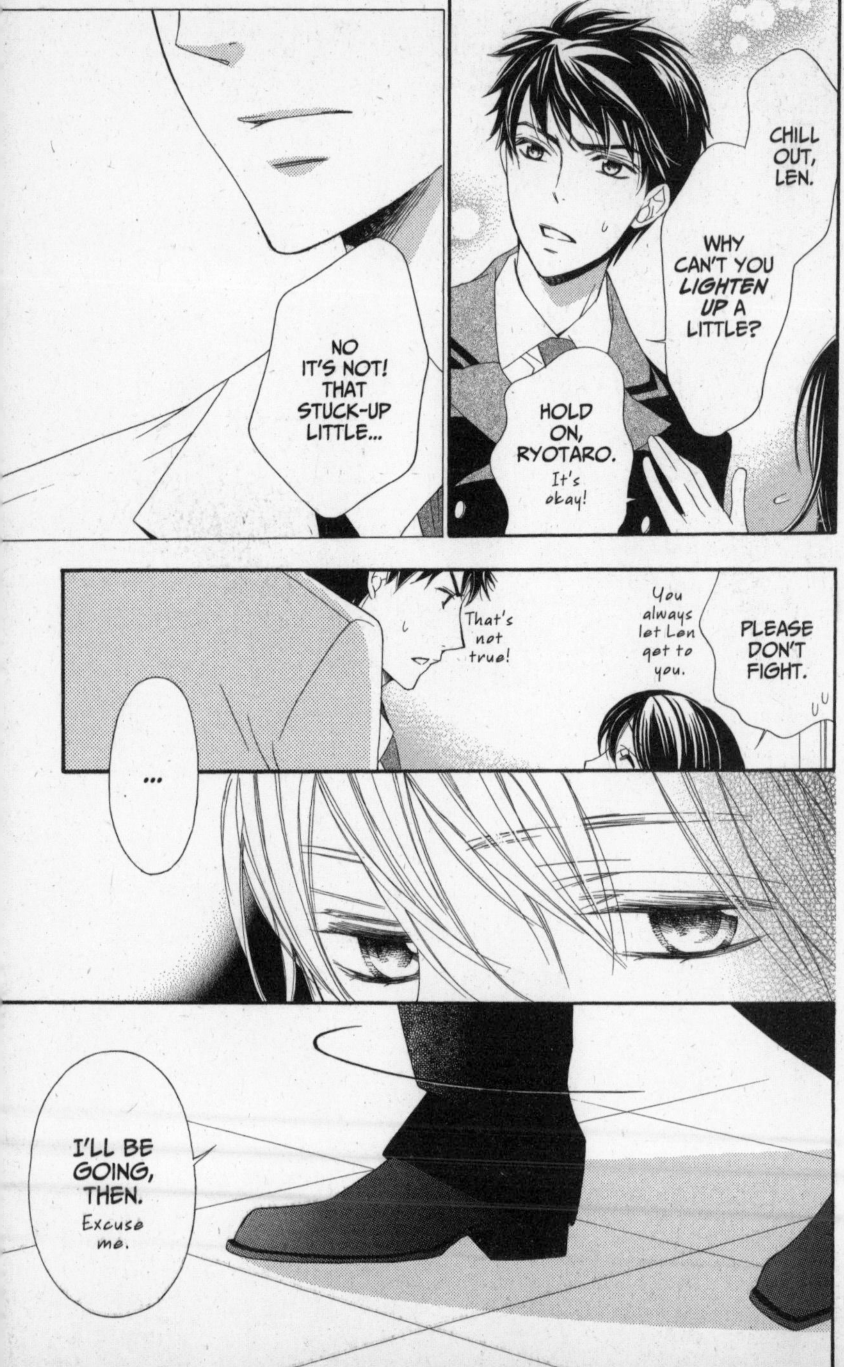
CHILL OUT, LEN.
WHY CAN'T YOU LIGHTEN UP A LITTLE?
HOLD ON, RYOTARO. It's okay!
NO IT'S NOT! THAT STUCK-UP LITTLE...
PLEASE DON'T FIGHT.
You always let Len get to you.
That's not true!
...
I'LL BE GOING, THEN. Excuse me.

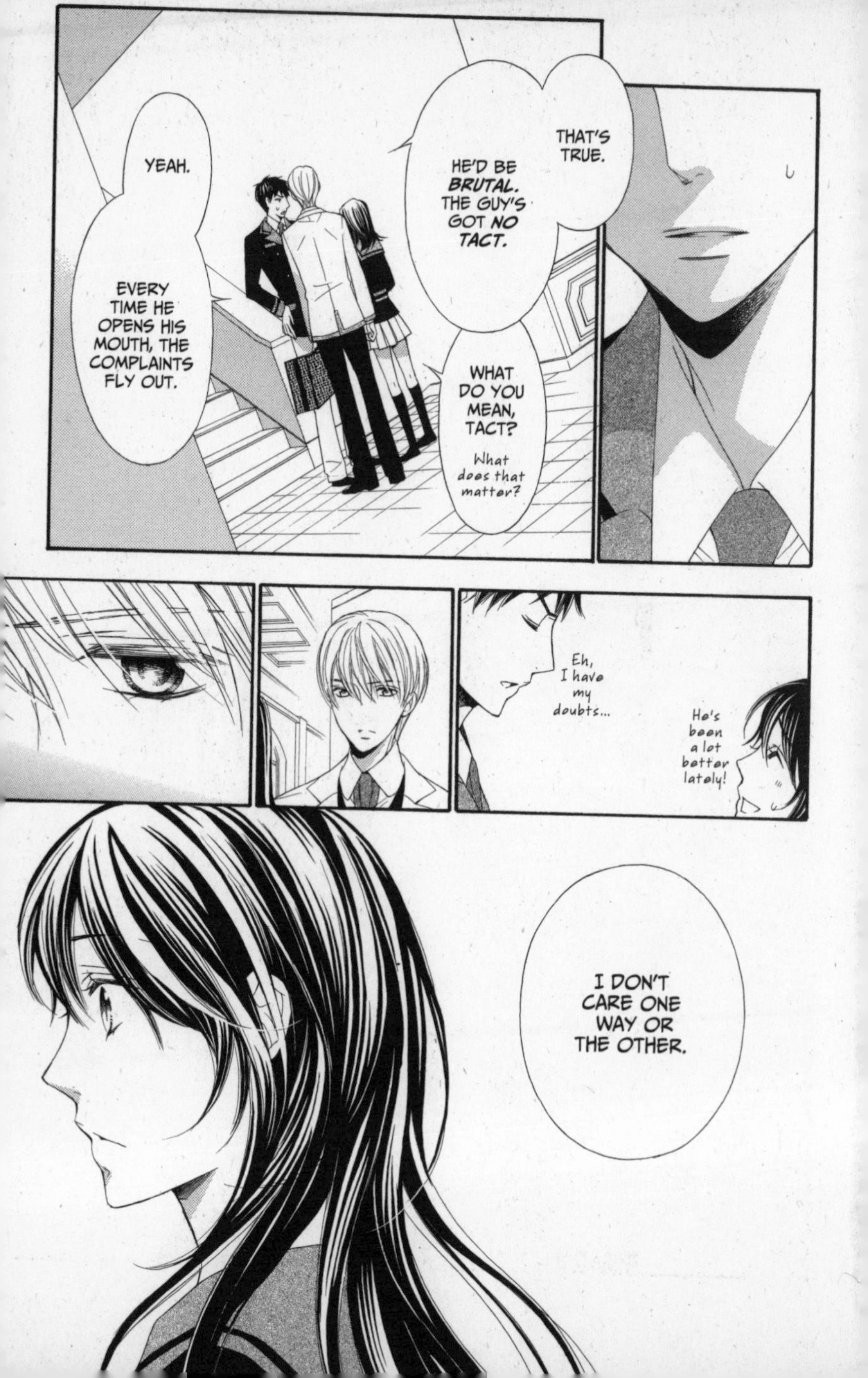
THAT'S TRUE.
HE'D BE ***BRUTAL.*** THE GUY'S GOT ***NO TACT.***
YEAH.
EVERY TIME HE OPENS HIS MOUTH, THE COMPLAINTS FLY OUT.
WHAT DO YOU MEAN, TACT?
What does that matter?
He's been a lot better lately!
Eh, I have my doubts...
I DON'T CARE ONE WAY OR THE OTHER.

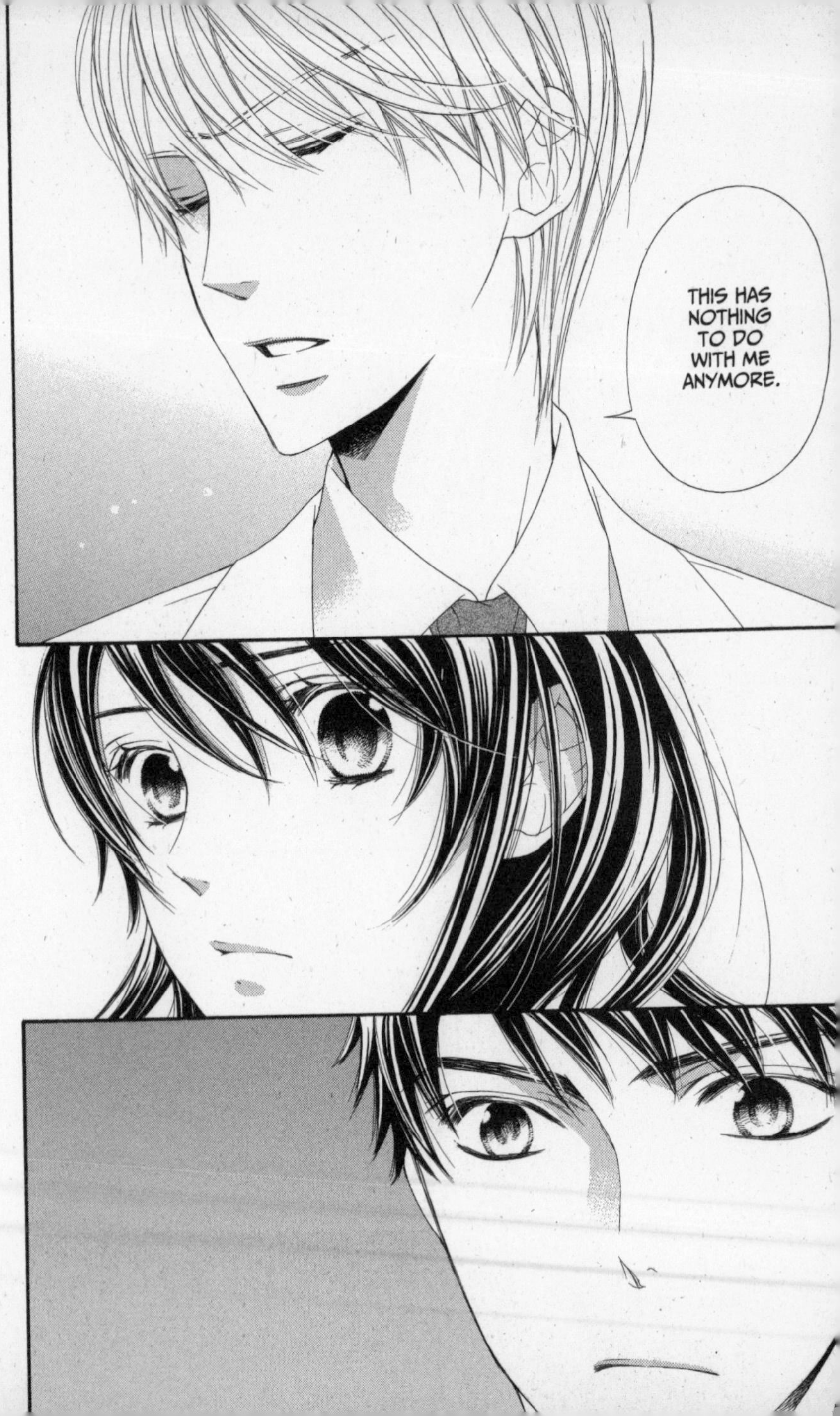
THIS HAS NOTHING TO DO WITH ME ANYMORE.

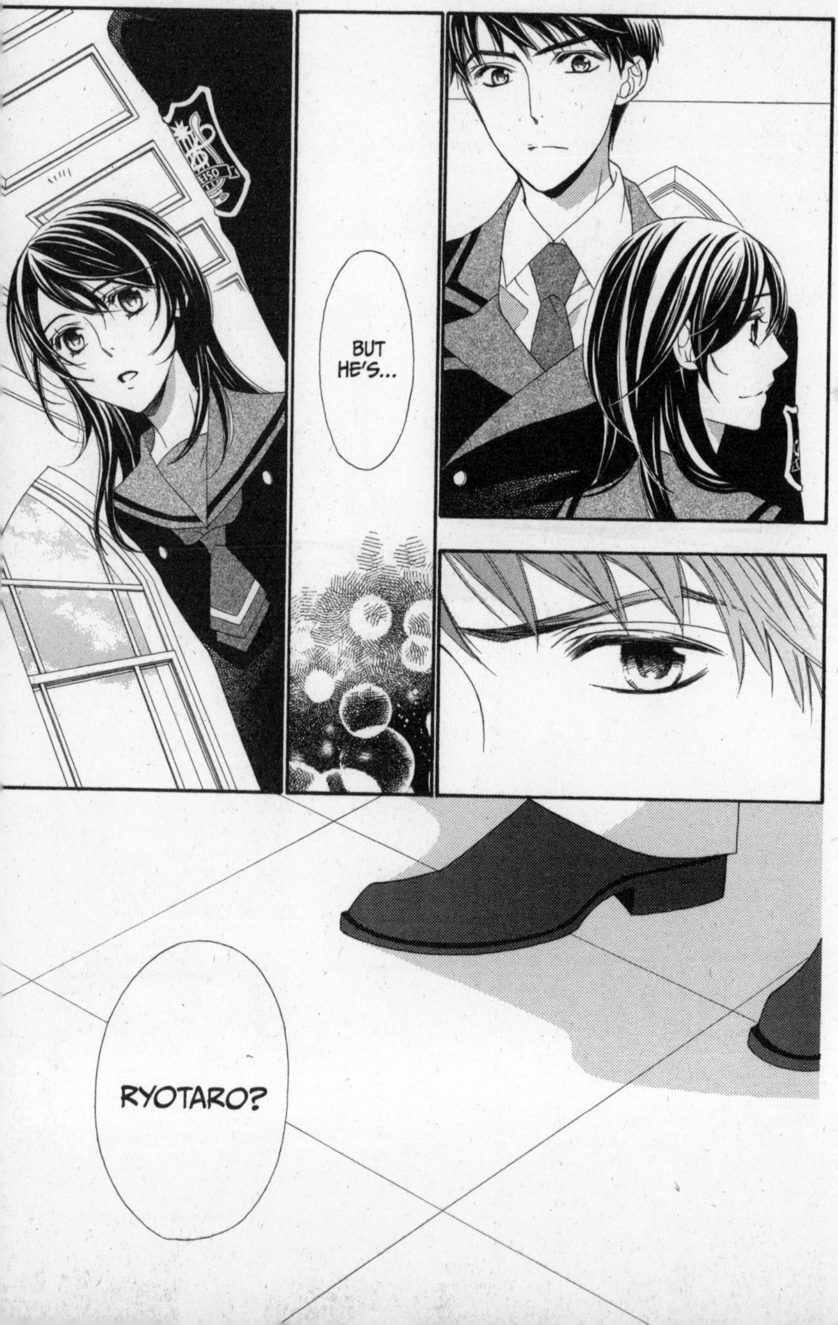
BUT HE'S...
RYOTARO?

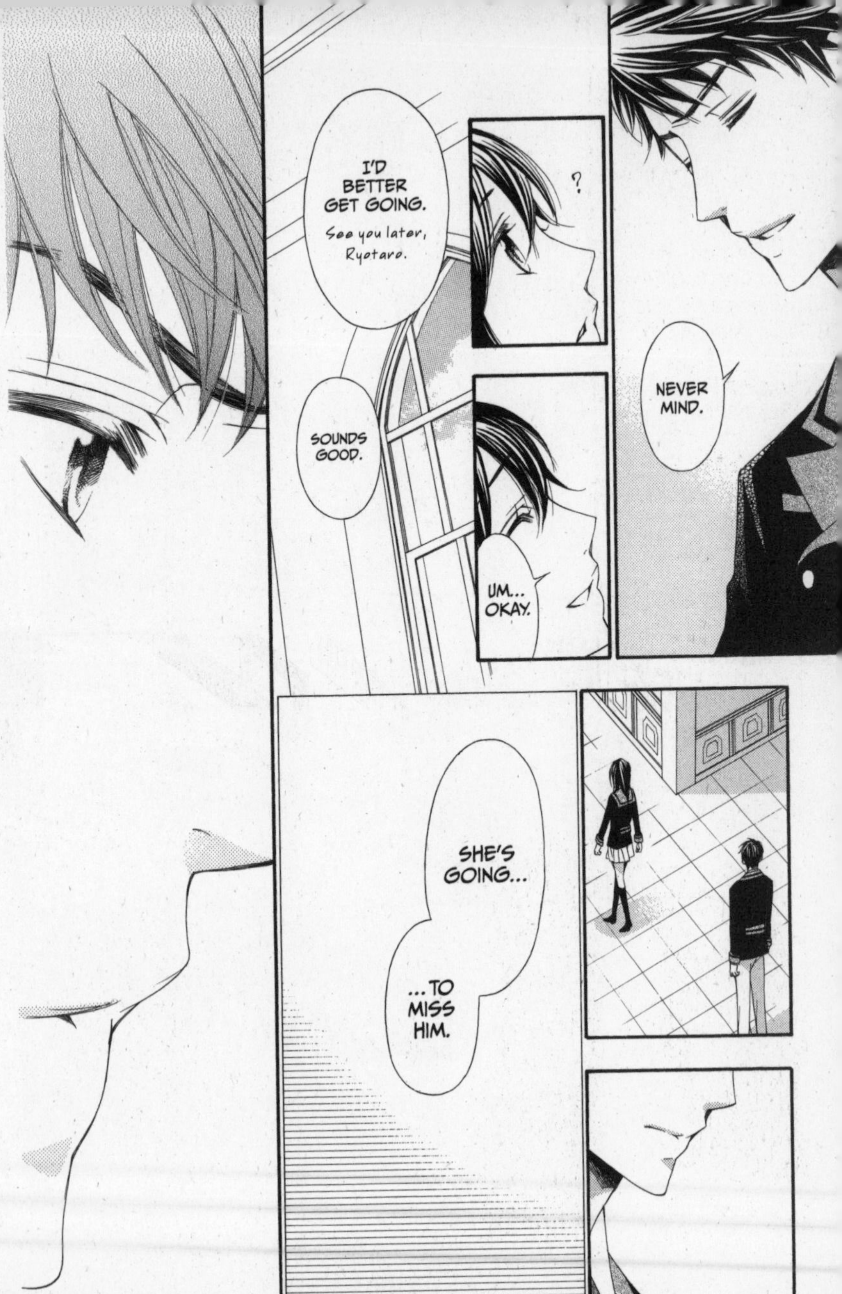
NEVER MIND.
?
UM... OKAY.
I'D BETTER GET GOING.
See you later, Ryotaro.
SOUNDS GOOD.
SHE'S GOING...
...TO MISS HIM.

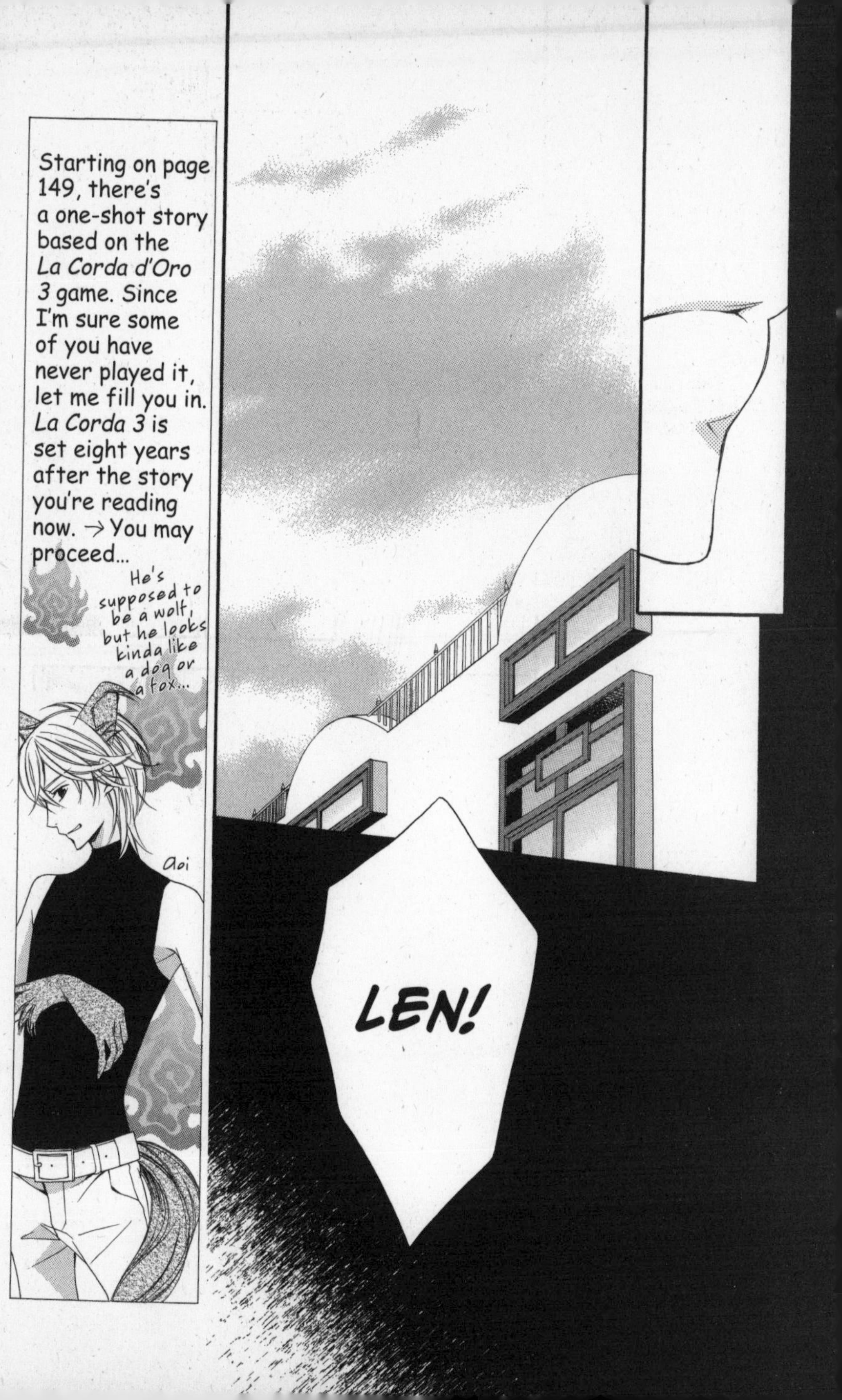
LEN!
Starting on page 149, there's a one-shot story based on the *La Corda d'Oro 3* game. Since I'm sure some of you have never played it, let me fill you in. *La Corda 3* is set eight years after the story you're reading now. → You may proceed...
He's supposed to be a wolf, but he looks kinda like a dog or a fox...
Aoi

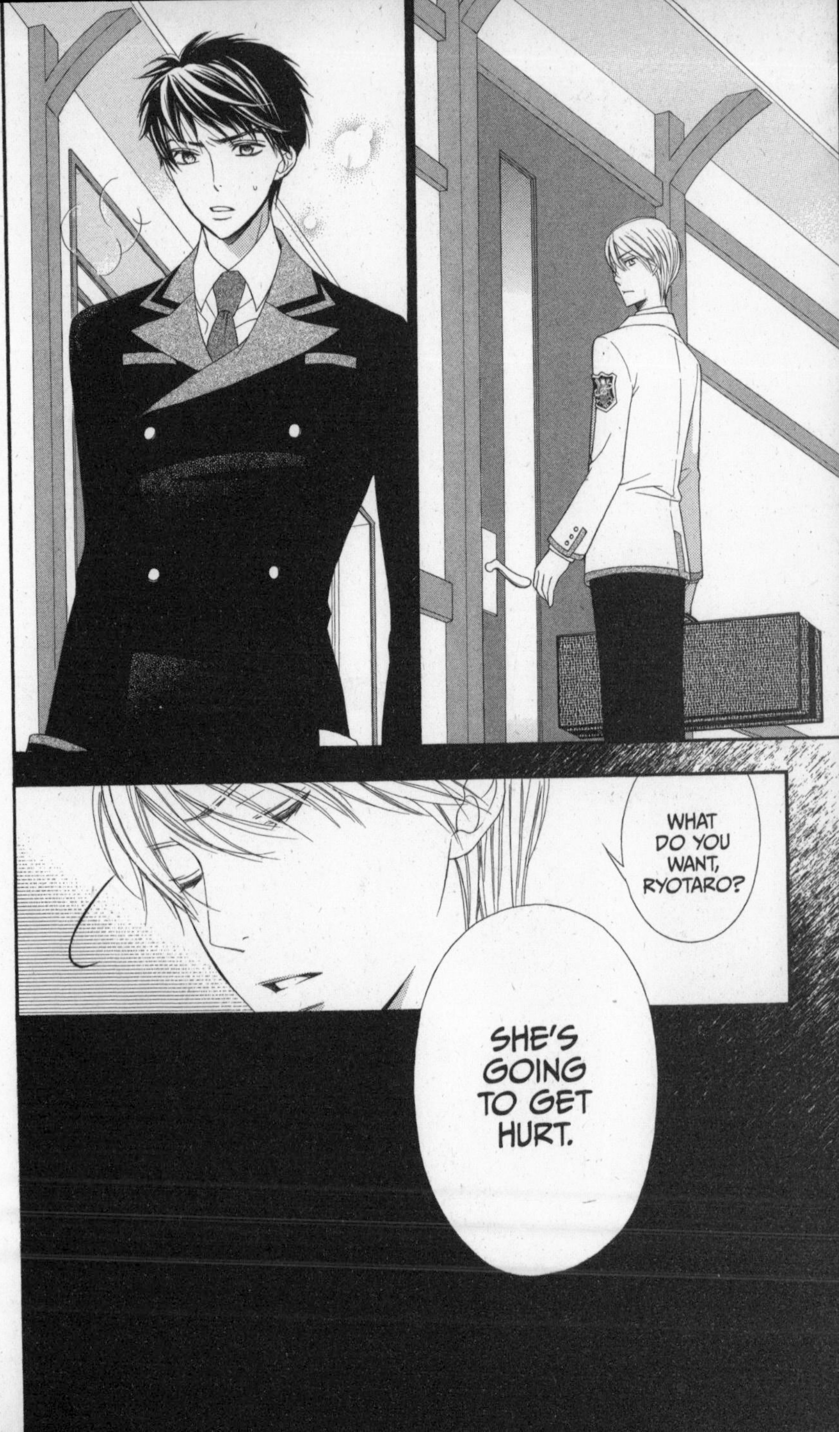
WHAT DO YOU WANT, RYOTARO?
SHE'S GOING TO GET HURT.

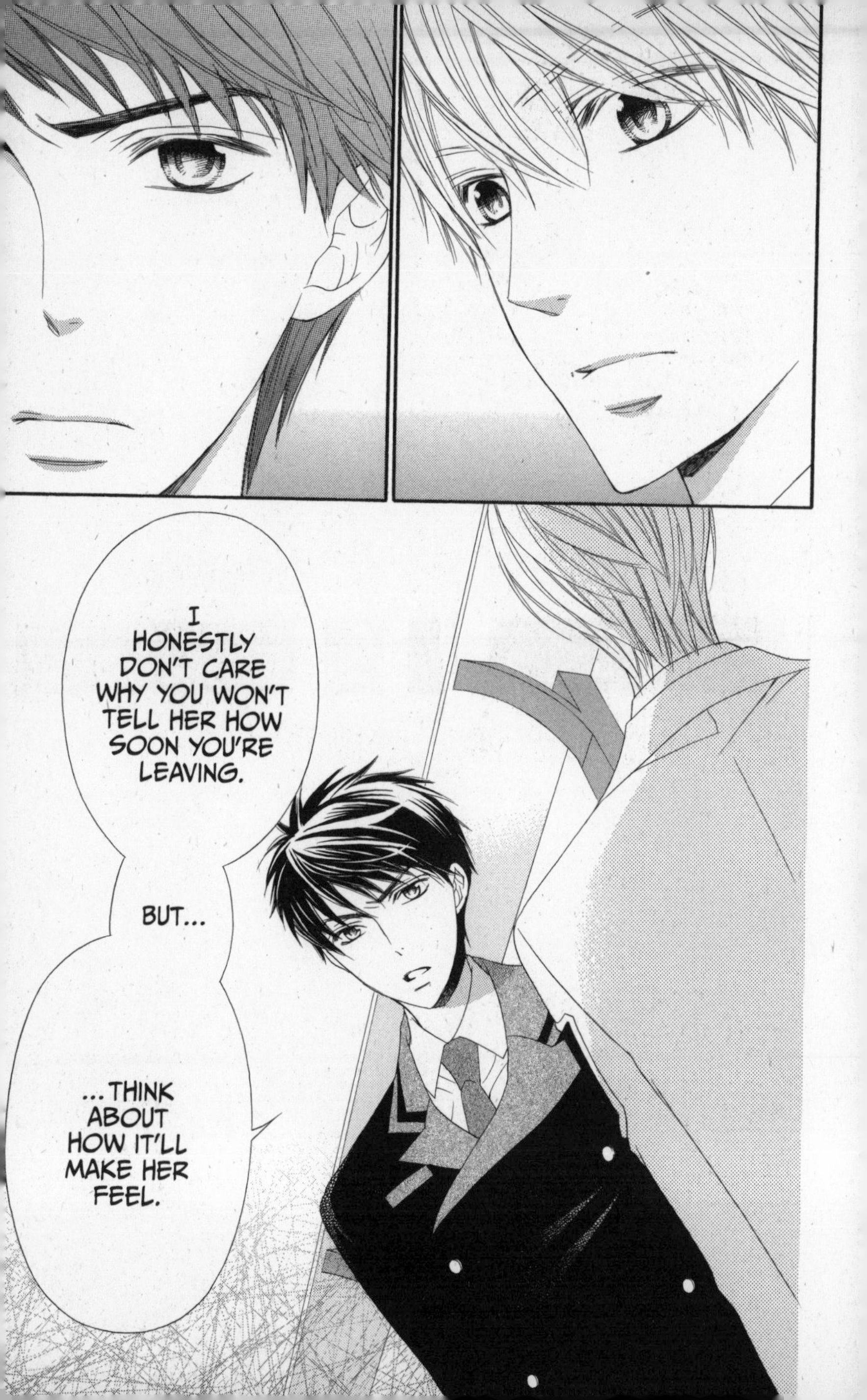
I HONESTLY DON'T CARE WHY YOU WON'T TELL HER HOW SOON YOU'RE LEAVING.
BUT...
...THINK ABOUT HOW IT'LL MAKE HER FEEL.

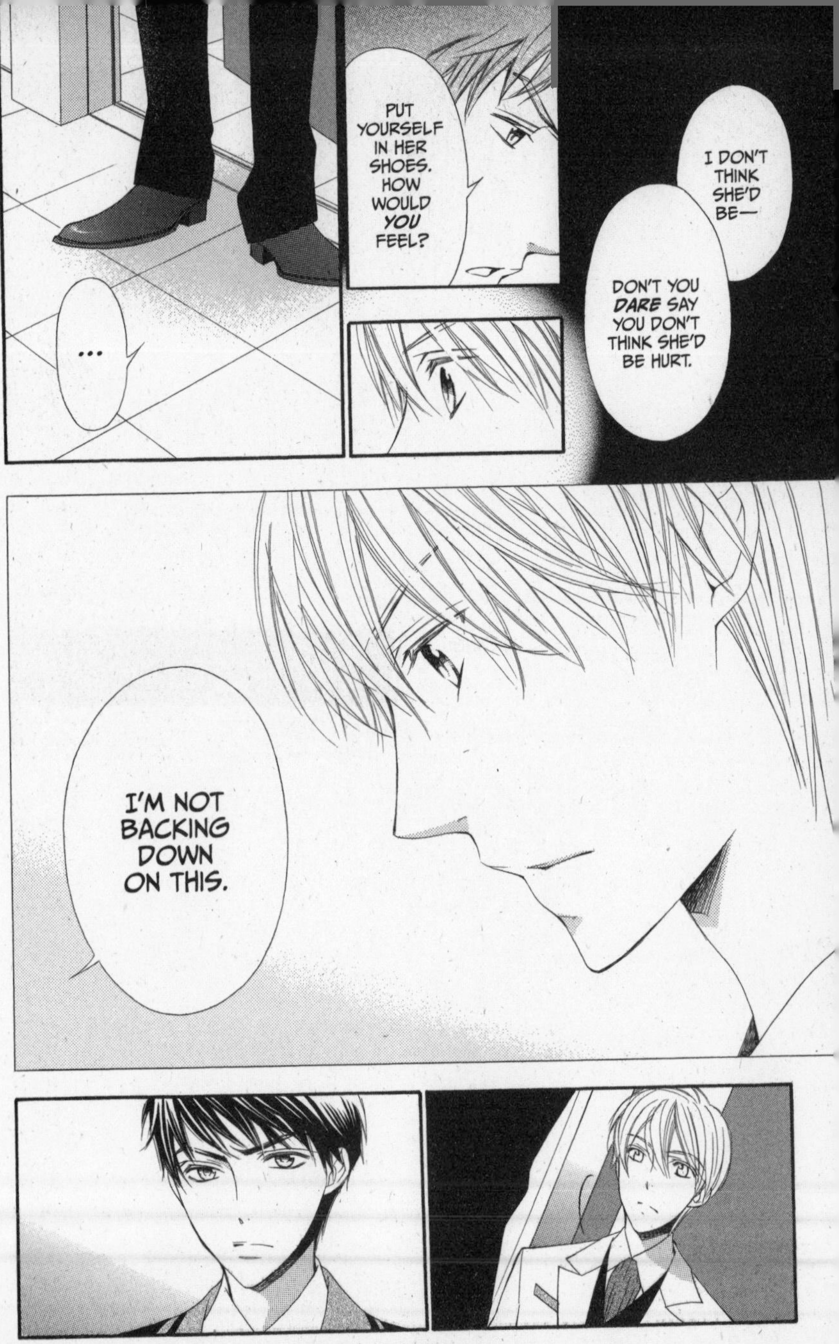
PUT YOURSELF IN HER SHOES. HOW WOULD *YOU* FEEL?
I DON'T THINK SHE'D BE—
DON'T YOU *DARE* SAY YOU DON'T THINK SHE'D BE HURT.
...
I'M NOT BACKING DOWN ON THIS.

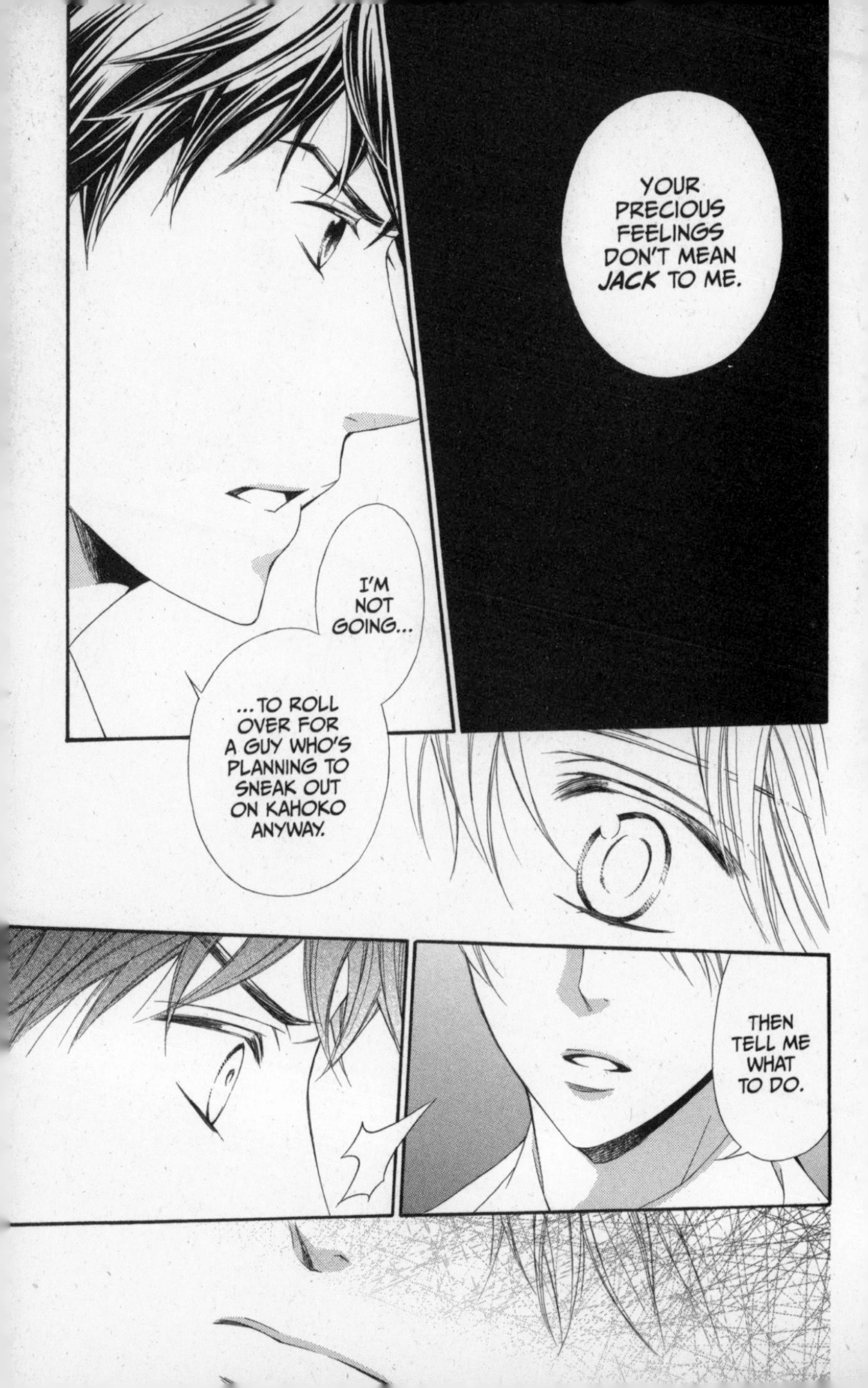
YOUR PRECIOUS FEELINGS DON'T MEAN *JACK* TO ME.
I'M NOT GOING...
...TO ROLL OVER FOR A GUY WHO'S PLANNING TO SNEAK OUT ON KAHOKO ANYWAY.
THEN TELL ME WHAT TO DO.

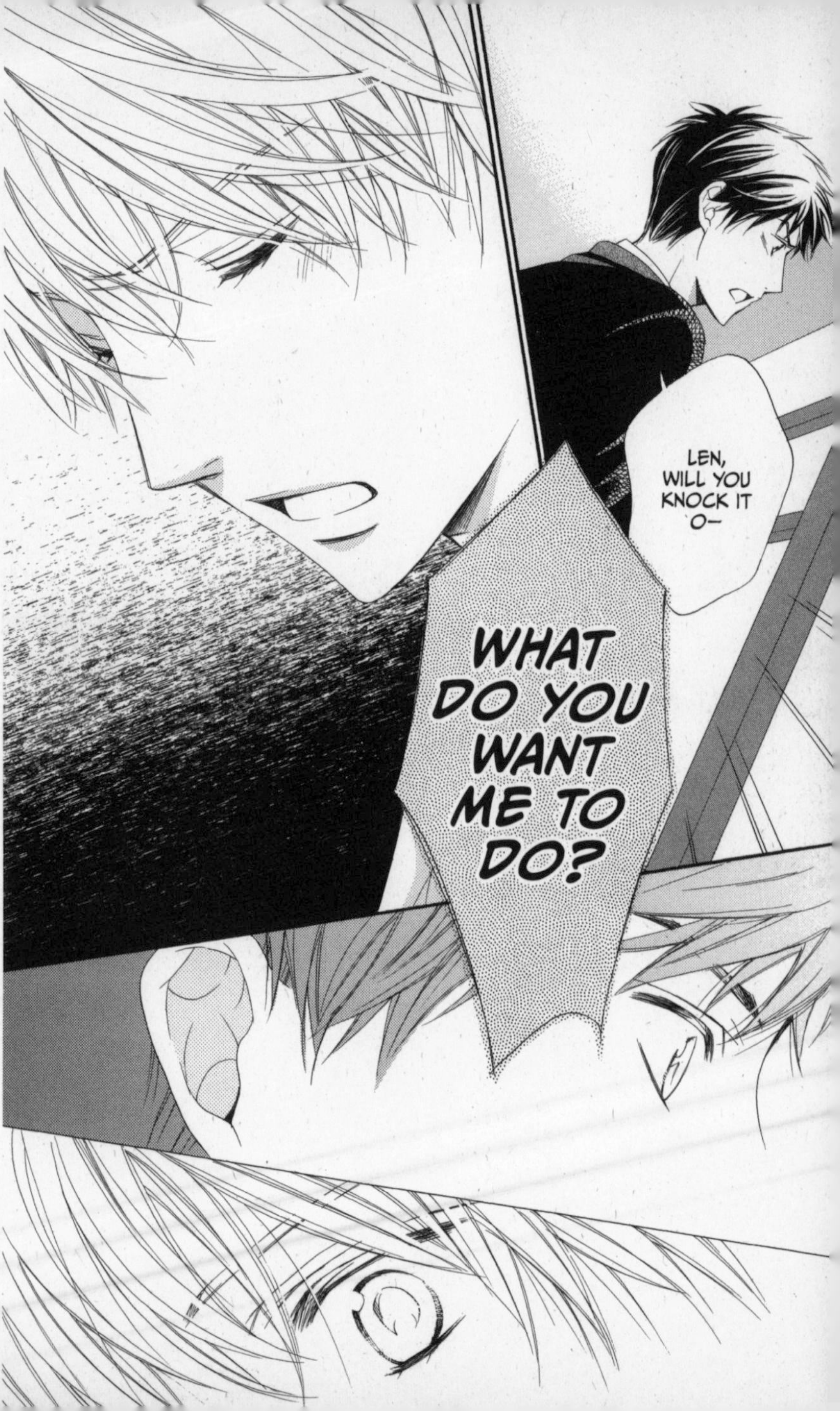
LEN, WILL YOU KNOCK IT O—
WHAT DO YOU WANT ME TO DO?

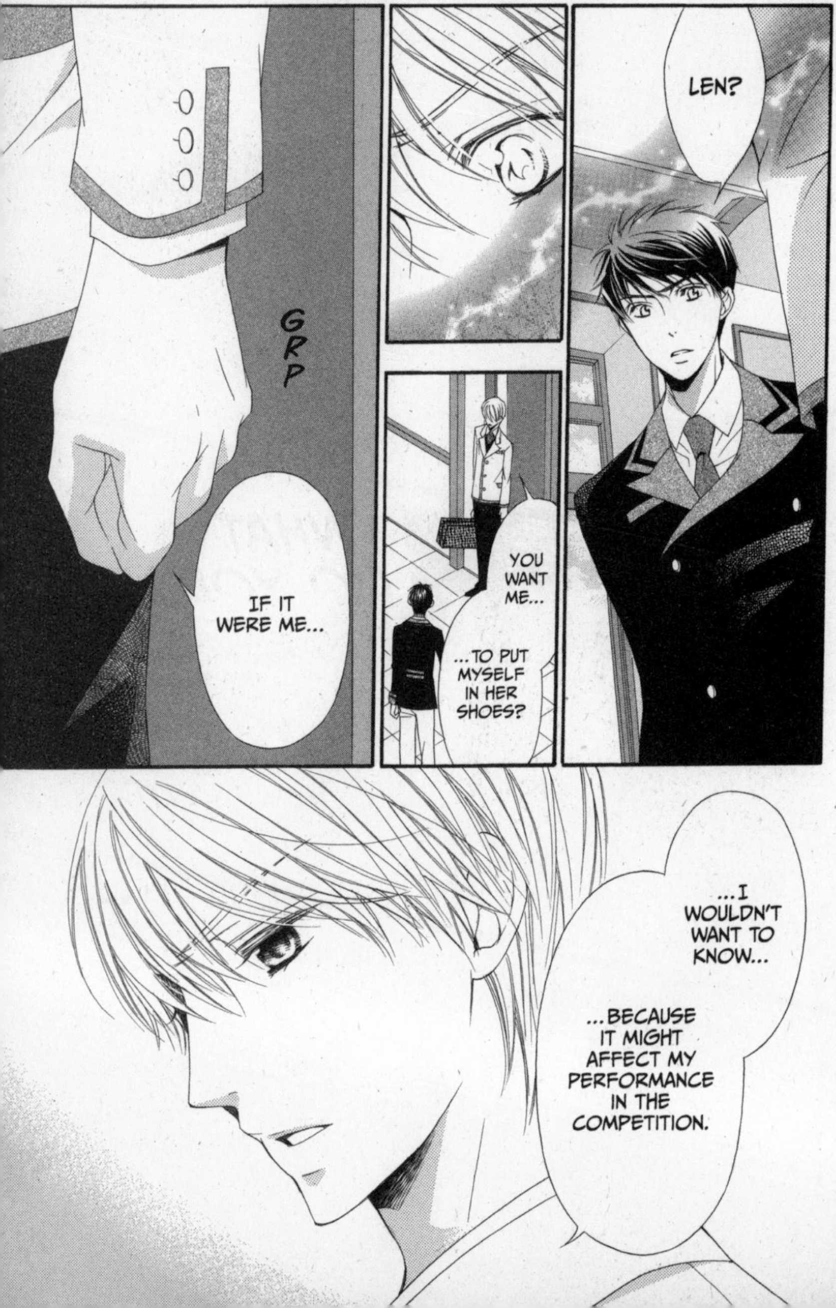
LEN?
YOU WANT ME...
...TO PUT MYSELF IN HER SHOES?
GRP
IF IT WERE ME...
...I WOULDN'T WANT TO KNOW...
...BECAUSE IT MIGHT AFFECT MY PERFORMANCE IN THE COMPETITION.

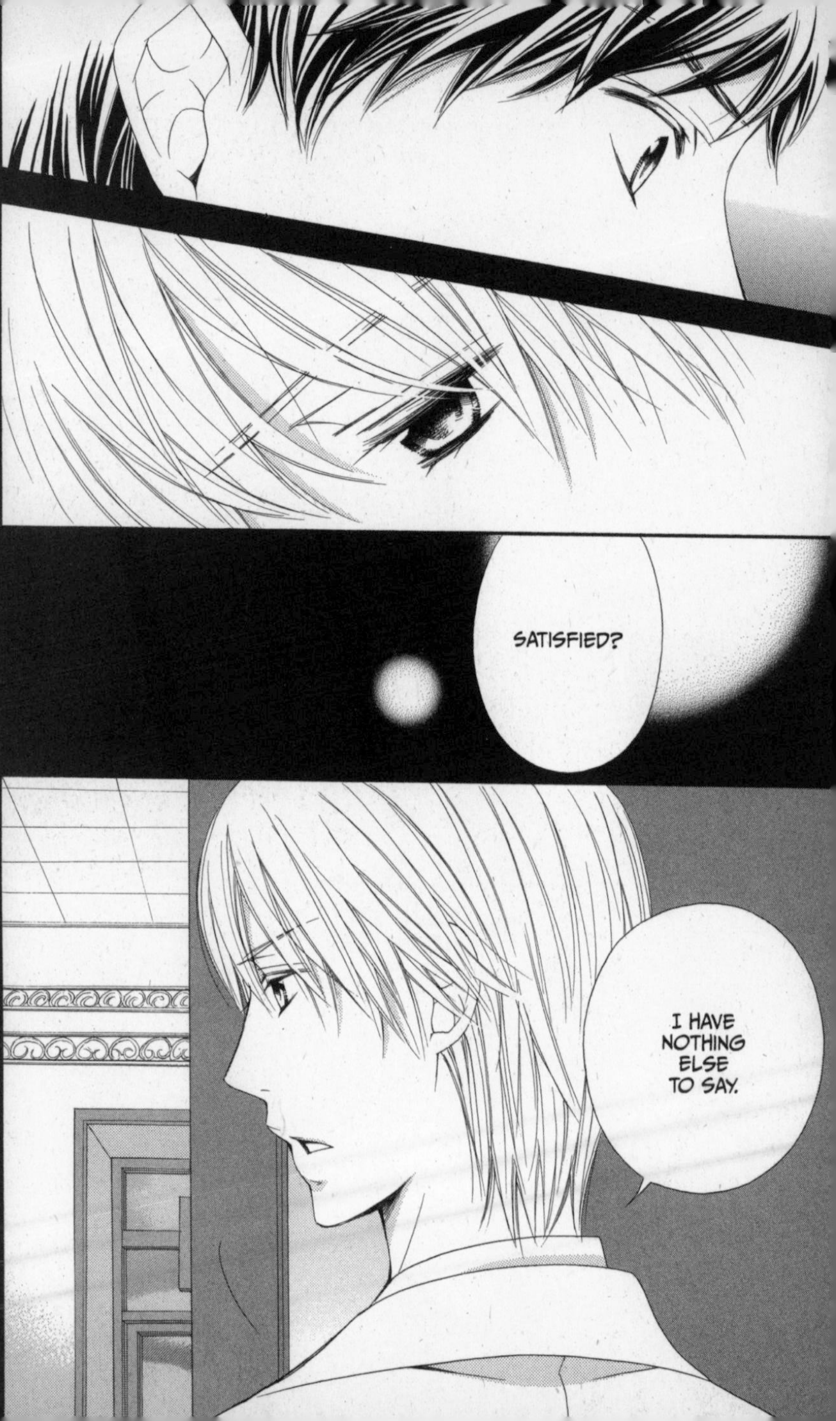
SATISFIED?
I HAVE NOTHING ELSE TO SAY.

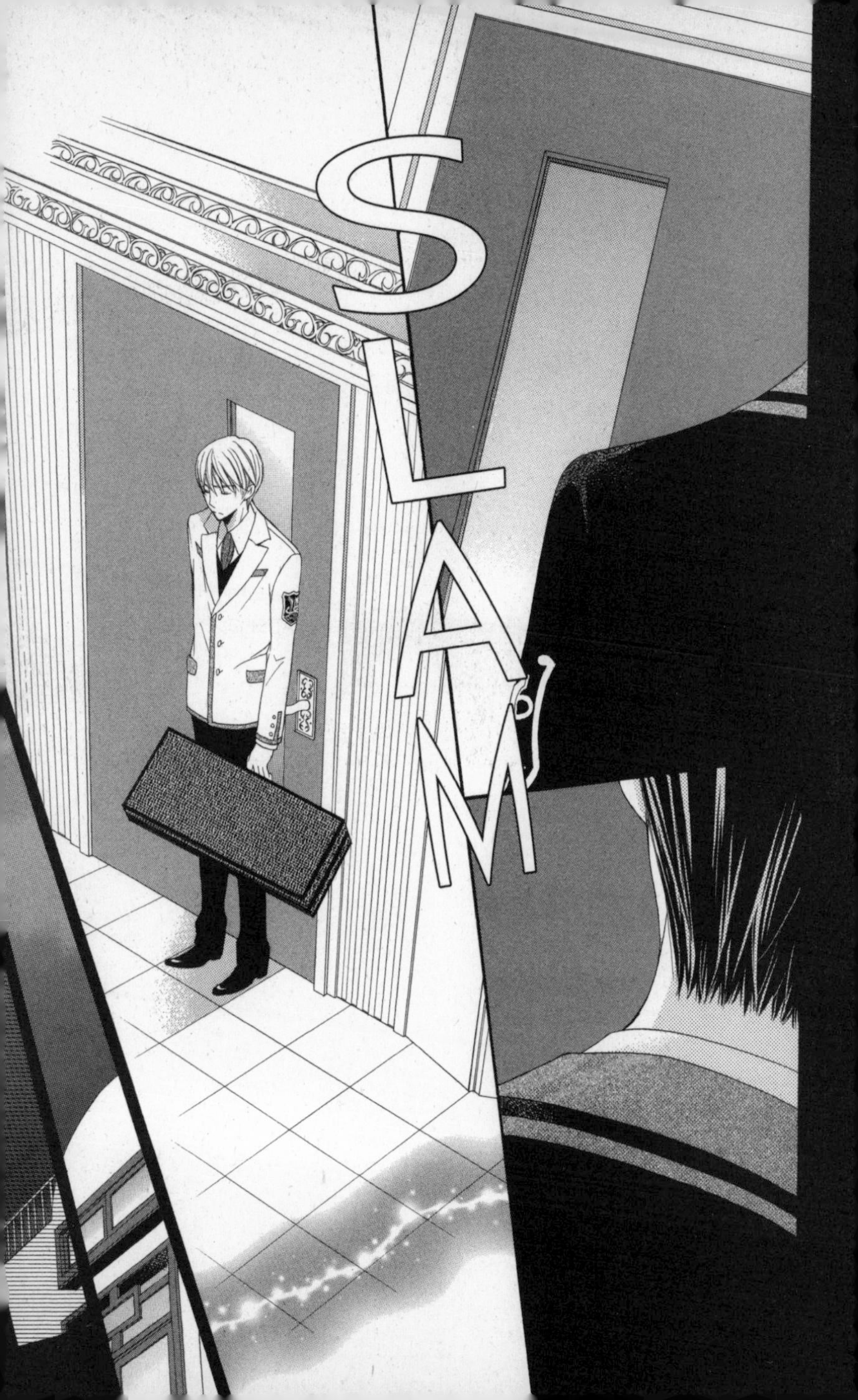
SLAM

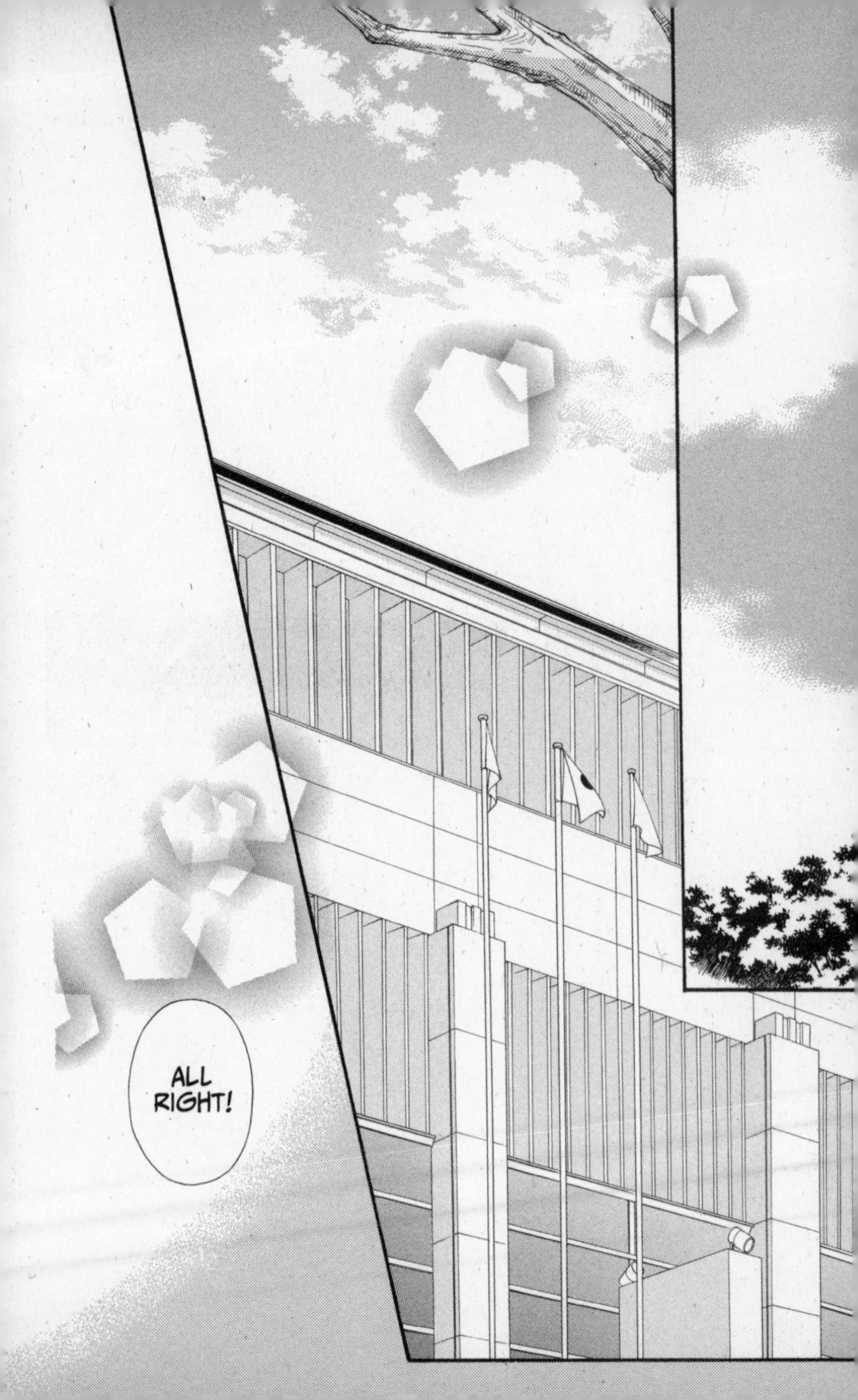
ALL RIGHT!

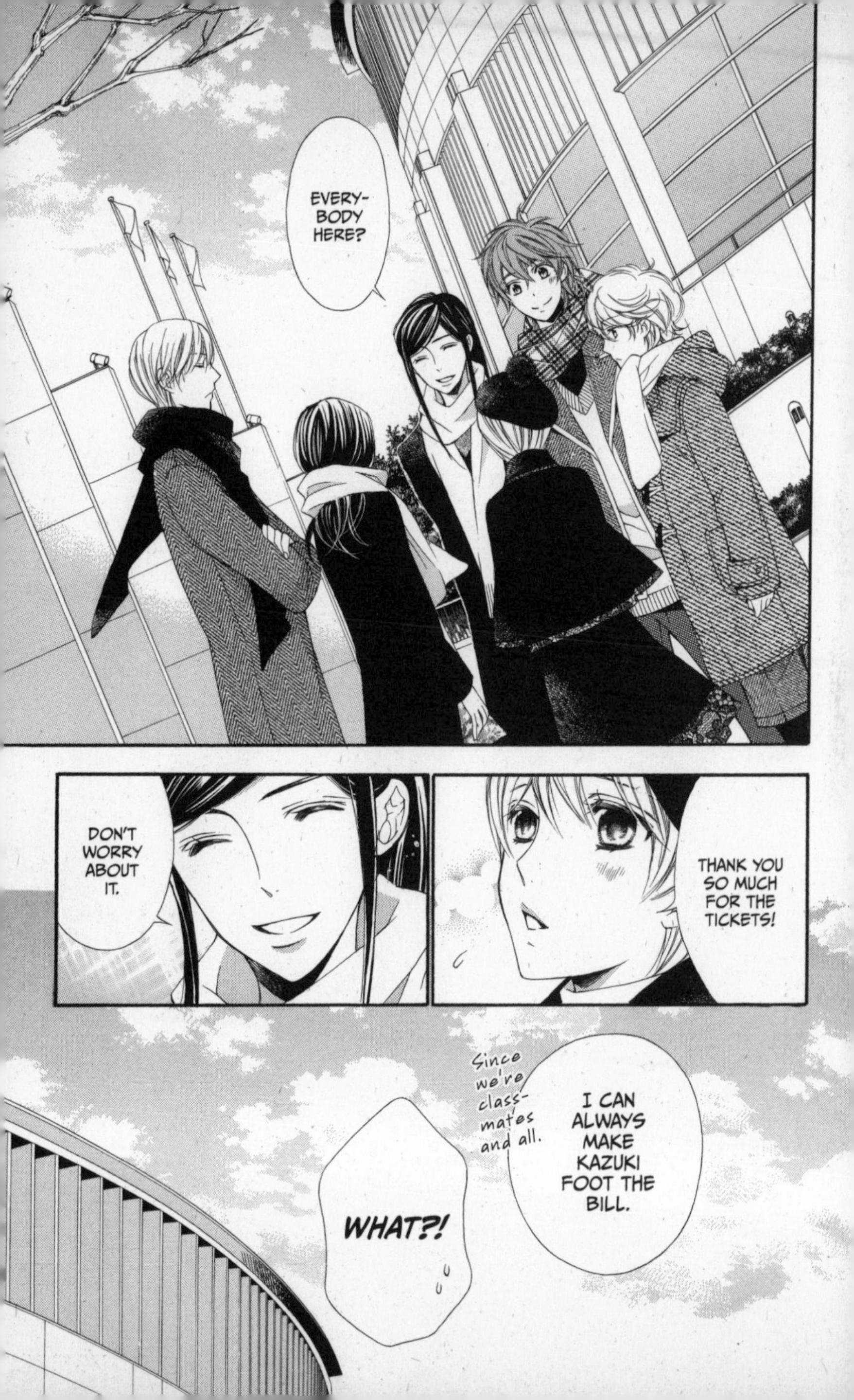
EVERY-BODY HERE?
THANK YOU SO MUCH FOR THE TICKETS!
DON'T WORRY ABOUT IT.
I CAN ALWAYS MAKE KAZUKI FOOT THE BILL.
Since we're class-mates and all.
WHAT?!

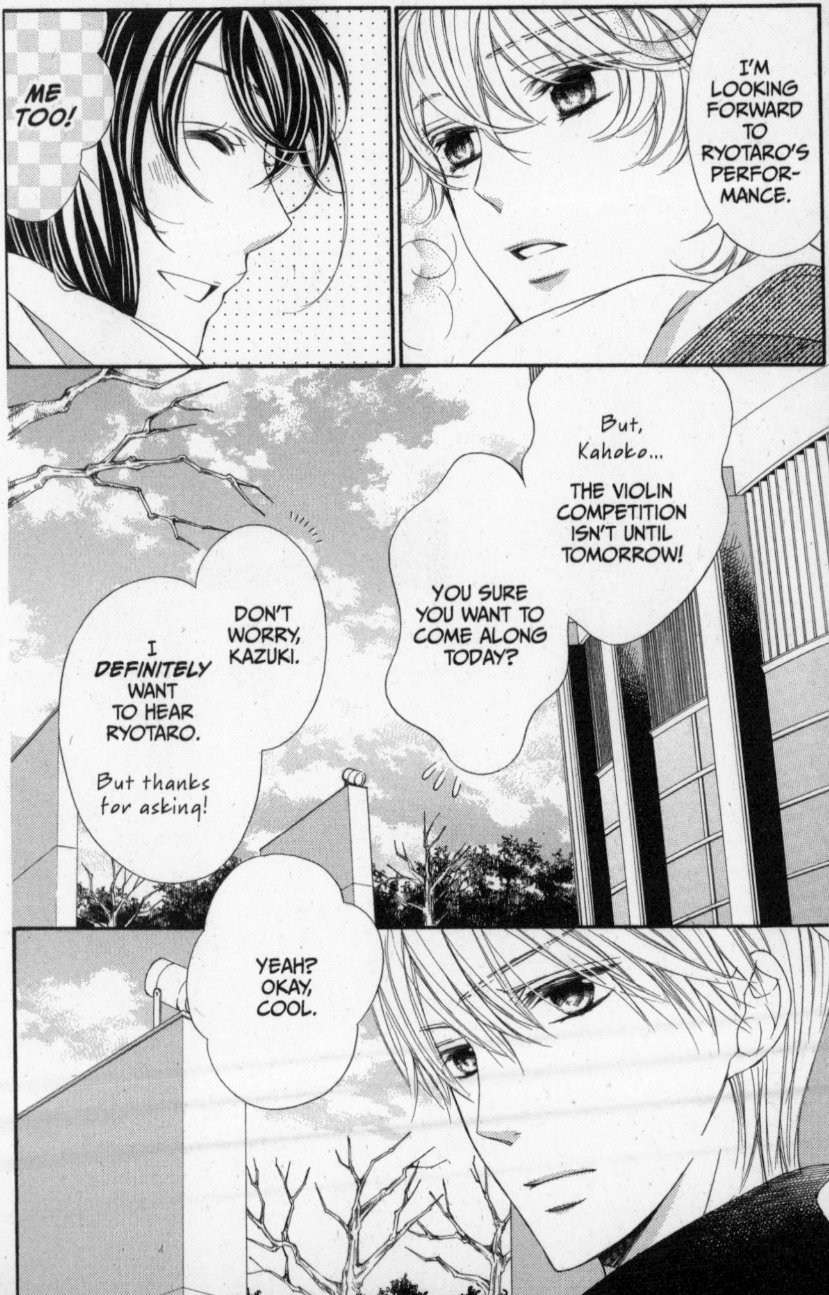
I'M LOOKING FORWARD TO RYOTARO'S PERFORMANCE.
ME TOO!
But, Kahoko... THE VIOLIN COMPETITION ISN'T UNTIL TOMORROW!
YOU SURE YOU WANT TO COME ALONG TODAY?
DON'T WORRY, KAZUKI.
I DEFINITELY WANT TO HEAR RYOTARO.
But thanks for asking!
YEAH? OKAY, COOL.

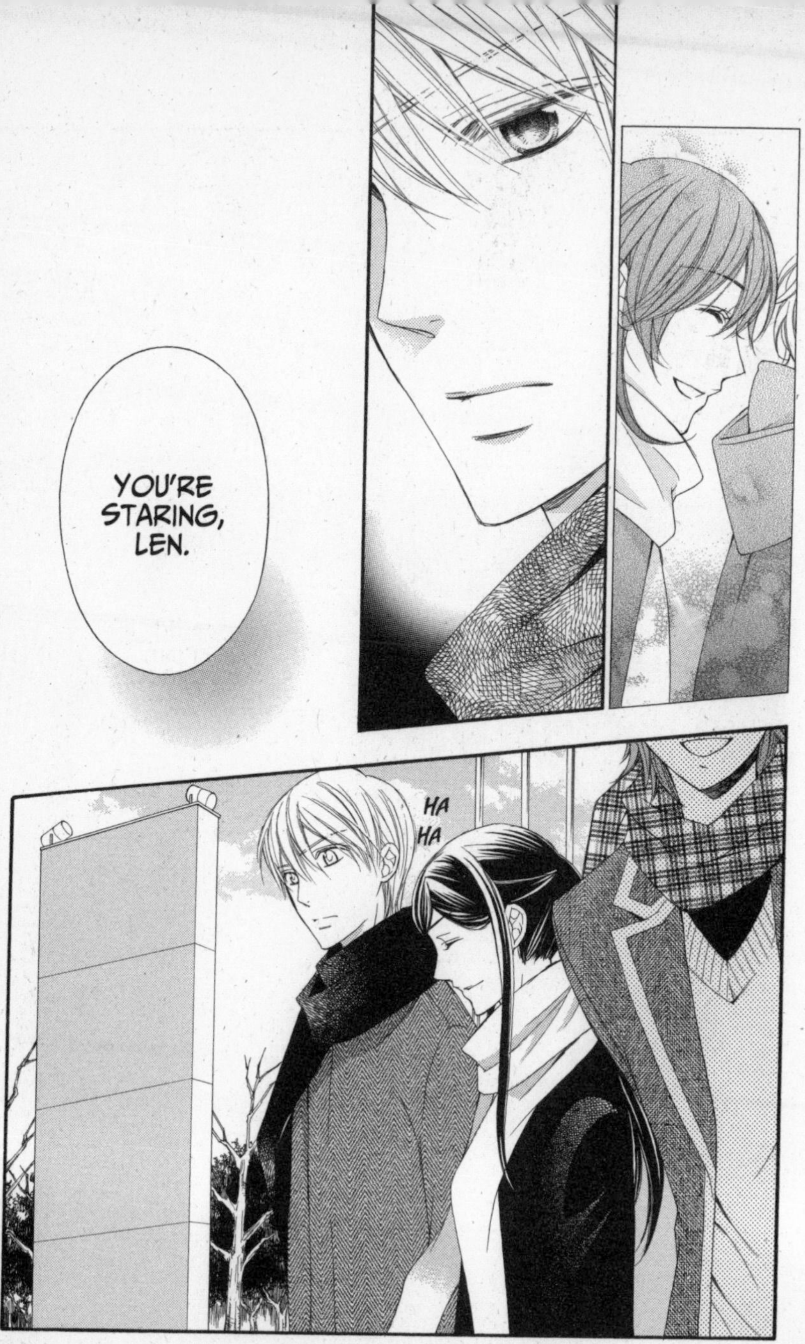
YOU'RE STARING, LEN.
HA HA

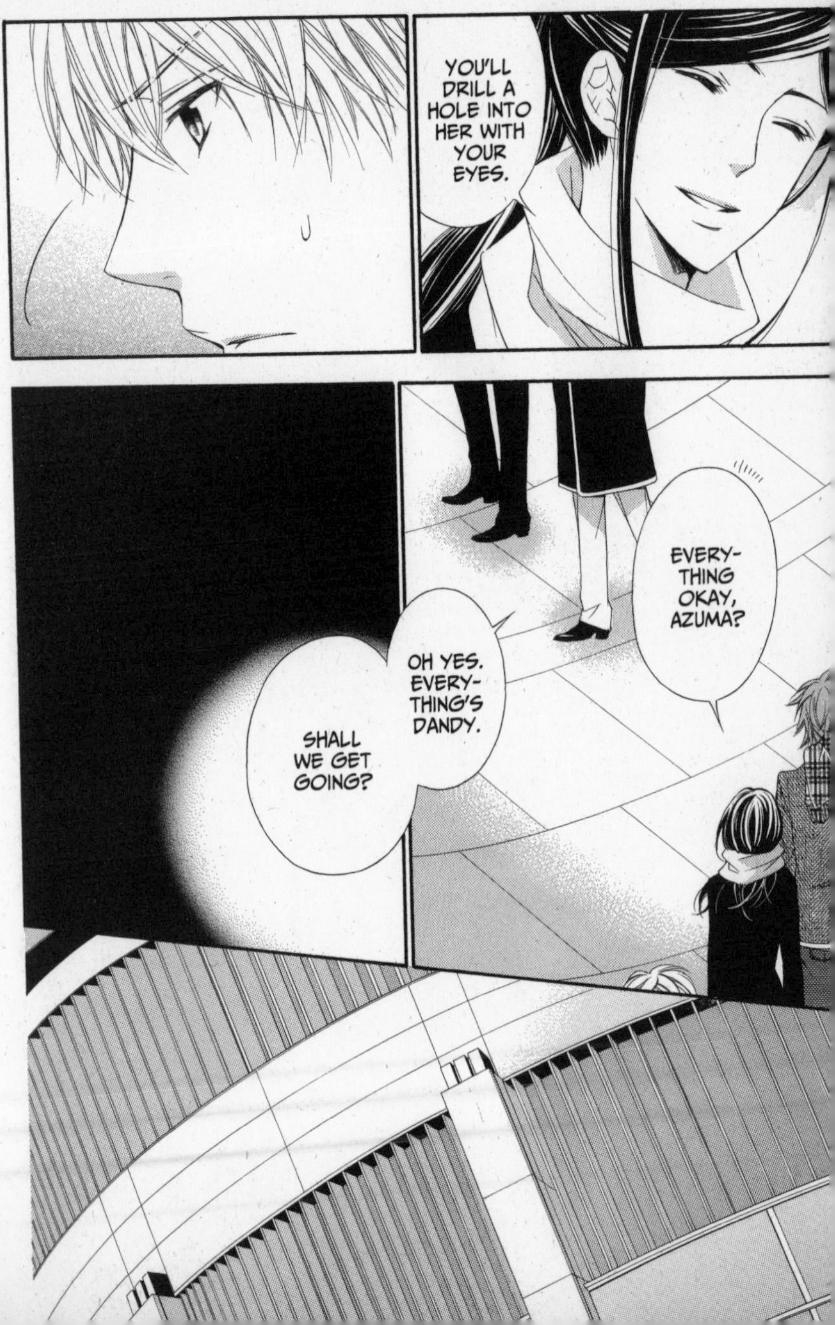
YOU'LL DRILL A HOLE INTO HER WITH YOUR EYES.
EVERY-THING OKAY, AZUMA?
OH YES. EVERY-THING'S DANDY.
SHALL WE GET GOING?

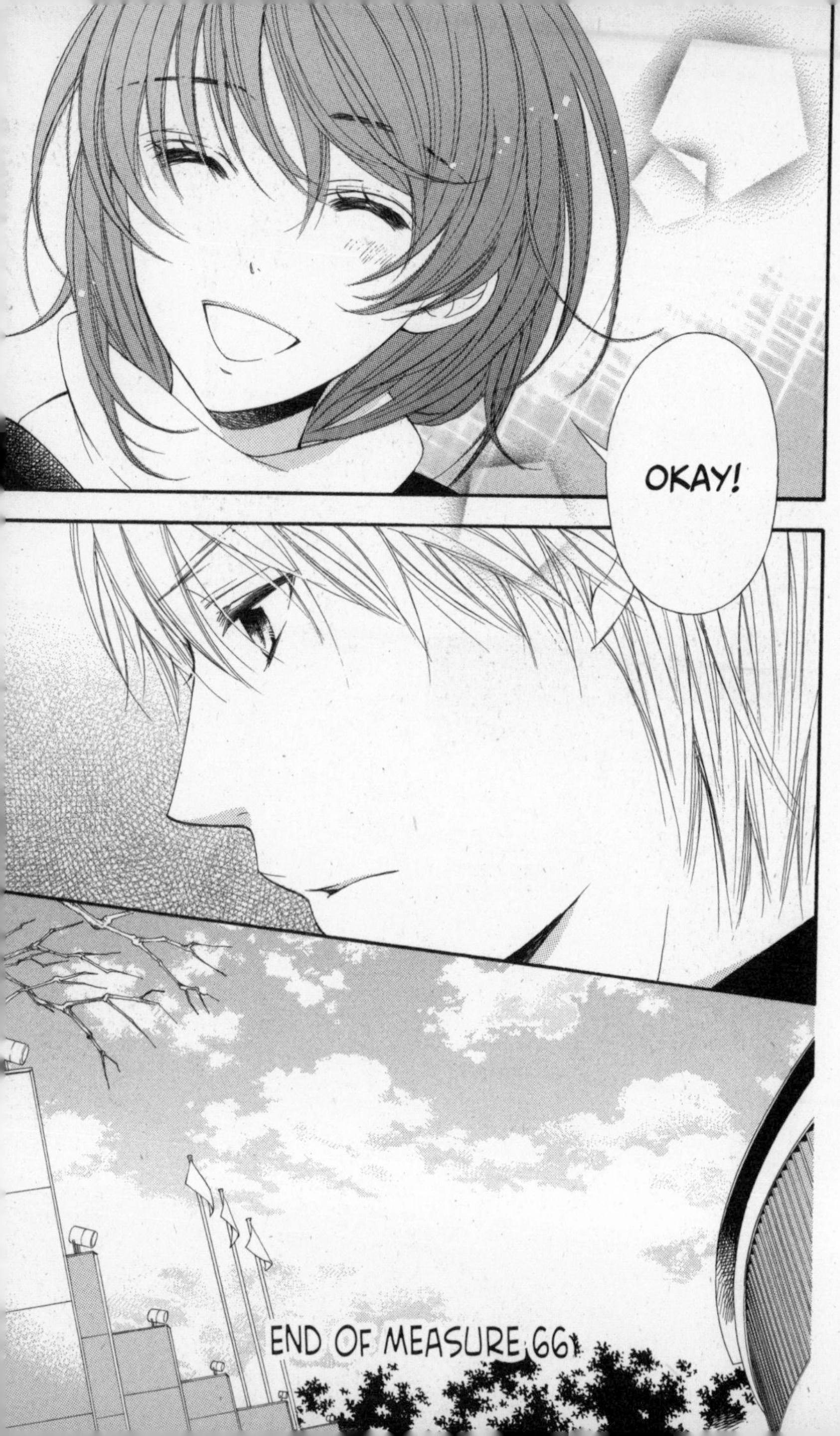
OKAY!
END OF MEASURE 66

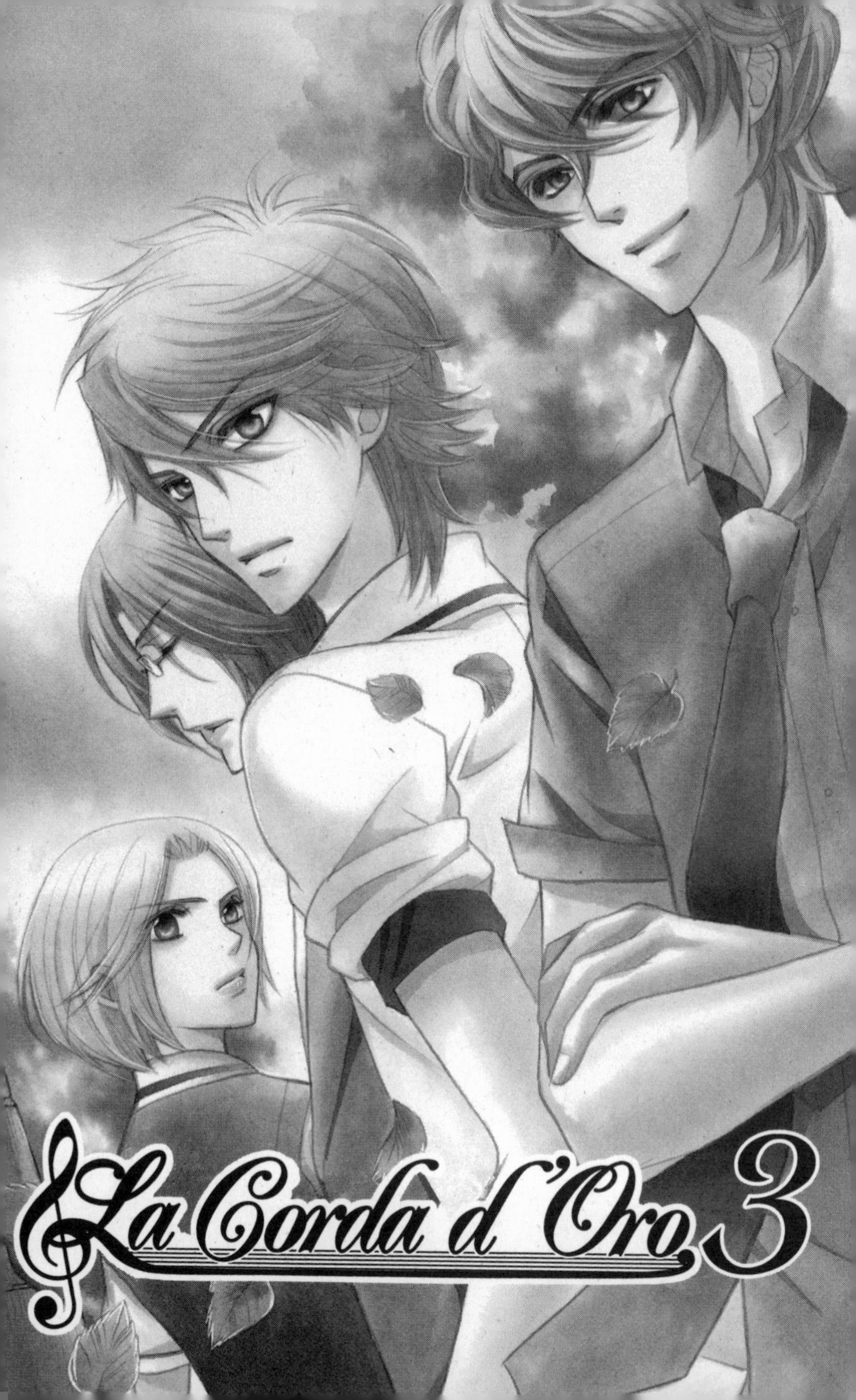
La Corda d'Oro 3

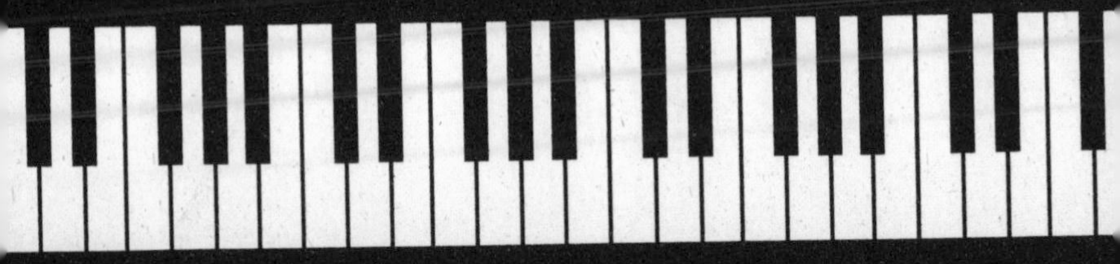

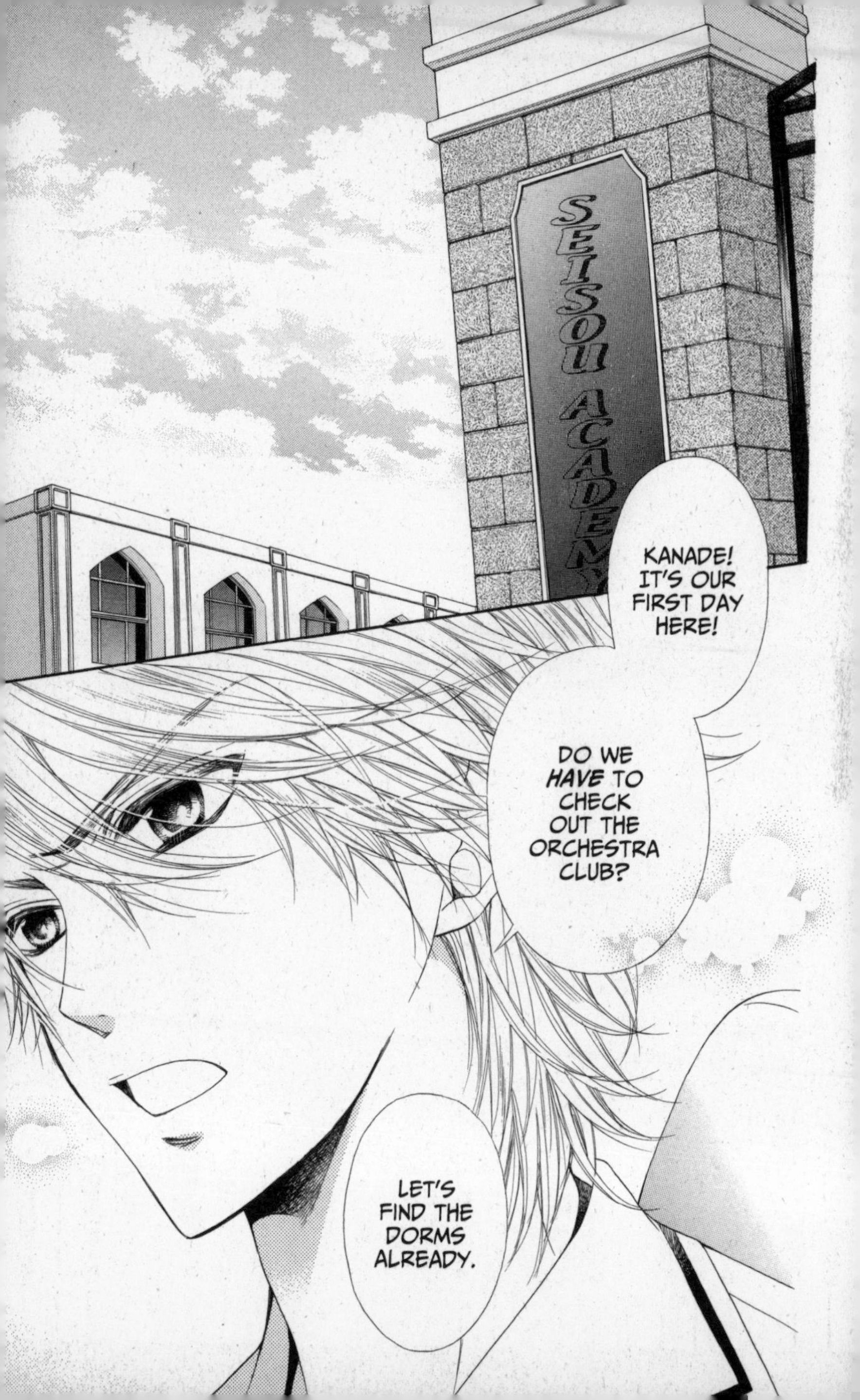
SEISOU ACADEMY
KANADE! IT'S OUR FIRST DAY HERE!
DO WE *HAVE* TO CHECK OUT THE ORCHESTRA CLUB?
LET'S FIND THE DORMS ALREADY.

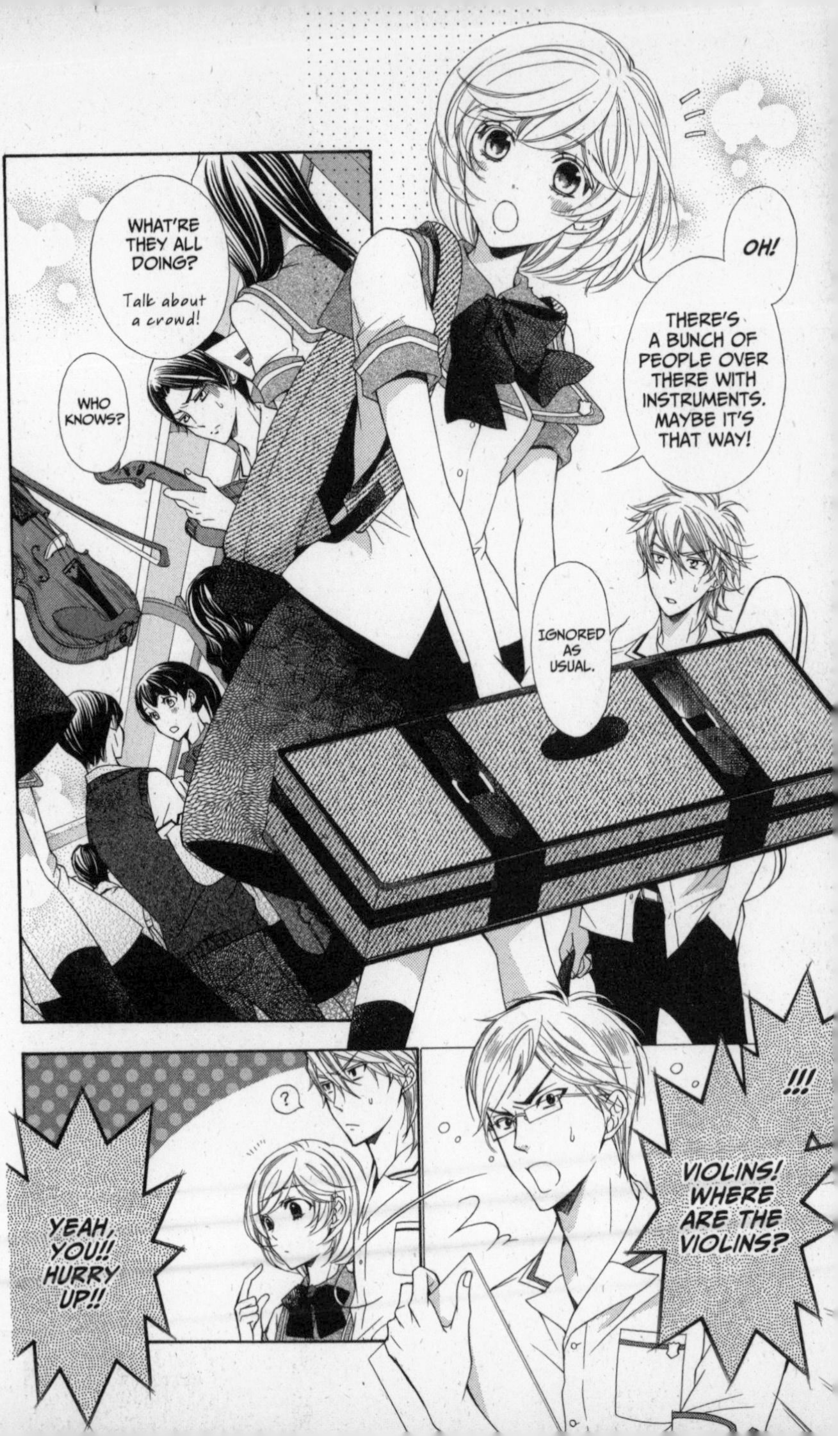
OH!
THERE'S A BUNCH OF PEOPLE OVER THERE WITH INSTRUMENTS. MAYBE IT'S THAT WAY!
IGNORED AS USUAL.
WHAT'RE THEY ALL DOING?
Talk about a crowd!
WHO KNOWS?
!!!
VIOLINS! WHERE ARE THE VIOLINS?
?
YEAH, YOU!! HURRY UP!!

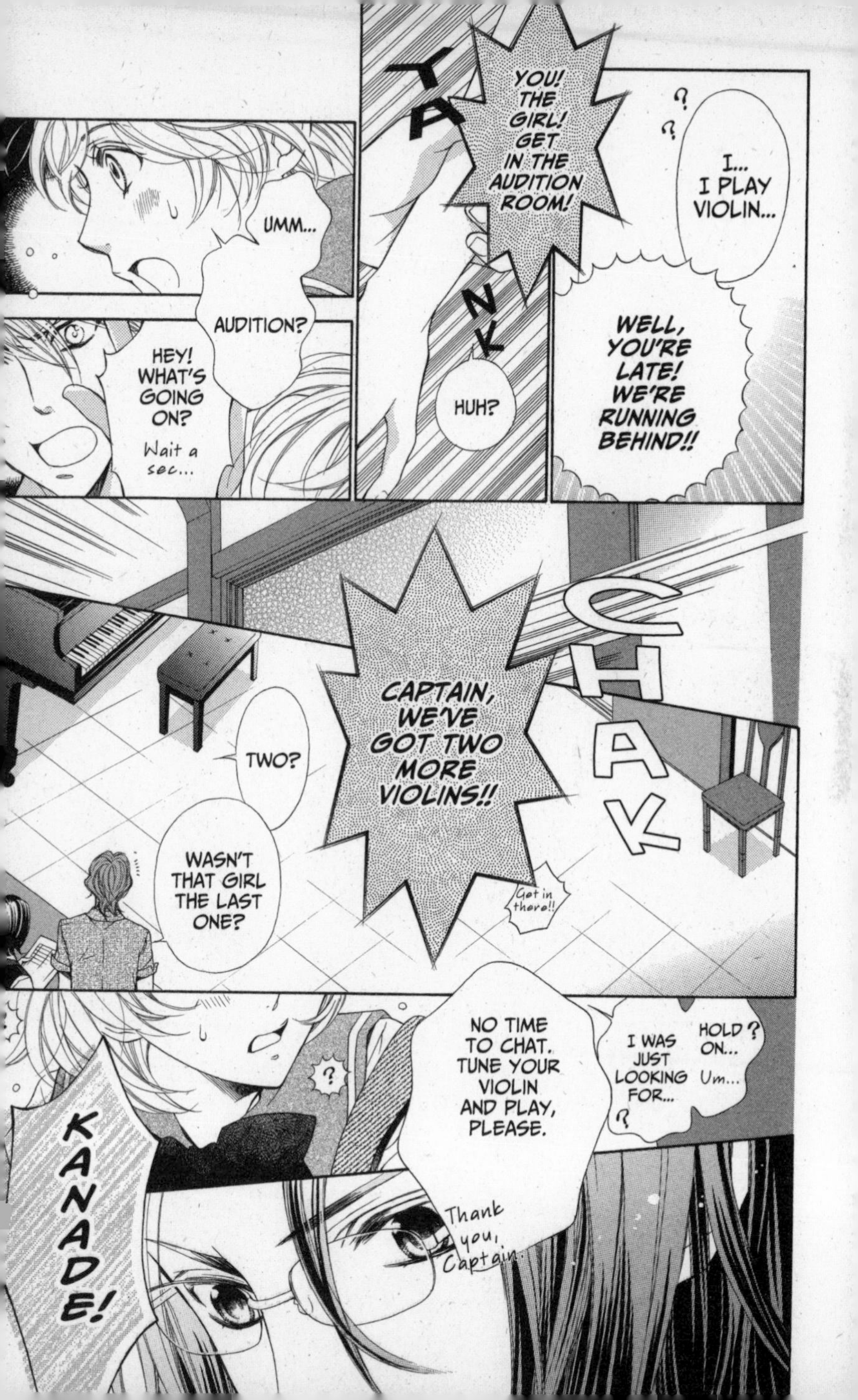
I... I PLAY VIOLIN...
WELL, YOU'RE LATE! WE'RE RUNNING BEHIND!!
YANK
YOU! THE GIRL! GET IN THE AUDITION ROOM!
HUH?
UMM... AUDITION?
HEY! WHAT'S GOING ON?
Wait a sec...
CHAK
CAPTAIN, WE'VE GOT TWO MORE VIOLINS!!
Get in there!!
TWO?
WASN'T THAT GIRL THE LAST ONE?
HOLD ON... Um...
I WAS JUST LOOKING FOR...
NO TIME TO CHAT. TUNE YOUR VIOLIN AND PLAY, PLEASE.
KANADE!
Thank you, Captain.

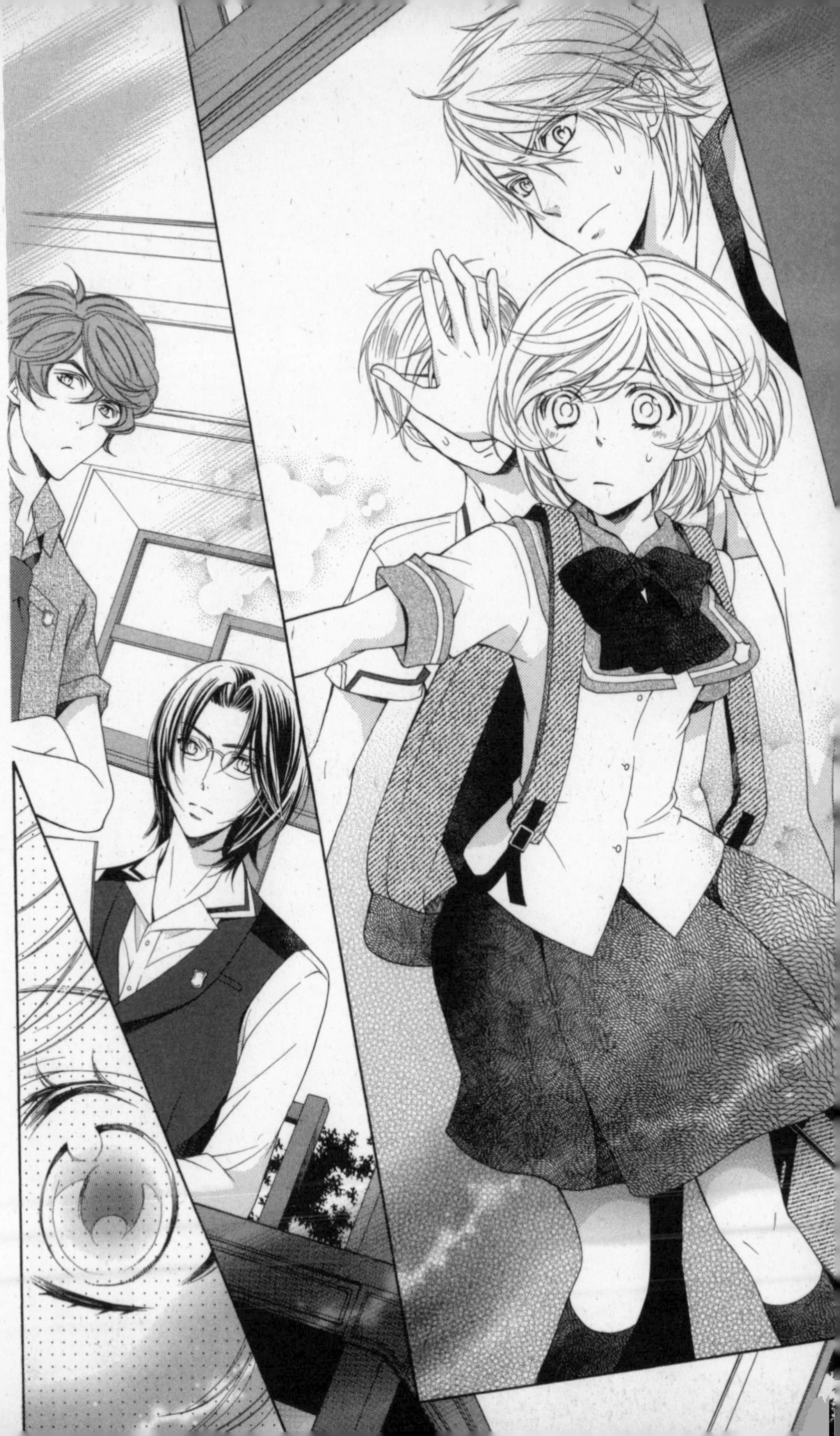

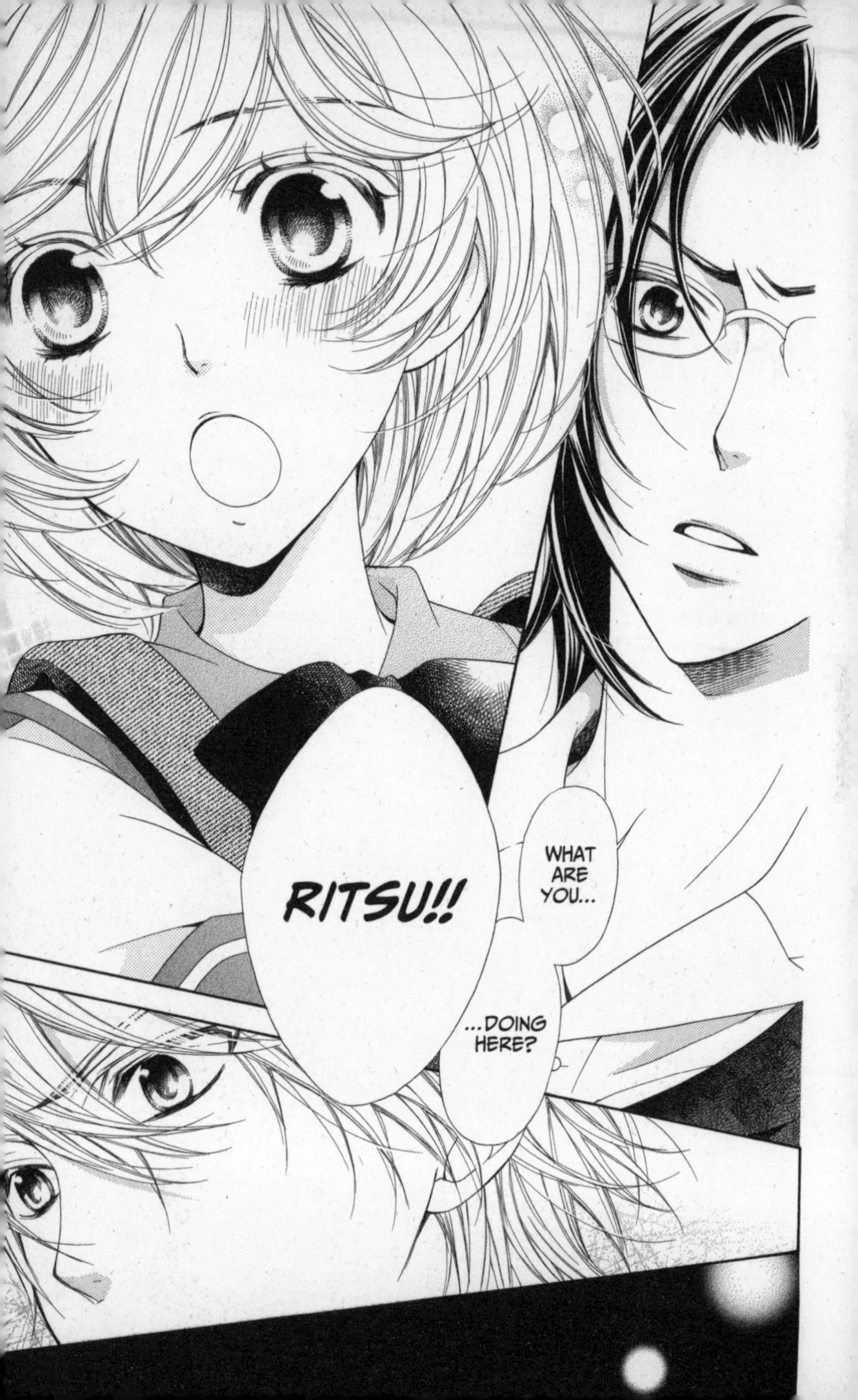
RITSU!!
WHAT ARE YOU...
...DOING HERE?

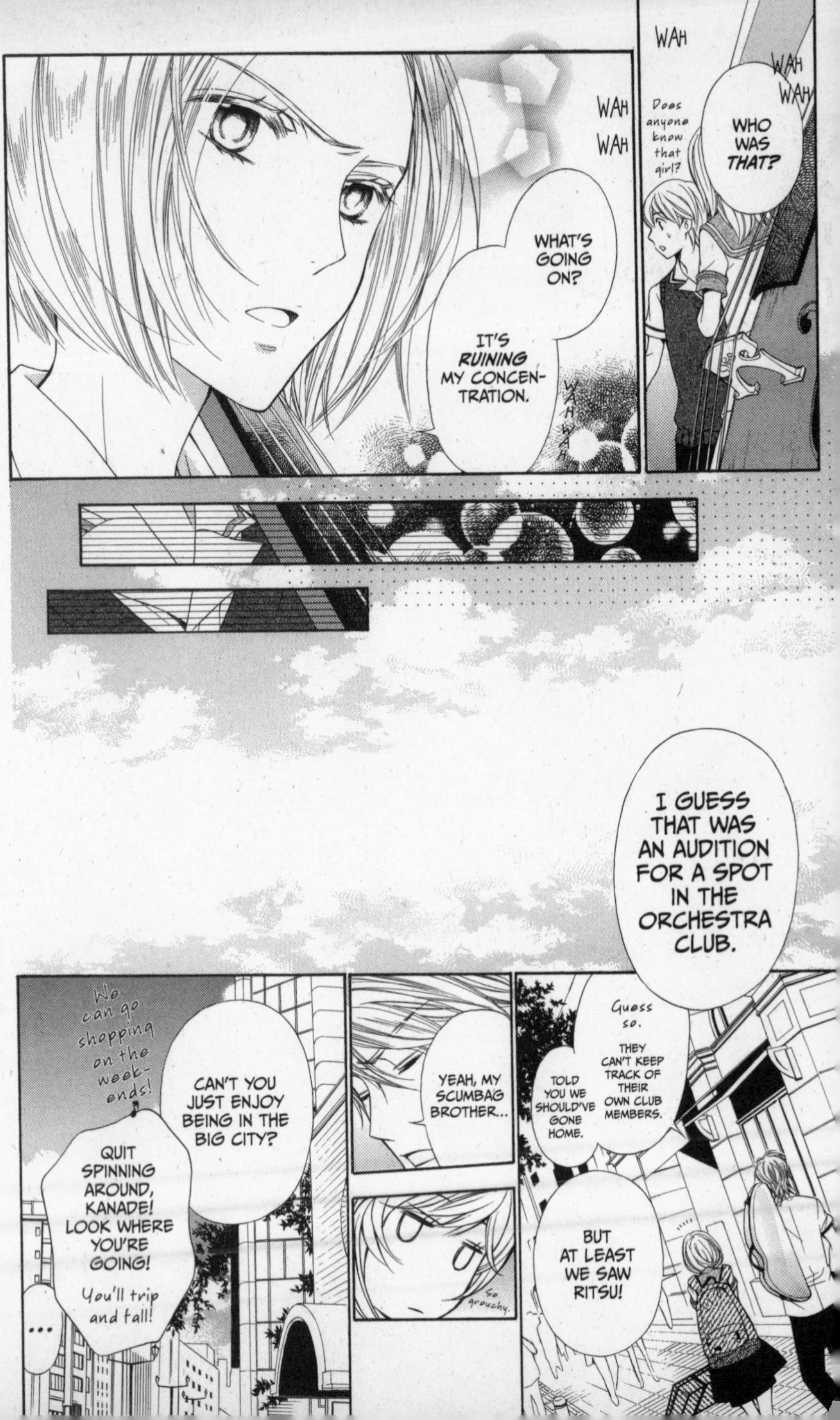
WAH
WAH WAH
WHO WAS THAT?
Does anyone know that girl?
WAH WAH
WHAT'S GOING ON?
IT'S RUINING MY CONCEN-TRATION.
WAH WAH
I GUESS THAT WAS AN AUDITION FOR A SPOT IN THE ORCHESTRA CLUB.
Guess so.
THEY CAN'T KEEP TRACK OF THEIR OWN CLUB MEMBERS.
TOLD YOU WE SHOULD'VE GONE HOME.
BUT AT LEAST WE SAW RITSU!
YEAH, MY SCUMBAG BROTHER...
So grouchy.
CAN'T YOU JUST ENJOY BEING IN THE BIG CITY?
We can go shopping on the week-ends!
QUIT SPINNING AROUND, KANADE! LOOK WHERE YOU'RE GOING!
You'll trip and fall!
...

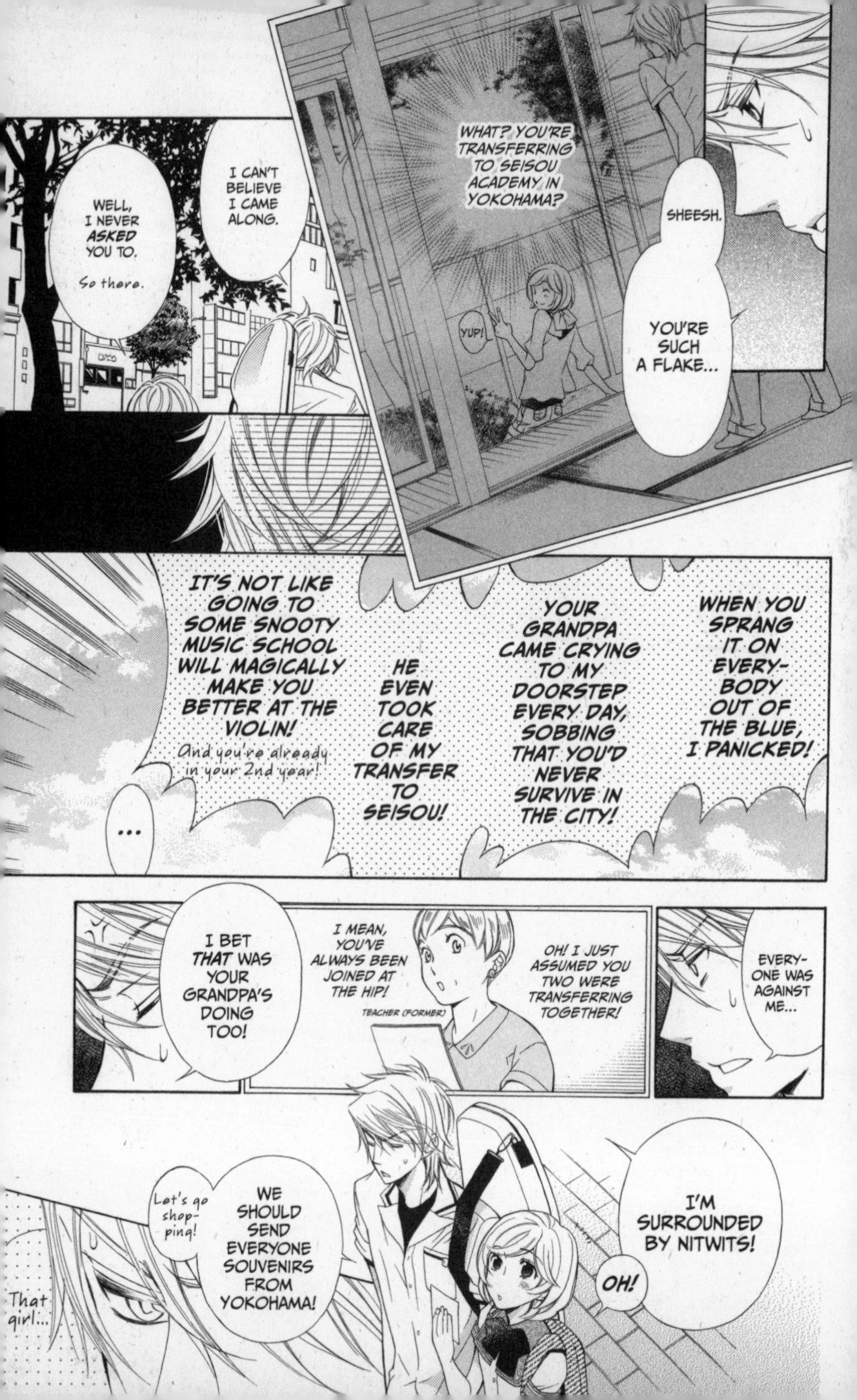
WHAT? YOU'RE TRANSFERRING TO SEISOU ACADEMY IN YOKOHAMA?
YUP!
SHEESH.
YOU'RE SUCH A FLAKE...
I CAN'T BELIEVE I CAME ALONG.
WELL, I NEVER ASKED YOU TO.
So there.
WHEN YOU SPRANG IT ON EVERYBODY OUT OF THE BLUE, I PANICKED!
YOUR GRANDPA CAME CRYING TO MY DOORSTEP EVERY DAY, SOBBING THAT YOU'D NEVER SURVIVE IN THE CITY!
HE EVEN TOOK CARE OF MY TRANSFER TO SEISOU!
IT'S NOT LIKE GOING TO SOME SNOOTY MUSIC SCHOOL WILL MAGICALLY MAKE YOU BETTER AT THE VIOLIN!
And you're already in your 2nd year!
...
EVERYONE WAS AGAINST ME...
OH! I JUST ASSUMED YOU TWO WERE TRANSFERRING TOGETHER!
I MEAN, YOU'VE ALWAYS BEEN JOINED AT THE HIP!
TEACHER (FORMER)
I BET THAT WAS YOUR GRANDPA'S DOING TOO!
I'M SURROUNDED BY NITWITS!
OH!
WE SHOULD SEND EVERYONE SOUVENIRS FROM YOKOHAMA!
Let's go shopping!
That girl...

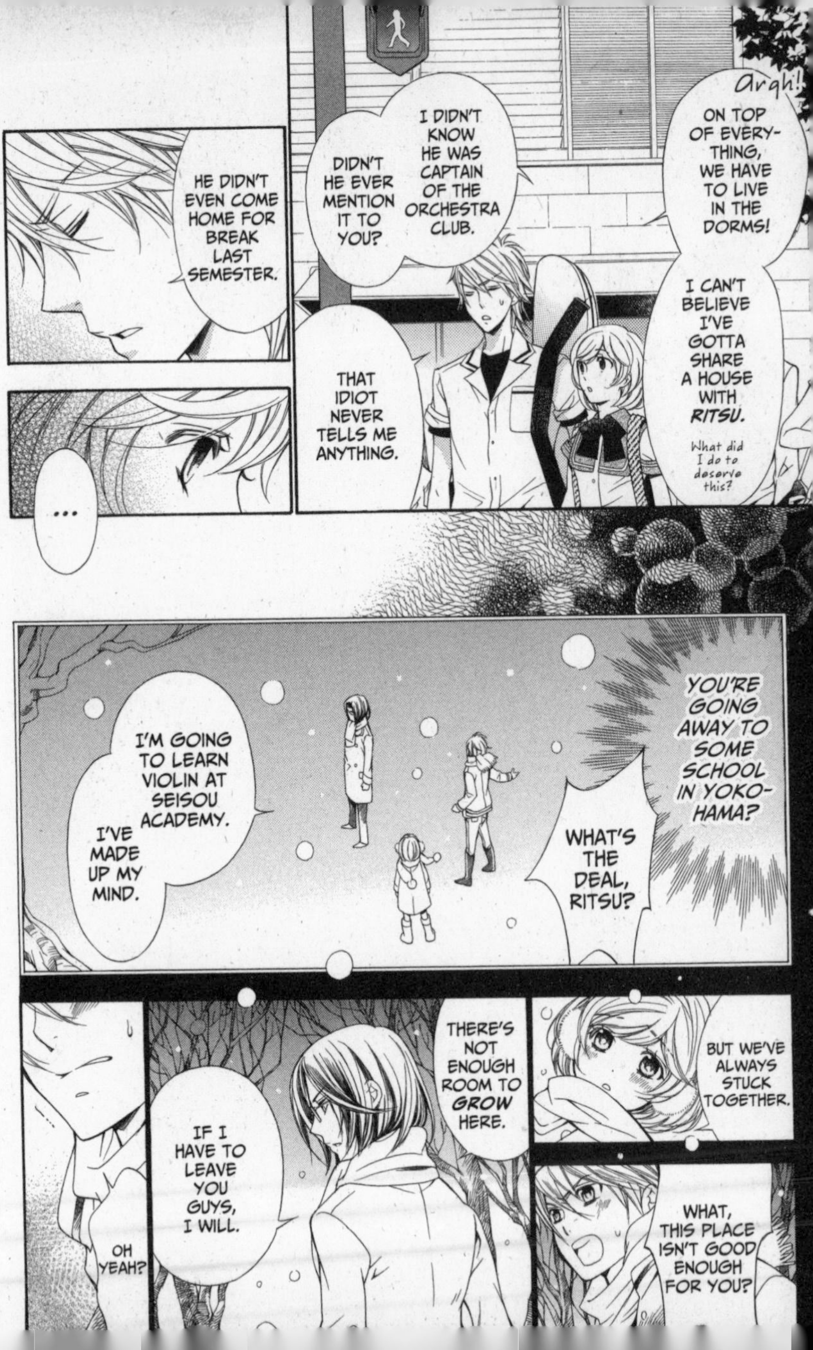
Argh!
ON TOP OF EVERYTHING, WE HAVE TO LIVE IN THE DORMS!
I CAN'T BELIEVE I'VE GOTTA SHARE A HOUSE WITH *RITSU.*
What did I do to deserve this?
I DIDN'T KNOW HE WAS CAPTAIN OF THE ORCHESTRA CLUB.
DIDN'T HE EVER MENTION IT TO YOU?
THAT IDIOT NEVER TELLS ME ANYTHING.
HE DIDN'T EVEN COME HOME FOR BREAK LAST SEMESTER.
...
YOU'RE GOING AWAY TO SOME SCHOOL IN YOKOHAMA?
WHAT'S THE DEAL, RITSU?
I'M GOING TO LEARN VIOLIN AT SEISOU ACADEMY.
I'VE MADE UP MY MIND.
BUT WE'VE ALWAYS STUCK TOGETHER.
WHAT, THIS PLACE ISN'T GOOD ENOUGH FOR YOU?
THERE'S NOT ENOUGH ROOM TO *GROW* HERE.
IF I HAVE TO LEAVE YOU GUYS, I WILL.
OH YEAH?

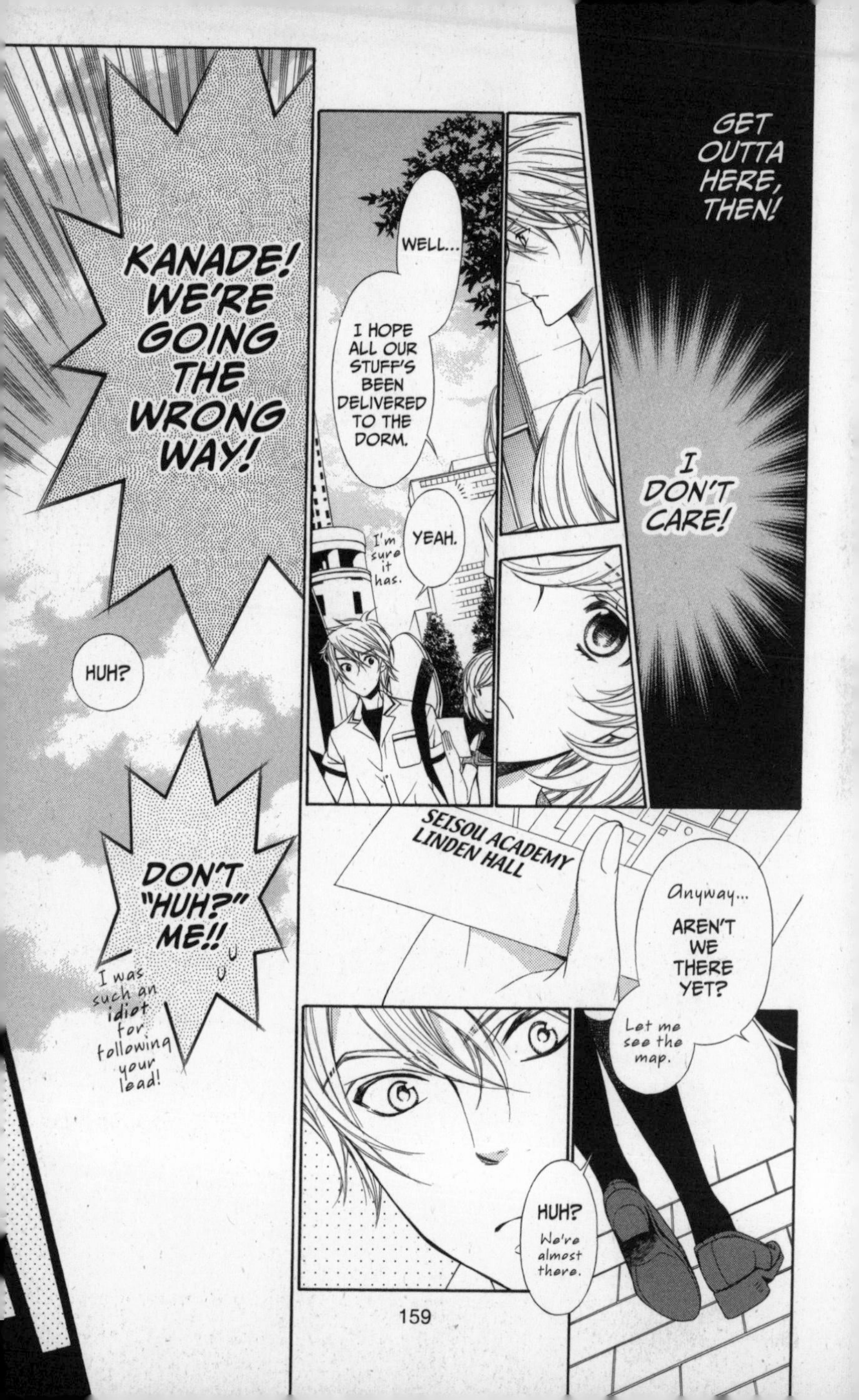
GET OUTTA HERE, THEN!
I DON'T CARE!
WELL...
I HOPE ALL OUR STUFF'S BEEN DELIVERED TO THE DORM.
YEAH.
I'm sure it has.
SEISOU ACADEMY LINDEN HALL
Anyway... AREN'T WE THERE YET?
Let me see the map.
HUH?
We're almost there.
KANADE! WE'RE GOING THE WRONG WAY!
HUH?
DON'T "HUH?" ME!!
I was such an idiot for following your lead!

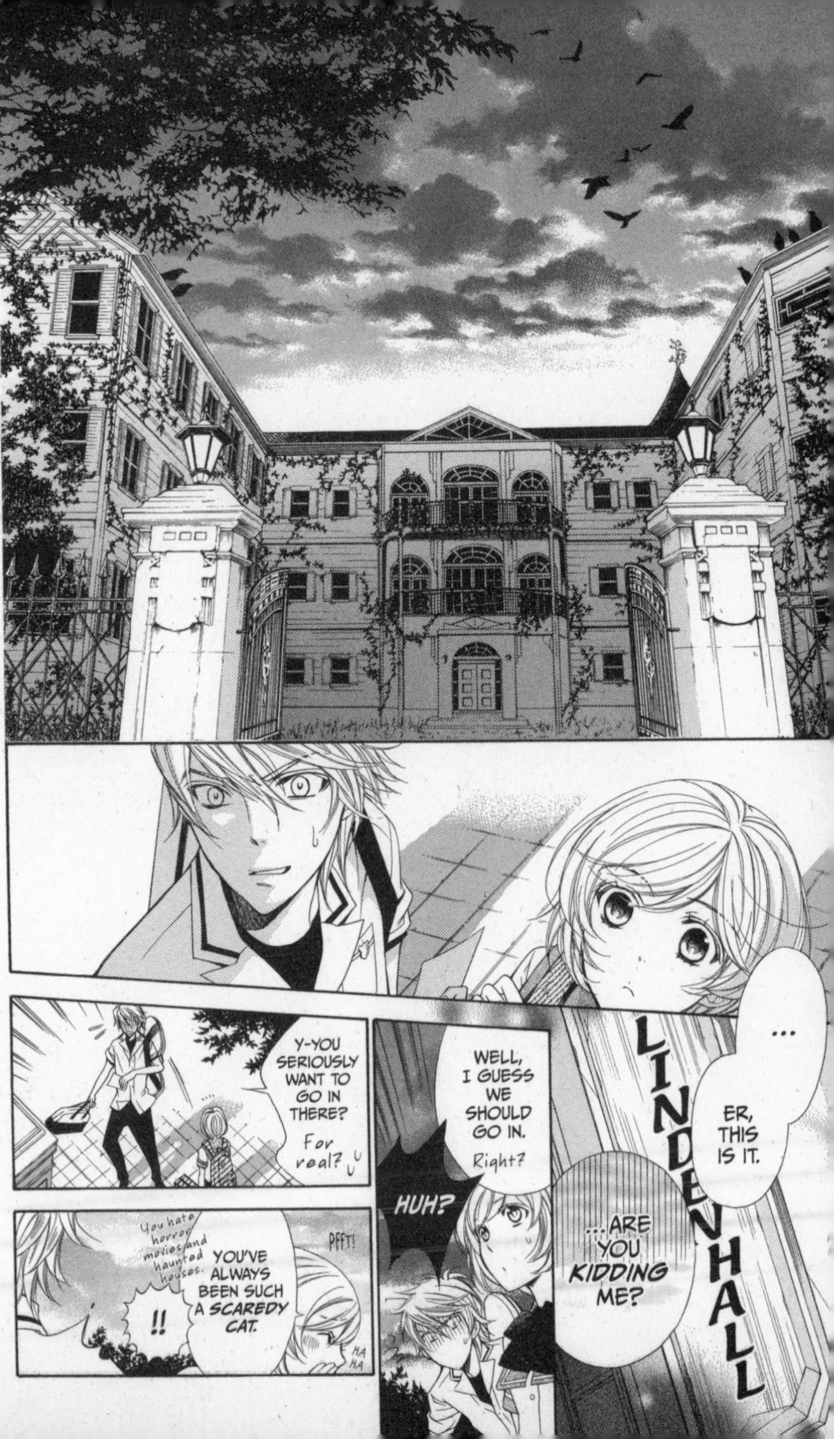
...
ER, THIS IS IT.
LINDENHALL
...ARE YOU KIDDING ME?
WELL, I GUESS WE SHOULD GO IN.
Right?
HUH?
Y-YOU SERIOUSLY WANT TO GO IN THERE?
For real?
PFFT!
YOU'VE ALWAYS BEEN SUCH A SCAREDY CAT.
You hate horror movies and haunted houses.
HA HA
!!

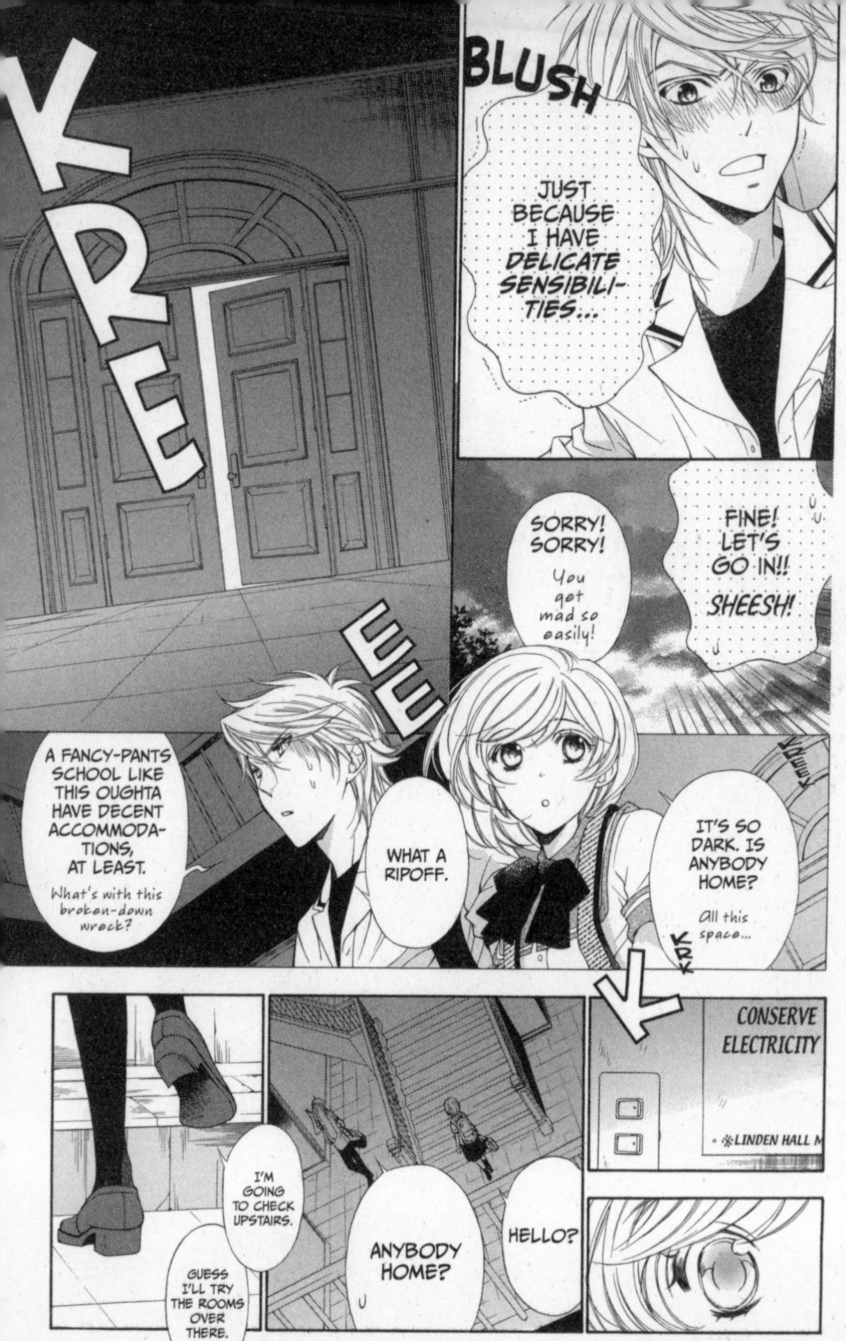
BLUSH
JUST BECAUSE I HAVE *DELICATE SENSIBILITIES*...
FINE! LET'S GO IN!! *SHEESH!*
SORRY! SORRY! You get mad so easily!
KREE
EEE
IT'S SO DARK. IS ANYBODY HOME? All this space...
WHAT A RIPOFF.
A FANCY-PANTS SCHOOL LIKE THIS OUGHTA HAVE DECENT ACCOMMODATIONS, AT LEAST. What's with this broken-down wreck?
KRK
K
CONSERVE ELECTRICITY
※LINDEN HALL M
HELLO?
ANYBODY HOME?
I'M GOING TO CHECK UPSTAIRS.
GUESS I'LL TRY THE ROOMS OVER THERE.

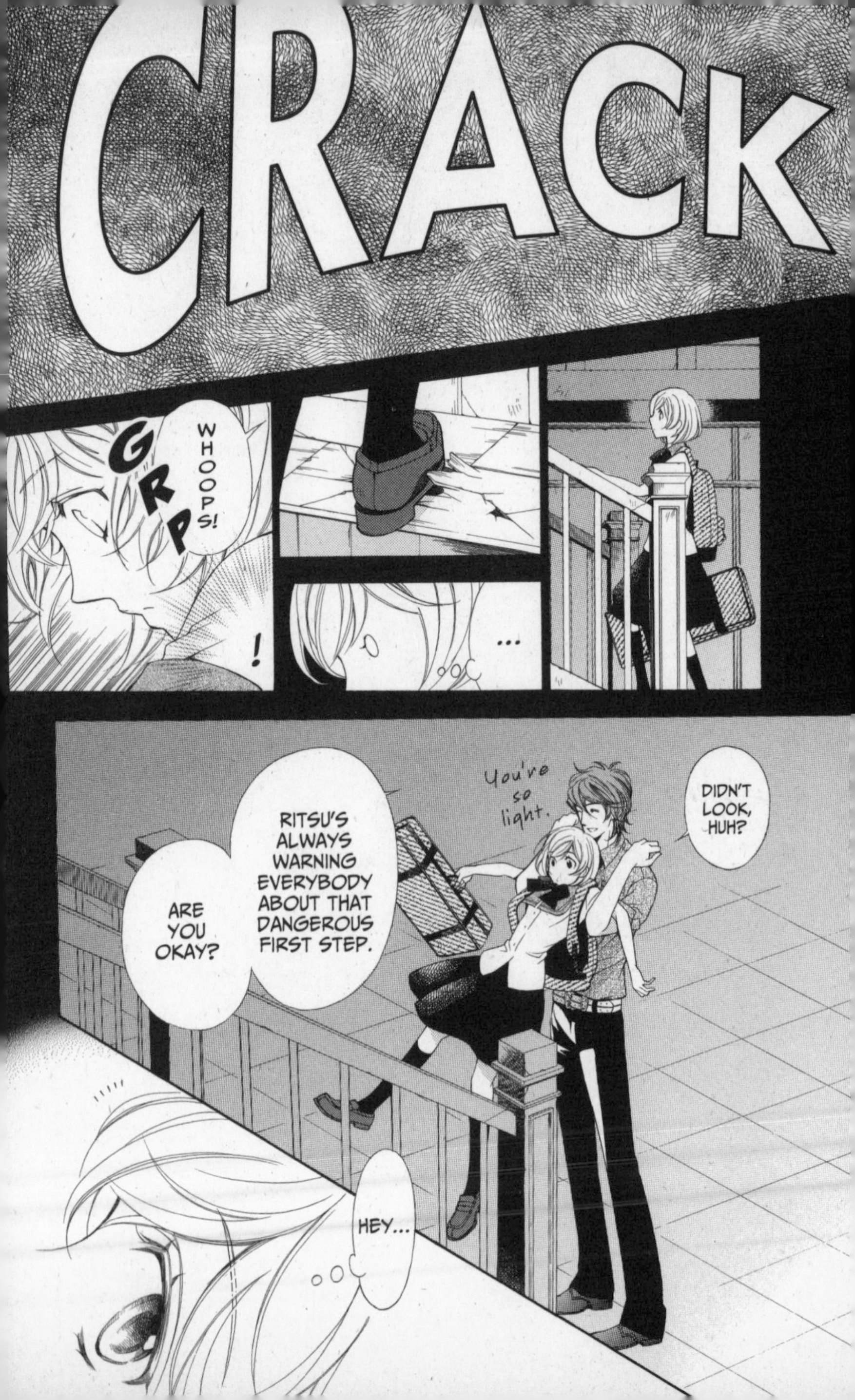
CRACK
...
WHOOPS!
GRP
!
DIDN'T LOOK, HUH?
You're so light.
RITSU'S ALWAYS WARNING EVERYBODY ABOUT THAT DANGEROUS FIRST STEP.
ARE YOU OKAY?
HEY...

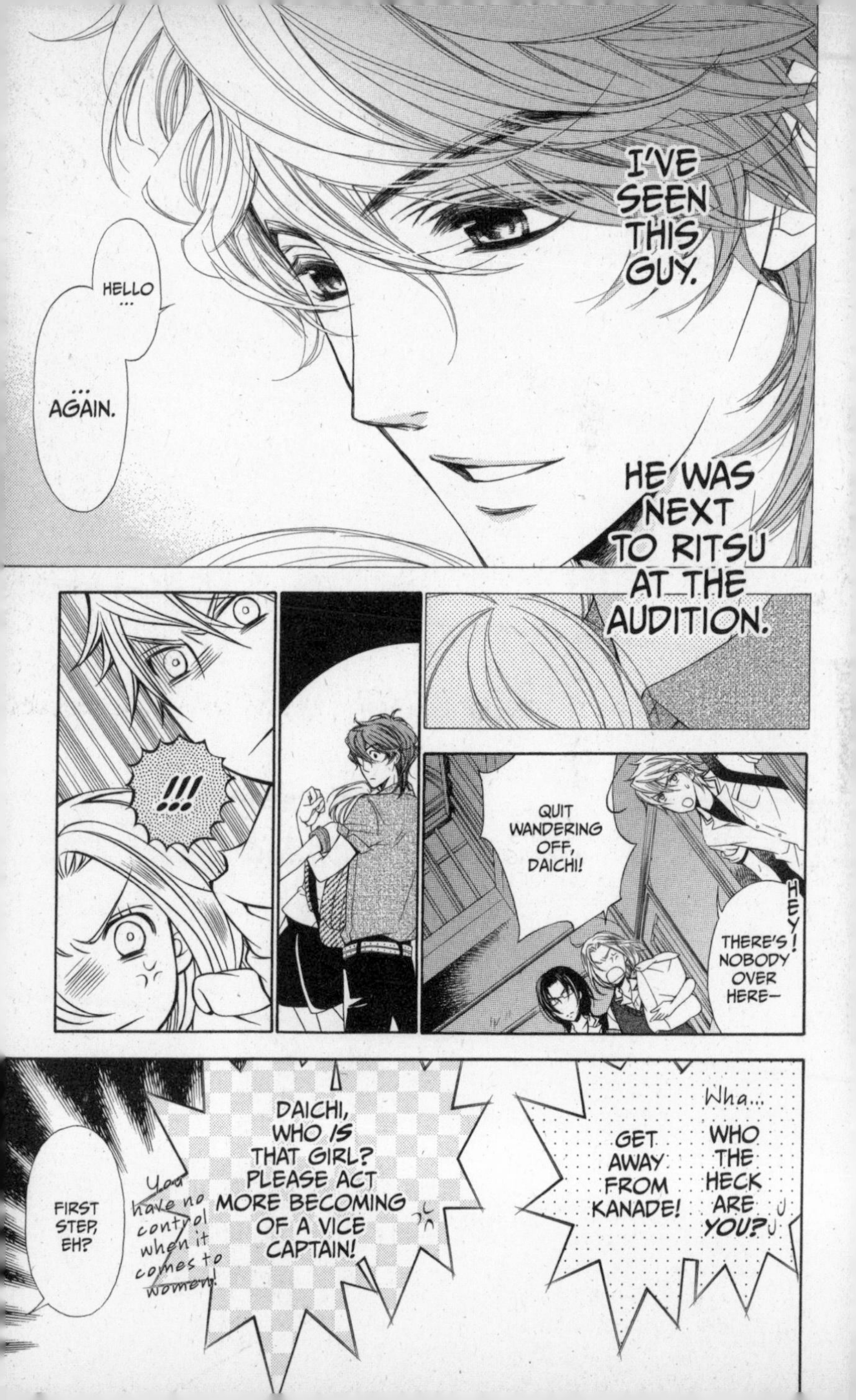
I'VE SEEN THIS GUY.
HELLO ...
... AGAIN.
HE WAS NEXT TO RITSU AT THE AUDITION.
HEY!
THERE'S NOBODY OVER HERE—
QUIT WANDERING OFF, DAICHI!
!!!
Wha...
WHO THE HECK ARE *YOU*?
GET AWAY FROM KANADE!
DAICHI, WHO *IS* THAT GIRL? PLEASE ACT MORE BECOMING OF A VICE CAPTAIN!
You have no control when it comes to women!
FIRST STEP, EH?

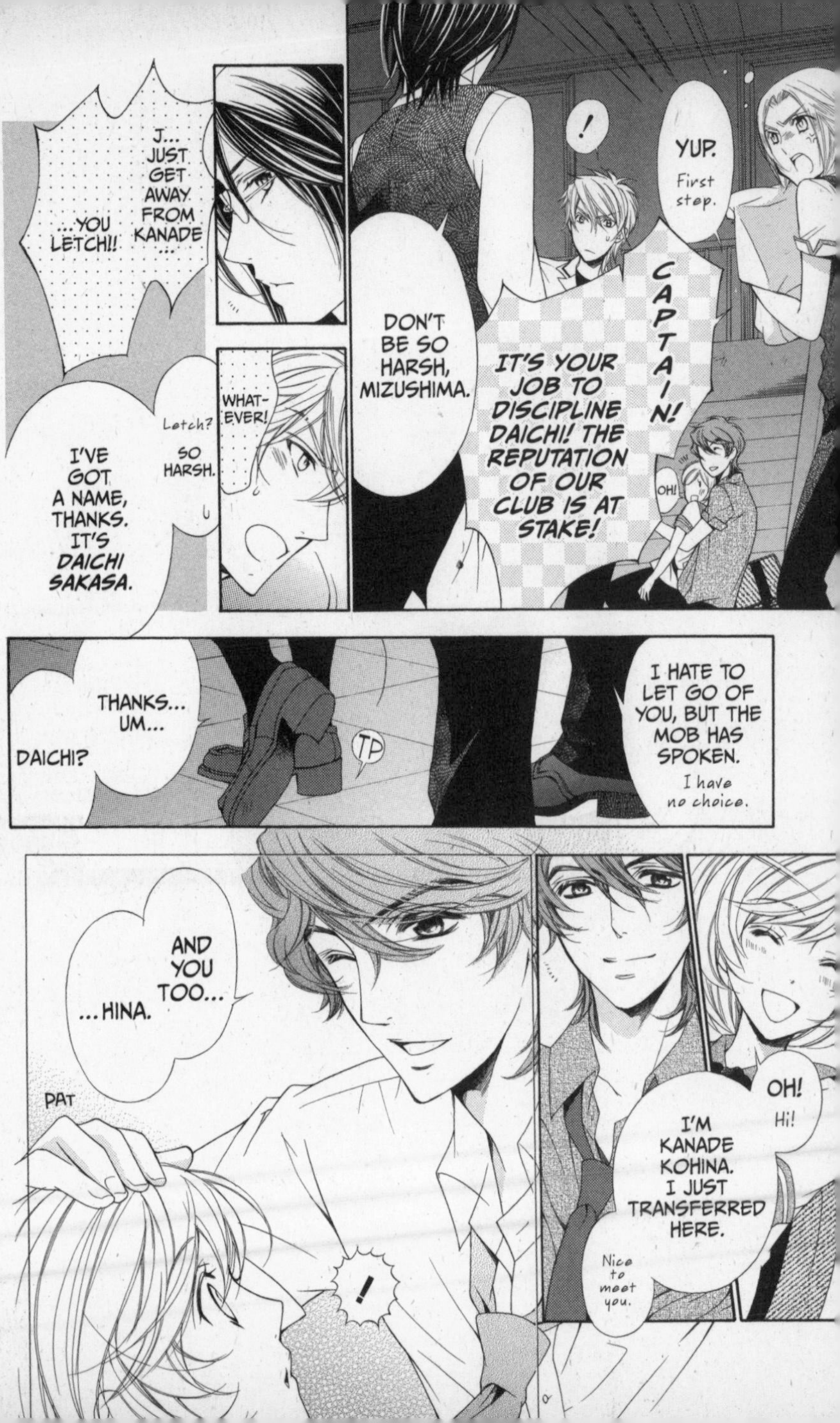

YUP.
First step.
CAPTAIN!
IT'S YOUR JOB TO DISCIPLINE DAICHI! THE REPUTATION OF OUR CLUB IS AT STAKE!
!
DON'T BE SO HARSH, MIZUSHIMA.
OH!
J... JUST GET AWAY FROM KANADE...
...YOU LETCH!!
WHAT-EVER!
SO HARSH.
Letch?
I'VE GOT A NAME, THANKS. IT'S DAICHI SAKASA.
I HATE TO LET GO OF YOU, BUT THE MOB HAS SPOKEN.
I have no choice.
TP
THANKS... UM...
DAICHI?
OH!
Hi!
I'M KANADE KOHINA. I JUST TRANSFERRED HERE.
Nice to meet you.
AND YOU TOO...
...HINA.
PAT
!

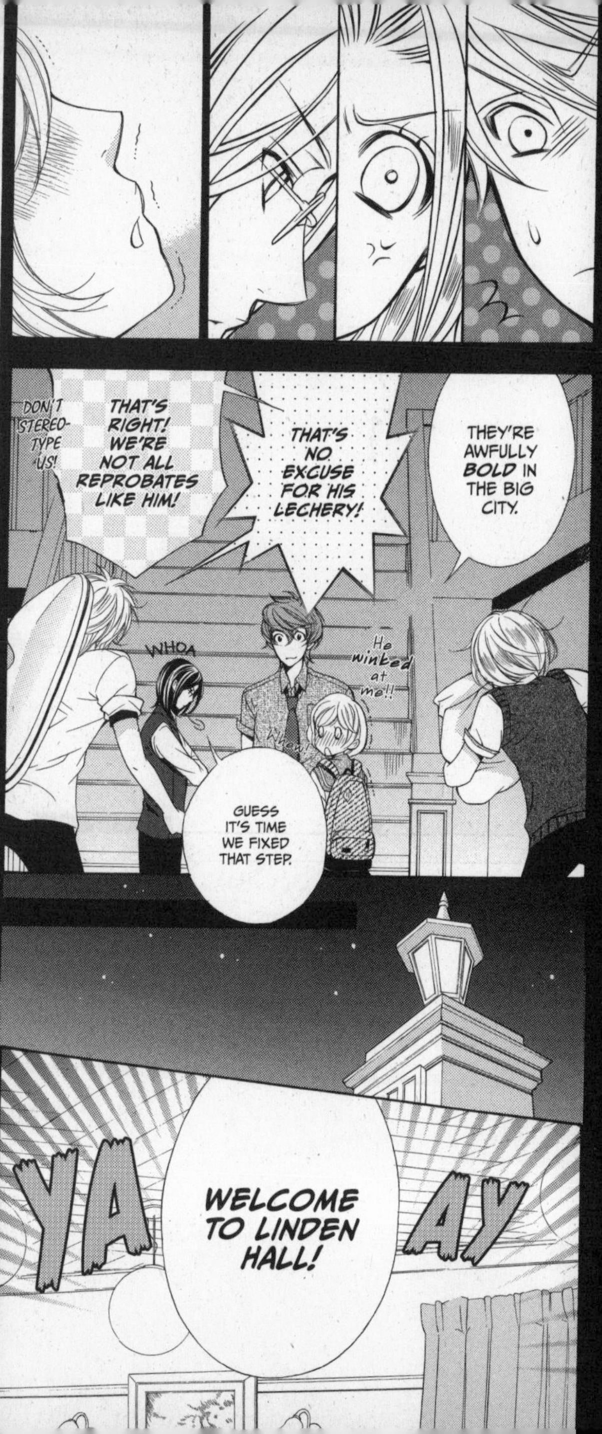
THEY'RE AWFULLY BOLD IN THE BIG CITY.
He winked at me!!
THAT'S NO EXCUSE FOR HIS LECHERY!
THAT'S RIGHT! WE'RE NOT ALL REPROBATES LIKE HIM!
DON'T STEREOTYPE US!
WHOA
Whew!
GUESS IT'S TIME WE FIXED THAT STEP.
WELCOME TO LINDEN HALL!
YA AY

→ The heroine of this story is Kahoko...I mean Kanade. She's in the Music school rather than Gen Ed. The guys are a lot different, but I hope you find some to your liking.

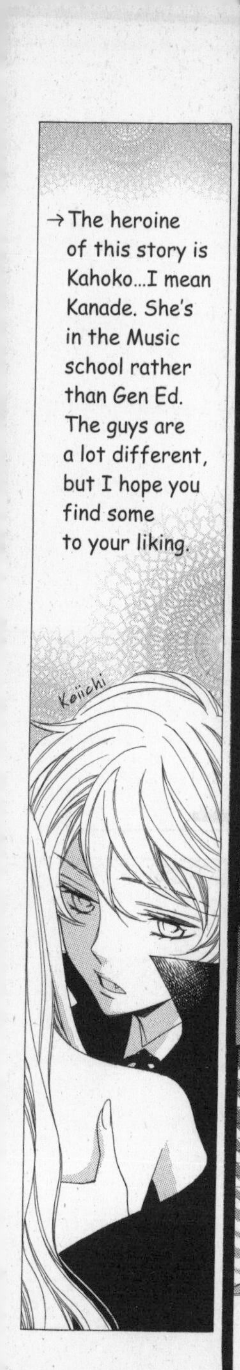
Keiichi

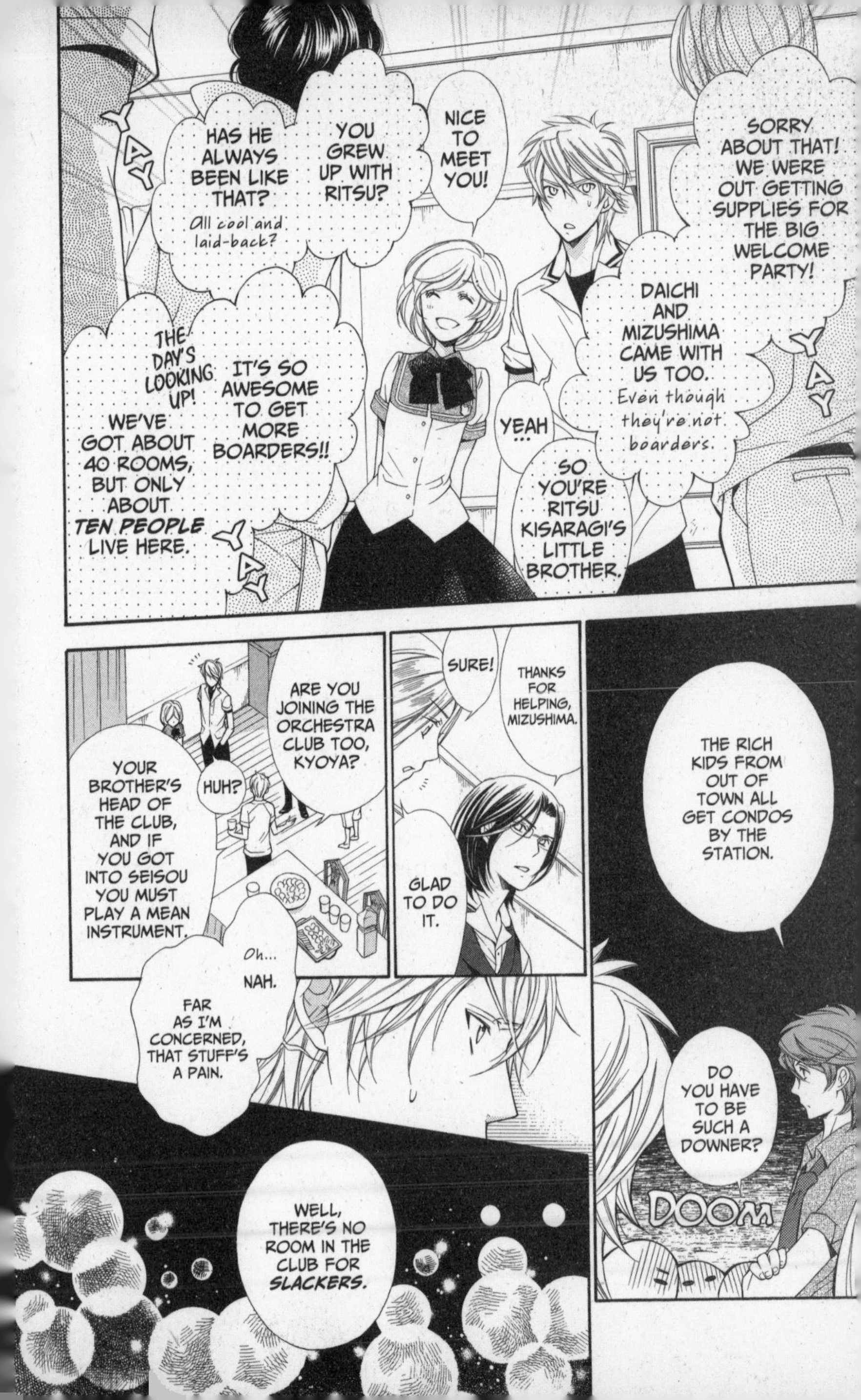
SORRY ABOUT THAT! WE WERE OUT GETTING SUPPLIES FOR THE BIG WELCOME PARTY!
YAY
NICE TO MEET YOU!
YOU GREW UP WITH RITSU?
HAS HE ALWAYS BEEN LIKE THAT?
All cool and laid-back?
YAY
DAICHI AND MIZUSHIMA CAME WITH US TOO.
Even though they're not boarders.
YEAH...
SO YOU'RE RITSU KISARAGI'S LITTLE BROTHER.
IT'S SO AWESOME TO GET MORE BOARDERS!!
THE DAY'S LOOKING UP!
WE'VE GOT ABOUT 40 ROOMS, BUT ONLY ABOUT *TEN PEOPLE* LIVE HERE.
YAY
THE RICH KIDS FROM OUT OF TOWN ALL GET CONDOS BY THE STATION.
DO YOU HAVE TO BE SUCH A DOWNER?
DOOM
THANKS FOR HELPING, MIZUSHIMA.
SURE!
GLAD TO DO IT.
ARE YOU JOINING THE ORCHESTRA CLUB TOO, KYOYA?
HUH?
YOUR BROTHER'S HEAD OF THE CLUB, AND IF YOU GOT INTO SEISOU YOU MUST PLAY A MEAN INSTRUMENT.
Oh...
NAH.
FAR AS I'M CONCERNED, THAT STUFF'S A PAIN.
WELL, THERE'S NO ROOM IN THE CLUB FOR *SLACKERS.*

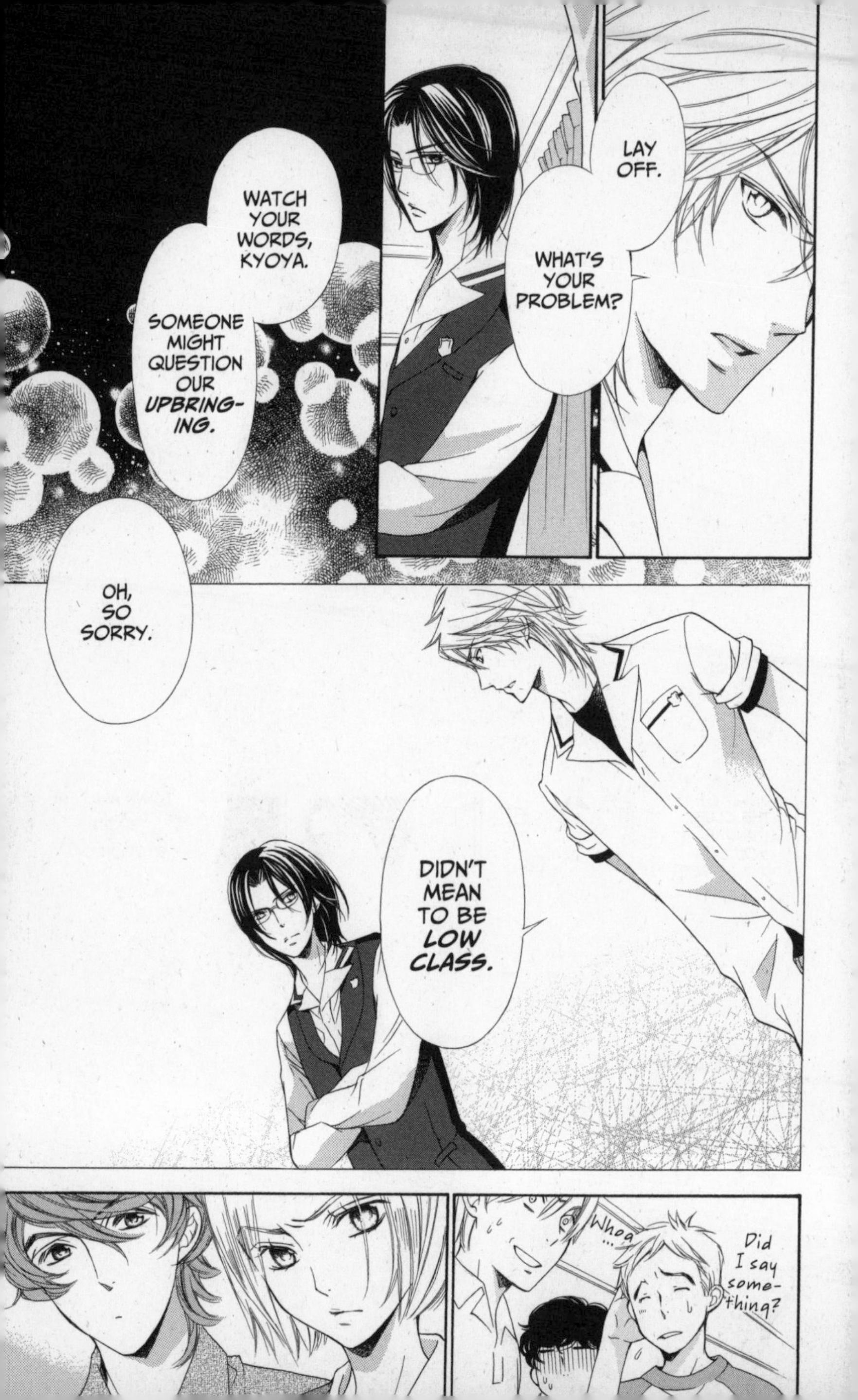
LAY OFF.
WHAT'S YOUR PROBLEM?
WATCH YOUR WORDS, KYOYA.
SOMEONE MIGHT QUESTION OUR *UPBRINGING.*
OH, SO SORRY.
DIDN'T MEAN TO BE *LOW CLASS.*
Whoa...
Did I say something?

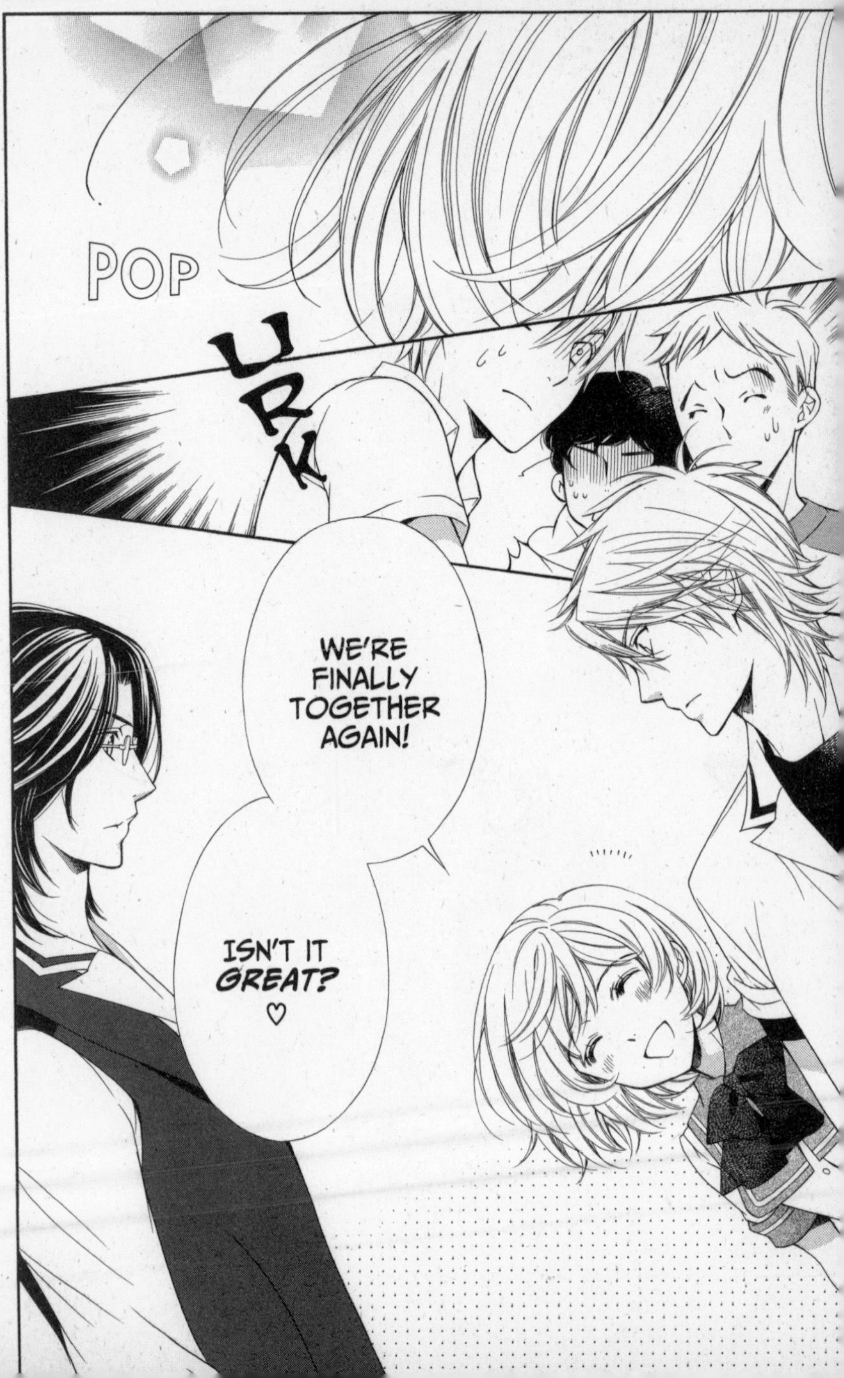
POP
URK
WE'RE FINALLY TOGETHER AGAIN!
ISN'T IT GREAT? ♡

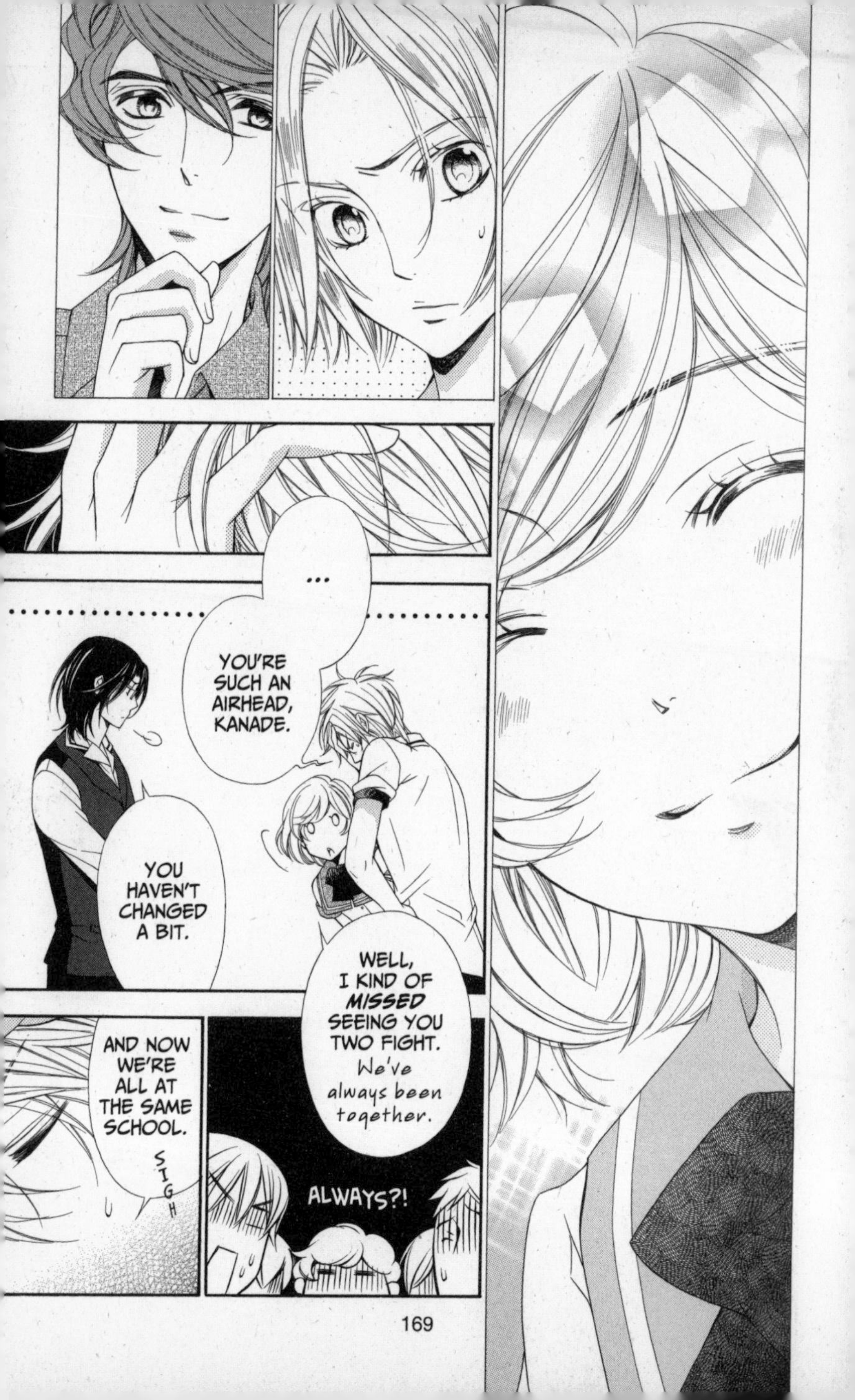
...
YOU'RE SUCH AN AIRHEAD, KANADE.
YOU HAVEN'T CHANGED A BIT.
WELL, I KIND OF ***MISSED*** SEEING YOU TWO FIGHT. We've always been together.
ALWAYS?!
AND NOW WE'RE ALL AT THE SAME SCHOOL.
SIGH

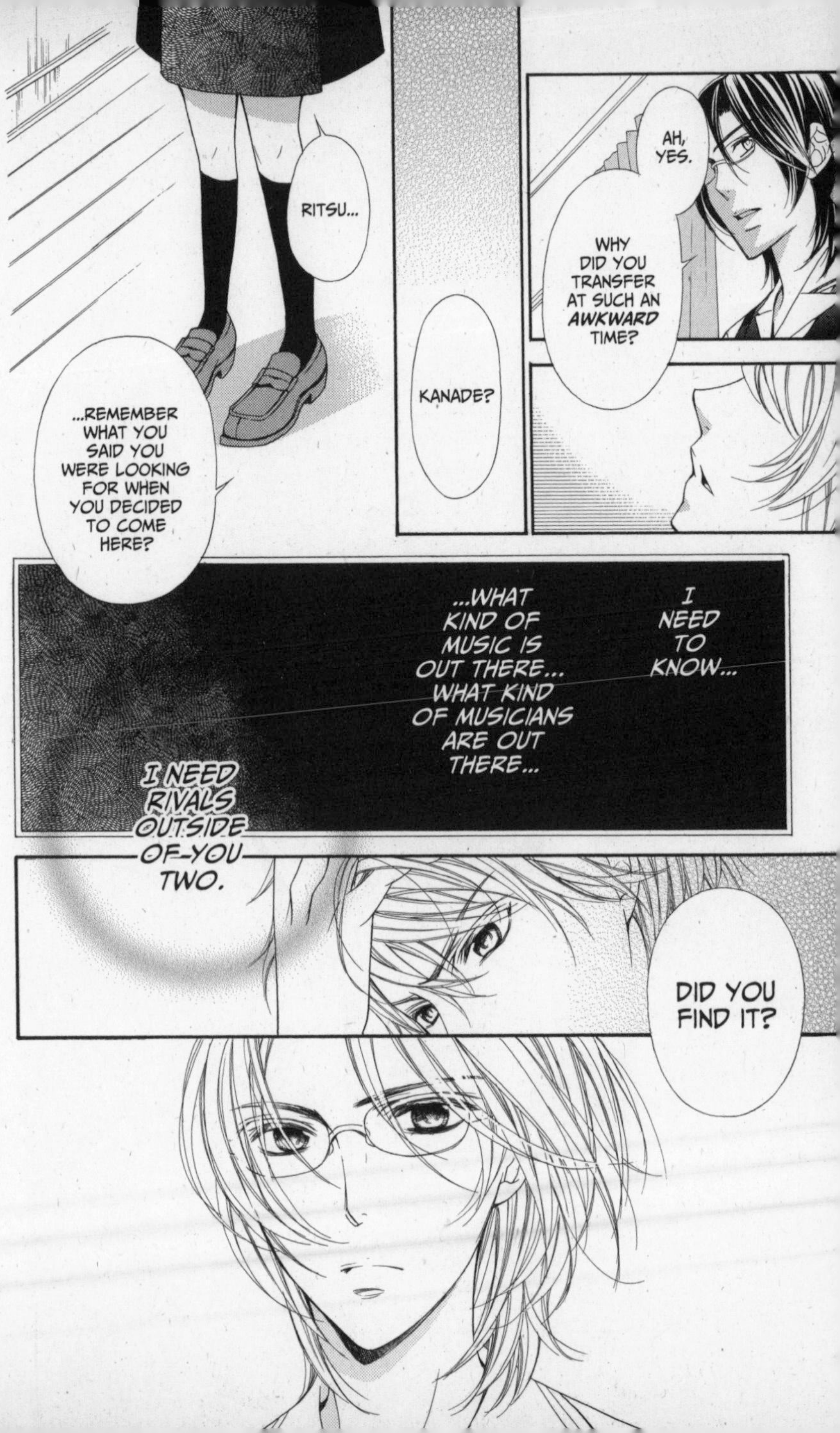
AH, YES.
WHY DID YOU TRANSFER AT SUCH AN *AWKWARD* TIME?
KANADE?
RITSU...
...REMEMBER WHAT YOU SAID YOU WERE LOOKING FOR WHEN YOU DECIDED TO COME HERE?
I NEED TO KNOW...
...WHAT KIND OF MUSIC IS OUT THERE... WHAT KIND OF MUSICIANS ARE OUT THERE...
I NEED RIVALS OUTSIDE OF YOU TWO.
DID YOU FIND IT?

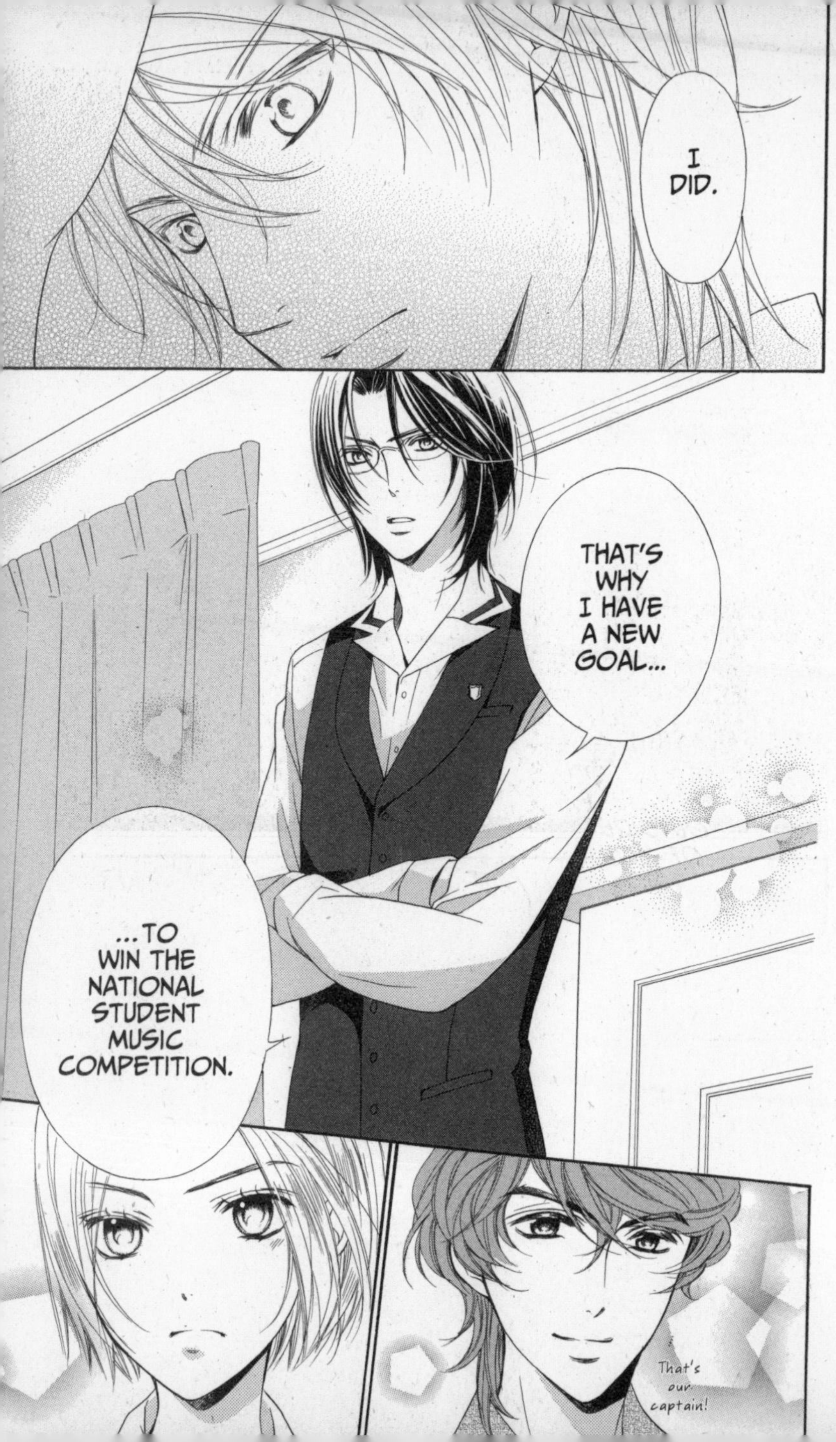
I DID.
THAT'S WHY I HAVE A NEW GOAL...
...TO WIN THE NATIONAL STUDENT MUSIC COMPETITION.
That's our captain!

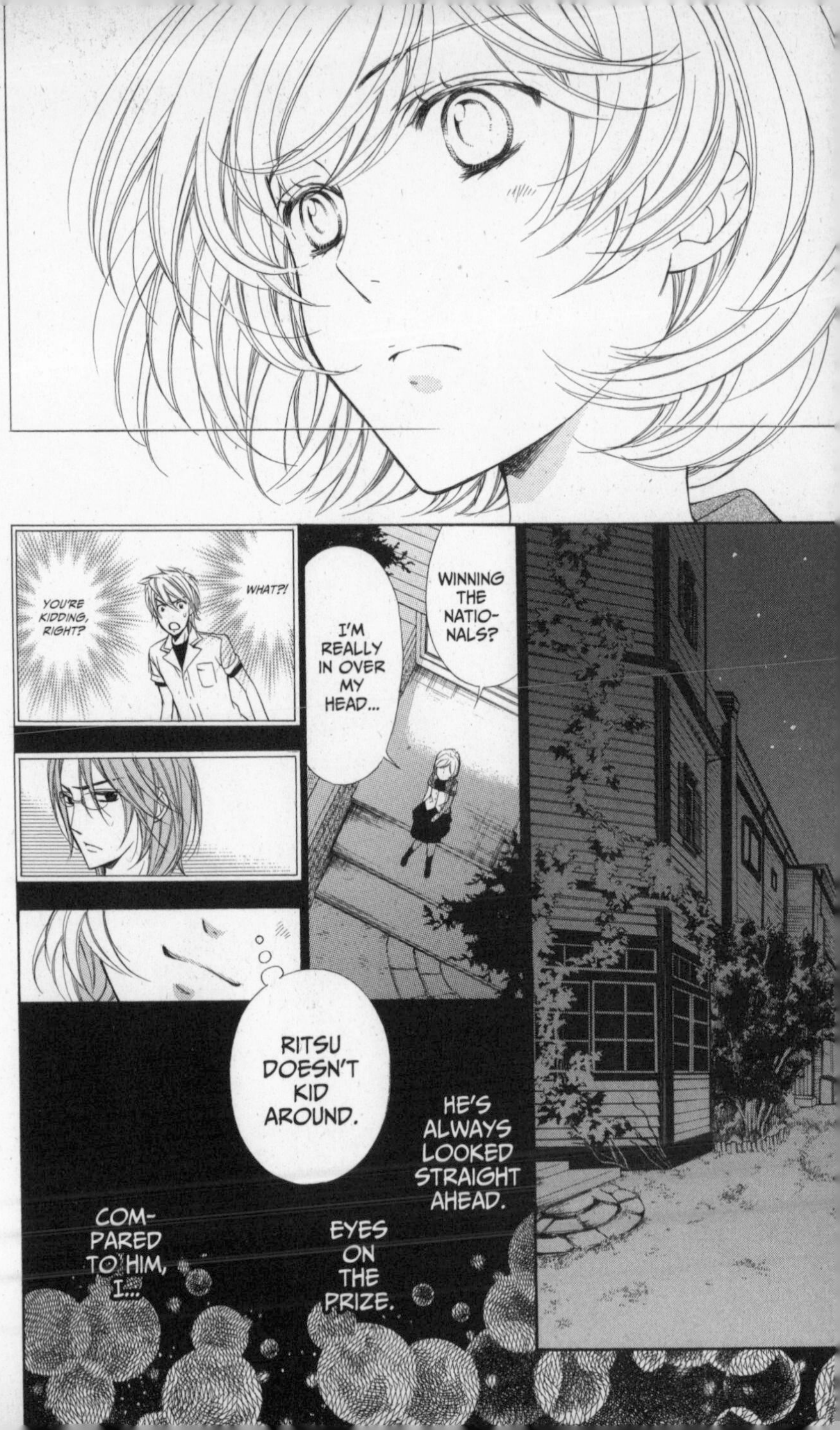
WINNING THE NATIO-NALS?
I'M REALLY IN OVER MY HEAD...
WHAT?!
YOU'RE KIDDING, RIGHT?
RITSU DOESN'T KID AROUND.
HE'S ALWAYS LOOKED STRAIGHT AHEAD.
EYES ON THE PRIZE.
COM-PARED TO HIM, I...

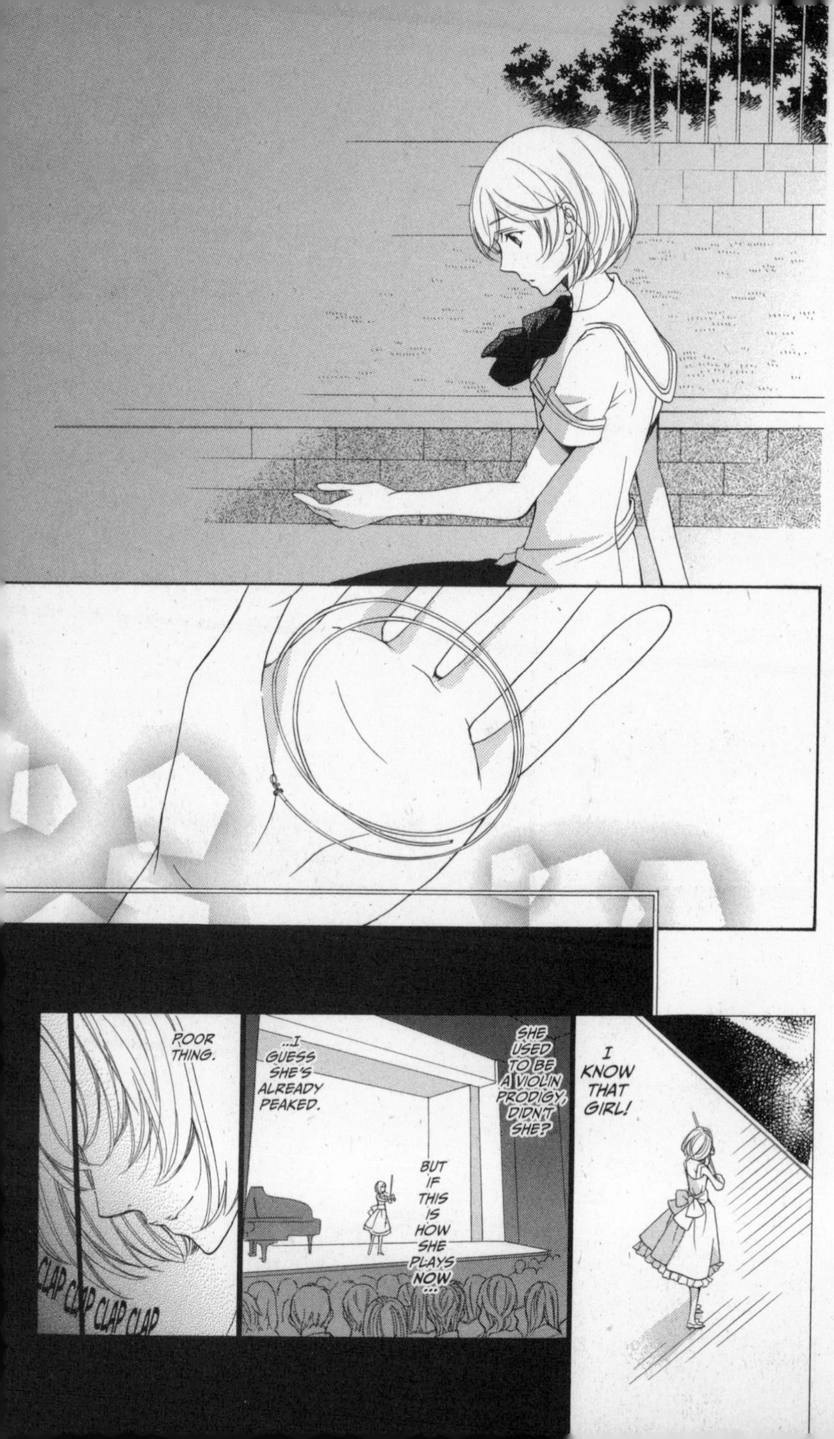
I KNOW THAT GIRL!
SHE USED TO BE A VIOLIN PRODIGY, DIDN'T SHE?
...I GUESS SHE'S ALREADY PEAKED.
BUT IF THIS IS HOW SHE PLAYS NOW...
POOR THING.
CLAP CLAP CLAP CLAP

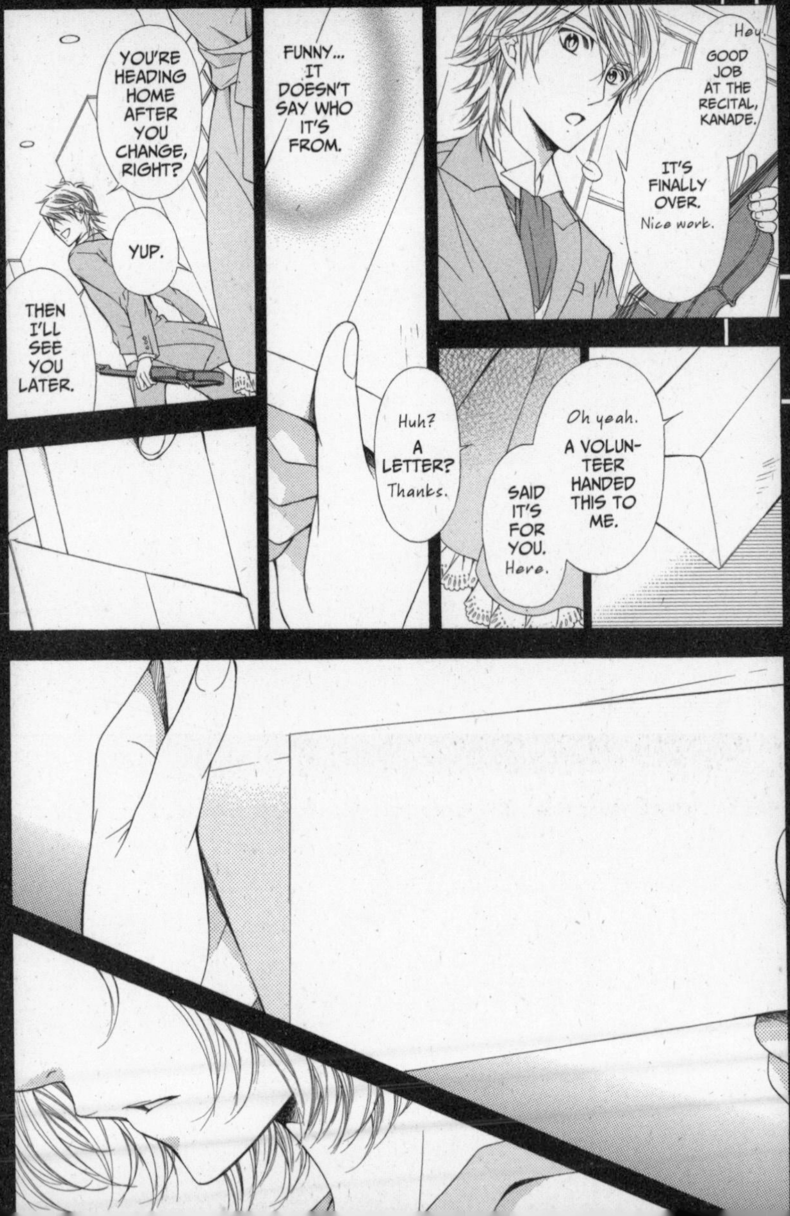
Hey.
GOOD JOB AT THE RECITAL, KANADE.
IT'S FINALLY OVER.
Nice work.
Oh yeah.
A VOLUNTEER HANDED THIS TO ME.
SAID IT'S FOR YOU.
Here.
Huh?
A LETTER?
Thanks.
FUNNY... IT DOESN'T SAY WHO IT'S FROM.
YOU'RE HEADING HOME AFTER YOU CHANGE, RIGHT?
YUP.
THEN I'LL SEE YOU LATER.

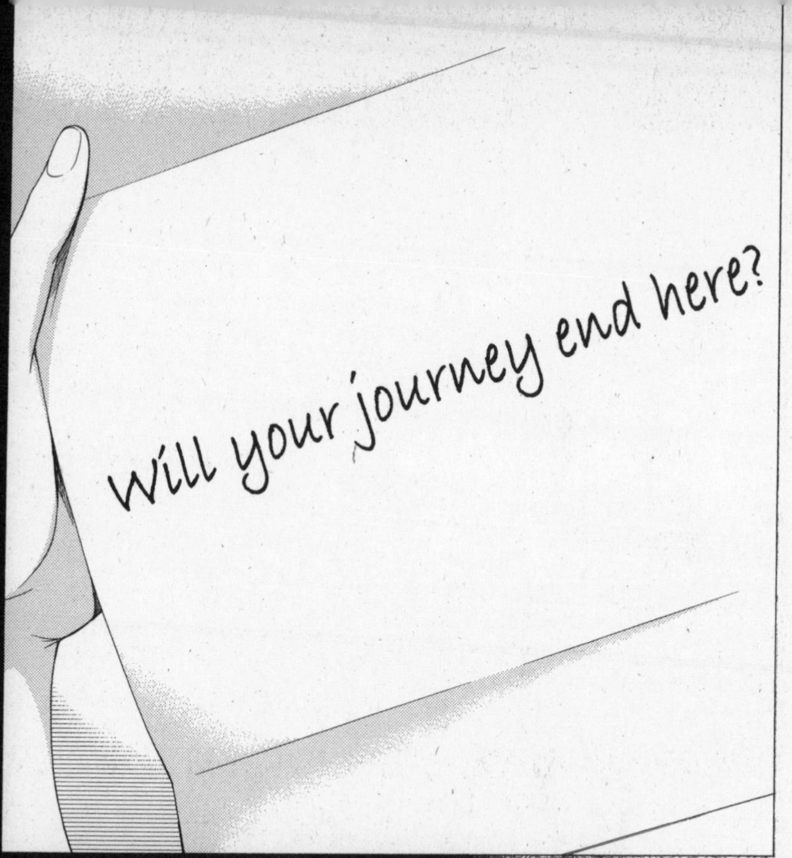
Will your journey end here?
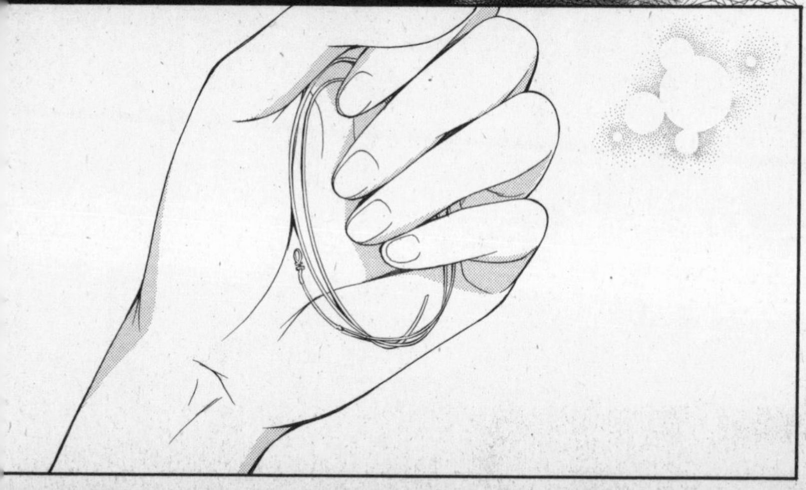

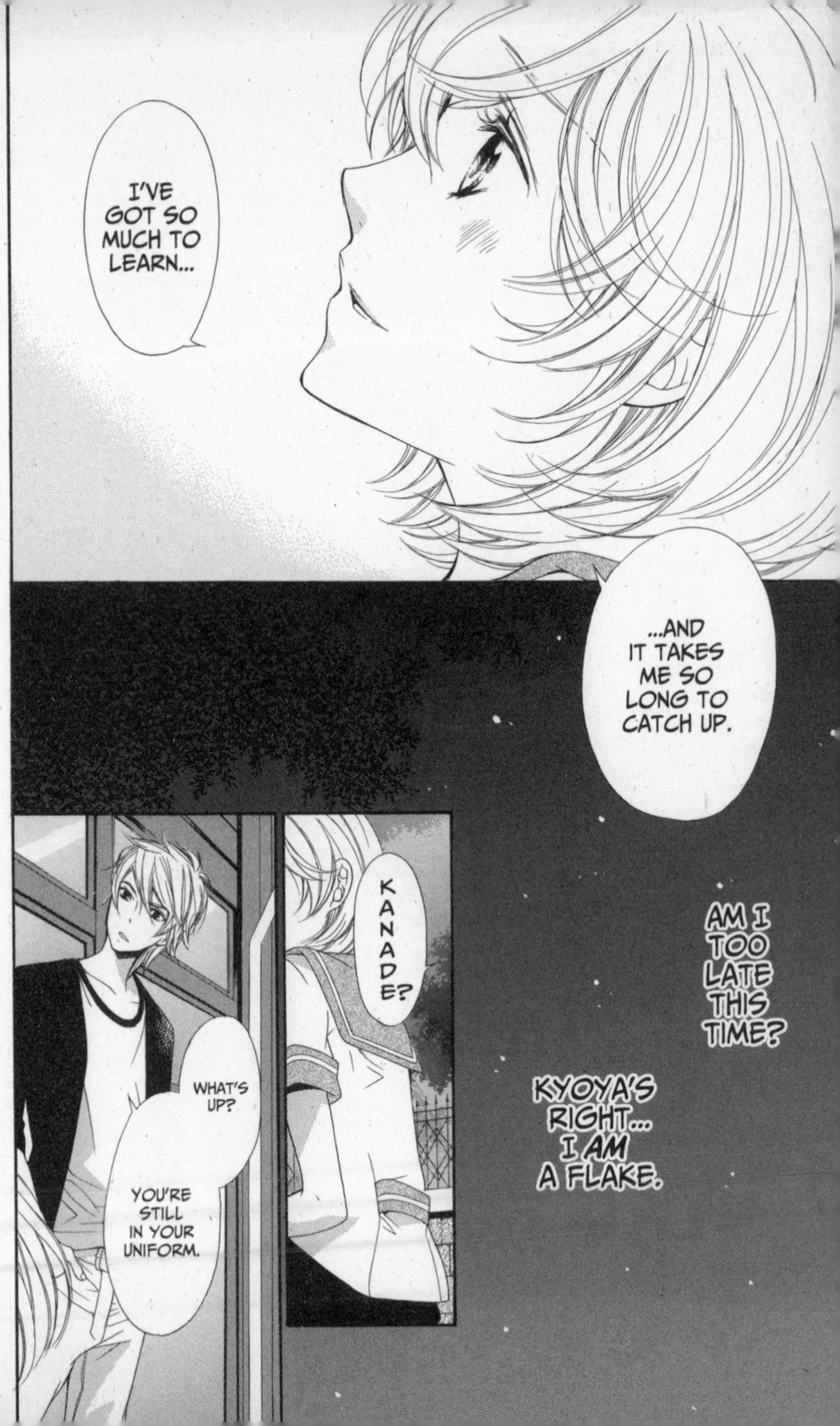
I'VE GOT SO MUCH TO LEARN...
...AND IT TAKES ME SO LONG TO CATCH UP.
AM I TOO LATE THIS TIME?
KYOYA'S RIGHT... I *AM* A FLAKE.
KANADE?
WHAT'S UP?
YOU'RE STILL IN YOUR UNIFORM.

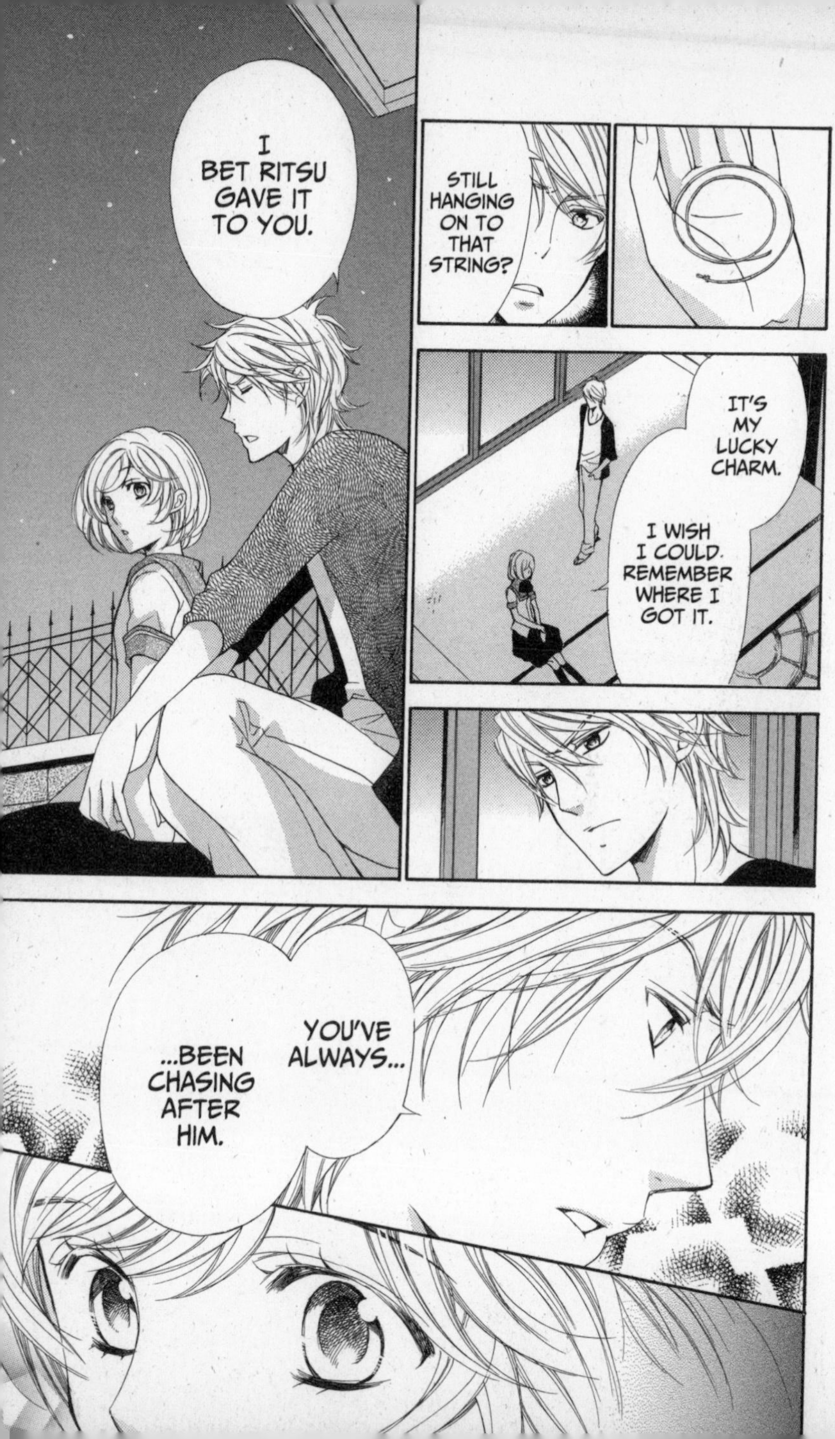
STILL HANGING ON TO THAT STRING?
IT'S MY LUCKY CHARM.
I WISH I COULD REMEMBER WHERE I GOT IT.
I BET RITSU GAVE IT TO YOU.
YOU'VE ALWAYS...
...BEEN CHASING AFTER HIM.

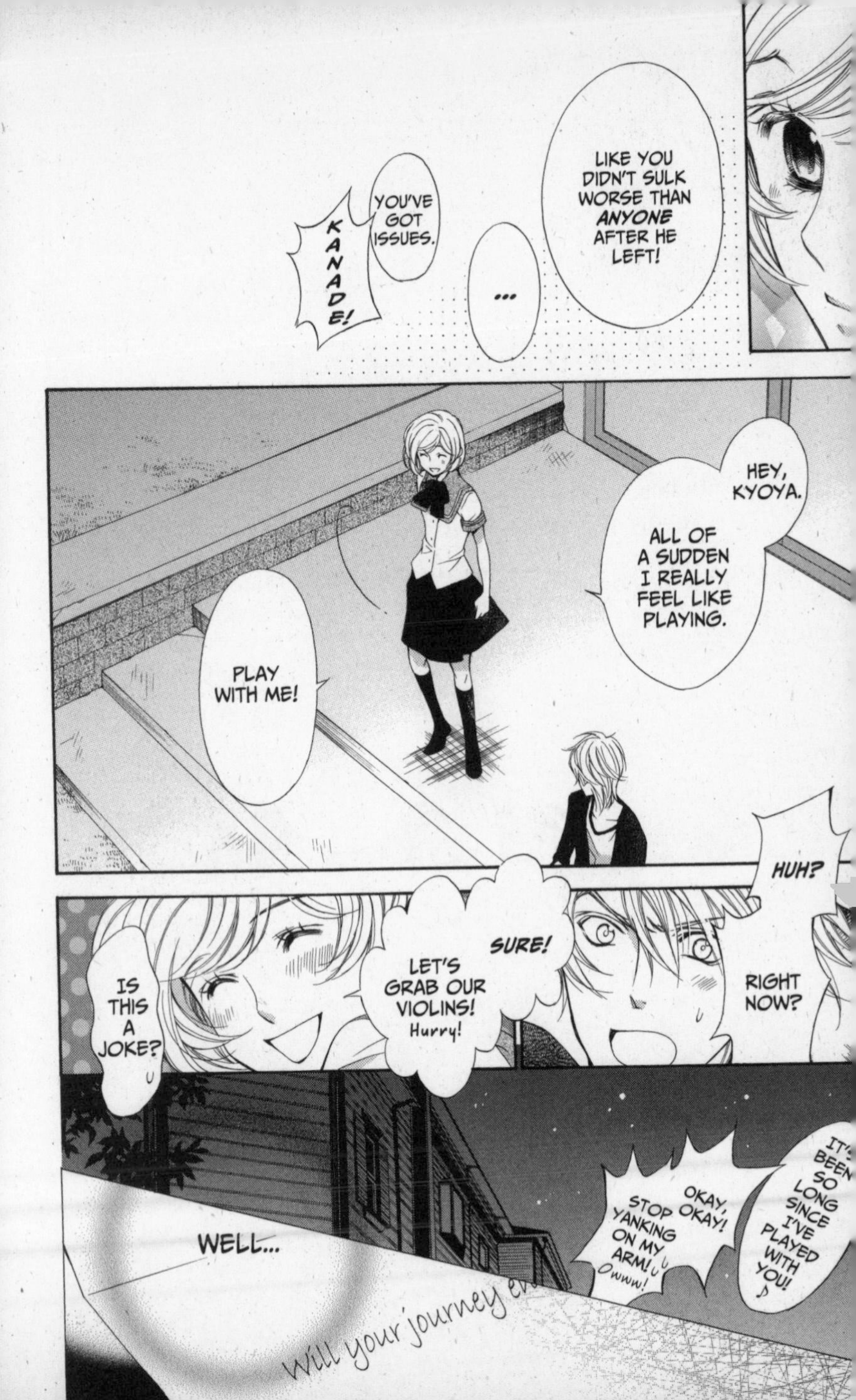
LIKE YOU DIDN'T SULK WORSE THAN ANYONE AFTER HE LEFT!
...
YOU'VE GOT ISSUES.
KANADE!
HEY, KYOYA.
ALL OF A SUDDEN I REALLY FEEL LIKE PLAYING.
PLAY WITH ME!
HUH?
RIGHT NOW?
SURE!
LET'S GRAB OUR VIOLINS! Hurry!
IS THIS A JOKE?
IT'S BEEN SO LONG SINCE I'VE PLAYED WITH YOU! ♪
OKAY, OKAY!
STOP YANKING ON MY ARM! Owww!
WELL...
Will your journey

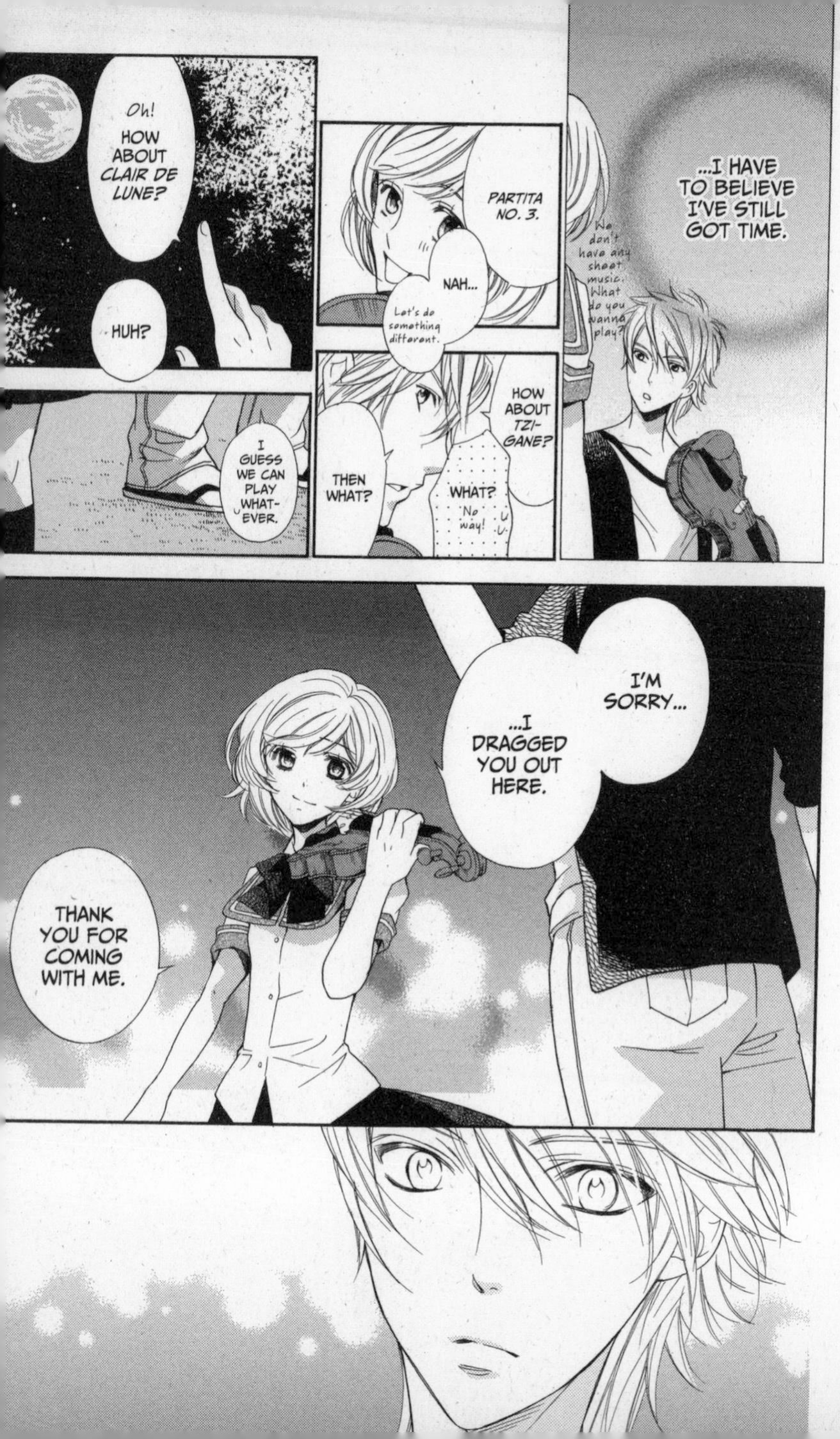
...I HAVE TO BELIEVE I'VE STILL GOT TIME.
We don't have any sheet music. What do you wanna play?
PARTITA NO. 3.
NAH...
Let's do something different.
HOW ABOUT TZI-GANE?
WHAT? No way!
THEN WHAT?
Oh! HOW ABOUT CLAIR DE LUNE?
HUH?
I GUESS WE CAN PLAY WHAT-EVER.
I'M SORRY...
...I DRAGGED YOU OUT HERE.
THANK YOU FOR COMING WITH ME.

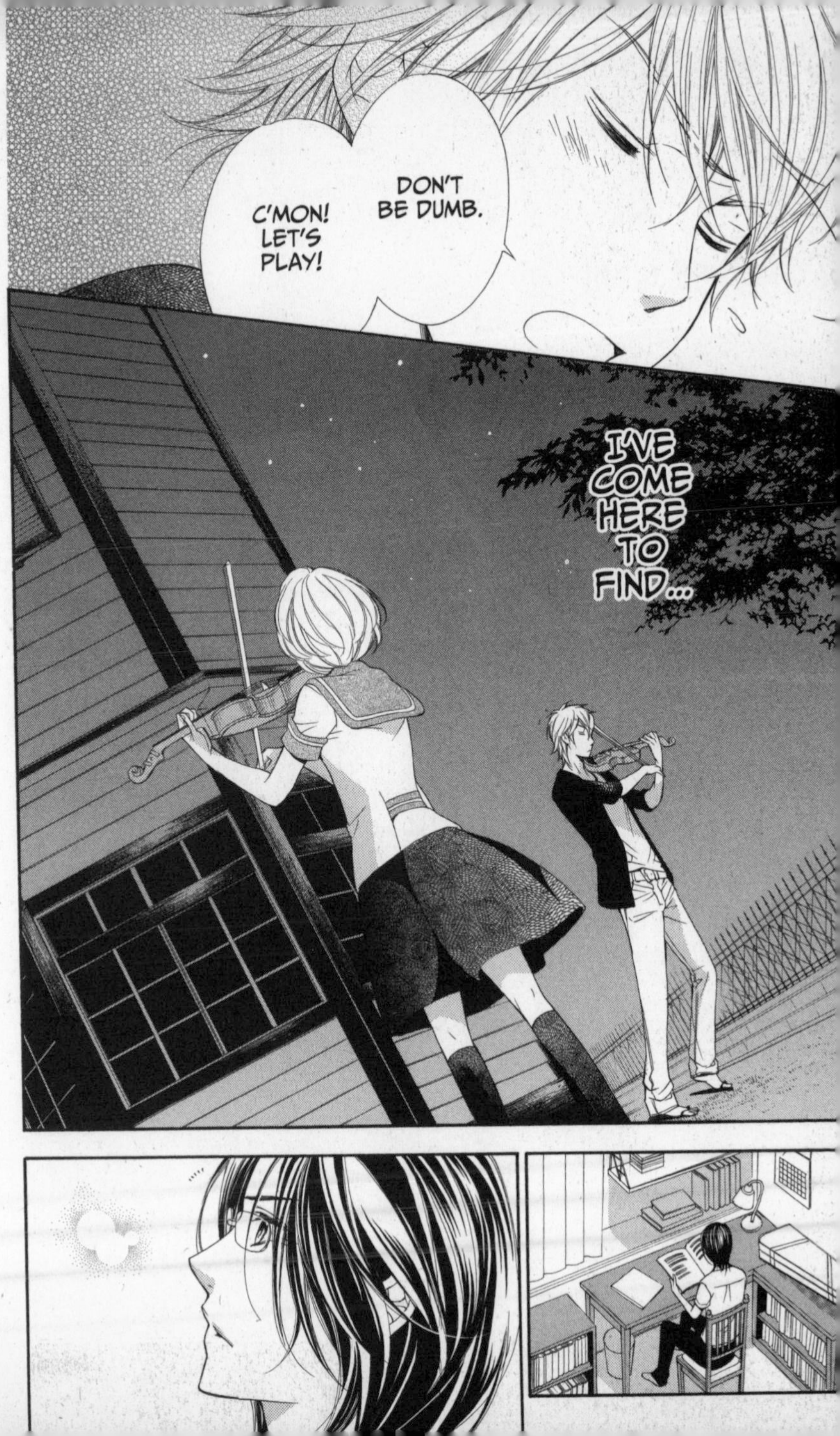
DON'T BE DUMB.
C'MON! LET'S PLAY!
I'VE COME HERE TO FIND...

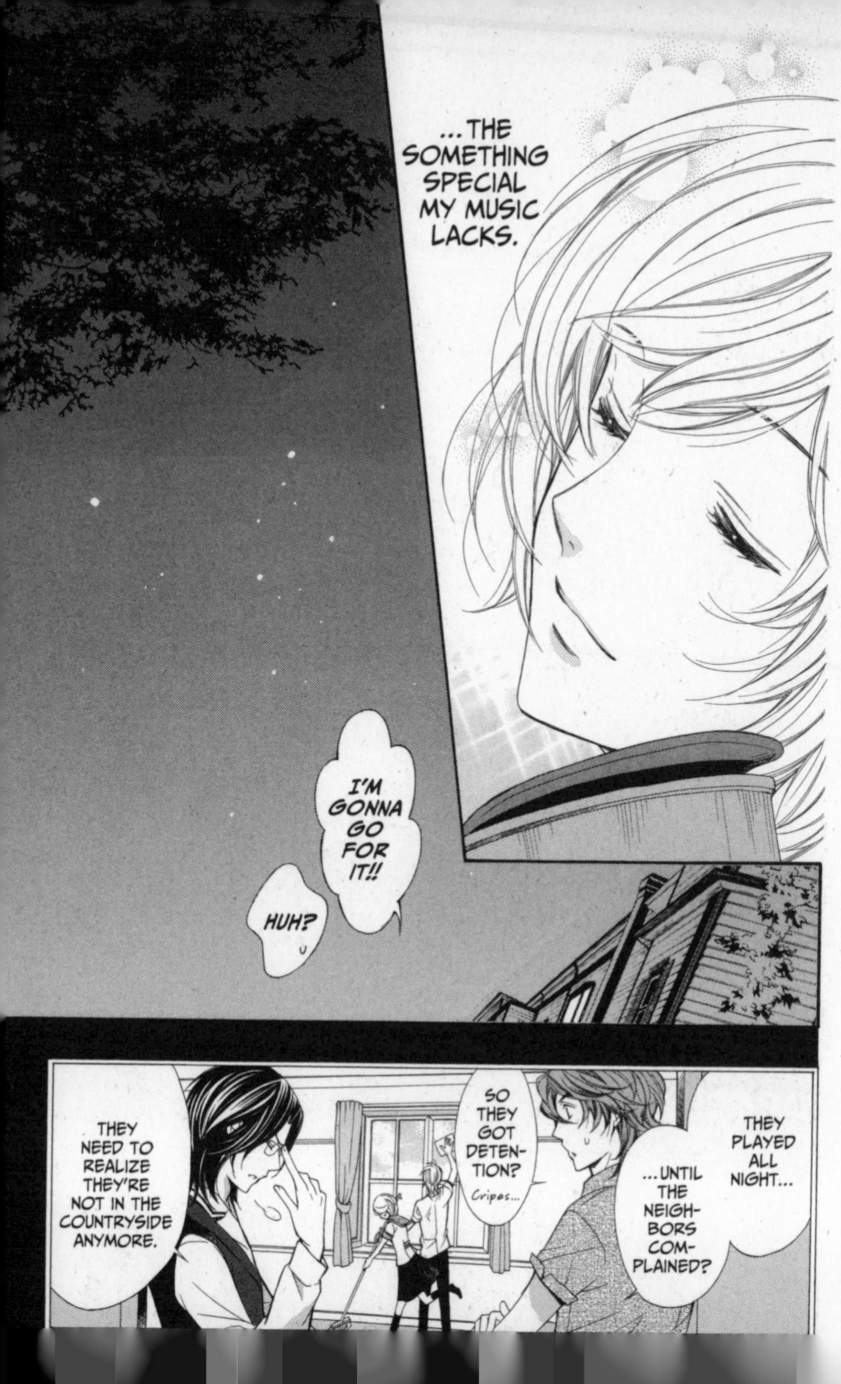
...THE SOMETHING SPECIAL MY MUSIC LACKS.
I'M GONNA GO FOR IT!!
HUH?
THEY PLAYED ALL NIGHT...
...UNTIL THE NEIGHBORS COMPLAINED?
SO THEY GOT DETENTION?
Cripes...
THEY NEED TO REALIZE THEY'RE NOT IN THE COUNTRYSIDE ANYMORE.

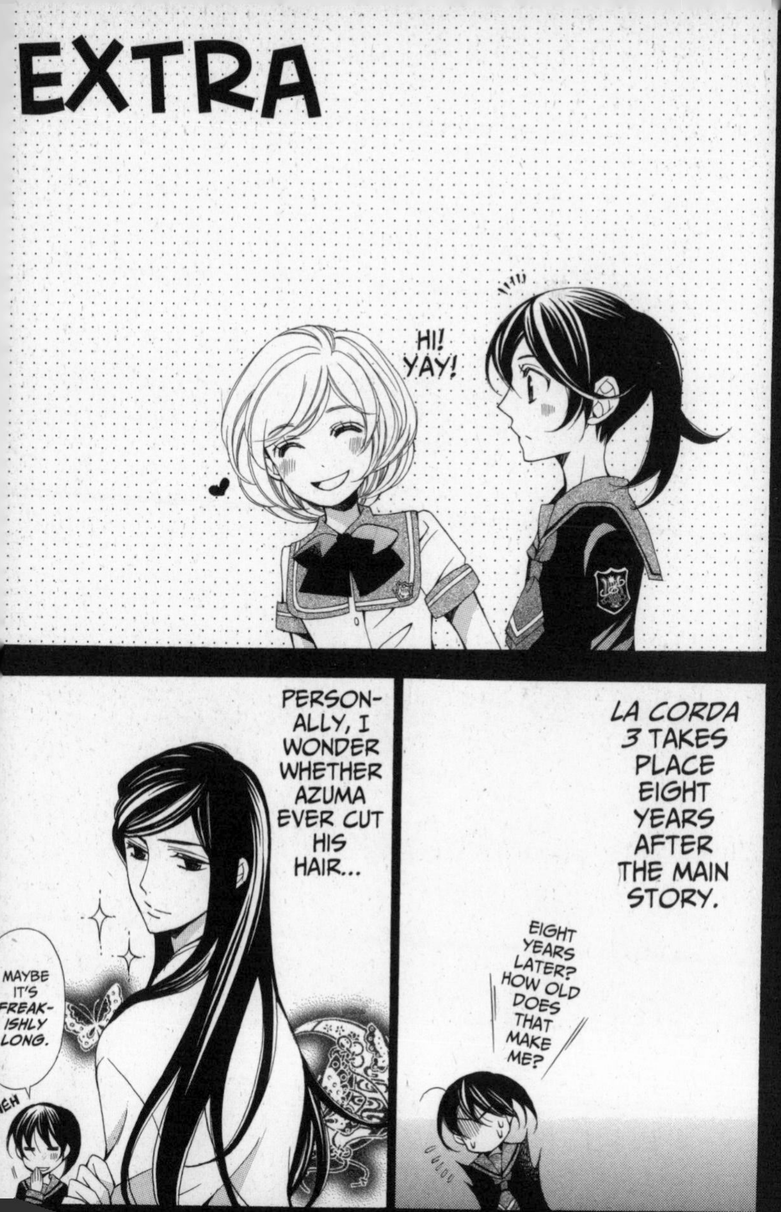
EXTRA
HI! YAY!
LA CORDA 3 TAKES PLACE EIGHT YEARS AFTER THE MAIN STORY.
EIGHT YEARS LATER? HOW OLD DOES THAT MAKE ME?
PERSON-ALLY, I WONDER WHETHER AZUMA EVER CUT HIS HAIR...
MAYBE IT'S FREAK-ISHLY LONG.
HEH

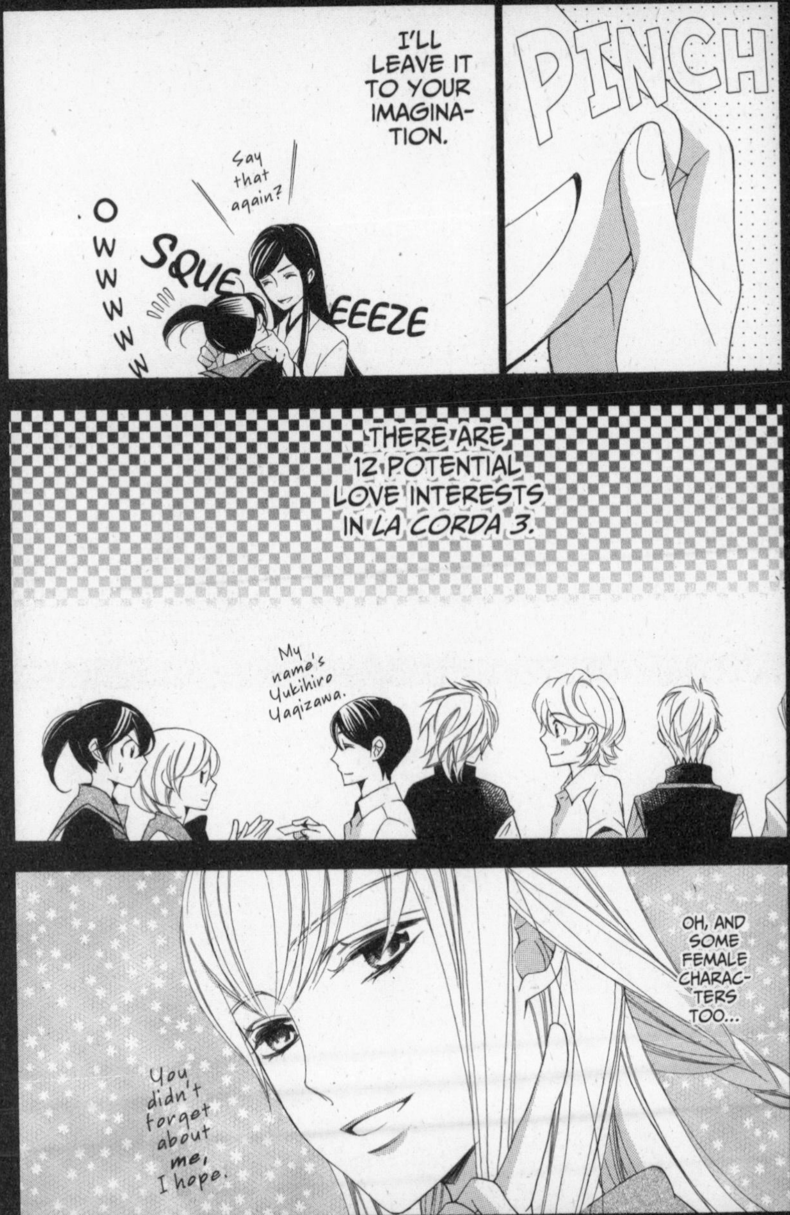
PINCH
I'LL LEAVE IT TO YOUR IMAGINATION.
Say that again?
SQUEEEEZE
OWWWWW
THERE ARE 12 POTENTIAL LOVE INTERESTS IN *LA CORDA 3*.
My name's Yukihiro Yagizawa.
OH, AND SOME FEMALE CHARACTERS TOO...
You didn't forget about me, I hope.

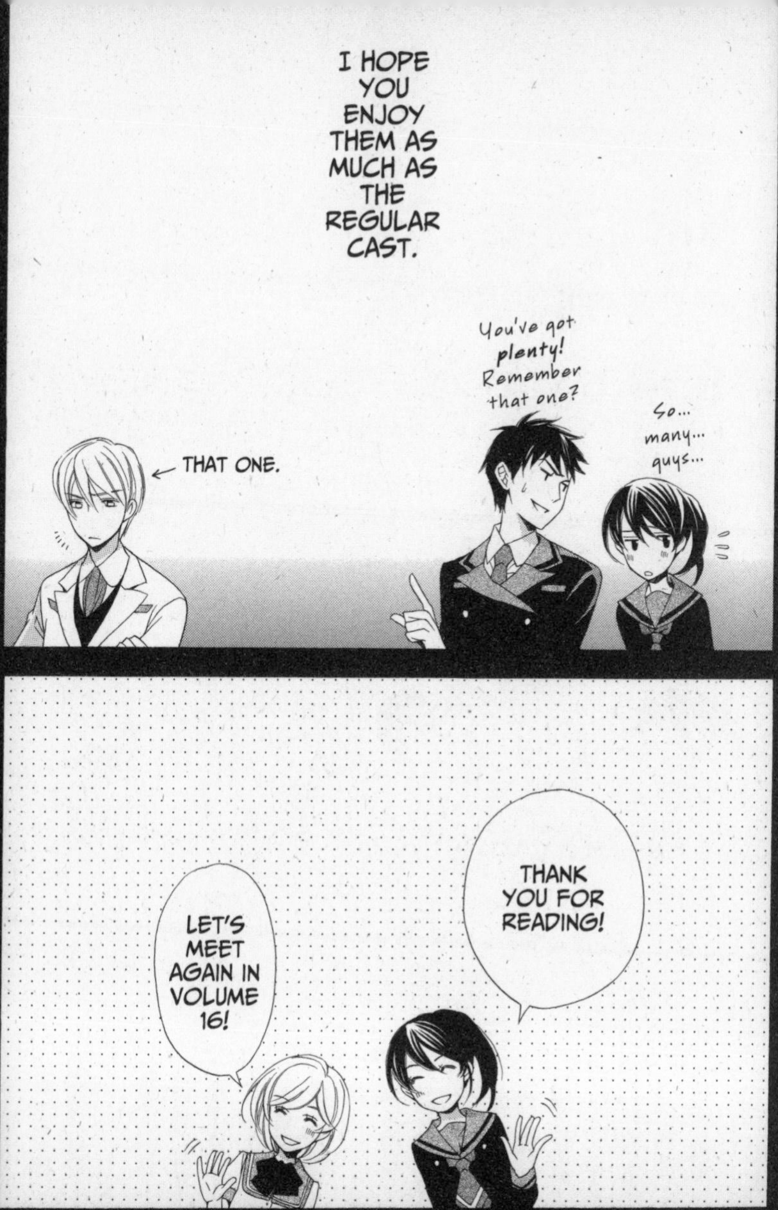
I HOPE YOU ENJOY THEM AS MUCH AS THE REGULAR CAST.
You've got plenty! Remember that one?
So... many... guys...
THAT ONE.
THANK YOU FOR READING!
LET'S MEET AGAIN IN VOLUME 16!

End of Extra

SPECIAL THANKS

M.Shiino
N.Sato
C.Nanai
M.Morinaga
S.Asahina
T.Yajima
E.Morishita
S.Kamiya

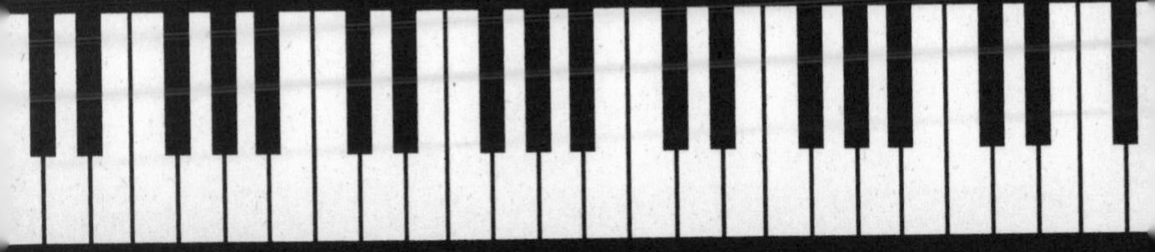

La Corda d'Oro End Notes

You can appreciate music just by listening to it, but knowing the story behind a piece can help enhance your enjoyment. In that spirit, here is background information about some of the topics mentioned in *La Corda d'Oro*. Enjoy!

Page 24, panel 2: *Ave Maria*
As mentioned in previous volumes, this piece is Franz Schubert's *Ellens dritter Gesang*, often called *Ave Maria* because the accompanying chorus opens with those words.

Page 24, panel 5: *Scherzo Tarantella*
Len played this demanding piece by Henryk Wieniawski, based on a traditional Italian dance, in the Second Selection. Most of Len's musical selections are fast-paced virtuoso pieces that require precise command of the bow but little personal expression.

Page 30, panels 1–3
The magazine Kahoko wants to buy is *Monthly LaLa*, the manga magazine in which *La Corda d'Oro* appears in Japan.

Page 179, panel 2: *Partita No. 3*
The term *partita* usually refers to a suite of short musical pieces. *Partita No. 3 in E Major* is a solo violin partita written in 1720 by Johann Sebastian Bach. A challenging, energetic composition, it provides a chance for advanced violinists to show off their technical skills.

Page 179, panel 2: *Tzigane*
Another fast, technically challenging piece, *Tzigane* is a 1924 composition by Maurice Ravel designed to evoke the wild spirit of Gypsy music. Len played *Tzigane* in the Third Selection.

Page 179, panel 3: *Clair de Lune*
Clair de Lune (French for "moonlight") is the third movement of *Suite Bergamasque*, a 1905 piano suite by Claude Debussy. The suite is Debussy's most famous work, and the delicate, melancholy *Clair de Lune*, named after a poem by Paul Verlaine, is by far his most beloved piece of music. It's been used in the soundtrack of many movies, including *Ocean's Eleven*, *Casino Royale* and *Twilight*.

Yuki Kure made her debut in 2000
with the story *Chijo yori Eien ni*
(Forever from the Earth), published
in monthly *LaLa* magazine.
La Corda d' Oro is her first manga
series published. Her hobbies are
watching soccer games and
collecting small goodies.

LA CORDA D'ORO
Vol. 15
Shojo Beat Edition

STORY AND ART BY
YUKI KURE
ORIGINAL CONCEPT BY
RUBY PARTY

English Translation & Adaptation/Mai Ihara
Touch-up Art & Lettering/HudsonYards
Design/Amy Martin
Editor/Shaenon K. Garrity

Kiniro no Corda by Yuki Kure © YUKI KURE/HAKUSENSHA, INC./
TECMO KOEI GAMES CO., LTD. 2010.
All rights reserved.
First published in Japan in 2010 by HAKUSENSHA, Inc., Tokyo.
English language translation rights arranged with HAKUSENSHA, Inc., Tokyo.

Printed in Canada

Published by VIZ Media, LLC
P.O. Box 77010
San Francisco, CA 94107

10 9 8 7 6 5 4 3 2 1
First printing, March 2012

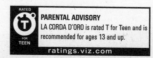

www.viz.com   www.shojobeat.com

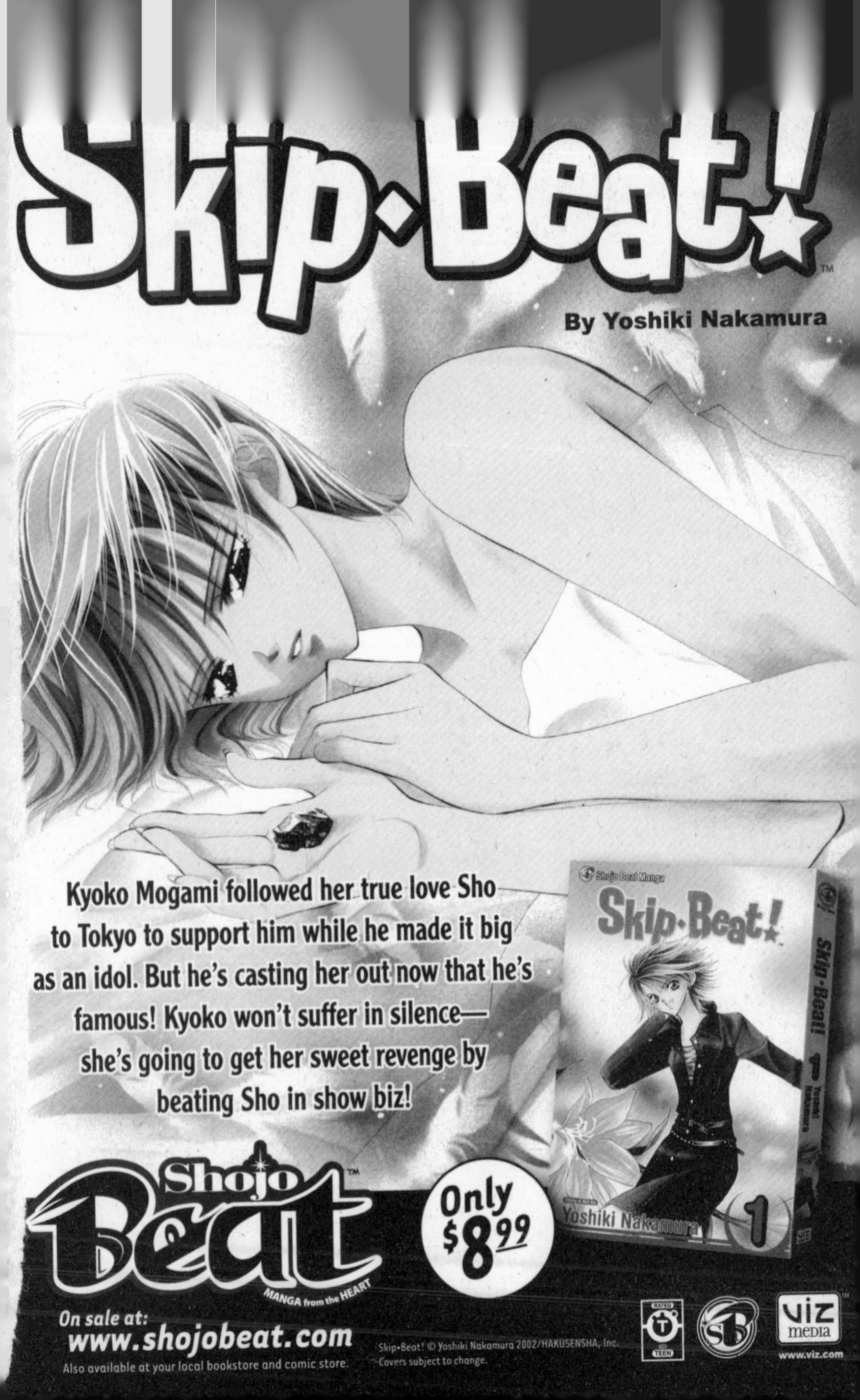

Don't Hide What's Inside

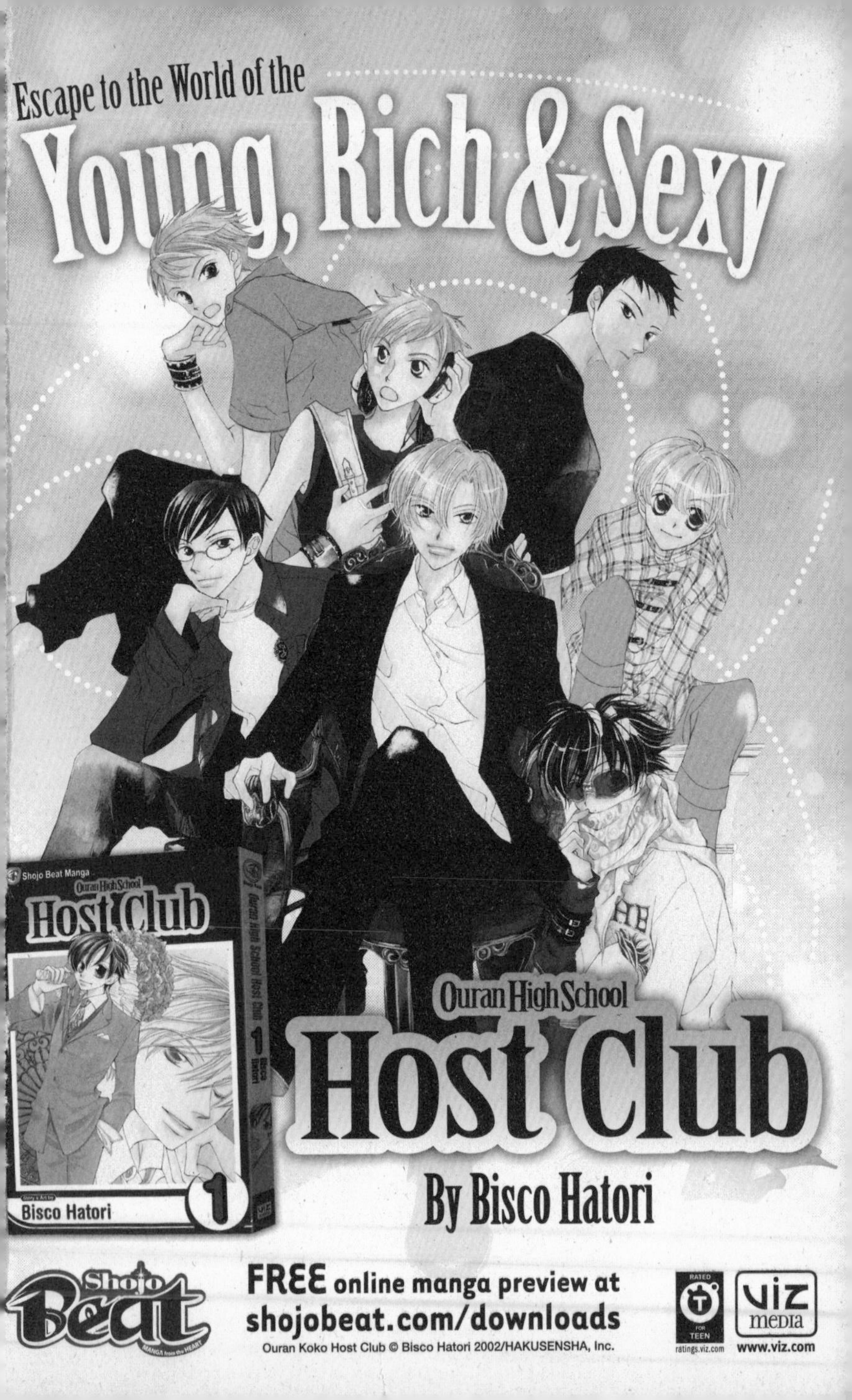
Escape to the World of the
Young, Rich & Sexy
Shojo Beat Manga
Ouran High School
Host Club
Ouran High School Host Club 1 Bisco Hatori
Bisco Hatori
1
Ouran High School
Host Club
By Bisco Hatori
Shojo Beat
FREE online manga preview at
shojobeat.com/downloads
Ouran Koko Host Club © Bisco Hatori 2002/HAKUSENSHA, Inc.
RATED T FOR TEEN
ratings.viz.com
viz media
www.viz.com